The Ice House

The Ice House

Minette Walters

St. Martin's Press

New York

Library of Congress Cataloging-in-Publication Data

Walters, Minette.
    The ice house / Minette Walters.
       p.   cm.
    ISBN 0-312-07801-3
    I. Title.
PR6073.A444I24   1992
823'.914—dc20   92-1262
                                CIP

First published in Great Britain by Macmillan London Limited.

First U.S. Edition: July 1992
10 9 8 7 6 5 4 3 2 1

To Alec

'Revenge is a kind of wild justice, which the more man's nature runs to, the more ought law to weed it out.'

FRANCIS BACON

'O wad some Pow'r the giftie gie us
To see oursels as others see us!
It wad frae mony a blunder free us,
     And foolish notion.'

ROBERT BURNS, 'To a Louse'

Southern Evening Herald – 23rd March

GROWING POLICE ANXIETY

Following intensive questioning at airports, docks and ferry terminals in the search for the missing businessman, David Maybury, police have expressed concern for his welfare. 'It is now ten days since he vanished,' said Inspector Walsh, the detective in charge of the investigation, 'and we cannot rule out the possibility of foul play.' Police efforts are being concentrated on a thorough search of Streech Grange Estate and the surrounding farmland.

There have been numerous reported sightings of the missing man over the past week, but none that could be substantiated. David Maybury, 44, was wearing a charcoal-grey pinstripe suit on the night he vanished. He is 5'10" tall, of average build, with dark hair and eyes.

Sun – 15th April

TO THE MANOR BURIED

Mrs Phoebe Maybury, 27, beautiful red-haired wife of missing businessman David Maybury, looked on in fury as police dug up her garden in their search for her husband. Mrs Maybury, an avid gardener herself, declared: 'This house has been in my family for years and the garden is the product of several generations. The police have no business to destroy it.'

Reliable sources say that David Maybury, 44, was in financial difficulties shortly before he disappeared. His wine business, funded by his wife and run from the cellars of her house, was virtually bankrupt. Friends talk of constant rows between the couple. Police are treating his disappearance as murder.

Daily Telegraph – 9th August
POLICE TEAM DISBANDED

POLICE admitted last night to being baffled over the disappearance of Hampshire man, David Maybury. In spite of a long and thorough investigation, no trace of him has been found, and the team involved in the enquiry has been disbanded. The file will remain open, according to police sources, but there is little confidence in solving the mystery. 'The public has been very helpful,' said a police spokesman. 'We have built a clear picture of what happened the night he vanished, but until we find his body, there's little more we can do.'

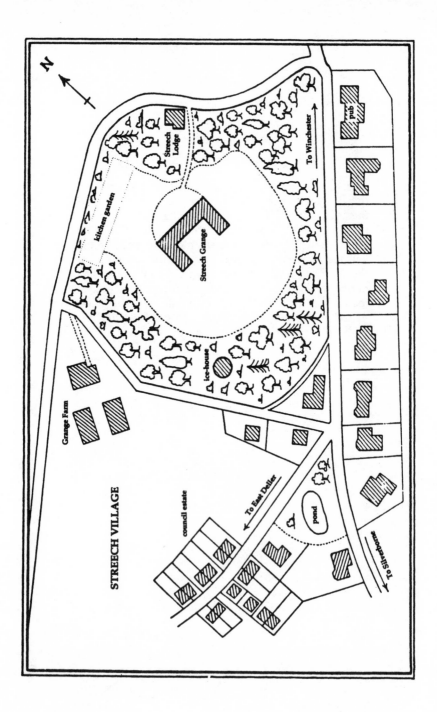

ONE

'Fred Phillips is *running*.' Anne Cattrell's remark burst upon the silence of that August afternoon like a fart at a vicar's tea-party.

Startled, her two companions looked up, Diana from her sketch-pad, Phoebe from her gardening book, their eyes watering at this abrupt transition from the printed page to brilliant sunlight. They had sat in contented stillness for an hour, grouped about a wrought-iron table on the terrace of their house where the wreckage of a lazy tea jostled with the flotsam of their professional lives: a pair of secateurs, an open paint-box, pages of manuscript, one with a circular tea stain where Anne had dumped a cup without thinking.

Phoebe was perched on an upright chair at right angles to the table, crossed ankles tucked neatly beneath her, red hair corkscrewing in flaming whorls about her shoulders. Her position was hardly changed from half an hour previously when she had finished her tea and guiltily buried her nose in her book instead of returning to the greenhouse to finish off a bulk order for five hundred Ivyleaf Pelargonium cuttings. Diana, unashamedly glistening with Ambre Solaire, reclined on a sun-lounger, the pleated skirt of her printed cotton dress spilling over the sides and brushing the flagstones. One elegant hand toyed with the underbelly of the Labrador lying beside her, the other drew swirling doodles in the margin of her sketch-pad which should have been filled – but was not – with commissioned designs for a cottage interior in Fowey. Anne, who had been struggling between intermittent dozes to conjure up a thousand words on 'Vaginal Orgasm – Fact or Fiction' for an obscure magazine, was drawn up tight against the table, chin on hands, dark eyes staring down the long vista of landscaped garden in front of her.

Phoebe glanced at her briefly then turned to follow her gaze, peering over her spectacles across the wide expanse of lawn. 'Good lord!' she exclaimed.

Her gardener, a man of massive proportions, was pounding across the grass, naked to the waist, his huge belly lapping at his trousers like some monstrous tidal wave. The semi-nudity was surprising enough, for Fred held strong views about his position at Streech Grange. Among other things, this required Phoebe to whistle a warning of her approach in the garden so that he might clothe himself suitably for what he referred to as a parley-vous, even in the heat of summer.

'Perhaps he's won the pools,' suggested Diana, but without conviction, as the three women watched his rapidly slowing advance.

'Highly unlikely,' countered Anne, pushing her chair away from the table. 'Fred's inertia would demand a more powerful stimulus than filthy lucre to prompt this bout of activity.'

They watched the rest of Fred's approach in silence. He was walking by the time he reached the terrace. He paused for a moment, leaning one hand heavily on the low wall bordering the flagstones, catching his breath. There was a tinge of grey to the weathered cheeks, a rasp in his throat. Concerned, Phoebe gestured to Diana to pull forward a vacant chair, then she stood up, took Fred's arm and helped him into it.

'Whatever's happened?' she asked anxiously.

'Oh, madam, something awful.' He was sweating profusely, unable to get the words out quickly. Perspiration ran in streams over his fat brown breasts, soft and round like a woman's, and the smell was all-pervading, consuming the sweet scent of the roses which nodded in beds at the edge of the terrace. Aware of this and of his nakedness, he wrung his hands in embarrassment. 'I'm so sorry, madam.'

Diana swung her legs off the lounger and sat up, twitching a rug off the back of her chair and placing it neatly across his shoulders. 'You should keep yourself warm after a run like that, Fred.'

He wrapped the rug around him, nodding his appreciation. 'What's happened, Fred?' Phoebe asked again.

'I don't rightly know how to say it' – she thought she saw compassion in his eyes – 'but it's got to be told.'

'Then tell me,' she prompted gently. 'I'm sure it can't be that bad.' She glanced at Benson, the golden Labrador, still lying placidly by Diana's chair. 'Has Hedges been run over?'

He reached out a rough, mud-caked hand from between the folds of the rug and with a familiarity that was quite out of character placed it on hers and squeezed gently. The gesture was as brief as it was unexpected. 'There's a body in the old ice house, madam.'

There was a moment's silence. 'A body?' echoed Phoebe. 'What sort of body?' Her voice was unemotional, steady.

Anne flicked a glance in her direction. There were times, she thought, when her friend's composure frightened her.

'To tell you the truth, madam, I didn't look too close. It was a

12

shock, coming on it the way I did.' He stared unhappily at his feet. 'Stepped on it, like, before I saw it. There was a bit of a smell afterwards.' They all looked in fascination at his gardening boots and he, regretting his impulsive statement, shuffled them awkwardly out of sight under the rug. 'It's all right, madam,' he said, 'wiped them on the grass soon as I could.'

The cup and saucer in Phoebe's hand rattled and she put them carefully on the table beside her secateurs. 'Of course you did, Fred. How thoughtful of you. Would you like some tea? A cake perhaps?' she asked him.

'No, thank you, madam.'

Diana turned away, suppressing an awful desire to laugh. Only Phoebe, she thought, of all the women she knew would offer cake in such circumstances. In its way it was admirable, for Phoebe, more than any of them, would be affected by Fred's shocking revelation.

Anne scrabbled among the pages of her manuscript in search of her cigarettes. With an abrupt movement she flicked the box open and offered it to Fred. He glanced at Phoebe for a permission he didn't need and she nodded gravely. 'Thank you kindly, Miss Cattrell. My nerves are that shook up.'

Anne lit it for him, holding his hand steady with hers. 'Let's get this straight, Fred,' she said, her dark eyes searching his. 'It's a person's dead body. Is that right?'

'That's right, Miss Cattrell.'

'Do you know who it is?'

'I can't say I do, miss.' He spoke with reluctance. 'I can't say anyone will know who it is.' He drew deeply on his cigarette, the sweat of suppressed nausea breaking out on his forehead. 'The truth is, from the quick look I had, there's not much of it left. It must have been there a while.'

The three women looked at him aghast. 'But surely it's got clothes on, Fred?' Diana asked nervously. 'At least you know if it's a man or woman.'

'No clothes that I could see, Mrs Goode.'

'You'd better show me.' Phoebe stood up with sudden decision and Fred rose awkwardly to his feet. 'I'd rather not, madam. You shouldn't see it. I don't want to take you down there.'

'Then I'll go on my own.' She smiled suddenly and laid a hand on his arm. 'I'm sorry but I have to see it. You do understand that, don't you, Fred?'

He stubbed out his cigarette and pulled the rug tighter about his shoulders. 'If you're that intent on going, I'll come with you. It's not something you should see alone.'

'Thank you.' She turned to Diana. 'Will you phone the police for me?'

'Of course.'

Anne pushed her chair back. 'I'll come with you,' she told Phoebe. Then she called after Diana as she followed the other two across the grass. 'You might lay on some brandy, I'll be needing some, even if no one else does.'

They grouped themselves in a nervous huddle a few yards from the entrance to the ice house. It was an unusual structure, designed and built in the eighteenth century to resemble a small hillock. Its function as an ice-store had ceased years ago with the advent of the refrigerator, and Nature had reasserted her dominion over it so that ranks of nettles marched in their hundreds around the base, making a natural fusion between the man-made dome and the solid earth. The only entrance, a wide low doorway, was set into the ice-house wall at the end of an overgrown pathway. The doorway, too, had long since lost itself in a mass of tangled brambles which grew over it in a thorny curtain from above and below. It was revealed now only because Fred had hacked and trampled the curtain aside to reach it.

A lighted torch lay abandoned on the ground at their feet. Phoebe picked it up. 'What made you go in there?' she asked Fred. 'We haven't used it for years.'

He pulled a face. 'I wish I hadn't, madam, God knows. What the eye doesn't see, the heart doesn't grieve over and that's a fact. I've been repairing the kitchen garden wall, where it collapsed a week ago. Half the bricks are unusable – I understood, when I saw the state of them, why the wall collapsed. Handful of dust, some of them. Anyway, I thought of the bricks we stored in here some years back, the ones from the outhouse we demolished. You said: "Hang on to the good ones, Fred, you never know when we might need them for repairs." '

'I remember.'

'So I wanted to use them for the wall.'

'Of course. You had to cut the brambles away?'

He nodded. 'I couldn't see the door, it was that overgrown.' He pointed to a scythe lying to one side of the ice house. 'I used that and my boots to reach it.'

'Come on,' said Anne suddenly. 'Let's get it over with. Talking isn't going to make it any easier.'

'Yes,' said Phoebe quietly. 'Does the door open any wider, Fred?'

'It does, madam. I had it full open before I stepped on what's in there. Pulled it to as far as I could when I left in case anyone came by.' He pursed his lips. 'To tell you the truth, it's wider now than when I left it.'

He walked forward reluctantly and, with a sudden movement, kicked the door. It swung open on creaking hinges. Phoebe crouched and shone the torch into the interior, bathing the contents with warm golden light. It wasn't so much the blackened and eyeless corpse that caused her to vomit, as the sight of Hedges rolling quietly and purposefully in the decomposing remains of the bowels. He came out with his tail between his legs and lay on the grass watching her, head between paws, as she heaved her tea on to the grass.

TWO

Silverborne Police Station, a modern triumph of polished chrome features and sealed tinted windows, baked in the sun amid its more traditional neighbours. Inside, the air-conditioning had broken down again and as the hours passed and the atmosphere overheated so did the policemen. They grew sticky and squabbled amongst themselves like young children. Those who could, got out; those who couldn't, jealously guarded their electric fans and prayed for a quick end to their shift. For Detective Chief Inspector Walsh, sweating profusely over some paperwork in his office, the order to take a team to Streech Grange came like a miraculous breath of air through the sealed windows. He whistled happily to himself as he made his way to the briefing room. But for Detective Sergeant McLoughlin, detailed to assist him, the knowledge that he was going to miss opening time and the cold lager he'd promised himself was the last straw.

Diana heard the approaching cars before the others. She finished her brandy and put the glass on the sideboard. 'Fingers out, girls. Here they come.'

Phoebe walked over to the mantelpiece, her face abnormally white against the vivid red hair. She was a tall woman who was rarely seen out of checked shirts and old Levis. But on her return from the ice house she had taken the trouble to change into a long-sleeved, high-collared silk dress. There was no doubting she looked at home in the elegant room with its pastel shades and draped velvet curtains but, to Anne at least, she had the air of a stranger. She smiled distantly at her two friends. 'I'm terribly sorry about this.'

Anne, as usual, was chain-smoking. She blew a stream of grey into the air above her where she sat on the sofa, head resting against the back. 'Don't be a fool,' she said bluntly. 'No one's going to hold you responsible because some idiot chooses to die on your property. There'll be a simple explanation: a tramp took shelter and had a heart attack.'

16

'My thoughts precisely,' said Diana, walking to the sofa. 'Give me a cigarette, there's a dear. My nerves are like piano wires, waiting for a Rachmaninov concerto to hit them.'

Anne chuckled and handed over the packet. 'Do you want one, Pheeb?'

She shook her head and started to polish her spectacles on her skirt hem, absent-mindedly lifting it to waist level and revealing her lack of knickers. Anne found the vagueness of the gesture reassuring.

'There won't be any glass left if you go on doing that,' she pointed out gently.

Phoebe sighed, dropped her skirt and put the spectacles back on. 'Tramps don't have heart attacks on other people's property in the nude,' she said.

The doorbell rang. They heard Molly Phillips, Fred's wife, walk to the front door and without a word, indeed quite by instinct, Anne and Diana positioned themselves on either side of the mantelpiece, flanking Phoebe. As the door opened it occurred to Diana that this might not have been a wise move. To the police mind, she feared, they would seem not so much to be supporting her – the intention – as guarding her.

Molly ushered in two men. 'Chief Inspector Walsh and Detective Sergeant McLoughlin, madam. There's a whole lot more outside. Shall I ask Fred to keep an eye on them?'

'No, that's all right, Molly. I'm sure they'll behave themselves.'

'If you say so, madam. Me, I'm not so sure. They've already scuffed their great clumsy feet over the gravel where Fred raked it so careful this morning.' She glared accusingly at the two men.

'Thank you, Molly. Perhaps you could make tea for everyone. I'm sure it will be welcome.'

'Right you are, madam.' The housekeeper closed the door behind her and stomped off down the corridor towards the kitchen.

George Walsh listened till her footsteps died away, then he came forward and held out his hand. He was a thin stooping man who had a bizarre habit of jerking his head from side to side, like a sufferer from Parkinson's disease. It gave him an appearance of vulnerability that was deceptive.

'Good afternoon, Mrs Maybury. We've met before, if you remember.' He could recall her vividly as she had been that first time, standing where she was now. Ten years, he thought, and she had hardly changed, still the lady of the manor, remote and aloof in the security of her position. The dramas of those years might never have been. There was certainly no evidence in the calm, unlined face which smiled at him now. There was a quality of stillness about her

17

that was unnatural. The village called her a witch, and he had always understood why.

Phoebe shook his hand. 'Yes, I do remember. It was your first big case.' Her voice was low-pitched, attractive. 'You had just been made Detective Inspector, I think. I don't believe you've met my friends, Miss Cattrell and Mrs Goode.' She gestured to Anne and Diana who shook hands solemnly in turn with the Chief Inspector. 'They live here now.'

Walsh studied the two women with interest. 'Permanently?' he asked.

'Most of the time,' said Diana, 'when our work doesn't take us away. We're both self-employed. I'm an interior designer, Anne's a freelance journalist.'

Walsh nodded, but Anne could see that Diana had told him nothing he didn't already know. 'I envy you.' He spoke the truth. He had coveted Streech Grange since the first time he had seen it.

Phoebe put out her hand to the other man. 'Good afternoon, Sergeant McLoughlin. May I introduce Mrs Goode and Miss Cattrell.'

He was in his mid thirties, of an age with the women, a dark, brooding man with cold eyes. In the twist of his lips, he had brought with him the irritability of the Police Station, concentrated, malignant. He regarded Phoebe and her friends with weary contempt and paid lip-service to etiquette by brushing their fingers with his in the briefest of exchanges. His dislike, uncalled-for, slapped against their unprotected cheeks.

To the consternation of her friends, who could feel the vibrations of her anger, Anne rose recklessly to the challenge. 'My, my, Sergeant, what *have* you been hearing about us?' She lifted a sardonic eyebrow then deliberately wiped her fingers down her Levis. 'You're scarcely off your mother's breast, so won't have been around the last time the Grange was the centre of police attention. Let me guess now. Our reputation – ' she indicated herself and the other two women – 'has preceded us. Which of our widely talked-about activities upsets you the most, I wonder? Child abuse, witchcraft or lesbianism?' She searched his face with scornful eyes. 'Lesbianism,' she murmured. 'Yes, you would find that the most threatening but, then, it's the only one that's true, isn't it?'

McLoughlin's temper, already fired by the heat of the day, nearly erupted. He breathed deeply. 'I've nothing against dykes, Miss Cattrell,' he said evenly. 'I just wouldn't stick my finger in one, that's all.'

Diana stubbed out her cigarette with rather more violence than was necessary. 'Don't tease the poor man, Anne,' she said dryly. 'He's going to need all his wits to sort out the mess in the ice house.'

Stiffly, Phoebe took the seat nearest her and gestured the others to sit down. Walsh sat in the chair opposite her, Anne and Diana on the sofa, leaving McLoughlin to perch on a delicate tapestry stool. His discomfort, as he folded his long legs awkwardly beneath him, was obvious to all.

'Take care you don't break that, Sergeant,' snapped Walsh. 'I don't like clumsiness any more than the housekeeper does. Well now, Mrs Maybury, perhaps you'd like to tell us why you called us out.'

'I thought Mrs Goode explained it on the telephone.'

He fished a piece of paper from his pocket. ' "Body in ice house, Streech Grange. Discovered at 4.35 p.m." Not much of an explanation, is it? Tell me what happened.'

'That's it, really. Fred Phillips, my gardener, found the body about that time and came and told us. Diana phoned you while Fred took Anne and me to look at it.'

'So you've seen it?'

'Yes.'

'Who is it? Do you know?'

'The body's unrecognisable.'

With an abrupt movement, Anne lit another cigarette. 'It's putrid, Inspector, black, disgusting. *No one* would know who it was.' She spoke impatiently, her deep voice clipping the words short.

Walsh nodded. 'I see. Did your gardener suggest you look at the body?'

Phoebe shook her head. 'No, he suggested I shouldn't. I insisted on going.'

'Why?'

She shrugged. 'Natural curiosity, I suppose. Wouldn't you have gone?'

He was silent for a moment. '*Is* it your husband, Mrs Maybury?'

'I've already told you the body is unrecognisable.'

'Did you insist on going because you thought it *might* be your husband?'

'Of course. But I've realised since it couldn't possibly be.'

'Why is that?'

'It was something Fred said. He reminded me that we stored some bricks in the ice house about six years ago when we demolished an old outhouse. David had been gone four years by that time.'

'His body was never found. We never traced him,' Walsh reminded her. 'Perhaps he came back.'

Diana laughed nervously. 'He couldn't come back, Inspector. He's dead. Murdered.'

'How do you know, Mrs Goode?'

'Because he'd have been back long before this if he wasn't. David always knew which side his bread was buttered.'

Walsh crossed his legs and smiled. 'The case is still open. *We've* never been able to prove he was murdered.'

Diana's face was suddenly grim. 'Because you concentrated all your energies on trying to pin the murder on Phoebe. You gave up when you couldn't prove it. You never made any attempt to ask me for a list of suspects. I could have given you a hundred likely names; Anne could have given you another hundred. David Maybury was the most out-and-out bastard who ever lived. He deserved to die.' She wondered if she had overdone it and glanced briefly at Phoebe. 'Sorry, love, but if more people had said it ten years ago, things might have been less hard for you.'

Anne nodded agreement. 'You'll waste a lot of time if you think that thing out there is David Maybury.' She stood up and walked over to sit on the arm of Phoebe's chair. 'For the record, Inspector, both Diana and I helped clear years of accumulated rubbish out of the ice house before Fred stacked the bricks in it. There were no corpses in there six years ago. Isn't that right, Di?'

Diana looked amused and inclined her head. 'It wouldn't have been the place to look for him, anyway. He's at the bottom of the sea somewhere, food for crabs and lobsters.' She looked at McLoughlin. 'Are you partial to crabs, Sergeant?'

Walsh intervened before McLoughlin could say anything. 'We followed up every known contact or associate Mr Maybury had. There was no evidence to connect any of them with his disappearance.'

Anne tossed her cigarette into the fireplace. 'Balls!' she exclaimed amiably. 'I'll tell you something, you never questioned me either and in my list of a hundred possible suspects *I* should have featured in the top ten.'

'You're quite mistaken, Miss Cattrell.' Inspector Walsh was unruffled. 'We went into your background very thoroughly. At the time of Mr Maybury's disappearance, in fact throughout most of our investigation, you were camped with your lady friends on Greenham Common under the eyes not only of the guards at the American Airforce base but also of the Newbury police and assorted television cameras. It was quite an alibi.'

'You're right. I'd forgotten. Touché, Inspector.' She chuckled. 'I was researching a feature for one of the colour supplements.' Out of the corner of her eye, she saw McLoughlin's lips thin to a disapproving line. 'But, hell, it was fun,' she went on in a dreamy voice. 'That camp is the best thing that's ever happened to me.'

Frowning, Phoebe laid a restraining hand on her arm and stood up. 'This is all irrelevant. Until you've examined the body, it seems to me quite pointless to speculate on whether or not it's David's. If you care to come with me, gentlemen, I will show you where it is.'

'Let Fred do it,' Diana protested.

'No. He's had enough shocks for one day. I'm all right. Could you make sure Molly's organising the tea?'

She opened the French windows and led the way on to the terrace. Benson and Hedges roused themselves from the warm flagstones and pushed their noses into her hand. Hedges's fur was still fluffy from his bath. She paused to stroke his head gently and pull his ears. 'There's one thing I really ought to tell you, Inspector,' she said.

Anne, watching from inside the drawing-room, gave a gurgle of laughter. 'Phoebe's confessing to Hedges's little peccadillo and the Sergeant's turned green around the gills.'

Diana pushed herself out of the sofa and walked towards her. 'Don't underestimate him, Anne,' she said. 'You're such a fool sometimes. Why do you always have to antagonise people?'

'I don't. I simply refuse to kowtow to their small-minded conventions. If they feel antagonised that's their problem. Principles should never be compromised. The minute they are, they cease to be principles.'

'Maybe, but you don't have to shove them down reluctant throats. A little common sense wouldn't come amiss at the moment. We do have a dead body on the premises. Or had you forgotten?' Her voice was more anxious than ironic.

Anne turned away from the window. 'You're probably right,' she agreed meekly.

'So you'll be careful?'

'I'll be careful.'

Diana frowned. 'I do wish I understood you. I never have, you know.'

Affection surged in Anne as she studied her friend's worried face. Poor old Di, she thought, how she hated all this. She should never have come to Streech. Her natural environment was an ivory tower where visitors were vetted and unpleasantness unheard of. 'You have no problem understanding me,' she pointed out lightly, 'you have a problem *agreeing* with me. My petty anarchies offend your sensibilities. I often wonder why you go along with them.'

Diana walked to the door. 'Which reminds me, next time you

want me to lie for you, warn me first, will you? I'm not as good at controlling my facial muscles as you are.'

'Nonsense,' said Anne, dropping into an armchair. 'You're the most accomplished liar I know.'

Diana paused with her hand on the doorknob. 'Why do you say that?' she asked sharply.

'Because,' Anne teased her rigid back, 'I was there when you told Lady Weevil that her choice of colours for her drawing-room was sophisticated. Anyone who could do that with a straight face must have unlimited muscle control.'

'Lady *Keevil*,' corrected Diana, looking round with a smile. 'I should never have let you come with me. That contract was worth a fortune.'

Anne was unrepentant. 'I needed the lift and you can hardly blame me if I got her name wrong. Everything she said sounded as if it had been squeezed through a wet flannel. Anyway, I did you a favour. Cherry-red carpets and lime-green curtains, for God's sake! Think of your reputation.'

'You know her father was a fruit wholesaler.'

'You *do* surprise me,' said Anne dryly.

THREE

Inside the ice house Chief Inspector Walsh firmly suppressed a slight movement in his bowels. Sergeant McLoughlin showed less control. He ran out of the building and was sick in the nettles alongside it. Unaware that she would have sympathised, he was thankful that Phoebe Maybury had returned to the Grange and was not there to see him.

'Not very nice, is it?' remarked Walsh when the Sergeant came back. 'Careful where you're stepping. There are bits all over the place. Must have been where the dog disturbed it.'

McLoughlin held a handkerchief to his mouth and retched violently. There was a strong smell of beer about him, and the Inspector eyed him with disfavour. A man of moods himself, he found inconsistency in others unendurable. He knew McLoughlin as well as any of the men he worked with, thought of him as a conscientious type, honest, intelligent, dependable. He even liked the man – he was one of the few who could cope with the notorious pendulum-swings of Walsh's temperament – but to see McLoughlin's weaknesses, disclosed like guilty secrets, irritated Walsh. 'What the hell's the matter with you?' he demanded. 'Five minutes ago you couldn't even be civil, now you're puking like a bloody baby.'

'Nothing, sir.'

'Nothing, sir,' mimicked Walsh savagely. He would have said more but there was an anger about the younger man that stilled his waspish tongue. With a sigh he took McLoughlin's arm and pushed him outside. 'Get me a photographer and some decent lights – it's impossible to see properly. And tell Dr Webster to get down here as fast as he can. I left a message for him so he should be at the Station by now.' He patted the Sergeant's arm clumsily, remembering perhaps that McLoughlin was more often his supporter than his detractor. 'If it's any consolation, Andy, I've never seen anything as nasty as this.'

As McLoughlin returned thankfully to the house, Inspector Walsh took a pipe from his pocket, filled it and lit it thoughtfully, then began a careful examination of the ground and the brambles around the door and pathway. The ground itself told him little. The summer had been an exceptional one and the last four weeks of almost perpetual sunshine had baked it hard. The only visible tracks were where feet, probably Fred's, had trampled the weeds and grass in front of the brambles. Previous tracks, if any, had long since been obliterated. The brambles might prove more interesting. It was evident, if there were no other entrance to the ice house, that the body had at some point traversed this thorny barrier, either alive on its own two legs or dead on the back of someone else's. The big question was, how long ago? How long had that nightmare been in there?

He walked slowly round the hillock. It would, of course, have been easier to satisfy himself that the door was the only entrance from inside the structure. He excused his reluctance to do this on the basis of not wishing to disturb the evidence more than was necessary but, being honest, he knew it was an excuse. The grisly tomb held no attractions for a man alone, even for a policeman intent on discovering the truth.

He spent some time investigating round the base of an untamed laurel which grew at the back of the ice house, using a discarded bamboo stake to stir up the leaf mould which had collected there. His efforts uncovered only solid brickwork, which looked strong enough to withstand another two hundred years of probing roots. In those days, he thought, they built to last.

He sat back on his heels for a moment, puffing on his pipe, then resumed his search, poking his stick at intervals into the nettles at the base of the ice-house roof but finding no other obvious points of weakness. He returned to the door and a closer examination of the brambles.

He was no gardener, he relied on his wife to tend their small patio garden where everything grew neatly in tubs, but even to his uneducated eye the brambles had a look of permanence. He spent some moments peering thoughtfully at the clods of earth and grass above the doorway, where roots had been torn free in handfuls, then, careful to avoid the grass which had been trodden on, he squatted beside the area of brambles which had been scythed and trampled flat. The broken stems were green with sap, most of the fruit was still unripe but the odd blackberry, more mature than its fellows, showed black and juicy amidst the ruins of its parent. With the end of the bamboo he carefully lifted the flattened mass of vegetation nearest to him and peered beneath it.

'Found anything, sir?' McLoughlin had returned.

'Look under here, Andy, and tell me what you see.'

24

McLoughlin knelt obligingly beside his superior and stared where Walsh was pointing. 'What am I looking for?'

'Stems with old breaks in them. We are safe in assuming our body didn't pole vault over this little lot.'

McLoughlin shook his head. 'We'd have to take the brambles apart for that, bit by bit, and I doubt we'd have much joy even then. Whoever flattened them did a thorough job.'

Walsh lowered the vegetation and removed the bamboo. 'The gardener, according to Mrs Maybury.'

'Looks as if he's put a steam-roller over it.'

'It's interesting, isn't it?' Walsh stood up. 'Did you get hold of Webster?'

'He's on his way, should be here in ten minutes. I've told the others to wait for him. Nick Robinson's already laid on the lights and the camera, so the gardener's showing them all down here once Webster arrives. Except young Williams. I've left him in the house to take background statements and keep his eyes open. He's a sharp lad. If there's anything to see, he'll see it.'

'Good. The mortuary van?'

'On stand-by at the station.'

Walsh moved a few yards away and sat down on the grass. 'We'll wait. There's nothing to be done until the photographs have been taken.' He blew a cloud of smoke out of the side of his mouth and squinted through it at McLoughlin. 'What is a nude corpse doing in Mrs Maybury's ice house, Sergeant? And what or, perhaps, who, has been eating it?'

With a groan, McLoughlin reached for his handkerchief.

PC Williams had taken statements from Mrs Maybury, Mrs Goode and Miss Cattrell and was now with Molly Phillips in the kitchen. For some reason that he couldn't understand, she was being deliberately obstructive and he thought with irritation that his colleagues had a knack of landing themselves the decent jobs. With ill-disguised satisfaction they had set off down the garden with Fred Phillips and the new arrivals and their assorted paraphernalia. Williams, who had seen Andy McLoughlin's face when he came up from the ice house, was consumed with curiosity as to what was down there. McLoughlin's nerves were sprung with Scottish steel, and he had looked as sick as a dog.

Reluctantly Constable Williams returned to the job in hand. 'So the first you knew about this body was when Mrs Goode came in to telephone?'

'What if it was?'

25

He looked at her in exasperation. 'Do you always answer questions with questions?'

'Maybe, maybe not. That's my business.'

He was only a lad, the sort that people looked at and said: Policemen are getting younger. He tried a wheedling approach that had worked for him on a couple of occasions in the past. 'Listen, Ma—'

'Don't you "Ma" me,' she spat at him viciously. 'You're no son of mine. I don't have kids.' She turned her back on him and busied herself slicing carrots into a saucepan. 'You should be ashamed of yourself. What would your mother say? She's the only one you've a right to call Ma like that.'

Frustrated old cow, he thought. He looked at the thin, drooping shoulders and reckoned her problem was that her old man had never given her a proper working over. 'I don't even know who she is.'

She was still for a moment, knife poised in mid-air, then went on with her slicing. She said nothing.

Williams tried another tack. 'All I'm doing, Mrs Phillips, is getting some background details on the discovery of the body. Mrs Goode has told me she came into the house to make the telephone call to us. She said you were in the hall when she made it and that afterwards she went down to the cellar to get some brandy because there was none left on the sideboard. Is that right?'

'If Mrs Goode says it is, that's enough for you. There's no need to come sneaking round here behind her back trying to find out if she's telling lies.'

He looked at her sharply. '*Is* she telling lies?'

'No, she's not. The very idea.'

'Then what's all the mystery?' he asked her angry back. 'What are you being so secretive about?'

She rounded on him. 'Don't you take that tone with me. I know your sort. None better. You'll not browbeat me.' She whisked the teacup from under his nose where he sat at the table and dumped it unceremoniously in her washing-up bowl. He could have sworn there were tears in her eyes.

The police photographer picked his way gingerly out of the doorway and lifted the camera strap over his neck. 'Finished, sir,' he told Walsh.

The Chief Inspector placed a hand on his shoulder. 'Good man. Back to the Station with you then and get that film developed.' He turned to the pathologist. 'Shall we go in, Webster?'

Dr Webster smiled grimly. 'Do I have a choice?'

'After you,' said Walsh maliciously.

The scene was lit now with battery-run arc-lights, every detail showing with stark clarity, no shadows to soften the shocking impact. Walsh gazed dispassionately on the body. It was true, he thought, that exposure to violence desensitised a man. He could barely recall his earlier repugnance, though perhaps the lights had something to do with this. As a child the dark had held terrors for him, with nightmare creations of his imagining lurking in the corners of his bedroom. His father, in other respects a kind man but fearing the embarrassment of an effeminate son, was unsympathetic and had closed his ears to the muffled weeping inside a bedroom from which all the light bulbs had been removed.

'Good God,' said Webster, surveying the ice-house floor with marked distaste. He picked his way carefully towards the centre of it, avoiding tattered pieces of hardened entrail which lay on the flagstones. He looked at the head. 'Good God,' he said again.

The head, still tethered to the upper torso by blackened sinew, was wedged in a gap in the top row of a neat stack of bricks. Dull grey hair, long enough to be a woman's, spilled out of the gap. Eyeless sockets, showing bone underneath, and exposed upper and lower jaw bones gleamed white against the blackened musculature of the face. The chest area, anchored by the head against the vertical face of bricks, looked as if it had been skilfully filleted. The lower half of the body lay unnaturally askew of its top half in a position that no living person, however supple, could have achieved. The abdominal region had all but disappeared though shreds of it lay about as mute witnesses that it had once existed. There were no genitals. The lower half of the left arm, propped on a smaller pile of bricks, was some four feet from the body, much of the flesh stripped away, but some sinews remaining to show it had been wrenched from its elbow. The right arm, pressed against the torso, had the same blackened quality as the head with patches of white bone showing through. Of the legs, only the calves and feet were immediately recognisable, but at a distance from each other in a grotesque parody of the splits and twisted upside down so that the soles pointed at the ice-house roof. Of the thighs, only splintered bones remained.

'Well?' said Walsh after some minutes during which the pathologist took temperature readings and made a rough sketch of the lie of the body.

'What do you want to know?'

'Man or woman?'

Webster pointed to the feet. 'From the size, I'd guess a man. We can't be sure until we've done some measurements, of course, but

27

it looks like it. If it's not a man, it was a big woman and a mannish one.'

'The hair's on the long side for a man. Unless it grew significantly after death.'

'Where have you been living, George? Even if it were down to the waist, it wouldn't tell you anything about the sex. And hair growth after death is minimal. No,' continued Webster, 'all things considered, I'd say we're dealing with a man, subject to confirmation, of course.'

'Any idea of age?'

'None, except that he's probably over twenty-one and even that's not certain. Some people go grey in their teens. I'll have to X-ray the skull for fusion between the plates.'

'How long has he been dead?'

Webster pursed his lips. 'That's going to be a bugger to decide. Old Fred out there said there was a bit of a stink when he stepped on it which would indicate a comparatively recent demise.' He sucked his teeth thoughtfully for some minutes, then shook his head and examined the floor carefully, using a spatula to loosen some dark material near the door. He sniffed the spatula. 'Excreta,' he announced, 'fairly recent, probably animal. You'd better take a cast of that to see if it's got Fred's boot prints. How long's he been dead?' He shivered suddenly. 'This is an ice house and several degrees cooler than it is outside. No obvious maggot infestation which implies the blowflies weren't attracted. If they had been, there'd be even less of it left. Frankly, George, your guess is as good as mine how long dead flesh would keep in this temperature. There is also the small matter of decomposition being hastened by consumption. We could be talking weeks, we could be talking months. I just don't know. I'll need to consult on this one.'

'Years?'

'No,' Webster said firmly. 'You'd be looking at a skeleton.'

'Supposing he was frozen when he came in. Would that make a difference?'

The pathologist snorted. 'You mean frozen as in fish fingers?' Walsh nodded. 'That's really too fantastic, George. You'd need a commercial freezer to freeze a man this size, and how would you transport him here? And why freeze him in the first place?' Webster frowned. 'It wouldn't make much difference as far as your investigation goes either. An ice house only keeps things frozen when it's full of ice. A frozen man would defrost in here just like a turkey in a larder. No, that's got to be out of the question.'

Walsh was staring thoughtfully at the severed arm. 'Has it? Odder

28

things have happened. Perhaps he's been in cold storage for ten years and was left here recently for someone to find.'

Webster whistled. 'David Maybury?'

'It's a possibility.' He squatted down and gestured to the distorted and tattered hand. 'What do you make of this? Looks to me as if the last two fingers are missing.'

Webster joined him. 'It's difficult to say,' he said doubtfully. 'Something's had a damn good go at it.' He glanced about the floor. 'You'll have to sweep up very thoroughly, make sure you don't miss anything. It's certainly odd. Could be coincidence, I suppose.'

Walsh stood up. 'I don't believe in coincidences. Any idea what he died of?'

'A first guess, George. Massive bleeding from a wound or wounds in his abdomen.'

Walsh glanced at him in surprise. 'You're very positive.'

'A guess, I said. You'll have to find his clothes to be sure. But look at him. The area from the abdomen down has been completely devoured, except for the lower halves of the legs. Imagine him sitting up, legs out in front of him, with blood pouring out of his belly. It would be seeping over precisely those parts which have been eaten.'

Inspector Walsh felt suddenly faint. 'Are you saying whatever it was ate him while he was still alive?'

'Well, don't have nightmares about it, old chap. If he was alive, he'd have been in a coma and wouldn't have known anything about it, otherwise he'd have scared the scavengers off. Stands to reason. Of course,' he continued thoughtfully, 'if he was defrosting slowly, the blood and water would liquefy to achieve the same result.'

Walsh performed the laborious ritual of lighting his pipe again, billowing clouds of blue smoke from the side of his mouth. Webster's mention of smell had made him aware of an underlying odour which he hadn't previously noticed. For some minutes he watched the doctor making a close examination of the head and chest, at one point taking some measurements. 'What sort of scavengers are we talking about? Foxes, rats?'

'Difficult to say.' He peered closely at one of the eye sockets, before indicating the fractured thigh bones. 'Something with strong jaws, I would guess. One thing's for certain, two of them have had a fight over him. Look at the way the legs are lying and that arm, pulled apart at the elbow. I'd say there's been a tug-of-war here.' He pursed his lips again. 'Badgers possibly. More likely dogs.'

Walsh thought of the yellow Labradors lying on the warm flag-stones, remembered how one of them had nuzzled the palm of his hand. With an abrupt movement, he wiped the hand down his trouser

29

leg. He puffed smoke relentlessly into the atmosphere. 'I follow your reasoning about why the animals should have gone for the abdomen and thighs, but they seem to have done a pretty good job on the top half as well. Why is that? Is it normal?'

Webster stood up and wiped his forehead with the sleeve of his shirt. 'God knows, George. About the only thing I'm sure of is that this whole thing is abnormal. I'll hazard a guess that the poor sod pressed his left hand to his belly to try to stop the blood running out or hold his guts in, whichever you prefer, then did what I just did – wiped the sweat off his face and smeared himself with blood. That would have attracted rats or whatever to his left hand and arm and the upper half of his body.'

'You said he'd have been in a coma.' Walsh's tone was accusing.

'Maybe he was, maybe he wasn't. How the hell should I know? Anyway, people move in comas.'

Walsh took his pipe out of his mouth and used its stem to point at the chest. 'Shall I tell you what that looks like to me?'

'Go on.'

'The bones on a breast of lamb after my wife's skinned the meat off it with a sharp knife.'

Webster looked tired. 'I know. I'm hoping it's deceptive. If it's not – well, you don't need me to spell out what it means.'

'The villagers say the women here are witches.'

Webster peeled off his gloves. 'Let's get out of here – unless there's anything else you think I can tell you. My own view is I'll find out more when I've got him on the slab.'

'Just one thing. Do you reckon he got his abdominal wound here or somewhere else?'

Webster picked up his case and led the way out. 'Don't ask me, George. The only thing I'm sure of is that he was alive when he got here. Whether he was *already* bleeding, I wouldn't know.' He paused in the doorway. 'Unless there's anything in this freezer theory, of course. Then he'd have been good and dead.'

FOUR

Three hours later, after the remains had been painstakingly removed under the direction of Dr Webster, and a laborious investigation of the ice-house interior had revealed little of note beyond a pile of dead bracken in one corner, the door was sealed and Walsh and McLoughlin returned to Streech Grange. Phoebe offered them the library to work in and, with a remarkable lack of curiosity, left them to their deliberations.

A team of policemen remained behind to comb the area in expanding circles round the ice house. Privately, Walsh thought this a wasted exercise – if too much time had elapsed between the body's arrival and its discovery, the surrounding area would tell them nothing. However, routine work had produced unlikely evidence before, and now various samples from the ice house were awaiting dispatch to the forensic labs. These included brick dust, tufts of fur, some discoloured mud off the floor and what Dr Webster asserted were the splintered remains of a lamb bone which McLoughlin had found amongst the brambles outside the door. Young Constable Williams, still ignorant of exactly what had been in the ice house, was summoned to the library.

He found Walsh and McLoughlin sitting side by side behind a mahogany desk of heroic proportions, the photographic evidence, developed at speed, spread fan-like in front of them. An ancient Anglepoise lamp with a green shade was the only lighting in the rapidly darkening room and, as Williams entered, Walsh bent the light away to soften the brightness of its glare. For the young PC, viewing the pictures upside down and in semi-darkness, it was a tantalising glimpse of the horrors he had so far only imagined. He read his small collection of statements with half an eye on McLoughlin's face, where black hollows were etched deep by the shadowy light. Jesus, but the bastard looked ill. He wondered if the whispers he'd heard were true.

'Their statements about the finding of the body are all consistent, sir. Nothing untoward in that direction.' He looked suddenly smug. 'But I reckon I've got a lead in another direction.'

'You do, do you?'

'Yes, sir. I'm betting Mr and Mrs Phillips were inside before they came to work here.' He consulted his neat and tiny script. 'Mrs Phillips was very peculiar, wouldn't answer any of my questions, kept accusing me of browbeating her, which I wasn't, and saying: "That's for me to know and you to find out." When I told her I'd have to take it up with Mrs Maybury, she damn near bit my head off. "Don't you go worrying madam," she said, "Fred and me's kept our noses clean since we've been out and that's all you need to know." ' He looked up triumphantly.

Walsh made a note on a piece of paper. 'All right, Constable, we'll look into it.'

McLoughlin saw the boy's disappointment and stirred himself. 'Good work, Williams,' he murmured. 'I think we should lay on sandwiches, sir. No one's had anything to eat since midday.' He thought of the liquid lunch he'd lost into the brambles. He'd have given his right arm for a beer. 'There's a pub at the bottom of the hill. Could Gavin get something made up for the lads?'

Testily, Walsh fished two tenners out of his jacket pocket. 'Sandwiches,' he ordered. 'Nothing too expensive. Leave some with us and take the rest to the ice house. You can stay and help the search down there.' He glanced behind him out of the window. 'They've got the arc-lights. Tell them to keep going as long as they can. We'll be down later. And don't forget my change.'

'Sir.' Williams left in a hurry before the Inspector could change his mind.

'He wouldn't be so bloody keen if he'd seen what was there,' remarked Walsh acidly, poking the photographs with a skinny finger. 'I wonder if he's right about the Phillips couple. Does the name ring a bell with you?'

'No.'

'Nor with me. Let's run through what we've got.' He took out his pipe and stuffed tobacco absent-mindedly into the bowl. Aloud, he sifted fussily through what facts they had, picking at them like chicken bones.

McLoughlin listened but didn't hear. His head hurt where a blood vessel, engorged and fat, was threatening to burst. Its roaring deafened him.

He picked a pencil off the desk and balanced it between his fingers. The ends trembled violently and he let it fall with a clatter. He forced himself to concentrate.

32

'So where do we start, Andy?'

'The ice house and who knew it was there. It has to be the key.' He isolated an exterior shot from the photographs on the desk and held it to the lamplight with shaking fingers. 'It looks like a hill,' he muttered. 'How would a stranger know it was hollow?'

Walsh clamped the pipe between his teeth and lit it. He didn't answer but took the photograph and studied it intently, smoking for a minute or two in silence.

Unemotionally, McLoughlin gazed on the pictures of the body. 'Is it Maybury?'

'Too early to say. Webster's gone back to check the dental and medical records. The bugger is we can't compare fingerprints. We weren't able to lift any from the house at the time of his disappearance. Not that we'd get a match. Both hands out there were in ribbons.' He tamped the burning tobacco with the end of his thumb. 'David Maybury had a very distinctive characteristic,' he continued after a moment. 'The last two fingers of his left hand were missing. He lost them in a shooting accident.'

McLoughlin felt the first flutterings of awakening interest. 'So it *is* him.'

'Could be.'

'That body hasn't been there ten years, sir. Dr Webster was talking in terms of months.'

'Maybe, maybe. I'll reserve judgement till I've seen the post-mortem report.'

'What was he like? Mrs Goode called him an out-and-out bastard.'

'I'd say that's a fair assessment. You can read up about him. It's all on file. I had a psychologist go through the evidence we took from the people who knew him. His unofficial verdict, bearing in mind he never met the man, was that Maybury showed marked psychopathic tendencies, particularly when drunk. He had a habit of beating people up, women as well as men.' Walsh puffed a spurt of smoke from the side of his mouth and eyed his subordinate. 'He put himself about a bit. We turned up at least three little tarts who kept warm beds for him in London.'

'Did she know?' He nodded towards the hall.

Walsh shrugged. 'Claimed she didn't.'

'Did he beat her up?'

'Undoubtedly, I should think, except she denied it. She had a bruise the size of a football on her face when she reported him missing and we found out she was twice admitted to hospital when he was alive, once with a fractured wrist and once with cracked ribs and a broken collar-bone. She told doctors she was accident-prone.'

He gave a harsh laugh. 'They didn't believe her any more than I did. He used her as his personal punch bag whenever he was drunk.'

'So why didn't she leave? Or perhaps she enjoyed the attention?'

Walsh considered him thoughtfully for a moment. He started to say something, then thought better of it. 'Streech Grange has been in her family for years. He lived here on sufferance and used her capital to run a small wine business from the house. Presumably most of the stock's still here if she hasn't drunk or sold it. No, she wouldn't leave. In fact I can't imagine any circumstances at all, not even fire, which would make her abandon her precious Streech Grange. She's a very tough lady.'

'And, I suppose, as he was in clover, he wouldn't go either.'

'That's about the size of it.'

'So she got rid of him.'

Walsh nodded.

'But you couldn't prove it.'

'No.'

McLoughlin's bleak face cracked into a semblance of a grin. 'She must have come up with one hell of a story.'

'Matter of fact, it was bloody awful. She told us he walked out one night and never returned.' Walsh wiped a dribble of tar and saliva off the end of his pipe with his sleeve. 'It was three days before she reported him missing, and she only did that because people had started to ask where he was. In that time she packed up all his clothes and sent them off to some charity whose name she couldn't remember, she burnt all his photos and went through this house with a vacuum cleaner and a cloth soaked with bleach to remove every last trace of him. In other words she behaved exactly like someone who had just murdered her husband and was trying to get rid of the evidence. We salvaged some hair that she'd missed in a brush, a current passport and photo that she'd overlooked at the back of a desk drawer, and an old blood donor card. And that was it. We turned this house and garden upside down, called in forensic to do a microscopic search and it was a waste of time. We scoured the countryside for him, showed his photo at all the ports and airports in case he'd somehow got through without a passport, alerted Interpol to look for him on the Continent, dredged lakes and rivers, released his photo to the national newspapers. Nothing. He simply vanished into thin air.'

'So how did she explain the bruise on her face?'

The Inspector chuckled. 'A door. What else? I tried to help her, suggested she killed her husband in self-defence. But no, he never touched her.' He shook his head, remembering. 'Extraordinary woman. She never made it easy for herself. She could have manufactured any number of stories to convince us he'd planned his disappearance – money troubles, for a start. He left her well-nigh penniless. But she did the reverse – she kept stolidly repeating that one night and for no reason he simply walked out and never came back. Only dead men disappear as completely as that.'

'Clever,' said McLoughlin reluctantly. 'She kept it simple, gave you nothing to pick holes in. So why didn't you charge her? Prosecutions have been brought without bodies before.'

The memories of ten years ago flooded back to try Walsh's patience. 'We couldn't put a case together,' he snapped. 'There wasn't one shred of evidence to dispute her bloody stupid story that he'd upped and left. We needed the body. We dug up half Hampshire looking for the blasted thing.' He fell silent for a moment, then tapped the photograph of the ice house which lay on the desk in front of him. 'You were right about this.'

'In what way?'

'It is the key. We searched Streech gardens from end to end ten years ago and none of us looked in here. I'd never seen an ice house in my life, never even heard of such a thing. So of course I didn't know the bloody hill was hollow. How the hell could I? No one told me. I remember standing on it at one point to get my bearings. I even remember telling one of my chaps to delve deep into those brambles. It was like a jungle.' He wiped the stem of his pipe on his sleeve again before putting it back in his mouth. Dried tar crisscrossed the tweed like black threads. 'I'll lay you any money you like, Andy, Maybury's body was in there all the time.'

There was a knock at the door and Phoebe came in carrying a tray of sandwiches. 'Constable Williams told me you were hungry, Inspector. I asked Molly to make these up for you.'

'Why thank you, Mrs Maybury. Come and sit down.' Phoebe put the tray of sandwiches on the desk, then seated herself in a leather armchair slightly to one side of it. The lamp on the desk shed a pool of light, embracing the three figures in a reluctant intimacy. The smoke from Walsh's pipe hung above them, floating in the air like curling tendrils of cirrus clouds. For one long moment there was complete silence, before the chiming mechanism of a grandfather clock whirred into action and struck the hour, nine o'clock.

Walsh, as if on cue, leant forward and addressed the woman. 'Why didn't you tell us about the ice house ten years ago, Mrs Maybury?'

For a moment he thought she looked surprised, even a little

35

relieved, then the expression vanished. Afterwards, he couldn't be sure it had been there at all. 'I don't understand,' she said.

Inspector Walsh gestured to McLoughlin to switch on the overhead lights. The muted lamplight disguised, deceived when he wanted to see every nuance of the extraordinarily impassive face. 'Its quite simple,' he murmured, after McLoughlin had flooded the room with brilliant white light, 'in our search for your husband, we never looked in the ice house. We didn't know it was there.' He studied her thoughtfully. 'And you didn't tell us.'

'I don't remember,' she said simply. 'If I didn't tell you, it was because I had forgotten about it. Did you not find it yourselves?'

'No.'

She gave a tiny shrug. 'Does it really matter, Inspector, after all this time?'

He ignored the question. 'Do you recall when the ice house was last used prior to your husband's disappearance?'

She leant her head tiredly against the back of her chair, her red hair splaying out around her pale face. Behind her glasses her eyes looked huge. Walsh knew her to be in her mid-thirties, yet she looked younger than his own daughter. He felt McLoughlin stir in the seat beside him as if her fragility had touched him in some way. Damn the woman, he thought with irritation, remembering the emotions she had once stirred in him. That appearance of vulnerability was a thin cloak for the sharp mind beneath.

'You'll have to let me think about it,' she said. 'At the moment, I honestly can't remember if we ever used it when David was alive. I have no recollection of it.' She paused briefly. 'I *do* recall my father using it as a darkroom one winter when I was on holiday from school. He didn't do it for very long.' She smiled. 'He said it was a confounded bore slogging all the way down there in the cold.' She gave a low ripple of laughter as if memories of her father made her happy. 'He took the films to a professional in Silverborne instead. My mother said it was because he enjoyed blaming someone else when the prints were disappointing, which they often were. He wasn't a very good photographer.' She looked steadily at the Inspector. 'I can't remember its being used after that, not until we decided to stack the bricks in there. The children might know. I suppose I could ask them.'

Walsh remembered her children, a gangling ten-year-old boy, arriving home from his boarding prep-school in the middle of the investigation, his eyes the same clear blue as his mother's, and an eight-year-old daughter with a bush of curling dark hair. They had protected her, he recalled, with the same fierce quality that her two friends had shown earlier in the drawing-room. 'Jonathan and Jane,' he said. 'Do they still live at home, Mrs Maybury?'

'Not really. Jonathan rents a flat in London. He's a medical student at Guy's. Jane is studying politics and philosophy at Oxford. They spend the odd weekend and holidays here. That's all.'

'They've done well. You must be pleased.' He thought sourly of his own daughter who had got herself pregnant at sixteen and who now, at the age of twenty-five, was divorced with four children, and had nothing to look forward to except life in a tatty council flat. He consulted his notes. 'You seem to have acquired a profession since I last saw you, Mrs Maybury. Constable Williams tells me you're a market gardener.'

Phoebe seemed puzzled by his change of direction. 'Fred's helped me build up a small Pelargonium nursery.' She spoke warily. 'We specialise in the Ivyleaf varieties.'

'Who buys them?'

'We have two main customers in this country, one's a supermarket chain and the other's a garden-supplies outlet in Devon and Cornwall. We've also had a few bulk orders from the States which we've air-freighted out.' She was intensely suspicious of him. 'Why do you want to know?'

'No particular reason,' he assured her. He sucked noisily on his pipe. 'I expect you get a lot of customers from the village.'

'None,' she said shortly. 'We don't sell direct to the public and, anyway, they wouldn't come here if we did.'

'You're not very popular in Streech, are you, Mrs Maybury?'

'So it would seem, Inspector.'

'You worked as a receptionist in the doctor's surgery ten years ago. Didn't you like that job?'

A flicker of amusement lifted the corners of her mouth. 'I was asked to leave. The patients felt uncomfortable with a murderess.'

'Did your husband know about the ice house?' He shot the question at her suddenly, unnerving her.

'That it was there, you mean?'

He nodded.

'I'm sure he must have done, though, as I say, I don't remember him ever going in there.'

Walsh made a note. 'We'll follow that up. The children may remember something. Will they be here this weekend, Mrs Maybury?'

She felt cold. 'I suppose if they don't come down, you'll send a policeman to them.'

'It's important.'

There was a tremor in her voice. 'Is it, Inspector? You have our word there was no body in there six years ago. What possible connection can that – that thing have with David's disappearance?' She took off her glasses and pressed her fingertips against her eyelids. 'I don't want the children harassed. They suffered enough when David went missing. To have the whole ghastly trauma played out a second time and for no obvious reason would be intolerable.'

Walsh smiled indulgently. 'Routine questions, Mrs Maybury. Hardly very traumatic, surely?'

She put her glasses on again, angered by his response. 'You were extraordinarily stupid ten years ago, of course. Why I ever assumed the passage of time would make you any brighter, I can't think. You sent us to hell and you call it "hardly traumatic". Do you know what hell is? Hell is what a little girl of eight goes through when the police dig up all the flowerbeds and question her mother for hours on end in a closed room. Hell is what is in your young son's eyes when his father deserts him without a word of explanation and his mother is accused of murder. Hell is seeing your children hurting and not being able to do a damn thing to stop it. You asked me if I was pleased with their achievements.' She leaned forward, her face twisted. 'Surely even you could have come up with something a little more imaginative? They have lived through the mysterious disappearance of their father, their mother being branded a murderess, their home being turned into a tourist attraction for the ghoulish and they have survived it relatively unscathed. I think "ecstatic" might be a better description of how I feel about the way they've turned out.'

'We suggested at the time you should send the children away, Mrs Maybury.' Walsh kept his voice carefully neutral. 'You chose to keep them here against our advice.'

Phoebe stood up. It was only the second time he had ever seen any violent emotion on that face. 'My God, I hate you.' She put her hands on the desk and he saw that the fingers trembled uncontrollably. 'Where was I to send them? My parents were dead, I had no brothers or sisters, neither Anne nor Diana was in a position to care for them. Was I supposed to entrust them to strangers when their own secure world was turning upside down?' She thought of her only relation, her father's unmarried sister, who had fallen out with the family years before. The old lady had read between every line of every newspaper with voracious delight and had penned her own small piece of poison to Phoebe on the subject of the sins of the parents. What her intentions were in writing the letter was anyone's guess but, in a strange way, her warped predictions for Jonathan and Jane had been a liberation for Phoebe. She had seen clearly

38

then – and for the first time – that the past was dead and buried and that regrets would achieve her nothing.

'How dare you speak to me of choice! My only choice was to smile while you shat on me and never once let the children know how frightened and alone I felt.' Her fingers gripped the edge of the desk. 'I will not go through all that again. I will not allow you to stick your dirty fingers into my children's lives. You've spread your filthy muck here once. You're bloody well not going to do it again.' She turned away and walked to the door.

'I've some more questions for you, Mrs Maybury. Please don't go.'

She looked round briefly as she opened the door. 'Fuck off, Inspector.' The door slammed behind her.

McLoughlin had listened to their exchange with rapt attention. 'Bit of a sea-change from this afternoon. Is she always as volatile?'

'Quite the reverse. Ten years ago we never rattled her composure once.' He sucked thoughtfully on his filthy briar.

'It's those two dykes she's shacked up with. They've turned her against men.'

Walsh was amused. 'I should think David Maybury did that years ago. Let's talk to Mrs Goode. Will you go and find her?'

McLoughlin reached for a sandwich and crammed it into his mouth before standing up. 'What about the other one? Shall I line her up too?'

The Chief Inspector thought for a moment. 'No. She's a dark horse, that one. I'll let her stew till I've checked up on her.'

From where he was standing, McLoughlin could see pink scalp shining through Walsh's thinning hair. He felt a sudden tenderness for the older man, as if Phoebe's hostility had exorcised his own and reminded him where his loyalties lay. 'She's your most likely suspect, sir. She'd have enjoyed cutting that poor sod's balls off. The other two would have hated it.'

'You're probably right, lad, but I'm betting he was dead when she did it.'

FIVE

Streech Grange was a fine old Jacobean mansion built of grey stone, with mullioned, leaded windows and steep slate roofs. Two wings, later additions, extended out at either end of the main body of the house, embracing the sides of the flagged terrace where the women had taken their tea. Stud partitions inside made each of these wings self-contained, with unlocked doors on the ground floor giving access to and from them. Sergeant McLoughlin, after a fruitless search of the drawing-room and the kitchen which were both empty, came to the communicating door with the east wing. He tapped lightly but, getting no response, turned the handle and walked down the corridor in front of him.

A door stood ajar at the end. He could hear a deep voice – unmistakably Anne Cattrell's – coming from inside the room. He listened.

'. . . stick to your guns and don't let the bastards intimidate you. God knows, I've had more experience of them than most. Whatever happens, Jane must be kept out of the way. You agree?' There was a murmur of assent. 'And, old love, if you can wipe the smirk off that Sergeant's face, you'll have my lifelong admiration.'

'I suppose it's occurred to you' – the lighter amused voice was Diana's – 'that he might have been born with that smirk. Perhaps it's a disability he's had to learn to cope with, like a withered arm. You'd be quite sympathetic if that were the case.'

Anne gave her throaty laugh. 'The only disabilities that idiot has are both in his trousers.'

'Namely?'

'He's a prick and an arsehole.'

Diana crowed with laughter and McLoughlin felt a dull flush creep up his neck. He trod softly to the communicating door, closed it behind him and knocked again, this time more loudly. When, after some moments, Anne opened the door, he was ready with his most sardonic smile.

'Yes, Sergeant?'

'I'm looking for Mrs Goode. Inspector Walsh would like a word with her.'

'This is my wing. She's not here.'

The lie was so blatant that he looked at her in astonishment. 'But—' He paused.

'But what, Sergeant?'

'Where will I find her?'

'I've no idea. Perhaps the Inspector would like to speak to me instead?'

McLoughlin pushed past her impatiently and walked down the corridor and into the room. There was no one in there. He frowned. The room was a large one with a desk at one end and a sofa and armchairs grouped about a wide fireplace at the other. Pot plants grew in profusion everywhere, cascading like green waterfalls from the mantelpiece, climbing up lattice-work on one of the walls, dappling the light from the lamps on low occasional tables. Floor to ceiling curtains in a herring-bone pattern of pale pinks, greys and blues were drawn along the length of the two outside walls, a royal blue carpet covered the floor, bright abstract paintings laughed merrily from the picture rails. Books in bookcases stood as straight as soldiers wherever there was a space. It was a delightful room, not one that McLoughlin would ever have associated with the tiny muscular woman who had followed him in and was now leaning her cropped, dark head against the door-jamb, waiting.

'Do you make a habit of forcing your way into people's private apartments, Sergeant? I have no recollection of inviting you in.'

'We have Mrs Maybury's permission to come and go as we please,' he said dismissively.

She walked over to one of the armchairs and slumped into it, taking a cigarette from a packet on the arm. 'Of course, in her house,' she agreed, lighting the cigarette. 'But this wing is mine. You have no authority to enter here except by permission or with a warrant.'

'I'm sorry,' he said stiffly. He felt suddenly uncomfortable, towering over her, conspicuously ill-at-ease while she, by contrast, was relaxed. 'I was not aware you owned this part of the house.'

'I don't own it, I rent it, but the legal position with regard to police entry is the same.' She smiled thinly. 'As a matter of interest, what possible reason had you for thinking Mrs Goode might be in here?'

He saw one of the curtain edges lift as a gentle breeze caught it, and realised Diana must have left by a French window. He cursed himself silently for allowing this woman to make a mockery of him.

'I couldn't find her anywhere else,' he said brusquely, 'and Inspector Walsh wants to speak to her. Does she live in the other wing?'

'She rents the other wing. As to living in it – surely you've guessed we all three rather muck in together. It's what's known as a ménage à trois, though in our case, rather loosely. The average threesome includes both sexes. We, I'm afraid, are more exclusive, preferring, as we do, our peculiarly – how shall I describe it? – spicy female sex. Three makes for more exciting encounters than two, don't you think. Or have you never tried?'

His dislike of her was irrational and intense. He jerked his head in the direction of the main part of the house. 'Have you corrupted her children the way you've corrupted her?'

She laughed softly and stood up. 'You'll find Mrs Goode in her sitting-room, I expect. I'll show you out.' She led the way along her corridor and opened the door. 'Walk straight through the main body of the house until you reach the west wing. It's a mirror image of this. You'll find a similar door to mine leading into it.' She pointed to a bell on the wall which he hadn't previously noticed. 'I should ring that if I were you. At the very least, it would be polite.' She stood watching him as he walked away, a scornful smile distorting her lips.

Andy McLoughlin had to pass the library door to reach the west wing so he looked in to tell Walsh it would be a few minutes yet before he returned with Diana Goode. To his surprise, she was in there already, sitting in the chair Phoebe had sat in. She and the Inspector turned their heads as the door opened. They were laughing together like people sharing a private joke.

'There you are, Sergeant. We've been waiting for you.'

He took his seat again and viewed Diana with suspicion. 'How did you know the Inspector wanted to talk to you?' He pictured her outside the French windows listening to Anne Cattrell making a fool of him.

'I didn't, Sergeant. I popped my head in to see if you wanted a cup of coffee.' She smiled good-humouredly and crossed one elegant leg over the other. 'What did you want to talk to me about, Inspector?'

There was an appreciative gleam in George Walsh's eye. 'How long have you known Mrs Maybury?' he asked her.

'Twenty-five years. Since we were twelve. We were at boarding school together. Anne, too.'

'A long time.'

'Yes. We've known her longer than anyone else, I suppose, longer

42

even than her parents did. They died when she was in her early twenties.' She came to a halt. 'But you know all about that from last time,' she finished awkwardly.

'Remind us,' Walsh encouraged.

Diana lowered her eyes to hide their expression. It was all very well for Anne to say don't let the bastards intimidate you. Knowledge itself was intimidating. With one casual reference, the sort she might make to anyone, she had rekindled the sparks of an old suspicion. No smoke without fire, everyone had said when David disappeared.

'They died in a car crash, didn't they?' Walsh prompted.

She nodded. 'The brakes failed. They were dead when they were cut out of the wreckage.' There was a long silence.

'If I remember correctly,' said Walsh to McLoughlin when Diana didn't go on, 'there were rumours of sabotage. Am I right, Mrs Goode? The village seemed to think Mrs Maybury caused the accident to get her hands prematurely on her inheritance. People have long memories. The story was resurrected at the time of Mr Maybury's disappearance.'

McLoughlin studied Diana's bent head. 'Why should they think that?' he asked.

'Because they're stupid,' she said fiercely. 'There was no truth in it. The Coroner's verdict couldn't have been clearer – the brakes failed because fluid had leaked from a corroded hose. The car was supposed to have been serviced three weeks before by a man called Casey who owned the garage in the village. He was just a bloody little crook. He took the money and didn't do the job.' She frowned. 'There was talk of a prosecution but it never came to anything. Not enough evidence, apparently. Anyway, it was Casey who started rumours that Phoebe had sabotaged the car to get her hands on Streech Grange. He didn't want to lose his customers.'

McLoughlin looked her up and down, but there was no appreciative gleam in his eyes. His indifference was complete and, to a woman like Diana who used flirtation to manipulate both sexes, it was daunting. Charm was powerless against a stone wall. 'There must have been more to it than that,' he suggested dryly. 'People aren't usually so gullible.'

She played with the hem of her jacket. 'It was David's fault. Phoebe's parents had given them a little house in Pimlico as a wedding present which David used as collateral for a loan. He lost the lot on some stock market gamble, couldn't make the repayments and they were in the throes of foreclosure at the time of the accident, with two small children, no money and nowhere to go.' She shook her head. 'God knows how, but that became public knowledge. The

43

locals lapped up what Casey was saying, put two and two together and made five. From the moment Phoebe took over this house, she was damned. David's disappearance a few years later simply confirmed all their prejudices.' She sighed. 'The sickening thing is, they didn't believe Casey either. He went bankrupt ten months later when all his customers deserted him. He had to sell up and move away, so there was some justice,' she said spitefully. 'Not that it did Phoebe any good. They were too damn stupid to see that if he was lying, she was innocent.'

McLoughlin leaned back in his chair, splaying strong fingers against the desk-top. He flicked her an unexpectedly boyish smile. 'It must have been awful for her.'

She responded guardedly. 'It was. She was so young and she had to cope with it alone. David either took himself off for weeks at a time or made matters worse by getting into rows with people.'

His eyes softened, as if he understood loneliness and could sympathise with it. 'And I suppose her friends here deserted her because of him?'

Diana thawed. 'She never really had any, that was half the trouble. If she had, it would have made all the difference. She went away to boarding school at the age of twelve, married at seventeen and only came back when her parents were dead. She's never had any friends in Streech.'

McLoughlin drummed his fingers softly on the mahogany. ' "The worst solitude is to be destitute of sincere friendship." Francis Bacon said that four hundred years ago.'

She was quite taken aback. Anne used Francis Bacon quotes as a matter of course but they tended to be flippant, throw-away lines, tossed into a conversation for careless effect. McLoughlin's dark voice lingered over the words. rolling them on his tongue, giving them weight. She was as surprised by their aptness as by the fact that he knew them. She regarded him thoughtfully.

'But he also said, "The mould of a man's fortune is in his own hands." ' His lips twisted cruelly. 'It's odd, isn't it, how Mrs Maybury brings out the worst in people? What's her secret, I wonder?' He stirred the photographs of crude death with the end of his pencil, turning them slowly so that Diana could see them. 'Why didn't she sell the Grange and move away, once she'd got rid of her husband?'

For all her surface sophistication, Diana was naive. Brutality shocked her because she never saw it coming. 'She couldn't,' she snapped angrily. 'It's not Phoebe's to sell. After a year of marriage to that bastard, she persuaded her father to change his Will and leave the house to her children. We three rent it from them.'

'Then why haven't her children sold it? Have they no sympathy for their mother?' He caught her eye. 'Or perhaps they don't like her? It seems to be a common problem for Mrs Maybury.'

Anger threatened to overwhelm Diana. She forced herself to stay calm. 'The idea, Sergeant, was to prevent David turning the house into ready cash and leaving Phoebe and the children homeless the minute the Gallaghers died. He'd have done it, too, given half a chance. He went through the money she inherited in record time. Colonel Gallagher, Phoebe's father, left instructions that the house could not be sold or mortgaged except under the most exceptional circumstances before Jane's twenty-first birthday. The responsibility for deciding whether those circumstances – principally financial distress on the part of Phoebe and her children – ever materialise was left to two trustees. In the view of the trustees, things have never got so bad that the sale of the Grange was the only option.'

'Was no other distress taken into account?'

'Of course not,' she said with heavy sarcasm. 'How could it have been? Colonel Gallagher wasn't clairvoyant. He did give discretion to the trustees but they have chosen to stick to the precise terms of the Will. In view of the uncertainty over David, whether he's dead or alive, it seemed the safest thing to do, even if Phoebe did suffer.' She glanced at Walsh to draw him back into the discussion. McLoughlin frightened her. 'The trustees have always put the children first, as they were instructed to do under the terms of the Will.'

McLoughlin's amusement was genuine. 'I'm beginning to feel quite sorry for Mrs Maybury. Does she dislike these trustees as much as they seem to dislike her?'

'I wouldn't know, Sergeant. I've never asked her.'

'Who are they?'

Chief Inspector Walsh chuckled. The lad had just hanged himself. 'Miss Anne Cattrell and Mrs Diana Goode. It was some Will, gave you two ladies a deal of responsibility when you were barely in your twenties. We've a copy on file,' he told the Sergeant. 'Colonel Gallagher must have thought very highly of you both to entrust you with his grandchildren's future.'

Diana smiled. She must remember to tell Anne how she'd wiped the smirk off McLoughlin's face. 'He did,' she said. 'Why should that surprise you?'

Walsh pursed his lips. 'I found it surprising ten years ago, but then I had never met you and Miss Cattrell. You were abroad at that time, I think, Mrs Goode.' He smiled and dropped one eyelid in what looked remarkably like a wink. 'I do not find it surprising now.'

She inclined her head. 'Thank you. My ex-husband is American. I was with him in the States when David vanished. I returned a year later after my divorce.'

She continued to look at Walsh but the hairs on her neck bristled under the weight of McLoughlin's gaze. She didn't want to catch his eye again. 'Did Colonel Gallagher know about the relationship you and Miss Cattrell had with his daughter?' he asked softly.

'That we were friends, you mean?' She kept her eyes on the Inspector.

'I was thinking more in terms of the bedroom, Mrs Goode, and the effect your fun and games might have on his grandchildren. Or didn't he know about that?'

Diana stared at her hands. She found people's contempt so difficult to handle and she wished she had one half of Anne's indifference to it. 'Not that it's any of your business, Sergeant,' she said at last, 'but Gerald Gallagher knew everything there was to know about us. He was not a man you had to hide things from.'

Walsh had been busily replenishing his pipe with tobacco. He put it into his mouth and lit it, belching more smoke into the already fuggy atmosphere. 'After they came back to the house, did either Mrs Maybury or Miss Cattrell suggest that they thought the body in the ice house was David Maybury's?'

'No.'

'Did either of them say who they thought it might be?'

'Anne said it was probably a tramp who had had a heart attack.'

'Mrs Maybury?'

Diana thought for a moment. 'Her only comment was that tramps don't die of heart attacks in the nude.'

'What's your view, Mrs Goode?'

'I don't have a view, Inspector, except that it isn't David. You've already had my reasons for that.'

'Why do you and Miss Cattrell want Jane Maybury kept out of the way?' McLoughlin asked suddenly.

There was no hesitation in her answer though she glanced at him curiously as she spoke. 'Jane was anorexic until eighteen months ago. She took a place at Oxford last September with her consultant's blessing, but he warned her not to put herself under unnecessary pressure. As trustees, we endorse Phoebe's view that Jane should be protected from this. She's still painfully thin. Undue anxiety would use up her reserves of energy. Do you consider that unreasonable, Sergeant?'

'Not at all,' he answered mildly.

'I wonder why Mrs Maybury didn't explain her daughter's condition to us,' asked Walsh. 'Has she a particular reason for keeping quiet about it?'

'None that I know of, but perhaps experience has taught her to be circumspect where the police are concerned.'

'How so?' He was affable.

'It's in your nature to go for the weak link. We all know that Jane can tell you nothing about that body, but Phoebe's probably afraid you'll question her until she cracks. And only when you've broken her will you be satisfied that she knew nothing in the first place.'

'You've a very twisted view of us, Mrs Goode.'

Diana forced a light laugh. 'Surely not, Inspector. Of the three of us, I'm the only one who retains some confidence in you. It is I, after all, who is giving you information.' She uncrossed her legs and drew them up on to the chair, covering them entirely with her knitted jacket. Her eyes rested briefly on the photographs. 'Is it a man's body? Anne and Phoebe couldn't tell.'

'At the moment we think so.'

'Murdered?'

'Probably.'

'Then take my advice and look in this village or the surrounding ones for your victim and your murderer. Phoebe is such an obvious scapegoat for someone else's crime. Shove the body on to her property and leave her to carry the can, that will have been the thinking behind this.'

Walsh nodded appreciatively as he pencilled a note on his pad. 'It's a possibility, Mrs Goode, a definite possibility. You're interested in psychology?'

He's quite a poppet after all, thought Diana, unleashing one of the calculatedly charming smiles she reserved for her more biddable customers. 'I use it all the time in my work,' she told him, 'though I don't suppose a clinician would call what I use psychology.'

He beamed back at her. 'So what would *he* call it?'

'Hidden persuasion, I should think.' She thought of Lady Keevil and her lime-green curtains. Lies, Anne would call it.

'Do your clients come here to consult you?'

She shook her head. 'No. It's their interiors they want designing, not mine. I go to them.'

'But you're an attractive woman, Mrs Goode.' His admiration for her was blatant. 'You must have a lot of friends who come visiting, people from the village, people you've met over the years.'

She wondered if he guessed how tender this particular nerve was, how deeply she felt the isolation of their lives. At first, bruised and battered from the break-up of her marriage, it had hardly mattered.

47

She had withdrawn inside the walls of Streech Grange to lick her wounds in peace, grateful for the absence of well-meaning friends and their embarrassing commiserations. The shock of discovery, as her scars healed and she tendered for one or two small design contracts, that Phoebe's exclusion had been imposed and not chosen had been a real one. She had learnt what it was to be a pariah; she had watched Phoebe nurture her hate; she had watched Anne's tolerance turn to cynical indifference; she had heard her own voice grow brittle. 'No,' she corrected him. 'We have very few visitors, certainly never from the village.'

His eyes were encouraging. 'Then tell me, assuming you're right and our victim and murderer are local, how could they know about the ice house and, if they did know about it, how did they find it? I think you'll agree it's well disguised.'

'Anyone could know about it,' she said dismissively. 'Fred may have mentioned it in the pub after he stacked the bricks in there. Phoebe's parents may have told people about it. I don't see that as a mystery.'

'All right. Now tell me how you find it if you haven't been shown where it is? Presumably none of you has noticed an intruder searching the grounds or you'd have mentioned it. And another thing, why was it necessary to put the body in there at all?'

She shrugged. 'It's a good hiding place.'

'How did the murderer know that? How did he or she know the ice house wasn't in regular use? And what was the point of hiding the body if the idea was to make Phoebe Maybury the scapegoat? You see, Mrs Goode, the picture is rather unclear.'

She thought for a moment. 'You can't rule out pure chance. Someone committed a murder, decided to get rid of the body in the Grange grounds in the hopes that, if it was discovered the police would concentrate their efforts on Phoebe, and stumbled on the ice house by accident while looking for somewhere to put the body.'

'But the ice house is half a mile from the gates,' Walsh objected. 'Do you seriously believe that a murderer staggered past the Lodge House and all the way down your drive and across your lawn in pitch darkness with a body on his shoulders? We can assume, I think, that no one would have been mad enough to do it during the daytime. Why didn't he simply bury the body in the wood near the gates?'

She looked uncomfortable. 'Perhaps he came over the wall at the back and approached the ice house from that direction.'

'Wouldn't that have meant negotiating his way through Grange Farm, which if I remember correctly adjoins the Grange at the back?'

She nodded reluctantly. 'Why run that danger? And why, having run it, not bury the body quickly, in the woodland there? Why was it so important to put him in the ice house?'

Diana shivered suddenly. She understood perfectly that he was trying to box her in, force her on to the defensive and admit that knowledge of the ice house and its whereabouts was a crucial element. 'It seems to me, Inspector,' she continued coolly, 'that you have made a number of assumptions which – correct me if I'm wrong – have yet to be substantiated. First, you are assuming the body was taken there. Perhaps whoever it was went under his – or her – own steam and met the murderer there.'

'Of course we've considered that possibility, Mrs Goode. It doesn't alter our thinking at all. We must still ask: Why the ice house and how did they know where to find it unless they had been there before?'

'Well, then,' she said, 'work on the assumption that people have been there and find out who they are. Off the top of my head, I could make several suggestions. Friends of Colonel Gallagher and his wife, for example.'

'Who would be in their seventies or eighties by now. Of course it's possible that an elderly person was responsible but, statistically, unlikely.'

'People to whom Phoebe or David pointed it out.'

McLoughlin moved on his chair. 'Mrs Maybury has already told us she'd forgotten all about it, so much so that she omitted to tell the police it was there when they were searching the grounds for her husband. It seems unlikely, if she had forgotten it to that extent, that she would have remembered to point it out to casual visitors who, from what you yourself have said, don't come here anyway.'

'David then.'

'Now you have it, Mrs Goode,' said the Inspector. 'David Maybury may well have shown the ice house to someone, to several people even, but Mrs Maybury has no recollection of it. Indeed, she cannot recall *him* ever using it though she did agree that he was probably aware of its existence. Frankly, Mrs Goode, at the moment I don't see how we can proceed in that direction unless Mrs Maybury or the children can remember occasions or names that might give us a lead.'

'The children,' said Diana, leaning forward. 'I should have thought of it before. They will have taken their friends there when they were younger. You know how inquisitive children are, there can't be an inch of this estate they won't have explored with their gang.' She sank back with sudden relief. 'That's it, of course. It'll be one of the village children who grew up with them, hardly a child now, though

49

– someone in his early twenties.' She noticed the smirk was back on McLoughlin's face.

Walsh spoke gently. 'I agree entirely that that is a possibility. Which is why it's so important for us to question Jonathan *and* Jane. It can't be avoided, you know, however much you and her mother may dislike the idea. Jane may be the only one who can lead us to a murderer.' He reached for another sandwich. 'The police are not barbarians, Mrs Goode. I can assure you we will be sympathetic and tactful in our dealings with her. I hope you will persuade Mrs Maybury of that.'

Diana uncurled her legs and stood up. Quite unaware of it, she leant on the desk in just the way Phoebe had done, as if close proximity had taught the women to adopt each other's mannerisms. 'I can't promise anything, Inspector. Phoebe has a mind of her own.'

'She has no choice in the matter,' he said flatly, 'except to influence her daughter over whether we question her here or in Oxford. Under the circumstances, I imagine Mrs Maybury would prefer it to be here.'

Diana straightened. 'Is there anything else you want to ask me?'

'Only two more things tonight. Tomorrow Sergeant McLoughlin will question you in more detail.' He looked up at her. 'How did Mrs Maybury come to employ the Phillipses? Did she advertise or did she apply to an agency?'

Diana's hands were fluttering. She thrust them into the pockets of her jacket. 'I believe Anne arranged it,' she said. 'You'll have to ask her.'

'Thank you. Now, just one more thing. When you helped clear the rubbish from the ice house what exactly was in there and what did you do with it?'

'It was ages ago,' she said uncomfortably. 'I can't remember. Nothing out of the way, just rubbish.'

Walsh looked at her thoughtfully. 'Describe the inside of the ice house to me, Mrs Goode.' He watched her eyes search rapidly amongst the photographs on the desk, but he had turned over all the general shots when she first came in. 'How big is it? What shape is the doorway? What's the floor made of?'

'I can't remember.'

He smiled a slow, satisfied smile and she was reminded of a stuffed timber wolf she had once seen with bared teeth and staring glass eyes. 'Thank you,' he said. She was dismissed.

SIX

Diana found Phoebe watching the ten o'clock news in the television room. The flickering colours from the set provided the only light and they played across Phoebe's glasses, hiding her eyes and giving her the look of a blind woman. Diana snapped on the table lamp.

'You'll get a headache,' she said, flopping into the seat beside Phoebe, reaching out to stroke the softly tanncd forearm.

Phoebe muted the sound of the television with the remote control on her lap, but left the picture running. 'I've got one already,' she admitted tiredly. She took off her glasses and held a handkerchief to her red-rimmed eyes. 'Sorry,' she said.

'What about?'

'Blubbing. I thought I'd grown out of it.'

Diana pulled a footstool forward with her toes and settled her feet on it comfortably. 'A good blub is one of my few remaining pleasures.'

Phoebe smiled. 'But not very helpful.' She tucked the handkerchief into her sleeve and replaced her glasses.

'Have you had anything to eat?'

'I'm not hungry. Molly left a casserole in the Aga if you are.'

'Mm, she told me before she left. I'm not hungry either.'

They lapsed into silence.

'It's a bloody mess, isn't it?' said Phoebe after a while.

'I'm afraid so.' Diana pushed her sandals off her feet and let them drop to the floor. 'The Inspector's no fool.' She kept her voice deliberately light.

Phoebe spoke harshly. 'I hate him. How old would you say he is?'

'Late fifties.'

'He hasn't aged much. He looked like a genial professor ten years ago.' She considered for a moment. 'But that's not his character. He's anything but genial. He's dangerous, Di. For God's sake don't forget it.'

The other woman nodded. 'And his incubus, Jock-the-Ripper? What did you make of him?'

51

Phoebe looked surprised as if the other woman had mentioned an irrelevance. 'The Sergeant? He didn't say much. Why do you ask?'

With rhythmical movements, as if she were stroking a cat, Diana smoothed the woollen pile on the front of her jacket. 'Anne's spoiling for a fight with him and I'm not sure why.' She glanced speculatively at Phoebe, who shrugged. 'She's making a mistake. She took one look at him in the drawing-room, labelled him "Pig-ignorant" and made up her mind to walk all over him. Damn!' she said with feeling. 'Why can't she learn to compromise occasionally? She'll have us up to our necks in shit if she's not careful.'

'Have they spoken to her yet?'

'No, they've told her they'll talk to her tomorrow. They seem very relaxed about it all. We have their official permission to go to bed.'

Phoebe closed her eyes and pressed long fingers against her temples. 'What did they ask you?'

Diana twisted in her chair to look at her friend. 'From what they implied, exactly what they asked you.'

'Except that I walked out and refused to answer their questions.' She opened her eyes and looked ruefully at the other woman. 'I know,' she said. 'It was very silly of me but they made me so angry. Strange, isn't it? I stood up to hours of interrogation when David went. This time, I lasted five minutes. I found myself hating that man so much, I wanted to claw his eyes out. I could have done it, too.'

Diana reached out again and briefly touched her arm. 'I don't think it's strange – any psychiatrist would tell you that anger is a normal reaction to stress – but it's probably unwise.' She pulled a face. 'Anne will say I've bottled out, of course, but my view is we should give them all the co-operation we can. The sooner they sort it out and leave us alone, the better.'

'They want to question the children.'

'I know and I don't think we can prevent it.'

'I could ask Jane's psychiatrist to write a report advising against it. Would that stop them?'

'For a day or two perhaps before they secured an order for a second opinion. That would declare her competent to answer questions. You know yourself, her own psychiatrist pronounced her fit eighteen months ago.'

'Not for this.' Phoebe massaged her temples vigorously. 'I'm frightened, Di. I really think she's managed to blot it all out. If they make her remember now, God knows what will happen.'

'Talk to Anne,' Diana said. 'She can be more objective than you.

You may find that you're underestimating Jane's strengths. She is your daughter, after all.'

'Meaning that I am less able to be objective?'

Go easy, Diana told herself. 'Meaning that she will have inherited the rigid Gallagher backbone, you oaf.'

'You're forgetting her father. However much I might like to pretend otherwise, there is some of David in each of them.'

'He wasn't all bad, Pheeb.'

Tears welled uncontrollably in Phoebe's eyes. She blinked them away angrily. 'But he was, and you know it as well as I do. You told the Inspector so this afternoon and you were right. He was rotten to the core. In time, if we hadn't got shot of him, he'd have turned me and the children rotten too. He had a damn good try in all conscience.' She was silent for a moment. 'It's the only thing I hold against my parents. If they hadn't been so conventional I need never have married him. I could have had Johnny and brought him up on my own.'

'It was difficult for them.' But I agree with her, thought Diana. There was no excuse for what her parents did, so why am I defending them? 'They did what they thought was right.'

'I was seventeen, for Christ's sake – ' Phoebe's nails bit deep into her palms – 'younger than Jane is now. I allowed myself to be married off to a bastard twice my age simply because he'd seduced me, and then I just stood by and watched him rewarded for it. Christ,' she spat, 'it makes me sick to think of the money he bled from my father.'

Then don't think about it, Diana wanted to say. You've tried to forget them, but there *were* good times, times at the beginning when Anne and I envied you because you were a woman and we were still gangling schoolgirls. One weekend in particular, it was still vivid in her memory, when David on some mad whim had taken the three of them on a business trip to Paris. She forgot which company he was working for, there had been so many, but the weekend she would never forget. David, so assured, so deft in his choice of where to go and what to do, so unaffected by the foreignness of it all; Phoebe, four months pregnant, lovely face framed in a glorious picture hat, so delighted with herself and with David; and Anne and Diana, out for half-term, in a fantasy of beautiful people in beautiful places. And it was fantasy, of course, for the reality of David Maybury was brutish, ugly – Diana had discovered that for herself – yet once, in Paris, they had known enchantment.

Phoebe stood abruptly, walked over to the television set and switched it off. She spoke with her back to Diana. 'Do you know what kept me going through all those hours of police questioning last time? How it was I managed to stay so calm in spite of what they were accusing me of?' She turned round and Diana saw that the tears had stopped as suddenly as they had started. 'It was relief, sheer bloody relief that I had got rid of the bastard so easily.'

Diana glanced at the curtains. It was cold for a night in August, she thought, and Phoebe must have left the window open. 'You're talking rubbish,' she said firmly. 'The last ten years have addled your brain. There was nothing easy about getting rid of David. Good God, woman, he's been an albatross round your neck since the day you married him, still is.' She pulled her jacket tighter about her. 'If only they'd found a body somewhere that you could have identified.'

'If pigs could fly,' reflected Phoebe as she tidied the room and punched the cushions ferociously into airy plumpness.

Diana picked up an empty coffee cup and walked through into the kitchen. 'They're concentrating their efforts on the ice house,' she announced over her shoulder. She ran the tap and washed the cup. 'They're working on the assumption that no one knows where it is.' She heard the sound of the window being closed in the television room. 'If I were you, I'd make a list of anyone you, David or the children have ever shown it to. I'm sure there'll be a lot of names.'

Phoebe laughed bitterly and drew a scrap of paper from her pocket. 'I've been racking my brains ever since I left the library. Result: Peter and Emma Barnes, and I can't swear to them.'

'You mean the awful Dilys's children?'

'Yes. They used to roam about the garden during one school holidays, looking for Jonathan and Jane. I'm sure Dilys put them up to it as a way of getting in with us.'

'But there must have been other children, Pheeb, in the early days.'

'No, not even schoolfriends. Jon was boarding, remember, and never wanted friends to stay, and Jane never wanted friends full stop. It was my fault. I should have encouraged them but things were just so difficult that I was really glad they were anti-social.'

'So what happened with Peter and Emma?'

'It all became rather unpleasant. Emma kept taking her knickers down in front of Jonathan.' She shook her head. 'I drew the line when he started taking his down, too. He was nine.' She sighed. 'Anyway, like a fool, I told David. So he promptly phoned Dilys and gave her an earful. He called her a vulgar bitch and said "like mother, like daughter". After that, they never came up here again, but I suppose Jon might have shown them the ice house before they were banned.'

54

Diana gave a guilty giggle. 'For once David was probably right. Emma hasn't improved much with the passing years, let's face it.'

'He had no business to speak to anyone like that,' said Phoebe coldly. 'God knows, I can't stand the woman, but Jon was behaving as badly as Emma. David never even told him off for it. He thought it was a great joke, talked about Jon becoming a man. I could have killed him for that. If anyone was vulgar, David was.'

Diana was disturbed by Phoebe's mood. She had known her to be bitter before but never with such a depth of feeling over something so petty. It was as if the events of the afternoon had caused a breach in her long-held defences, releasing the pent-up emotions of years. She saw the dangers of it only too clearly. She and Anne had thought of Jane as the weak link. Were they wrong? Was it not Phoebe, after all, who was the more vulnerable?

'You're tired, old thing,' she said calmly, putting her arm through the other woman's. 'Let's go to bed and sleep on it.'

Phoebe's head drooped wearily. 'I've got such a bloody awful headache.'

'Hardly surprising in the circumstances. Take some aspirin. You'll be a new woman in the morning.'

They walked arm in arm down the corridor. 'Did they ask you about Fred and Molly?' queried Phoebe suddenly.

'A bit.'

'Oh, lord.'

'Don't worry about it.' They had reached the stairs. Diana gave her a kiss and released her. 'Walsh also asked me to describe the ice house,' she said with reluctance.

'I told you he was dangerous,' said Phoebe, walking up the stairs.

Diana's footsteps were loud in the silence. The phrase 'quiet as the grave' came to haunt her as she took off her shoes and tip-toed along the corridor. She eased Anne's door open and looked round it. Anne was at the desk, working at her word-processor. Diana whistled quietly to attract her attention, then pointed at the ceiling. Together they crept up the stairs to Anne's bedroom.

Anne followed her in, eyes alight with mischief and laughter. 'My God, Di, this is so unlike you. You're always such a stickler for appearances. You do realise the place is still crawling with filth?'

'Don't be an idiot. It's not a game this time, so just shut up and listen.'

She pushed Anne on to the bed and perched, cross-legged, beside her. As she spoke, her hands worked nervously, kneading and pummelling the softness of the duvet.

SEVEN

The curtain was drawn aside and Phoebe Maybury appeared at the window. She stared out for a moment, her hair a fiery red where the lamplight caught it from behind, her eyes huge in her strained white face. Looking at her, George Walsh wondered what emotions had stirred her. Fear? Guilt? Madness even? There was something amiss in those staring eyes. She was so close he could have touched her. He held his breath. She reached out, caught the handle and pulled the window to. The curtain fell back into place and moments later the light was switched off. The murmur of Phoebe's and Diana's voices continued in the kitchen, but their words were no longer audible.

Walsh beckoned to McLoughlin, whom he could dimly see, and led the way on soft feet across the terrace and on to the grass. He had been keeping a wary eye on the lighted windows of Anne's wing where her silhouette, seated at her desk, showed up strongly against the curtains. She had changed position frequently in the last half hour, but had not moved from her seat. Walsh was as sure as he could be that his and McLoughlin's short spell of eavesdropping had been unobserved.

They set off silently in the direction of the ice house, McLoughlin lighting their way with a torch which he kept shaded with one hand. When Walsh judged them far enough away from the house to be unheard, he stopped and turned to his colleague.

'What did you make of that, Andy?'

'I'd say we just heard the clearest admission of guilt we're ever likely to hear,' the other threw out.

'Hm.' Walsh chewed thoughtfully on his lower lip. 'I wonder. What was it she said?'

'She admitted to relief at having got rid of her husband so easily.' He shrugged. 'Seems clear enough to me.'

Walsh started to walk again. 'It wouldn't stand up in a court of law for a minute,' he mused. 'But it's interesting, definitely interesting.' He came to an abrupt halt. 'I think she's cracking at long last.

I got the impression that Mrs Goode certainly thinks so. What's her part in this? She can't have been involved in Maybury's disappearance. We had her thoroughly checked and there's no doubt she was in America at the time.'

'Accessory after the fact? She and the Cattrell woman have known Mrs Maybury did it but have kept quiet for the sake of the children.' He shrugged again. 'Bar that, she seems straight enough. She doesn't know much about the ice house, that's for sure.'

'Unless she's bluffing.' He pondered for a few minutes. 'Doesn't it seem odd to you that she can have lived here for eight years and not have seen inside that place?'

The moon came out from behind a cloud and lit their way with a cold grey lustre. McLoughlin switched off the torch. 'Perhaps she didn't fancy it,' he observed with grim humour. 'Perhaps she knew what was in there.'

This remark brought Walsh up short again. 'Well, well,' he murmured, 'I wonder if that's it. It makes sense. No one's going to poke around in a place where they know there's a dead body. They're a hard-bitten trio. I can't see any of them going out of her way to do what's morally right. They'd harbour a corpse quite happily, provided it was out of sight. What do you think?'

His Sergeant scowled. 'Women are a closed book to me, sir. I wouldn't even pretend to understand them.'

Walsh chuckled. 'Kelly been playing you up again?'

The laugh pierced McLoughlin's brain, scintillating and sharp as a needle. He turned away and thrust his hands and the torch deep into the pockets of his bomber jacket. Tempt me, he thought, just tempt me. 'We've had a row. Nothing serious.'

Walsh, who knew enough of McLoughlin's prolonged marital problems to be sympathetic, grunted. 'Funnily enough, I saw her a couple of days ago with Jack Booth. She was swinging along without a care in the world, never seen her so cheerful. She's not pregnant, I suppose? She had a real bloom on her.'

The bastard should have hit him. It would have hurt less. 'That's probably because she's gone to live with Jack,' he said casually. 'She left last week.' Now laugh, you sod, laugh, laugh, laugh, and give me an excuse to smash your face in.

Walsh, at a loss, gave McLoughlin's arm an awkward pat. He understood now why the lad had been so touchy the last few days. To lose your wife was bad enough, to lose her to your closest friend was a belter. My God! Jack Booth, of all people! He'd been best man at their wedding. Well, well. It explained a good deal. Why McLoughlin walked alone these days. Why Jack had suddenly

decided to leave the force to work for a security firm in Southampton.
'I had no idea. I'm sorry.'

'It's no big deal, sir. It was all very amicable. No hard feelings on
either side.'

He was very cool about it. 'Perhaps it's a temporary infatuation,'
Walsh suggested lamely. 'Perhaps she'll come back when she's got
over it.'

McLoughlin's teeth gleamed white inside his grin, but the night
hid the black rage in his eyes. 'Do me a favour, sir, that's about the
last thing I want to hear. God knows we never had much to say to
each other before she went. What the hell would we talk about if
she came back?' Jesus, he wanted to hit someone. Did they all
know? Were they all laughing? He would kill the first person who
laughed.

He quickened his pace. 'Thank God we didn't have children. This
way, no one loses.'

Walsh, following a few steps behind, pondered the capriciousness
of human nature. He could recall a conversation he had had with
McLoughlin only months before when the younger man had blamed
his marital problems on the fact that he and Kelly had no children.
She was bored, he claimed, found her job as a secretary unsatisfying,
needed a baby to keep her occupied. Walsh had wisely kept silent,
knowing from experience with his daughter that advice on domestic
disputes was rarely appreciated, but he had hoped quite fervently
that Fate would intervene to prevent some wretched baby being born
to keep this ill-matched couple occupied. His own daughter's first
pregnancy at the age of sixteen when she was still at school and
unmarried had been a shock to him, but the greater shock was to
discover that his wife and daughter had never really liked each other.
His daughter blamed two disastrous marriages and four children on
her restless seeking after love; while his wife blamed their daughter
for her wasted opportunities and lack of self-esteem. George tried
to make up for past failings by taking an interest in his grandchildren,
but he found it difficult. His interest tended to be critical. He thought
them wild and undisciplined and blamed this on his daughter's leni-
ency and their lack of a father-figure.

Walsh's recurring nightmare was that with the careless conception
of his daughter he had sown seeds of unhappiness which would grow
and mature with every succeeding generation.

He caught up with McLoughlin. 'Life's a puzzle, Andy. You'll
look back at the end and see where all the pieces fitted, even if you
can't see it now. Things will work out for the best. They always do.'

'Of course they will, sir. "All is for the best in the best of all possible worlds." You believe that crap, do you?'

Walsh was crushed. 'Yes, as a matter of fact.'

They were approaching the ice house which stood silhouetted against the arc-lights on the far side. McLoughlin jerked his head at the open doorway and the blackness inside. 'I can guess where he would have told you to stick your little aphorism. He wouldn't agree with it.'

'But his murderer might.' And so might your wife, Walsh thought acidly, tucked up in bed with a little warm and jovial humanity in the shape of Jack Booth. He raised a hand in greeting to DC Jones as they rounded the building. 'Found anything?'

Jones pointed to a piece of canvas on the ground. 'That's it, sir. We've worked a fifty-metre radius round the ice house. I've told the lads to leave the woodland along the back wall until tomorrow. The lights throw too many shadows to see properly.'

Walsh squatted on his haunches and used a pencil to sort and turn the collection of empty crisp packets, sweet wrappers, two threadbare tennis balls and other odds and ends. He isolated three used condoms, a pair of faded bikini underpants and several spent cartridges. 'We'll follow these up. I don't think the rest is going to tell us anything.' He pushed himself to his feet. 'Right, I think we'll call it a day. Jones, I want you to continue searching the grounds tomorrow. Concentrate on the areas of woodland, along the back wall and up by the front gates. Get a team together to help you. Andy, you carry on with the questioning until I join you. Ask Fred Phillips if he's used a shotgun recently. We'll check at the station to see whether he or anyone else here is licensed to use one. Sergeant Robinson and the PCs can go door to door in the village.' He indicated the condoms and the knickers. 'They seem unlikely objects for anyone in the Grange to have abandoned in the garden though you' – he looked at McLoughlin – 'might ask tactfully.' He turned to Jones. 'Were they together in the same place?'

'Scattered about, sir. We marked the positions.'

'Good man. It looks as if a local Lothario is in the habit of bringing his girlfriends up here. If so, he may be able to give us some information. I'll have Nick Robinson concentrate on that.'

There was a sour look on McLoughlin's face. He didn't relish the prospect of discussing used condoms with the women at the Grange. 'And you, sir?' he asked.

'Me? I'm going to check back through one or two files, particularly our friend Ms Cattrell's. That's a tough nut. I don't fancy it, not one little bit.' He pursed his lips and tugged at them with a finger and thumb.

'There's a Special Branch file on her as long as your arm, dating back to when she was a student. I had access to bits of it when Maybury went missing. It's how I knew she was at Greenham Common. She's thrown a few spanners in the works over the years. Do you remember that furore a couple of years ago over creative accounting in the Defence Ministry? Someone added a nought to a three million pound tender and the Ministry paid out ten times what the contract was worth. That was an Anne Cattrell scoop. Heads rolled. She's a dab hand at getting heads to roll.' He fingered his jaw thoughtfully. 'I suggest you remember that, Andy.'

'You're coming it a bit strong, aren't you, sir? If she's that good, what the hell's she doing stuck out here in the wilds of Hampshire? She should be in London on one of the big nationals.' Walsh's tones of amused admiration had needled him.

'Oh, she's good,' said Walsh waspishly, 'and she did work on a London national before she chucked it all up to come down here and turn freelance. Don't make the mistake of underestimating her. I've seen some of the comments on her file. She's a gutsy little bitch, not the sort to cross swords with lightly. She has a history of left-wing involvement and she knows everything there is to know about civil rights and police powers. She's been a press officer with CND, she's an outspoken feminist, active trades' unionist, she's been linked with the Militant Tendency and at one time she was a member of the British Communist Party—'

'Jesus Christ!' McLoughlin broke in angrily. 'What the hell's she doing living in a bloody mansion? Damn it all, sir, they've got a couple of servants working for them.'

'Fascinating, isn't it? What made her jack in her job *and* her principles? I suggest you ask her tomorrow. It's the first damn chance we've had to find out.'

The old man reeked of whisky. He sat like a lumpy Guy Fawkes in the doorway of a tobacconist in Southampton, his legs encased in incongruously bright pink trousers, his ancient hat awry on his bald head, a jolly song on his lips. It was nearly midnight. As drunks will, he called out to passers-by between snatches of song; they, with sidelong glances, crossed the road or scurried by with quickened pace.

A policeman approached and stood in front of him, wondering what to do with the silly old fool. 'You're a pain in the flaming arse,' he said amiably.

The tramp glared at him. 'A blooming bluebottle,' he said, showing his age, before a gleam of recognition crept into the rheumy eyes. 'Gawd love me, it's Sergeant Jordan,' he cackled. He fished a brown-paper-covered bottle from the recesses of his coat, pulled the cork out with brown teeth and offered it to the bobby. 'Have a drink, me old mate.'

Sergeant Jordan shook his head. 'Not tonight, Josephine.'

The old man tipped up the bottle and emptied the contents into his mouth. His hat fell off and rolled across the doorstep. The Sergeant bent down and retrieved it, clapping it firmly on the tramp's head. 'Come on, you old fool.' He put his hand under an unsavoury arm and heaved the filthy object to its feet.

'You nicking me?'

'Is that what you want?'

'Wouldn't mind, son,' he whined. 'I'm tired. Could just do wiv a decent kip.'

'And I can just do without fumigating the cell after you've been in it,' the policeman muttered, pulling a card out of his pocket and reading the address on it. 'I'm going to do you a favour, probably the first one you've had in years that didn't involve free booze. Come on, you're going to sleep in the Hilton tonight.'

George Walsh dropped Sergeants Robinson and McLoughlin at the Lamb and Flag in Winchester Road for a quick pint before closing time, then drove to Silverborne Police Station. His route took him along the High Street past the war memorial and the old cornmarket, now a bank, and between the two rows of darkened shops. Beyond its rapid expansion, Silverborne's only claim to fame in the last ten years had been its physical proximity to Streech Grange and the mystery surrounding David Maybury's disappearance. That Streech should again be the centre of police attention was no coincidence in Walsh's view. There was an inexorability about murder investigations, he believed, with comparatively few remaining unsolved. Certainly lightning like this never struck twice. He was whistling tunelessly as he pushed through the front doors.

Bob Rogers was on duty behind the desk. He looked up as Walsh came in. 'Evening, sir.'

'Bob.'

'The word is you've found Maybury.'

Walsh leant an arm on the desk. 'I'm not taking anything for granted,' he growled. 'The bastard's eluded me for ten years. I can wait another twenty-four hours before I pop the champagne. Any word from Webster?'

Rogers shook his head.

'Busy tonight?'

'Not so you'd notice.'

'Do me a favour then. Get me a list of all persons, men and women, reported missing in our area in, say, the last six months. I'll be in my office.'

Walsh went upstairs, his feet echoing loudly in the deserted corridor. He liked the place at night, empty, silent, with no ringing telephones and no inane chatter outside his door to intrude on his thoughts. He went into his office and snapped on the light. His wife had bought him a painting two Christmases ago to lend a personal touch to his bleak white walls. It hung on the wall opposite the door and greeted him every time he entered the room. He loathed it. It was a symbol of her taste, not his, a herd of glossy black horses with flowing manes galloping through an autumnal forest. He would have preferred some Van Gogh prints for the same price but his wife had laughed at the suggestion. Darling, she had said, anyone can have a print; surely you'd rather have an original? He glared at the pretty picture and wondered, not for the first time, why he found it so hard to say no to his wife.

He went to his filing cabinet and sorted through the C's. 'Cairns', 'Callaghan', 'Calvert', 'Cambridge', 'Cattrell'. He gave an exclamation of satisfaction, withdrew the file from the drawer and took it over to his desk. He opened it and settled into his chair, loosening his tie and kicking off his shoes.

The information was set out in the form of a CV, giving details of Anne Cattrell's history as far as it was known to the Silverborne police at the time of Maybury's disappearance. Additional, more recent information had been added from time to time on the last page. Walsh fingered his lips thoughtfully as he read. It was disappointing on the whole. He had hoped to find a chink in her armour, some small point of leverage he could use to his advantage. But there was nothing. Unless the fact that the last nine years of her life was contained on one page, while the previous ten years covered several, was worth consideration. Why *had* she given up a promising career? If she'd stayed in London she'd have been a top name by now. But in nine years her biggest success had been the Defence Ministry scoop and that, published in a monthly magazine, had been hijacked by staff reporters on the nationals. She had got little credit for it. Indeed, Walsh had only known it was her story because the name had registered in connection with Maybury. If she'd got hitched, her sudden drop in profile would have made sense, but – his face creased into a deep scowl. Was it that simple? Had she and those women entered into some sort of perverted marriage the minute they were all free? He found the idea oddly reassuring. If Mrs Maybury had always been a lesbian, it explained so much. He was gathering the file together when Bob Rogers came in.

'I've got those names for you, sir, and a cup of tea.'

'Good man.' He took the cup gratefully. 'How many?'

Sergeant Rogers consulted his list. 'Five. Two women and three men. The women are pretty obvious runaways – both adolescent or late adolescent, both left home after rows with parents and haven't been seen since. The youngest was fourteen, Mary Lucinda Phelps, known as Lucy. We mounted quite a search for her, if you remember, but never found anything.'

'Yes, I do remember. Looked about twenty-five from her photograph.'

'That's the one. Parents swore she was a virgin, but it turned out she'd had an abortion at the age of thirteen. Poor kid's probably on the streets in London by now. The other one's a Suzie Miller, aged eighteen, last seen in early May hitching on the A31 with an older man. We have a witness to that who said she was all over him. Her parents wanted us to treat it as a murder, but there was nothing to suggest anything untoward had happened and we've certainly never found a body. Of the three men, one's a probable suicide, though again we've not found a body, one's semi-senile and gone walkabout, and the other's bolted. That's a young Asian lad of twenty-one, with a history of depression, Mohammed Mirahmadi, five previous suicide attempts, all attempted drownings. Left home three months ago. We dragged some nearby quarry pits but without success. The second on the list's an old man, Keith Chapel, who wandered out of sheltered accommodation in the middle of March, that's nearly five months, and hasn't come back. Mind you, it's odd no one's spotted him. It says here he was wearing bright pink trousers. And finally, a Daniel Clive Thompson, fifty-two, reported missing by his wife nine, ten weeks ago. Inspector Staley looked into that one quite thoroughly. The man's business had gone bust and left a lot of people hopping mad, including most of the employees. The Inspector's view is that he's done a bunk to London. He was last seen getting off a train on Waterloo station.' He looked up.

'Any of them live near Streech?'

'One of the men, Daniel Thompson. Address: Larkfield, East Deller. That's the neighbouring village, isn't it?'

'What's the description?'

'Five feet eleven, grey hair, hazel eyes, well-built, wearing a brown suit, forty-four-inch chest and brown shoes, size eight. Other information: blood group O, appendectomy scar, full set of dentures, tattoos on both forearms. Last sighting, May 25th, at Waterloo. Last seen by his wife on same day when she dropped him at Winchester station. That's all I've got here, but Inspector Staley's got quite a file on him. Shall I look it out for you?'

'No,' Walsh growled angrily. 'It's Maybury.' He watched Bob Rogers walk to the door. 'Damn and blast it! It's like leaving your umbrella behind on a fine day. It always rains. Leave me the list. If I hang on to it, it's bound to be Maybury.' He waited till the door closed, then stared glumly at the description of Daniel Thompson. His face looked ten years older.

EIGHT

When Anne entered the library the following morning she found McLoughlin standing by the window, gazing broodingly out over the gravel drive. He turned as she came in and she noticed the black rings of a sleepless night round his eyes and the tell-tale nicks of a clumsy shave on his neck and chin. He smelled of anger and frustration and yesterday's beer. He gestured for her to sit down, waited until she had done so, then settled himself in the chair behind the desk. Particles of dust shimmered and danced in the sunlight that shafted between them. They eyed each other with open dislike.

'I won't keep you long, Miss Cattrell. Chief Inspector Walsh will be here later and I know he has some questions to ask you. For the moment, I'd like to concentrate on the finding of the body and one or two related matters. Perhaps you could start by running through the events of yesterday afternoon, beginning with the arrival of the gardener.'

Anne did as she was asked, knowing it would be a waste of time to point out that she had already done this the previous afternoon for PC Williams. From time to time she glanced at McLoughlin but looked away again when he refused to drop his gaze. There was a new awareness in his eyes which meant he was better informed about her. And how tiresome that was, she thought. Yesterday, he had despised her; today, he saw her as a challenge. With an inward sigh she began to prepare her defences.

'You don't know who he was, how he got there, or when. Had you seen inside the ice house before yesterday?'

'No.'

'Then why did you tell us that you and Mrs Goode had cleared the rubbish out of it six years ago?'

Anne had been well prepared for this by Diana. 'Because it seemed like a good idea at the time.' She fished a cigarette out of her pocket and lit it. 'I wanted to save you time and trouble. You should be looking outside the Grange for your victim and your suspects. It's nothing to do with anyone here.'

65

He was unimpressed. 'It's never a good idea to tell lies to the police. With your experience you should know that.'

'My experience?' she queried silkily.

'If you don't mind, we'll dispense with the word games, Miss Cattrell. It'll save a lot of time.'

'You're quite right, of course,' she agreed mildly. What a prig the man was!

His eyes narrowed. 'Did you lie because you understood the significance of the ice house and the importance of knowing where it was?'

She was silent for a moment. 'I certainly understood that *you* would consider it significant. You have yet to persuade me that it is. I share Mrs Good's view that its location is probably known to a number of people, or that chance played a part in the body's being there.'

'We have found some used condoms in the area round the icehouse,' McLoughlin said, abruptly changing the subject. 'Have you any idea who would have left them there?'

Anne grinned. 'Well, it wasn't me, Sergeant. I don't use them.'

He showed his irritation. 'Have you had intercourse there with someone who does, Miss Cattrell?'

'What, with a *man*?' She gave her throaty chuckle. 'Is that a very sensible question to ask a lesbian?'

He gripped his knees tightly with trembling fingers as a sudden black rage hammered in his head. He felt terrible, his eyes smarting from lack of sleep, his mouth tasting foul. What a loathsome bloody bitch she was, he thought. He took a few shallow breaths and eased his hands on to the desk. They shook with a life of their own. 'Have you?' he asked again.

She watched him closely. 'No, I haven't,' she answered calmly. 'Nor, as far as I know, has anyone else in the house.' She leaned forward and tapped the end of her cigarette against the side of an ashtray. He moved his hands to his lap.

'Perhaps you could clear up something that puzzles both Chief Inspector Walsh and myself,' he continued. 'We understand you and Mrs Goode have been living here for several years. How is it neither of you has seen inside the ice house?'

'In the same way that most Londoners have never seen inside the Tower. One doesn't tend to explore things on one's own doorstep.'

'Did you know of its existence?'

'I suppose so.' She thought for a moment. 'I must have done. I don't remember being surprised at Fred mentioning it.'

'Did you know where it was?'

'No.'

'What did you think the hillock was?'

'I can only recall walking right round these gardens once and that was when I first came here. I expect I thought the hillock was a hillock.'

McLoughlin didn't believe her. 'Don't you go for walks? With the dogs, with your friends?'

She turned her cigarette in her fingers. 'Do I look like someone who takes exercise, Sergeant?'

He studied her briefly. 'As a matter of fact you do. You're very slim.'

'I eat very little, drink only neat spirits and smoke like a chimney. It does wonders for the figure but leaves me gasping for breath halfway up the stairs.'

'Don't you help with the gardening?'

She raised an eyebrow. 'I'd be a liability. I couldn't tell the difference between a rose-bay willow-herb and a Michaelmas daisy. In any case, when would I find the time? I'm a professional woman. I work all day. We leave the gardening arrangements to Phoebe, that's her province.'

He thought of the pot plants in her room. Was she lying again? But why lie about gardening, for Christ's sake? His hand wandered to the uneven stubble on his jaw, touching, testing, fingering. Without warning, a shutter of panic snapped shut in his brain, blanking his memory. Had he shaved? Where had he slept? Had he had breakfast? His eyes glazed and he looked straight through Anne into a darkness beyond her, as if she was in a dimension outside his narrow line of vision.

Her voice was remote. 'Are you all right?'

The shutter opened again and left him with the nausea of relief. 'Why are you living here, Miss Cattrell?'

'Probably for exactly the same reason you're living in your house. It's as nice a roof over my head as I could find.'

'That's hardly an answer. How do you square Streech Grange and its two servants with your conscience? Isn't it rather too – privileged for your taste?' His voice grated with derision.

Anne stubbed out her cigarette. 'I simply can't answer that question. It's based on so many false premises that it's entirely hypothetical. Nor, frankly, do I see its relevance.'

'Who suggested you come here? Mrs Maybury?'

'No one. It was my suggestion.'

'Why?'

'Because,' she repeated patiently, 'I thought it would be a nice place to live.'

'That's crap,' he said angrily.

She smiled. 'You're forgetting the sort of woman I am, Sergeant. I have to take my pleasures where I find them. Phoebe wouldn't – couldn't – leave this house to come to London, so I had to come here. It's very simple really.'

There was a long silence. 'Pleasures don't last,' he said softly. The shutter flickered horribly in his brain. ' "Pleasures are like poppies spread, You seize the flower, its bloom is shed; Or like the snow falls in the river, A moment white – then melts for ever." ' He spoke the words to himself. There was another silence. 'In your case, Miss Cattrell, the price of pleasure would seem to be hypocrisy. That's a high price to pay. Was Mrs Maybury worth it?'

If he'd turned a knife in her gut, he couldn't have hurt her more. She took refuge in anger. 'Let me give you a brief résumé of what led up to this line of questioning. Someone, probably Walsh, told you: she's a feminist, a lefty, a member of CND, an ex-Commie, and God knows what other rubbish besides. And you, exulting in your superiority because you're male and heterosexual, leapt at the chance of having a go at me on matters of principle. You're not interested in truth, McLoughlin. The only issue here is whether you and your inflated ego can make a dent in mine and, Jesus,' she spat at him, 'you're hardly original in that.'

He, too, leant forward so that they were facing each other across the desk. 'Who are Fred and Molly Phillips?'

She was unprepared, as he had known she would be, and she couldn't hide the flash of concern in her eyes. She sat back in her chair and reached for another cigarette.

'They work for Phoebe as housekeeper and gardener.'

'Mrs Goode told us you arranged their employment here. How did you find them?'

'I was introduced to them.'

'Through your work, through your political contacts? Perhaps penal reform is one of your interests?'

Damn him to hell and back, she thought, he wasn't a complete clod after all. 'I'm on the committee of a London-based group for the rehabilitation of ex-prisoners. I met them through that.'

She expected triumph and gave him reluctant credit when he didn't show it. 'Have they always been called Phillips?'

'No.'

'What was their surname?'

'I think you should ask them that.'

He passed a weary hand across his face. 'Well, of course, I can, Miss Cattrell, and that will simply drag out the agony for everybody. We will find out one way or the other.'

She looked out of the window, over his shoulder, to where Phoebe was pinching the dead-heads off the roses bordering the drive. She had lost her tension of the previous evening and squatted contentedly in the sun, tongues of flame curling in her shining hair, nimble fingers snapping through the flower stems. Benson sat hotly beside her, Hedges lay panting in the shade of a dwarf rhododendron. The sun's heat, still far from its peak, shimmered above the warm gravel.

'Jefferson,' said Anne.

The Sergeant made the connection immediately. 'Five years each for the murder of their lodger, Ian Donaghue.'

Anne nodded. 'Do you know why the sentences were so lenient?'

'Yes, I do. Donaghue buggered and killed their twelve-year-old son. They found him before the police did and hanged him.'

She nodded.

'Do you approve of personal vengeance, Miss Cattrell?'

'I sympathise with it.'

He smiled suddenly and for a brief moment she thought he looked quite human. 'Then at last we've found something we can agree on.' He tapped his pencil on the desk. 'How well do the Phillipses get on with Mrs Maybury?'

'Extremely well.' Surprisingly, she giggled. 'Fred treats her like royalty and Molly treats her like muck. It's a stunning combination.'

'I expect they're grateful to her.'

'The reverse. I'd say Phoebe is more grateful to them.'

'Why? She's given them a new home and employment.'

'You see the Grange as it is now but when I moved in nine years ago, Phoebe had been managing on her own for a year. She was shunned by everybody. No one from the village or even Silverborne would work for her. She had to do the gardening, the housework and house maintenance herself and the place was like a tip.' A stone lurched sickeningly in her mind as memories struggled to get out. It was the stench of urine, she thought. Everywhere. On the walls, the carpets, the curtains. She would never forget the terrible stench of urine. 'Fred and Molly's arrival a couple of months after us changed her life.'

McLoughlin stared about the library. There was a good deal that was original, the carved oak bookcases, moulded plaster cornices, the panelled fireplace, but there were other things that were new, the paintwork, a radiator under the window, secondary glazing in white stove-enamel frames, all certainly under ten years old.

'Have the local people changed their attitude to Mrs Maybury now?'

She followed his gaze. 'Not at all. They still won't do any work for her.' She flicked ash from her cigarette. 'She tries from time to time without success. Silverborne's a dead duck. She's been as far as Winchester and Southampton with the same result. Streech Grange is notorious, Sergeant, but then you already know that, don't you?' She smiled cynically. 'They all seem to think they're going to be murdered the minute they set foot in the place. With some justification, it would seem, after yesterday's little discovery.'

He jerked his head at the window. 'Then who put in the central heating and the double glazing? Fred?'

'Phoebe.'

He laughed with genuine amusement. 'Oh, for God's sake! Look, I know you're on some personal crusade to prove that women are the be-all and end-all, but you can't expect me to swallow *that*.' He got up and strode across to the window. 'Have you any idea how much glass like this weighs?' He tapped a pane of the double-glazing and drew the unwelcome attention of Phoebe outside. She looked at him curiously for a moment then, seeing him turn away, resumed her gardening. He came back to his chair. 'She couldn't begin to lift it, let alone set it professionally in its frame. It would need at least two men, if not three.'

'Or three women,' said Anne, unmoved by his outburst. 'We all lend a hand with the lifting. There are five of us after all, eight on the week-ends when the children come home.'

'Eight?' he queried sharply. 'I thought there were only two children.'

'Three. There's Elizabeth, Diana's daughter, as well.'

McLoughlin ruffled his fingers through his hair, leaving a dark crest pointing towards the ceiling. 'She never mentioned a daughter,' he said sourly, wondering what other surprises lay in store.

'You probably didn't ask her.'

He ignored this. 'You said Mrs Maybury also did the central heating. How?'

'The same way plumbers do it, presumably. I remember she favoured capillary joints so there was a lot of wire wool involved and flux and soldering equipment. There were also numerous lengths of fifteen- and twenty-two-millimetre copper piping lying around. She hired a pipe-bending machine for several weeks with different sized pre-formers to make S-bends and right angles. I got a damned good article on women and DIY out of it.'

He shook his head. 'Who showed her how to do it? Who connected up the boiler?'

'She did.' She was amused by his expression. 'She got a book from the library. It told her exactly what to do.'

Andy McLoughlin was intensely sceptical. In his experience, a woman who could connect a central-heating boiler simply didn't exist. His mother, who held unenlightened ideas about a woman's place in the home, rooted herself firmly in the kitchen, scrubbed and cleaned, washed and cooked and refused adamantly even to learn how to change an electric plug, maintaining it was man's work. His wife, who by contrast had claimed enlightened ideas, had enrolled as a temporary secretary and called herself a career woman. In reality she had idled her days away, painting her nails, playing with her hair, complaining constantly of boredom but doing nothing about it. She had reserved her energies for when her husband came home, unleashing them in a fury of recriminations over his long hours of work, his neglect of her, his failure to notice her appearance, his inability to be the admiring prop her insecure personality demanded. The irony was that he had been attracted to her in the first place because his mother's kitchen mentality appalled him and yet, of the two of them, his mother had the brightest intellect. He had come away from both relationships with a sense, not of his own inadequacy, but of theirs. He had looked for equality and found only an irritating dependence.

'What else has she done?' he demanded curtly, eyeing the professional finish on the rag-rolled emulsion. 'The decorating?'

'No, that's mostly Diana's work, though we've all lent a hand. Di's also done the upholstery and curtaining. What else has Phoebe done?' She thought for a moment. 'She's rewired the house, made two extra bathrooms and put up the stud partitions between our wings and the main body. At the moment, she and Fred are working out how best to tackle a complete overhaul of the roof.' She felt the weight of his scepticism and shrugged. 'She's not trying to prove anything, Sergeant, nor am I by telling you. Phoebe's done what everyone else does and has adapted herself to the situation she finds herself in. She's a fighter. She's not the type to throw in her hand when the cards go against her.'

He thought of his own circumstances. Loneliness frightened him.

'Were you and Mrs Goode worried about Mrs Maybury's mental condition after twelve months alone in this house? Was that your real reason for moving here?'

Could reality be quantified, Anne wondered, any more than truth? To say yes to such a question from such a man would be a betrayal.

His capacity for understanding was confined by his prejudices. 'No, Sergeant,' she lied. 'Diana and I have never had a moment's concern over Phoebe's mental condition, as you put it. She's a good deal more stable than you are, for example.'

His eyes narrowed angrily. 'You're a psychiatrist, are you, Miss Cattrell?'

'Put it this way,' she said, leaning forward and studying him coolly. 'I can always recognise a chronic drink problem when I see one.'

The speed with which his hand shot out and gripped her throat was staggering. He pulled her relentlessly towards him across the desk, his fingers biting into her flesh, a tumult of confused emotions governing his actions. The kiss, if the brutal penetration of another's mouth can be called a kiss, was as unplanned as the assault. He released her abruptly and stared at the red weals on her neck. A cold sweat drenched his back as he realised how vulnerable he had made himself. 'I don't know why I did that,' he said. 'I'm sorry.' But he knew that under the same circumstances he would do it again. At last he felt revenged.

She wiped his saliva from her mouth and pulled her shirt collar up round her neck. 'Did you want to ask me anything else?' She spoke as if nothing had happened.

He shook his head. 'Not at the present.' He watched her stand up. 'You can report me for that, Miss Cattrell.'

'Of course.'

'I don't know why I did it,' he said again.

'I do,' she said. 'Because you're an inadequate little shit.'

NINE

Sergeant Nick Robinson looked up and saw with relief that he had only two more houses to do before he reached the pub. Off to his right rose the hill which passed Streech Grange gates; behind him, some miles distant, lay Winchester; ahead of him, the brick wall which surrounded the southern flank of the Grange Estate hugged the road to East Deller. He checked his watch. It was ten minutes to opening time and he could murder a pint. If there was one thing he loathed, it was door-to-door questioning. With a lighter step he walked up the short drive to Clementine Cottage and – he checked his list – Mrs Amy Ledbetter. He rang the bell.

After some minutes and the laborious rattle of an anti-burglar chain, the door opened six inches. A pair of bright eyes examined him. 'Yes?'

He held out his identification. 'Police, Mrs Ledbetter.'

The card was taken by an arthritically deformed hand and disappeared inside. 'Wait there, please,' said her voice. 'I intend to phone the Police Station and make sure you are who you say you are.'

'Very well.' He leaned against the side of her porch and lit a cigarette. This was the third telephoned check on him in two hours. He wondered if the uniformed constables were having as much trouble as he was.

Three minutes later the door opened wide and Mrs Ledbetter gestured him into the living-room. She was well into her seventies with a leathery skin and a no-nonsense look about her. She returned his warrant and told him to take a seat. 'There's an ashtray on the table. Well, Sergeant, what can I do for you?'

No need to beat about the bush with this old bat, he thought. Not like her twee little neighbour who claimed that to hear about murder on the television gave her palpitations. 'The remains of a murdered man were discovered in the garden of the Grange yesterday afternoon,' he said baldly. 'We're making enquiries to see if anyone in the village knows anything about it.'

'Oh, no,' said Amy Ledbetter. 'Poor Phoebe.'

73

DS Robinson looked at her with interest. This was a reaction he hadn't met with before. The mood of the other villagers he had spoken to had been one of vituperative satisfaction.

'Would it surprise you,' he asked the old lady, 'if I said you're the only person so far who's expressed any sympathy for Mrs Maybury?'

She wrinkled her lips into a moue of disgust. 'Of course it wouldn't. The lack of intelligence in this community is staggering. I'd have moved away years ago if I wasn't so fond of my garden. I suppose it's David's body?'

'We don't know yet.'

'I see.' She considered him thoughtfully. 'Well, fire away. What do you want to ask me?'

'Do you know Mrs Maybury well?'

'I've known her all her life. Gerald Gallagher, Phoebe's father, and my husband were old friends. I used to see a lot of her when she was younger and my husband was still alive.'

'And now?'

She frowned. 'No, I see very little of her now. My fault.' She raised one of her gnarled hands. 'Arthritis is the devil. It's more comfortable to stay at home and potter than go out paying calls and it makes you irritable. I was very short with her last time she came to see me and she hasn't been back since. That was about twelve months ago. My fault,' she said again.

Game old bird, he thought, and probably more reliable than the others he'd talked to who had dealt in innuendo and gossip. 'Do you know anything about her two friends, Mrs Goode and Miss Cattrell?'

'I've met them, knew them quite well at one time. Phoebe used to bring them home from school. Nice girls, interesting, full of character.'

Robinson consulted his notebook. 'One of the villagers told me – ' he looked up briefly – 'and I quote: "Those women are dangerous. They have made several attempts to seduce girls in the village, they even tried to get my daughter to join one of their lesbian orgies." ' He looked up again. 'Do you know anything about that?'

She brushed a stray hair from her forehead with the back of her curled hand. 'Dilys Barnes, I suppose. She won't thank you for describing her as a villager. She's a shocking snob, likes to think she's one of us.'

He was intrigued. 'How did you know?'

'That it was Dilys? Because she's a very silly woman who tells lies. It's lack of breeding, of course. That type will do anything to avoid being laughed at. They've ruined their children with all their snobbish ideas. They sent the boy off to public school, and he's come back with a chip on his shoulder the size of a mountain. And the daughter, Emma,' she pulled a wry face. 'I'm afraid poor little Emma has become very loose. I think it's her way of getting back at her mother.'

'I see,' he said, completely lost.

She chuckled at his expression. 'She copulates in the woods at Streech Grange,' she explained. 'It's a favourite spot for it.' She chuckled again as the Sergeant's mouth dropped open. 'Emma was seen sneaking out of the grounds late one night and the story her mother put about the next day was that absurd one she's repeated to you.' She shook her head. 'It's nonsense, of course, and no one really believes it, but they pay lip-service to it because they don't like Phoebe. And she's her own worst enemy. She will let them see how much she despises them. That's always a mistake. Anyway, ask Emma. She's not a bad girl. If you keep what she says confidential, she'll tell you the truth I expect.'

He made a note. 'Thank you, I will. You say the woods are a favourite spot for – er – copulation.'

'Very much so,' she said firmly. 'Reggie and I used them a lot before we were married. They're particularly nice in the spring. Bluebell woods, you know. Very pretty.'

He boggled at her.

'Well, well,' she said calmly, 'that surprises you, I see, but the young are really very ignorant about sex. People were no more able to control their desire for it in my day than they are now and, thanks to Marie Stopes, we were not unprotected.' She smiled. 'When you're as old as I am, young man, you'll know that where human nature is concerned, very little changes. Life, for most of us, is the pursuit of pleasure.'

Well, that's true, he thought, thinking of his pint. He abandoned his inhibitions. 'We've found some used condoms on the Grange Estate which ties in with what you've been saying, Mrs Ledbetter. Apart from Emma Barnes, do you know of anyone else who might have been making love up there?'

'Precise knowledge, no. Guesses, yes. If you promise to be tactful in approaching the people concerned, I'll give you two more names.'

He nodded. 'I promise.'

'Paddy Clarke, the landlord at the pub. He's married to a harridan who has no idea how highly sexed he is. She thinks he takes the dog for a walk after closing time while she clears up inside, but I've seen the dog running loose in the moonlight too often to believe that. I don't sleep well,' she added, by way of explanation.

'And the other?'

'Eddie Staines, one of the farmhands up at Bywater Farm. A good-looking young devil, out with a different girlfriend every month. I've seen him set off up that hill a few times.' She nodded in the direction of the Grange.

'That's very helpful,' he said.

'Anything else?'

'Yes.' He looked a little sheepish. 'Have you noticed any strangers about? In the last six months, say?' This question had been greeted with universal amusement.

Mrs Ledbetter cackled. 'Twenty-five years ago I might have been able to give you a sensible answer to a question like that. Nowadays, impossible.' She shrugged. 'There are always strangers about, especially in the summer. Tourists, people driving through and stopping at the pub for lunch, campers from the site at East Deller. We've had a few caravans get stuck in the ditch on the corner, usually French ones, such bad drivers they are. Ask Paddy. He pulls them out with his jeep. No, I can't help you there, I'm afraid.'

'Sure?' he prompted. 'Someone on foot perhaps, someone you remember from years ago?'

She gave an amused snort. 'David Maybury, you mean? I certainly haven't seen him in the last few months. I'd have reported that. The last time I saw David was a week before he disappeared. It was in Winchester in the days when I could still drive and I came across him in Woolworths buying a teddy-bear for Jane. He was a strange character. Vile one day, charming the next, what my husband would have called a cad, the sort of man that women are invariably attracted to.' She lapsed into silence for a moment. 'There was the tramp, of course,' she said.

'What tramp?'

'He came through the village some weeks back. Funny old man with a brown trilby hanging off the back of his head. He was singing "Molly Malone", I remember. Quite beautifully. Ask Paddy. I'm sure he went into the pub.' Her head sank wearily against the back of her chair. 'I'm tired. I can't help you any more. Show yourself out, young man, and don't forget to shut the gate.' She closed her eyes.

DS Robinson rose smartly to his feet. 'Thank you for giving me so much of your time, Mrs Ledbetter.'

She was snoring quietly as he tip-toed out.

Inspector Walsh replaced the telephone receiver and stared thoughtfully into the middle distance. Dr Webster had been irritatingly unhelpful.

'Can't prove it is Maybury, can't prove it isn't,' he had said cheerfully along the wire, 'but my professional guess is it isn't.'

'Why, for God's sake?'

'Too many discrepancies. I can't make a match on the hair for a kick-off, though I'm not saying that's the end of it. I've sent samples off to a friend of mine who claims to be an expert in these things but don't get your hopes up. He warned me that the sample you got off Maybury's hairbrush may have deteriorated too far. Certainly I couldn't do anything with it.'

'What else?'

'Teeth. Did you notice our corpse was toothless? Not an incisor or molar in sight. Indications that he had dentures, but there were none with him. Looks like something or someone removed them. Now, Maybury on the other hand had all his teeth ten years ago and his records show they were in pretty good shape, only four fillings between them. That's a very different picture, George. He'd have to have suffered appalling gum disease to necessitate having all his teeth out within ten years.'

Walsh pondered for a moment. 'Let's say, for whatever reason, he wanted to lose his old identity. He could have had them taken out on purpose.'

Webster chuckled good-humouredly. 'Far-fetched though not impossible. But why would Mrs Maybury remove his dentures in that case, assuming she's our murderer? She, of all people, would know they couldn't identify him. To be honest, George, I'd say it's the other way round. Whoever murdered our chap in the ice house removed anything that would show he *wasn't* Maybury. He's had all his toes and fingertips mauled, for example, as if someone wanted to prevent us taking prints. Yet everyone at that house knows you didn't manage to lift a single workable print ten years ago.'

'God damn it,' exploded Walsh. 'I thought I had the bastard at last. Are you sure, Jim? What about the missing fingers?'

'Well, they're certainly missing, but it looks as though they've been chopped off with a meat cleaver. I've compared them with the records of Maybury's amputations and they're nothing like. Maybury had lost the top two joints of both fingers. Our corpse has had his severed at the base of each finger.'

'Doesn't prove it's not Maybury.'

'I agree, but it does look as if someone who knew only that he'd lost his last two fingers has tried to make us think it's Maybury. To be honest, George, I'm not even positive at the moment that a human agency is involved. It is quite conceivable, if a little bizarre, that very sharp teeth have mutilated him in the way I've described. Take that filleting you pointed out. I've taken some close-ups of some furrows on the ribs and it's damned hard to say what they are. I can't rule out tooth marks.'

'Blood group?'

'Yup, you've got a match there all right. Both O positive, just like fifty per cent of the population. And, talking of blood, you must find his clothes. There's very little in that mud we scraped off the floor.'

'Great,' Walsh had growled, 'so what good news have you got for me?'

'I'm getting the report typed now, but I'll give you the gist. Male, white, five feet ten inches – give or take an inch on either side, both femurs have been well and truly smashed so I wouldn't be too dogmatic on that one – broad build probably running to fat, hair on chest and shoulder blades, indication of tattoo discolouration on right forearm, size eight shoe. No idea of hair colour but hair was probably dark brown before it went grey. Age, over fifty.'

'Oh, for God's sake, Jim. Can't you be more precise?'

'It's not a precise science as people get older, George, and a few teeth would have helped. It's all a question of fusion between the skull plates, but somewhere between fifty and sixty is my guess at the moment. I'll come back to you when I've done some more homework.'

'All right,' said Walsh grudgingly. 'When did he die?'

'I've taken some advice on this one. The consensus is, weighing the heat of the summer against the cool of the ice house – bearing in mind that the ambient temperature in the ice house may have been quite high if the door was open – and balancing that against the acceleration in decomposition after the scavengers had pulled him open and devoured him, plus possible mutilation by human agency but minus severe maggot infestation because the blowflies didn't lay in numbers, though I've sent some larvae off for further examination – '

'All right, all right, I didn't ask for a bloody biology lesson. How long's he been dead?'

'Eight to twelve weeks or two to three months, whichever you prefer.'

'I don't prefer either of them. They're too vague. There's a month's difference. Which do you favour, eight or twelve?'

'Probably somewhere in the middle, but don't quote me.'

'You'll be lucky,' was Walsh's parting shot. He slammed the phone

78

down crossly, then buzzed his secretary on the intercom. 'Mary, love, could you get me all the details on a man who was reported missing about two months ago? Name: Daniel Thompson, address: somewhere in East Deller. I think you'll find Inspector Staley covered it. If he's free, ask him to give me five minutes, will you?' 'Sure thing,' she breezed back.

His eyes strayed to the huge file on David Maybury which he'd resurrected from the archives that morning, and which, refurbished and glossy in its pristine new folder, sat now on the edge of his desk like a promise of spring. 'You bastard!' said Chief Inspector Walsh.

TEN

Summoned by urgent telephone calls, Jonathan Maybury and Elizabeth Goode arrived early that afternoon in Jonathan's battered red Mini. As he drove it in through the gates and past the Lodge, Elizabeth turned to him with a worried frown. 'You won't tell anyone, will you?'

'Tell anyone what?'

'You know perfectly well. Promise me, Jon.'

He shrugged. 'OK, but I think you're mad. Much better to come clean now.'

'No,' she said firmly. 'I know what I'm doing.'

He glanced out of the window at the azaleas and rhododendrons, long past their best, which hedged the length of the driveway. 'I wonder if you do. From where I stand, there's very little difference between your paranoia on the subject and your mother's. You'll have to find the guts to speak out sooner or later, Lizzie.'

'Don't be an idiot,' she snapped.

He slowed as the wide sweep of gravel in front of the house opened up before them. Two cars were already parked there. 'Plain-clothes police cars,' he said with grim humour, drawing the Mini alongside one of them. 'I hope you're ready for the thumbscrews.'

'Oh, for God's sake grow up,' she exploded angrily, her worry and her uncertain temper getting the better of her. 'There are times when I could quite happily murder you, Jon.'

'We've found a pair of shoes, sir.' DC Jones placed a transparent plastic bag on the ground at Walsh's feet.

Walsh, who was sitting on a tree stump at the edge of the woodland surrounding the ice house, leaned forward to peer at the bag's contents. The shoes were good quality brown leather with irregular cloudy patches on the surface where damp had penetrated and then dried. One shoe had a brown lace, the other a black lace. Walsh turned the bag over and looked at the soles.

'Interesting,' he said. 'New heels with metal studs. There's hardly a mark on them. What size are they?'

'Eights, sir.' Jones pointed to the shoe with the brown lace. 'You can just make it out on that one.'

Walsh nodded. 'Tell one of your men to go up to the house and find out what size shoes Fred Phillips and Jonathan Maybury wear, then on down to the village to see how Robinson and his chaps are getting on. If they've finished, I want them up here.'

'Righto,' said Jones irreverently.

Walsh stood up. 'I'll be at the ice house with Sergeant McLoughlin.'

DS Robinson returned to the pub as the last customers left.

'Sorry, mate,' said the landlord amiably, recognising him from the pint he had bought earlier. 'Too late. Can't serve you now.'

Robinson proffered his identification. 'DS Robinson, Mr Clarke. I'm asking questions around the village. You're my last port of call.'

Paddy Clarke leaned his elbows on the bar and chuckled. 'The body at the Grange, I suppose. There's been talk of nothing else all lunchtime. Sod all I can tell you about it.'

Nick Robinson perched himself on a bar stool and offered Paddy a cigarette before taking one himself. 'You'd be surprised. People often know more than they think they do.'

He assessed his man rapidly and decided here was another where a straightforward approach would pay. Paddy was a big, bluff man with a ready smile and a shrewd eye. But not a person to cross, Robinson thought. His hands were the size of meat plates.

'We're interested in any strangers who may have been through Streech in the last few months, Mr Clarke.'

Paddy guffawed with laughter. 'Give me a break. I get strangers in here every day, people taking the back roads down to the West Country, stopping off for a quick lunch. Can't help you there.'

'Fair enough, but someone mentioned seeing an old tramp a while back, thought he may have come in here. Does that ring a bell?'

Paddy squinted through the smoke from his cigarette. 'Funny. I wouldn't have remembered him myself, but now you mention it, we did have one in here, said he'd walked from Winchester. Looked like a bundle of old rags, sat in the corner over there.' He nodded to a corner by the fireplace. 'The wife wanted me to turn him away, but I'd no reason to. He had money and he behaved himself, made a couple of pints last through to closing time then shambled off along the Grange wall. You think he's involved?'

'Not necessarily. We're just looking for leads at the moment. When was this? Can you remember?'

The big man thought for a moment. 'It was pissing down outside. Reckon he came in to dry off. The wife might remember when. I'll ask her and give you a ring if you like.'

'She's not here then?'

'Gone to the Cash and Carry. She'll be back soon.'

Nick Robinson checked his notebook. 'I gather you also do a Good Samaritan act with stranded caravans.'

'About twice a year when idiots cut the corner. It's good for business, mind. They usually feel obliged to come in and eat something.' He nodded towards the window. 'It's the Council's fault. They've stuck a bloody great sign for the East Deller campsite at the top of the hill. I've complained about it but nobody takes any notice.'

'Anything strike you about the people you've rescued, anything unusual?'

'There was a one-legged German midget once with a wife like Raquel Welsh. That struck me as unusual.'

Nick Robinson smiled as he made a note. 'Nothing unusual.'

'You don't have much to go on, do you?'

'That depends on you.' Unconsciously, the policeman lowered his voice. 'Is anyone else here?'

Paddy's eyes narrowed slightly. 'No one. What are you after?'

'A confidential chat, sir, preferably with no eavesdroppers,' said Robinson, eyeing the large hands.

Paddy squeezed the glowing end of his cigarette into an ashtray with fingers the size of sausages. 'Go ahead.' His tone was not inviting.

'The body was found in the ice house at the Grange. Do you know the ice house?'

'I know there is one. I couldn't lead you to it.'

'Who told you about it?'

'Probably the same person who told me there's a two-hundred-year-old oak in the woods,' said Paddy with a shrug. 'Maybe I got it from David Maybury's booklet. I couldn't say.'

'What booklet?'

'I've some copies somewhere. David had this idea of fleecing the tourists, wanted to turn the Grange into another Stourhead. He produced a map of the grounds with a short history of the house and had a hundred or so copies printed. It was a dead duck from the word go. He wouldn't spend any money on advertising and who the hell's ever heard of Streech Grange?' Paddy gave a derogatory snort. 'Stupid bastard. He was a cheapskate, always expected something for nothing.'

Robinson's eyes were alight with interest. 'Do you know who else has this booklet?'

'We're talking twelve to thirteen years, Sergeant. As far as I remember, David handed them out to anyone who would pass them on to tourists. Testing the water, he said. Whether anyone else's still got a copy I wouldn't know.'

'Can you look yours out?'

The other man was doubtful. 'Christ knows where they are, but I'll have a go. The wife might know.'

'Thanks. I gather you knew Maybury quite well.'

'As well as I wanted to.'

'What sort of man was he? What was his background?'

Paddy stared thoughtfully at the ceiling, dredging up memories. 'Upper-middle-class, I'd say. He was the son of an Army major who was killed during the war. I don't think David ever really knew his father but old Colonel Gallagher certainly did. I imagine that's why he let Phoebe's marriage go ahead, he thought the son would take after his father.' His lips twisted into a cynical smile. 'Fat chance. David was a bastard through and through. The story goes that when his mother died he had the choice of going to her funeral or going to the Derby. He chose the Derby because he had a fortune riding on the favourite.'

'You didn't like him?'

Paddy accepted another cigarette. 'He was a shit – the kind who enjoys putting people down – but he kept me supplied with fairly decent plonk, plus he was one of my best customers. Bought all his beer from me and drank in here most nights.' He took a deep inhalation of smoke. 'Nobody regretted his disappearance, except me. He left owing me over a hundred quid. I wouldn't have minded so much if I hadn't just settled my wine account with his blasted company.'

'You say "he left". You don't think he was murdered?'

'I've no views on it. Left, murdered, same result. It doubled our trade overnight. With all the media coverage, Streech became quite famous. The ghouls dropped in here for local colour before setting off up the hill to gawp through the Grange gates.' He saw a look of distaste on the Constable's face and shrugged. 'I'm a businessman. The same thing'll happen this time which is why the wife's gone to the Cash and Carry. Take my word for it, there'll be a horde of pressmen in here tonight. I pity those wretched women. They'll not be able to set foot outside their gates without being hounded.'

'How well do you know them?'

A guarded expression came over the big man's face. 'Well enough.'

'Do you know anything about their lesbian activities?'

Paddy Clarke chuckled. 'Who's been winding you up?' he asked.

'Several people have mentioned it,' said Robinson mildly. 'There's no truth in it then?'

'They've got minds like sewers,' said Paddy with disgust. 'Three women living together, keeping themselves to themselves, minding their own business and tongues start to wag.' He gave his derogatory snort again. 'Two of them have kids. That hardly ties in with lesbianism.'

'Anne Cattrell hasn't any and she admitted being a lesbian to a colleague of mine.'

Paddy gave such a shout of laughter that he choked on the smoke from his cigarette. 'For your information,' he said with watering eyes, 'Anne could give Fiona Richmond lessons on sex. 'Struth, man, she's had more lovers than you've had hot dinners. What's your colleague like? A pompous jerk, I'll bet. Anne would enjoy taking the piss out of someone like that.'

DS Robinson refused to be drawn on the subject of Andy McLoughlin. 'How come no one's mentioned this? Surely the people here would find promiscuity as titillating as lesbianism.'

'Because she's discreet, for crying out loud. Do you crap on your doorstep? Anyway, there's no one in this dump she'd give houseroom to.' He spoke scathingly. 'She prefers her men with brain as well as brawn.'

'How do you know all this, Mr Clarke?'

Paddy glared at him. 'Never mind how I know. Confidential, you said, and confidential it is. I'm setting the record straight. There's enough bullshit been talked about those women to fill a midden. You'll be telling me next they run a witches' coven. That's another favourite, with poor old Fred cast in the rôle of satanic stallion because of his prison record.'

'Confidentially, sir,' said Robinson after a brief hesitation while he contemplated Fred Phillips in the rôle of satanic stallion, 'I've heard from a number of sources that you might know something about several used condoms we've found near the ice house at the Grange.'

Clarke, he thought, looked positively murderous. 'What sources?'

'A number,' said Robinson firmly, 'but I'm not going to divulge them, just as I won't divulge anything you say to me without your permission. We're in the dark, sir. We need information.'

'To hell with information,' said Paddy aggressively, thrusting his face close to Robinson's. 'I'm a publican, not a bloody policeman. You're the one who's being paid. You do your own dirty work.'

Ten years on the force had given Nick Robinson a certain wiliness. He tucked his pen into his jacket and got off the barstool. 'That's your privilege, sir, but as things stand at the moment the finger's pointing at Mrs Maybury and her friends. They seem to be the only ones with enough knowledge of the grounds to have hidden the body in the ice house. I'll guarantee that if we don't get more information, the three of them will be charged with conspiracy.'

There was a long silence while the publican stared at the policeman. Robinson felt he ought to disapprove of Clarke – if Amy Ledbetter was right, the man was a highly sexed stud – but instead he found himself liking him. Whatever his sexual morality, the man looked you in the eye when he spoke to you.

'God damn it!' said Paddy suddenly, slamming a massive fist on to the bar. 'Sit down, man. I'll get you a beer, but if you ever breathe a word of this to my wife I'll string you up by your balls.'

McLoughlin was waiting at the entrance to the ice house when Walsh arrived with the plastic bag containing the shoes. 'I was told you wanted to see me, sir.'

Walsh removed his jacket and lowered himself on to the sun-baked ground, folding the jacket neatly beside him. 'Sit down, Andy. I'm after a few quiet words away from the house. This whole damned thing's getting more complicated by the minute and I don't want any flapping ears around.' He studied the Sergeant's drawn face with sudden irritability. 'What's the matter with you?' he snapped. 'You look terrible.'

McLoughlin transferred his wallet and loose change from his rear trouser pockets and sat down at a short distance from his boss. 'Nothing,' he said, trying without success to find a comfortable position for his legs. He regarded the other man through half-closed lids. He could never decide whether he liked or disliked Walsh. The Inspector, for all his irascibility, could surprise with a kindness. But not today.

He looked across at Walsh and saw only an insignificant, skinny man, playing tough because the system allowed it. He was tempted to make the Inspector a free gift of his assault on Anne Cattrell that morning just to see his reaction. Would he bark? Or would he bite? Bark, McLoughlin thought with amused contempt. Walsh was no more able to face an unpleasantness than the next man. It would be different, of course, when she put in her written complaint. Then, the machinery of justice would roll and action would be as mechanical as it was inevitable. His certainty that this would happen lifted rather than depressed him. The cut would be clean and final, so much cleaner and so much more final than if he administered it himself. He even felt a stirring of anger against the woman that she hadn't delivered the blow already.

Walsh finished summarising the pathologist's report. 'Well?' he demanded.

The shutter clicked maddeningly in McLoughlin's brain. He stared at Walsh with vacant eyes for a moment, then shook his head. 'You say he's exploring the possibility of mutilation. He's not sure yet?'

Walsh snarled sarcastically. 'Won't commit himself. Claims he hasn't enough experience of eaten bodies. But it's a damned odd rat that chews selectively on the only two fingers Maybury had missing.'

'You'll have to tie Webster down on that,' McLoughlin pointed out thoughtfully. 'It makes a hell of a difference to the case if there was no mutilation.' Dreadful black-and-white footage of Mussolini's corpse, strung by its feet from a lamppost after an angry mob had emasculated it, floated into his mind. Violent, angry, hating faces, jeering their revenge. 'A hell of a difference,' he said quietly.

'Why?'

'It's less likely to be Maybury.'

'You're as bad as Webster,' growled Walsh. 'Jumping to bloody conclusions. Let me tell you, Andy, that body is *more* likely to be Maybury's than anyone else's. It is a statistical improbability that this house should be the centre of two unconnected police investigations in ten years, and it is a statistical *probability*, as I've said all along, that his wife murdered him.'

'Even she couldn't murder him twice, sir. If she did it ten years ago, then it wasn't him in the ice house. If it was him in the ice house, then, by God, she's had a raw deal.'

'She brought it on herself,' said Walsh coldly.

'Maybe, but you've let Maybury grow into an obsession with you, and you can't expect the rest of us to chase red herrings just to prove a point.'

Walsh poked around amongst the folds of his jacket for his pipe. He stuffed it in thoughtful silence. 'I've got this gut feeling, Andy,' he said at last, holding his lighter flame to the tobacco and puffing. 'The moment I saw that mess yesterday, I knew. Found you, you bastard, I said to myself.' He looked up and caught McLoughlin's eye. 'OK, OK, lad, I'm not a fool. I'm not about to tie you all down because of my gut feeling, but the fact remains that the blasted body is unidentifiable. And why? Because someone, somewhere, doesn't want it identified, that's why. Who took the clothes? Where are the dentures? Why no fingerprints? Oh, it's been mutilated all right, and it was as likely to be mutilated because it *was* Maybury as because it wasn't.'

'So where do we go from here? Missing persons?'

'Checked. Our area, anyway. We'll go further afield if necessary, but on the evidence so far a local connection seems probable. We've one likely candidate. A Daniel Thompson from East Deller. The description matches very closely and he went missing around the time Webster thinks our man was killed.' He nodded to the shoes in the plastic bag. 'When he disappeared, he was wearing brown lace-ups. Jones found these in the woods adjoining the farm.'

McLoughlin whistled through his teeth. 'If they're his, is there anyone who can identify them?'

'A wife.' Walsh watched McLoughlin push himself awkwardly to his feet. 'Not so fast,' he snapped petulantly. 'Let's hear how you got on. You spoke to Miss Cattrell? Learn anything?'

McLoughlin plucked at the grass beside him. 'The Phillipses' real name is Jefferson. They were sentenced to five years each for the murder of their lodger Ian Donaghue who buggered and killed their son. He was an only child, twelve years old, born when Mrs Jefferson was forty. Miss Cattrell arranged their employment here.' He looked up. 'They're a possibility, sir. What they've done once, they might do again.'

'Different MO. As far as I remember, they made no secret of Donaghue's execution, even carried out a mock trial in front of his girlfriend and hanged him when he confessed. She was a star witness in their defence, wasn't she? It doesn't square with this murder.'

'Maybe,' said McLoughlin, 'but they've proved they're capable of murdering for revenge and they're pretty attached to Mrs Maybury. We can't ignore it.'

'Have you questioned them yet?'

McLoughlin winced. 'Up to a point. I had her in after Miss Cattrell. It was like trying to prise information out of an oyster. She's a cantankerous old biddy.' He pulled his notebook out of his shirt pocket and riffled through the pages. 'She let slip one thing which struck me as interesting. I asked her if she was happy here. She said: "The only difference between a fortress and a prison is that in a fortress the doors are locked on the inside." '

'What's interesting about that?'

'Would you describe your house as a fortress?'

'She's senile.' Walsh waved him on impatiently. 'Any more?'

'Diana Goode has a daughter, Elizabeth, who spends odd week-ends here. Aged nineteen, has a flat in London which was given her by her father, works as a croupier in one of the big West End casinos. She's a bit wild, or that's the impression her mother gave.'

Walsh grunted.

'Phoebe Maybury has a licensed shotgun,' McLoughlin continued, reading down his notes. 'She's responsible for the spent cartridges. According to Fred, there's a colony of feral cats in and around Grange Farm which use his kitchen garden as their private bog. Mrs Maybury scares them off with a blast from the shotgun but Fred claims she's rather lost interest lately, says it's like trying to hold back the tide.'

'Anyone know anything about the condoms?'

McLoughlin raised a sardonic eyebrow. 'No,' he said with feeling. 'But they all found it very amusing, at my expense. Fred said he's raked up quite a few in the past. I questioned him again about finding the body. His story's the same, no discrepancies.' He ran through the sequence for Walsh's benefit.

When Fred arrived at the ice house, the door was completely obscured by the brambles. He returned to his shed to fetch a torch and a scythe, and trampled the brambles so thoroughly because he had intended to take a wheelbarrow in to remove the bricks and had wanted a clear path. The door had been half-open when he finally came to it. There had been no indication that anyone had been that way recently. After he had found the body, he had paused long enough to swing the door to as far as it would go, then he had taken to his heels.

'Did you press him hard?' Walsh asked.

'I went over it with him three or four times, but he's like his wife. He's single-minded and he doesn't volunteer information. That's the story and he's sticking to it. If he did flatten the brambles after he found the body, he's not going to admit to it.'

'What's your guess, Andy?'

'I'm with you, sir. I'd say it's odds on he found plenty of evidence to show there'd been traffic that way and did his utmost to obliterate it after he found the body.' McLoughlin glanced at the mass of torn vegetation on either side of the doorway. 'He did a good job, too. There's no way of knowing now how many people went in there or when.'

Elizabeth and Jonathan found their mothers and Anne drinking coffee in the drawing-room. Benson and Hedges roused themselves from the carpet to greet the newcomers, sniffing hands, rubbing delightedly against legs, rolling over in an ecstasy of joyful welcome.

By contrast the three women were positively diffident. Phoebe held out a hand to her son. Diana patted the seat beside her in tentative invitation. Anne nodded.

Phoebe spoke first. 'Hello, darling. Journey down all right?'

Jonathan perched on the arm of her chair and bent down to peck her cheek. 'Fine. Lizzie persuaded her boss to give her the night off and met me at the hospital. I've skipped an afternoon's lectures. We were on the M3 by midday. We haven't eaten yet,' he added as an afterthought.

Diana stood up. 'I'll get you something.'

'Not yet,' said Elizabeth, catching her hand and pulling her on to the sofa again. 'A few minutes won't make any difference. Tell us what's been happening. We had a quick word with Molly in the kitchen but she didn't exactly lavish us with detail. Do the police know whose body it is? Have they said anything about how it was done?' She blurted the questions, insensitive to feelings, eyes over-bright.

Her questions were greeted with surprised silence. In twenty-four hours, the women had unconsciously adjusted themselves to a climate of suspicion. A question must be thought about; answers carefully considered.

Predictably, it was Anne who broke the silence. 'It's really quite frightening, isn't it? Your judgement becomes impaired.' She flicked ash into the fireplace. 'Imagine what it must be like in a police state. You wouldn't dare trust anybody.'

Diana threw her a grateful glance. 'You tell them. I'm not trained for this sort of thing. My forte is amusing anecdotes with a punchline. When this is over, I'll polish it up, exaggerate the more titillating bits and give everyone something to laugh about over dinner.' She shook her head. 'But not now. At the moment, it's not very funny.'

'Oh, I don't know,' said Phoebe surprisingly. 'I had a good laugh this morning when Molly caught Sergeant McLoughlin in the downstairs cupboard. She chased him out with a broom. The poor man looked absolutely terrified. Apparently he was trying to find the bog.'

Elizabeth giggled nervously. 'What's he like?'

'Confused,' said Anne dryly, catching the points of her shirt collar and holding them together. 'Now, Lizzie, what was it you asked? Do they know whose body it is? No. Have they said anything about how it was done? No.' She leant forward and held up her fingers to tick off points. 'The situation, as far as we know it, is this.' Slowly and lucidly she ran through the details of the finding of the body, its removal, the police examination of the ice house and grounds and their subsequent questioning. 'The next step, I think, will be a search warrant.' She turned to Phoebe. 'It would be logical. They'll want to go through the house with a fine-tooth comb.'

'I don't understand why they didn't do it last night.'

Anne frowned. 'I've been wondering about that but I suspect they've been waiting for the results of the post-mortem. They'll want to know what they're looking for. In some ways it makes it worse.'

Jonathan turned to his mother. 'You said on the phone they wanted to question us. What about?'

Phoebe took off her glasses and polished them on her shirt hem. 'They want the names of anyone you showed the ice house to.' She looked up at him and he wondered, not for the first time, why she wore glasses. Without them she was beautiful; with them she was ordinary. Once, when he was a child, he had looked through them. It had been a kind of betrayal to discover the lenses were clear glass.

'What about Jane?' he said immediately. 'Are they going to question her too?'

'Yes.'

'You mustn't let them,' he said urgently.

She took his hand and held it between hers. 'We don't think we can stop them, darling, and if we try we may make it worse. She'll be home tomorrow. Anne says we should trust her.'

Jonathan stood up angrily. 'You're mad, Anne. She'll destroy herself and Mum.'

Anne shrugged. 'We have very little option, Johnny.' She used his childhood diminutive deliberately. 'I suggest you have more faith in your sister and keep your fingers crossed. Frankly, there's bugger all else we can do.'

90

ELEVEN

In dribs and drabs, as messages got through, Walsh's men assembled on the grass in front of the ice house to make their reports. The day was at its hottest and the company shed their jackets gratefully and sat or reclined on the ground like family men at the beach. McLoughlin, lying now on his stomach, frowned into the middle distance like an anxious father with far-off boisterous children. Sergeant Robinson, oblivious to anyone's needs but his own, guzzled happily on a packet of sandwiches and gave the whole the spurious air of an impromptu picnic.

In the background the brambles which had once flourished as a magnificent green curtain quietly leached their sap through shattered stems and turned brown in the sun.

Walsh drew out his handkerchief and wiped the sweat from his forehead. 'Let's hear what you've got then,' he snarled into the contented silence as if he had already made the suggestion once and been ignored. He was sitting with his legs stretched wide apart and a notebook on the ground between his knees. He turned to a blank page. 'Shoes,' he said, making a pencilled note then tapping the brown shoes in the bag beside him. 'Who went up to the house?'

'I did, sir,' said one of Jones's search party. 'Fred Phillips takes size ten and his feet are about as broad as they are long. He took off his boots to show me.' He chuckled at the memory. 'He's not just built like an elephant, he's got feet to match.' He caught Walsh's eye and peered hurriedly at the shoes in the bag. He shook his head. 'No chance. I doubt he'd even get those over his big toes. Jonathan Maybury takes size nine.' He looked up. 'Incidentally, he and Mrs Goode's daughter have arrived, sir. They're with their mothers now.'

Walsh murmured acknowledgement as he jotted down the sizes. 'OK, Robinson, what have you got?'

The DS crammed the last of his sandwich into his mouth and fished out his pad. 'Promotion,' he muttered under his breath to the man next to him.

'What was that?' demanded Walsh coldly.

'Sorry, sir, wind,' replied Robinson, thumbing through his pages. 'I hit upon a mine of information, sir. I'll put it all in my report, but the important bits are these: one, these woods are used regularly by local courting couples, have been for years apparently; two, David Maybury had a hundred copies of a booklet printed, showing a map of the grounds and giving a potted history of the place.' He glanced at Walsh. 'He wanted to attract tourists,' he explained, 'and gave the booklets away to anyone in the village who would pass them on.'

'Damn,' said the Chief Inspector with feeling. 'Have you got a copy?'

'Not yet. It was the landlord at the pub who told me about it and he's looking for his copies now. If he finds them, he'll give me a ring.'

'Anything else?'

'Do me a favour, sir, I've hardly started,' said Nick Robinson plaintively. 'I asked about strangers. Several people remembered seeing an old tramp hanging around the village about two, three months ago but I couldn't get a definite date on him. He had money because he bought a couple of drinks in the pub.'

'I've a date, sir,' Constable Williams interrupted eagerly. 'He knocked at two houses on the council estate asking for food and money. The first was an old lady called Mrs Hogarth who gave him a sandwich; the second was a Mrs Fowler who sent him off with a flea in his ear because he came in the middle of her son's birthday party. The twenty-seventh of May,' he finished triumphantly. 'I've got a good description, too. He shouldn't be too hard to find. Old brown trilby, green jacket and, this is the clincher, bright pink trousers.'

Walsh was doubtful. 'There's probably no connection. Tramps are two a penny round here in the summer. They follow the sun and the scenic routes just like the tourists. Any more?'

DS Robinson caught a sardonic gleam in McLoughlin's eye which told him what he'd already guessed, that the old man was in another of his moods. God rot his soul, he thought. It was like working with a yo-yo, up one minute, down the next. Any other time and all his efforts of the morning would have earned him a pat on the back. As things stood now, he'd be lucky if he got away with a kick in the pants.

He returned to his notebook. 'I followed a lead I was given and spoke to one of the condom users,' he went on. 'He comes up here with his girlfriend when it's warm enough, usually around eleven o'clock—'

'Name,' snapped Walsh.

'Sorry, sir. Promised I wouldn't reveal his name, not unless it became absolutely necessary for a prosecution and, even then, not without his permission.' In Sergeant Robinson's view, Paddy Clarke's threat to string him up by the balls had been no idle one. The big man had offered no reasons for his promiscuity but Robinson had guessed them when Mrs Clarke returned unexpectedly as he was leaving. She was big, meaty and domineering with a brittle smile and hard eyes. A Gorgon who wore the trousers. God knows, Robinson had thought, no one could blame Paddy for wanting something soft, sweet and compliant to cuddle from time to time.

'Go on,' said Walsh.

'I asked him if he'd seen anything unusual up here in the last six months. Seen, no, he said, but heard, yes. According to him it's normally pretty quiet, the odd owl or nightjar, dogs barking in the distance, that sort of thing.' He consulted his notebook. 'On two occasions in June, during the first two weeks, he reckons, he and his girlfriend were – and I'm quoting him, sir – "scared shitless by the most god-awful racket you've ever heard. Like souls crying out in hell." The first time it happened, his girlfriend was so frightened she took to her heels and ran. He followed pretty sharpish and when they reached the road, she told him she'd left her knickers behind.'

A muted snigger rippled round the seated men like a soft breeze through the grass. Even Walsh smiled. 'What was it, did they know?'

'They sussed it the second time. They came up a week later and it happened again but to a much lesser degree. This time, my man hung on to his girl and made her listen. It was cats yowling and spitting, either at each other or something else – he thought he could hear growling as well. He couldn't say where it was coming from, but it was fairly close.' He looked at Walsh. 'They've been up several times since but it's not happened again.'

McLoughlin stirred himself. 'The colony of feral cats at the farm,' he said, 'fighting over the body. If that's right and the date's accurate it gives us the beginnings of a timescale. Our victim was murdered during or before the first week in June.'

'How sure is your man of his dates?' Walsh asked Robinson.

'Pretty sure. He's going to check with the girlfriend but he remembers it being during that spell of very hot weather at the beginning of June, said the ground was dry as a bone both times so he didn't need to take anything for them to lie on.'

Walsh made some notes on his pad. 'Is that it?'

'I've had some conflicting reports about the three women up here. Almost everyone agrees they're lesbians and that they try to seduce the village girls into lesbian orgies. But two of them – in my view, sir, the two most sensible – said it was malicious rubbish. One's an old lady in her seventies or eighties who knows them pretty well, the other's my informant. He said that Anne Cattrell's had so many lovers she could give Fiona Richmond lessons on sex.' He took a cigarette out and lit it, glancing through the smoke at McLoughlin. 'If it's true, sir, it might give us another angle. *Crime passionnel*, or whatever the Frogs call it. It strikes me she's gone out of her way to make us think she's only interested in women. Why? Could be because she's done away with a jealous lover and doesn't want us to make the connection.'

'Your informant's talking crap,' McLoughlin said bluntly. 'Everyone knows they're lesbians. Hell, I've heard more old jokes about that than I can remember.' Jack Booth had had a fund of them. 'It's hardly something new that Miss Cattrell's invented for our benefit. And if it's not true, why do they pretend it is? What on earth do they gain by it?'

Walsh was stuffing tobacco into his pipe. 'Your problem, Andy, is that you generalise too much,' he said acidly. 'The fact that everyone knows something doesn't make it true. Everyone knew my brother was a tight-fisted bastard until he died and we discovered he'd been paying out two hundred quid a year for fifteen years to educate some black kids in Africa.' He nodded approvingly at Robinson. 'You may have something, Nick. Personally, I couldn't give a monkey's what their sexual habits are and, from what I've seen of them, they couldn't give a monkey's what people say or think about them. Which is why' – he glared at McLoughlin – 'they wouldn't trouble to deny or confirm anything. But,' he continued thoughtfully, lighting his pipe, 'I *am* interested in the fact that Anne Cattrell's been shoving lesbianism down our throats since we got here. What's her motive?' He fell silent.

DS Robinson waited a moment. 'Let me have a go at her, sir. A new face, she might open up. No harm in trying.'

'I'll think about it. Has anyone else got anything?'

A constable raised a hand. 'Two people I spoke to reported hearing a woman sobbing one night, sir, but they couldn't remember how long ago.'

'Two people in the same house?'

'No, that's why I thought it worth mentioning. Different houses. There's a couple of farm cottages just off the East Deller road, belong to Grange Farm. Both sets of occupants remembered hearing the woman but said they didn't do anything about it because they thought it was a lovers' tiff. Neither cottage could remember exactly when it was.'

'Go and see them again,' said Walsh abruptly. 'You, too, Williams. Find out if they were watching telly when it happened, what programme was on, were they eating supper? Or if they were in bed, how late was it, were they awake because it was hot, because it was raining? Anything to give us an idea of time and date. If she wasn't sobbing because she'd just killed a man, she might have been sobbing because she'd just seen him killed.' He pushed himself awkwardly to his feet, gathering his notebook and jacket as he did so. 'McLoughlin, you come with me. We're going to have a chat with Mrs Thompson. Jones, you and your squad pack up here and get everything back to the Station. You can take an hour's break, then I want you all here for a search of the house. There'll be warrants on my desk,' he told Jones. 'Bring them with you.' He turned to Nick Robinson. 'OK, lad, you go and have your quiet little chat about sex with Ms Cattrell but don't go putting the wind up her. If she did chop our body up, I want to be able to prove it.'

'Leave it to me, sir.'

Walsh smiled his reptilian smile. 'Just remember one thing, Nick. In her time she's eaten Special Branch men for breakfast. You represent a small bag of peanuts.'

The door opened after some moments to reveal a drab little woman in a high-buttoned, long-sleeved black dress. She had sorrowful eyes and a pinched mouth. A gold cross on a long chain lay between her flat breasts and she needed only a coif and an open prayer book to complete the picture of devoted suffering.

Walsh proffered his identity card. 'Mrs Thompson?' he asked.

She nodded but didn't bother to look at the card.

'Chief Inspector Walsh and Sergeant McLoughlin. Could we come in? We'd like to ask you some questions about your husband's disappearance.'

She pinched her lips into an unattractive moue. 'But I've told the police all I know,' she whimpered, the sorrowful eyes welling with tears. 'I don't want to think about it any more.'

Walsh groaned inwardly. His wife would be like this, he thought, if anything happened to him. Inadequate, tearful, irritating. He smiled kindly. 'We'll only keep you a minute,' he assured her.

Reluctantly, she pulled the door wide and gestured towards the living-room, though *living*-room, thought McLoughlin as he entered it, was a misnomer. It was clean to the point of obsession and bare of anything that might display character or individuality, no books, no ornaments, no pictures, not even a television. In his mind's eye, he compared it with the vivid and colourful room that Anne Cattrell lived in. If the two rooms were an outward expression of the inner person, he had no doubt who was the more interesting. Living with Mrs Thompson would be like living with an empty shell.

They sat on the sterile chairs. Mrs Thompson perched on the edge of the sofa, crumpling a lace handkerchief between her fingers, dabbing her eyes with it from time to time. Inspector Walsh took his pipe from his pocket, glanced around the room as if noticing it for the first time, then put the pipe away again.

'What size shoes does your husband take?' he asked the little woman.

Her eyes opened wide and she stared at him as if he'd made an improper suggestion. 'I don't understand,' she whispered.

Walsh felt his irritation mounting. If Thompson had done a runner, who could blame him? The woman was ridiculous. 'What size shoes does your husband take?' he asked again patiently.

'Does?' she repeated. 'Does? Have you found him then? I've been so sure he was dead.' She became quite animated. 'He's lost his memory, hasn't he? It's the only explanation. He'd never leave me, you know.'

'No, we haven't found him, Mrs Thompson,' said the Inspector firmly, 'but you reported him missing and we are doing our best to trace him for you. It would help if we knew his shoe size. The missing person's report says size eight. Is that correct?'

'I don't know,' she said vacantly. 'He always bought his shoes himself.' She peeped at him from under her lashes and, rather shockingly, flashed him a coy smile.

McLoughlin leaned forward. 'Could you take me upstairs, Mrs Thompson, and we'll find out from the pairs he left behind?'

She shrank into the sofa. 'I couldn't possibly,' she said. 'I don't know you. It was a young policewoman who came before. Where is she? Why isn't she here?'

Inspector Walsh counted to ten and considered that Daniel Thompson must have been a saint. 'How long have you been married?' he asked curiously.

'Thirty-two years,' she whispered.

The man *was* a saint, he thought. 'Could you pop up and fetch a pair of his shoes?' he suggested. 'Sergeant McLoughlin and I will wait down here for you.'

She accepted this without demur and slipped out of the room, shutting the door behind her as if the door would somehow stop them were they really intent on raping her in her bedroom. Walsh raised his eyebrows to heaven. 'She needs her head examined.'

McLoughlin replied seriously, 'She's ill. Looks to me as if her husband's disappearance has sent her off the rails. Don't you think we ought to get her some help?'

Walsh pondered. 'There was a vicarage a few houses down, wasn't there? We'll stop off on our way back to the Grange.'

They looked up as the door opened again and Mrs Thompson reappeared with a pair of highly polished black leather shoes clasped against her chest. 'Size eight,' she said, 'and a narrow fitting. I never realised what dainty feet he had. He wasn't a short man, you know.'

Reluctantly, Walsh opened his briefcase and produced the clear plastic bag containing the brown shoes. He placed the shoes, in the bag, on the flat of one hand and held them out for the woman to examine. 'Are these your husband's shoes, Mrs Thompson? Do you remember him having a pair like this?'

There was no hesitation in her reply. 'Certainly not,' she said. 'My husband wouldn't dream of wearing co-respondent shoes.'

'The white patches are where the shoes have got damp, Mrs Thompson, not white leather. The shoes were uniformly brown once.'

'Oh.' She moved closer, then after a few moments, shook her head. 'No, I've never seen them before. They're certainly not Daniel's. He had only one pair of brown shoes and he was wearing them the day he' – she gave a little sob – 'the day he vanished.' She used the sodden scrap of lace to dab at her eyes again. 'They were very expensive Italian shoes with pointed toes. Nothing like those. He was very conscientious about his appearance,' she finished.

Walsh put the shoes back in his briefcase. 'When you reported your husband missing, Mrs Thompson, you said he'd had some business worries recently. What exactly did you mean?'

She shied away from him as if he'd tried to touch her. 'He wouldn't leave me,' she said again.

'Of course he wouldn't, Mrs Thompson, but pressure at work does make some men act irrationally. Perhaps he couldn't cope with his problems and needed time on his own to sort them out. Is that what you meant?'

Tears poured from the sorrowful eyes in a flood. She wore her despair like a tatty cardigan, something she had grown used to and was comfortable with in spite of its ugliness. She sank on to the sofa. 'His business is bankrupt,' she explained. 'He owes money all over the place. It's all being sorted out by his assistant but people –

creditors – keep ringing me. There's nothing I can do. I've told them he's dead.'

'How do you know?' asked Walsh gently.

'He wouldn't leave me,' she said, 'not if he was alive.'

Walsh looked at McLoughlin and nodded towards the door. They stood up. 'Thank you for giving us your time, Mrs Thompson. There's just one thing. Has your husband ever been to Streech Grange or had dealings with the people living there?'

Her lips thinned to an angry slit. 'Is that where those awful women live?' she spat. Walsh nodded. 'Daniel would sooner walk into the lion's den' – she fingered her cross – 'than be contaminated by their sin.' She kissed the cross and started to undo the buttons of her dress.

'Fair enough,' said Walsh with some embarrassment. 'We'll let ourselves out.'

Andy McLoughlin paused in the living-room doorway and looked back at her. 'We're going to ask the Vicar to pop round and see you, Mrs Thompson. It might do you good to have a chat with him.'

The Vicar listened to the expressions of police concern with ill-disguised panic. 'Frankly, Inspector, there's nothing I can do. Believe me, our little community has bent over backwards to assist poor Mrs Thompson. We've enlisted the aid of her doctor and a social worker, but they're powerless to act unless she herself requests psychiatric help. She's not mad, you see, nor, in the accepted sense, even depressed. In fact, outwardly, she's coping magnificently.' He had a pronounced Adam's apple which bobbed up and down as he spoke. 'It's only when people visit her, particularly men, that she acts – er – strangely. The doctor's sure it's only a matter of time before she snaps out of it.' He wrung his hands. 'The truth is neither he nor I like to go there any more. She seems to have developed sex and religious mania. I'll send my wife, though to be honest her last encounter with Mrs Thompson was less than happy, some accusation about seeing me in church with only my socks and shoes on.' The Adam's apple crowded nervously towards his chin. 'Poor woman. Such a tragedy for her. Leave it with me, Inspector. I'm sure it's only a matter of time, of coming to terms with Daniel's disappearance. There must be a text to deal with it. Leave it with me.'

Detective Sergeant Robinson rang Anne's doorbell and waited. The door was slightly ajar and a voice called: 'Come in,' from a distance. He went down the corridor to the room at the end. Anne was sitting at her desk, a pencil tucked behind her ear, one booted foot propped on an open drawer and tapping time to 'Jumping Jack Flash' playing quietly from her stereo. She looked up and waved him to an empty chair. 'I'm Anne Cattrell,' she said, taking the pencil from behind her ear and marking a correction on a page of typed paper. 'Vaginal Orgasm – Fact or Fiction', had struggled its way towards some sort of climax on five sheets of A4.

He sat down. 'Detective Sergeant Robinson,' he introduced himself.

She smiled. 'What can I do for you?'

Hell, he thought, she's OK – more than OK. With her cap of dark hair and wide-spaced eyes, she reminded him of Audrey Hepburn. From the way McLoughlin had talked the previous evening, he'd been expecting a real dog. 'It's not much,' he said, 'just something that doesn't square.'

'Fire away. Does the music worry you?'

'No. One of my favourites,' he said truthfully. 'It's like this, Miss Cattrell, both you and the majority of people in Streech village have made out that you and your friends are lesbians.' He paused.

'Go on.'

'Yet when I mentioned it to Mr Clarke at the pub this morning, he roared with laughter and said, though not in quite these words, that you were very definitely heterosexual.'

'What were his actual words?' she asked curiously.

He noticed the full ashtray on her desk. 'Do you mind if I smoke, Miss Cattrell?'

She offered him one of hers. 'Be my guest.' She watched him light the cigarette in silence.

'He said you've had more men than I've had hot dinners,' he said in a rush.

She chuckled. 'Yes, that well-worn cliché sounds like Paddy. So, you want to know if I'm a lesbian, and if I'm not why I've given the impression that I am.' He could almost hear her mind clicking. 'Why would a woman give people reason to despise her unless it's to put them off the track of something else?' She levelled her pencil at him. 'You think I've murdered one of my lovers and left him to rot in the ice house.' Her hands were as small and delicate as a child's.

'No,' he lied gamely. 'To be honest, it's not very important one way or the other, it's just something that's puzzled us. Also,' he went on, taking a shot in the dark, 'I took to Mr Clarke more than any of the others I spoke to, and I can't really believe he's the one who's wrong.'

'Clever of you,' said Anne appreciatively. 'In matters unconnected

99

with sex, Paddy has more sense in his little finger than the whole of Streech put together.'

'Well?' he asked.

'Was his wife there when you spoke to him?'

He shook his head. 'We spoke entirely in confidence though what he said about you was intended to be passed on. He said he was fed up with the b— er – rubbish that was spoken about the three of you.'

'Bullshit?' she supplied helpfully.

'Yes.' He grinned boyishly. 'Actually, I met his wife as I was leaving. She scared the hell out of me.'

Anne lit a cigarette. 'She was a nun once and incredibly pretty. She met Paddy in church and he swept her off her feet and persuaded her to break her vows. She's never forgiven him for it. As she gets older, her fall from grace assumes larger and larger proportions. She thinks it's God's punishment that she hasn't any children.' She was amused by his astonishment.

'You're having me on?' He couldn't believe Mrs Clarke had ever been pretty.

Her dark eyes sparkled. 'God's truth, m'lud.' She blew a smoke ring into the air. 'Fifteen years ago she set Paddy on fire. The spark's still there. It flashes out occasionally when she forgets herself, though Paddy can't see it. He's accepted the surface image and forgotten that nine-tenths of her lies hidden.'

'You could say that about anyone,' Robinson pointed out.

'You could indeed.'

'Jumping Jack Flash' had given way to 'Mother's Little Helper'. Her foot tapped out a new rhythm.

He waited for a moment but she didn't go on. 'Was Mr Clarke's information about you correct, Miss Cattrell?'

'Hopelessly wrong on numbers unless your mother's deprived you of hot dinners, but the general drift's accurate.'

'So why did you tell Sergeant McLoughlin you were a lesbian?'

She made another pencilled note on the page. 'I didn't,' she said, without looking up. 'He heard what he wanted to hear.'

'He's not a bad sort,' he said lamely, wondering why he felt a need to defend McLoughlin. 'He's been going through a rough patch lately.'

She raised her eyes. 'Is he a friend of yours?'

Robinson shrugged. 'I suppose so. He's done me some favours, stood by me a couple of times. We have the odd drink together.'

Anne found his answer depressing. Who listened, she wondered, when a man needed to talk? Women had friends; men, it seemed, had drinking companions. 'Whatever I said wouldn't have made any difference,' she told the Sergeant. 'It doesn't matter twopence to this case whether we bonk women every night or men every night. Or if,' she waved her pencil at her bookcase, 'we go to bed for the simple pleasures of reading ourselves to sleep. When you've solved your murder, you'll see I'm right.' She bent to her corrections once more.

TWELVE

Chief Inspector Walsh gathered his men about him on the drive in front of the Grange and divided them into four groups. Three to search the properties inside, and a fourth to comb the outhouses behind the kitchen, the garage block, the greenhouses and the cellars. Robinson had come out of the house to join them.

'What are we looking for, sir?' asked one man.

Walsh handed some typed sheets round the groups. 'Read these pointers, then use your common sense. If anyone here is connected with this murder, they are not going to make you a free gift of their involvement so keep your wits about you and your eyes open. The important facts to remember are these; one, our man died approximately ten weeks ago; two, he was stabbed; three, his clothes and dentures were removed; four, and most importantly, it would help if we knew who the hell he was. David Maybury and Daniel Thompson seem the most likely contenders and there's a brief description of both of them on those sheets.' He paused to let the men read the descriptions. 'You will notice that in terms of height, colouring and shoe size, the two are not dissimilar, but bear in mind, please, that Maybury will have aged ten years since his description was written. I shall head up the search in Mrs Maybury's house, McLoughlin will take Miss Cattrell, Jones, Mrs Goode and Robinson will mastermind the outhouses. If anyone finds anything, notify me immediately.'

With a sense of reluctance, McLoughlin presented himself and his two men outside Anne's door and rang her bell. Nick Robinson's crowing account of his chat with her had set a pile-driver beating in his head. 'Got your wires crossed there, old son,' Nick had said breathily into his ear. 'Given half a chance, I'd have a shot myself. They always say the bright ones are the least inhibited.'

McLoughlin, starved of alcohol, poked stiff fingers into the fat man's beer gut and listened to the satisfying ejection of air. 'You mean they stick a knife between your ribs when the performance is lousy,' he hissed into the other man's face.

Robinson notched up a direct hit and chuckled between deep breaths. 'I wouldn't know. I never have that problem.'

McLoughlin tried to remember a time when his head hadn't hurt, when shutters stayed open in his mind, and when he hadn't felt sick. His feelings see-sawed violently between intense dislike of Anne coupled with certainty that she was responsible for the mangled body in the ice house, and a hot shame that set the sweat pouring under his arms whenever he thought of his behaviour of the morning. He bunched his fist till the knuckles gleamed white. 'So why did she say she was a dyke?'

With a wary eye on the fist, Nick Robinson took a pace or two backwards. 'Claims she didn't. Face it, Andy, she reckons you're a pompous ass so she took the piss.' And it'll do you good, he thought. He liked McLoughlin, he had no reason not to, but the man fancied himself a cut above the rest of them which was why his wife's desertion had come so hard. The joke was that the Station had known about it for days, ever since Jack Booth had spilled the beans to Bob Rogers, but they had waited tactfully for McLoughlin to tell them himself. He never had. For two weeks he had come in every morning with a ferocious hangover and rambling stories about what Kelly had said or done the night before. Only his pride was hurt, they all knew it, and that not for much longer the way the WPCs were queuing up to get between his sheets. The clever money was on WPC Brownlow. And for Nick, fat, prematurely bald and with a penchant for WPC Brownlow himself, Anne's indifference to McLoughlin had been a soothing balm.

Anne opened the door and gestured them inside. McLoughlin removed the search warrant from his briefcase and gave it to her. She read it through carefully before handing it back with a shrug. There was no change in her manner towards him, no indication to him or his colleagues that he had overstepped that invisible mark beyond which behaviour is censured.

'Go ahead,' she said, nodding towards the small staircase leading to her upper rooms. 'I'll be in my study if you want me.' She returned to her desk in the big sunlit room. 'I Can't Get No Satisfaction' throbbed in the amplifiers.

Her spare room revealed nothing. McLoughlin doubted if it had been used for months, even years. There was a depression in the counterpane of one of the twin beds which implied that Benson or Hedges had found a comfortable retreat there, but no indication of a human presence. They moved on to her bedroom.

'Not bad,' said one of the men approvingly. 'The wife's just paid a fortune for pink frills, white melamine and mirrors. Can't get into the bloody bedroom now. Bet we could have done something like this for half the price.' He ran his hand along the front of a low oak chest.

The room gave an impression of space because it contained so little: only the chest, a delicate wicker chair, and a low double bed with a pile of pillows and a bottle-green duvet. In a recess in one corner was a built-in wardrobe. A white carpet stretched to infinity with no line to show where carpet ended and white skirting boards began. Huge colour close-ups of glorious flowers against jet-black backgrounds marched in a brilliant band round white walls. The room both challenged the eye and relaxed it.

'You two go through the chest and wardrobe,' said McLoughlin. 'I'll have a look in the bathroom.' He retreated gratefully to the normality of a pale pink bathroom but found nothing exceptional, unless two tins of shaving foam, a large packet of disposable razors and three used toothbrushes could be considered unusual possessions for a spinster. As he turned to the door, the corner of his eye caught a movement behind him. He spun sharply, heart struggling like a live thing in his mouth, and hardly recognised himself in the drawn and angry man who stared out of the mirror. He flicked the tap and splashed water over his face, dabbing it dry with a towel which smelt of roses. His head ached unbearably. He was at war with himself and the effort of trying to hold the warring parts together was destroying him. It was nothing to do with Kelly. The thought, unprompted, surprised him. It was inside him and had been inside him for a long time, a simmering rage that he could neither direct nor control, but which Kelly's departure had fired.

He went into the bedroom.

'Here's something, Sarge,' said DC Friar. He was on the bed, reclining against the pillows in a posture absurdly reminiscent of Manet's 'Olympia'. He held a small leather-bound book in one hand and was chuckling over it. 'Jesus, it's obscene.'

'Off,' said McLoughlin with a jerk of his head. He watched the man slide his feet reluctantly to the floor. 'What is it?'

'Her diary. Listen to this. "I cannot look on a penis, post-ejaculation, in a condom without laughing. I am transported immediately to my childhood and the time when my father's finger turned septic. He constructed a finger-stall out of industrial polythene – 'to keep an eye on the bugger' – and summoned my mother and me to witness the exciting climax when the finger, after much squeezing, burst. It was a jolly occasion." Jesus, that's sick!' He twitched the book out of McLoughlin's reach. 'And this one, listen to this one – ' he flicked a page – "'Phoebe and Diana sunbathed nude on the terrace today. I could have watched them for hours, they were so beautiful.''' Friar grinned. 'She's a dirty little bugger, isn't she? I wonder if the other two know she's a peeper.' He looked up and was surprised by the expression of distaste on McLoughlin's face. He took it for prudery. 'I was reading the entries for end of May, beginning of June,' he said. 'Take a look at June second and third.'

McLoughlin turned the pages. Her handwriting was black and strong and not always legible. He found Saturday, June 2nd. She had written: 'I have looked into the grave and eternity frightens me. I dreamed there was awareness after death. I hung alone in a great darkness, unable to speak or move, but knowing' (this word was underscored three times) 'that I had been abandoned to exist for ever without love and without hope. I could only yearn, and the pain of my yearning was terrible. I shall keep my light on tonight. Just at the moment, the darkness frightens me.' He read on. June 3rd: 'Poor Di. "Conscience does make cowards of us all." Should I have told her?' June 4th: 'P. is a mystery. He tells me he screws fifty women a year, and I believe him, yet he remains the most considerate of lovers. Why, when he can afford to take women for granted?'

McLoughlin snapped the diary shut in his palm. 'Anything else? Anything on her clothes?' The two men shook their heads. 'We'll tackle the living-room.'

Anne looked up as they went in. She saw the diary in McLoughlin's hand and a faint colour washed her cheeks. Damn, she thought. Why, of all things, had she forgotten that? 'Is that necessary?' she asked him.

'I'm afraid so, Miss Cattrell.' The Stones struck a final chord which lingered as a vibration in the air before fading into silence.

'There's nothing in it,' she said. 'Nothing that will help you, at least.'

DC Friar muttered into his colleague's ear, loud enough for McLoughlin to hear. 'Like hell there isn't! It's packed with fucking information!'

He wasn't prepared for the sudden grip of McLoughlin's fingers on the underside of his upper arm. They bit into the tender flesh like iron marlinspikes, gouging, probing, unrelenting in their viciousness. Quite unwittingly, he had reminded McLoughlin of Jack Booth.

A head taller than Friar, McLoughlin smiled gently down on him. His voice, curling lovingly round the Scots vernacular, murmured softly and sweetly: ' "Ye ugly, creepin blastit wonner, Destested, shunn'd by saunt and sinner, How daur ye set a fit upon her, sae fine a Lady! Gae somewhere else and seek your dinner, on some poor body." ' There was no emotion in his dark face but his knuckles whitened. 'Recognise that, Friar?'

The DC pulled himself free with an effort and rubbed his arm. He looked thoroughly startled. 'Give over, Sarge,' he muttered uncomfortably. 'I didn't understand a bloody word.' He looked to the other constable for support but Jansen was staring at his feet. He was new to Silverborne and Andy McLoughlin scared the shit out of him.

McLoughlin placed his briefcase on the corner of Anne's desk and opened it. 'It's from a poem by Robert Burns,' he told Friar affably. 'It's called "To A Louse". Now, Miss Cattrell,' he went on, turning his attention to her, 'this is a murder investigation. Your diary will help us establish your movements during the last few months.' He removed a pad of receipts and wrote on the top one. 'It will be returned as soon as we've finished with it.' He tore off the piece of paper and held it out to her and, for a brief moment, his eyes looked into hers and saw the laughter in them. A surge of warmth lapped around the frozen heart of his solitude. She bent her head to study the receipt and his gaze was attracted to the soft curls round the base of her neck, tiny inverted question marks which posed as many problems for him as she did herself. He wanted to touch them.

'I don't record my movements in that diary,' she told him after a moment, 'only my thoughts.' She looked up and her eyes laughed still. 'It's poor fare, Sergeant, just bees in my bonnet. I fear ye'll dine but sparely on sic a place.'

He smiled. Burns had written his poem after seeing a louse on a lady's bonnet in church. 'Ye've nae got the accent, Miss Cattrell. Ye grate ma lug wi' your crabbet sound.' She laughed out loud, and he hooked his foot round a chair and drew it forward to sit on. It was such a tiny face, he thought, and so expressive. Too expressive? Did sorrow come as easily as laughter? 'You recorded some interesting thoughts in your diary on June second. You wrote' – he pictured the written page in his mind – "I have looked into the grave and eternity frightens me." ' He examined her closely. 'Why did you write that, Miss Cattrell, and why did you write it then?'

'No reason. I often write about death.'

'Had you just seen inside a grave?'

'No.'

'Does death frighten you?'

'Not in the least. It annoys me.'

'In what way?'

Her eyes were amused. They would always betray her, he thought.

'Because I'll never know what happened next. I want to read the whole book, not just the first chapter. Don't you?'

Yes, he thought, I do. 'Yet you feared it at the beginning of June. Why?'

'I don't remember.'

' "I dreamed there was awareness after death," ' he prompted her. 'You went on to say that you would keep your light on that night because the darkness frightened you.'

She thought back. 'I had a dream and my dreams are very real. That one was particularly vivid. I woke early, when it was still dark, and I couldn't think where I was. I thought the dream was true.' She shrugged. 'That's what frightened me.'

'You told Mrs Goode something on June third which troubled her conscience. What was that?'

'Did I?' He opened the diary and read the extract to her. She shook her head. 'It was probably something trivial. Di has a sensitive conscience.

'Perhaps,' he suggested, 'you'd decided to tell her about the corpse you'd found in the ice house?'

'No, it certainly wasn't that.' Her eyes danced wickedly. 'I'd remember that.'

He was silent for a moment. 'Tell me why you don't feel sorry for that wretched man out there, Miss Cattrell.'

She turned away to look for a cigarette. 'I do feel sorry for him.'

'Do you?' He picked up her lighter and flicked the flame for her. 'You've never said so. Neither has Mrs Maybury or Mrs Goode. It's hardly normal. Most people would have expressed some sympathy, said "Poor man" as the minimum gesture of regret. The only emotion any of you has shown so far is irritation.'

It was true, she thought. How stupid they had been. 'We save our sympathies for ourselves,' she told him coolly. 'Compassion is a frail thing. It dies at the first touch of frost. You would have to live at Streech Grange to understand that.'

'You depress me. I assumed compassion was one of your muses.' He splayed his hands on the desk, then stood up. 'You would have felt sorry for a stranger, I think. But you knew him and you didn't like him, did you?' His chair scraped back. 'Right, Friar, Jansen, let's get on with it. We'll be as quick as we can, Miss Cattrell. At the end I will ask you to go upstairs with a WPC who will search you for anything you may have concealed in your clothing. You are welcome to stay while we work in here but, if you prefer to wait outside, one of the constables will wait with you.'

She puffed a smoke ring into the air and stabbed its centre with the end of her cigarette. 'Oh, I'll stay, Sergeant,' she told him. 'Police searches are meat and drink to me. It should run to a couple of thousand words on a woman's page somewhere. I rather fancy a headline like THE PRY TRADE or LICENCE TO SNOOP. What do you think?'

Sallow-faced bitch, he thought, as he watched the smoke drift from her mouth. The room stank of her cigarettes. 'Please yourself, Miss Cattrell.' He turned away. The blood swelled and throbbed and thickened in his head till he thought only a scream would relieve its pressure.

They went through everything with a fine-tooth comb and with infinite patience. Inside books, behind pictures, beneath chairs, through drawers; they ran long needles into the earth in the plant pots, felt for lumps under the fitted carpet, upended the sofa and poked deftly into its soft cushions; and when they had finished, the room looked exactly as it had done before they started. Anne, who had been moved courteously from her place behind her desk, was duly impressed.

'Very professional,' she told them. 'I congratulate you. Is that it?'

'Not quite,' said McLoughlin. 'Would you open the safe for me, please?'

She gave him a startled look. 'What on earth makes you think I've got a safe?'

He walked over to the oak-panelled mantelpiece which was an exact replica of the one in the library. He pressed on the edge of the middle panel and slid it back, revealing the dull green metal of a wall-safe with a chromium handle and lock. He glanced at Friar and Jansen. 'I found the one in the library this morning,' he said. 'Neat, isn't it?' He couldn't look at her. Her panic, brief though it had been, had shocked him.

She walked back to her desk, collecting her thoughts. She had always believed Phoebe the better judge of character, but it was Diana who was scared of McLoughlin.

'Would you open it, please?' he asked her again.

She took an unbroached packet of cigarettes from a carton of two hundred in her top drawer and tore the seal off it. He watched her patiently, saying nothing.

'Just who do you think you are?' snapped DC Friar angrily. 'You heard the Sergeant. Open the bloody safe.'

She ignored him, flipped the lid of the packet and turned the whole thing upside down, shaking a key into the palm of her hand. 'How are you on Spenser?' she asked McLoughlin with a quirky

smile. ' "A man by nothing is so well betrayed as by his manners."
It might have been written for your friend here.'

She's stalling, he thought, she's afraid, and I hate her. God, how
I hate her. 'The safe, please, Miss Cattrell.'

She walked over with a tiny shrug, unlocked the door and pulled
it open. The safe was empty except for a carving knife with a blood-
stained rag wrapped around its handle. The blade was black and
crusted. McLoughlin felt sick. For all his anger, he hadn't wanted
this. With a detached part of his mind, he wondered if he was ill.
His head was burning as if he had a fever. He leant his shoulder
against the mantelpiece to steady himself. 'Can you explain this,
please?' He heard his voice from a distance, harsh and unnatural.

'What's to explain?' she asked, taking out a cigarette and lighting it.

What indeed? The shutter clicked open and shut, open and shut,
behind his eyes. He glanced at the cigarette packet on the desk.
'Let's start with why you went to so much trouble to hide the key?'

'Habit.'

'That's a lie, Miss Cattrell.'

Tension had tightened the skin around his nose and mouth, giving
him a curiously flat look. She thought of the steel hawser she had
once seen in Shanghai, winding on to a huge capstan and drawing a
crippled tanker into the docks. As the slack was taken up, it had
risen from the concrete, shaking itself free of dust as it thinned and
tautened, and then had come a moment of pure horror when it
snapped under the strain and whipped with frightening speed through
the defenceless flesh of a man's neck. He had seen it coming, she
remembered, had put up his hands to protect himself. She looked
at McLoughlin and felt an urge to do the same. 'I want to phone
my solicitor,' she said. 'I will not answer any more questions until
he gets here.'

McLoughlin stirred. 'Friar, find Inspector Walsh for me and ask
him to come to Miss Cattrell's wing, will you? Tell him it's urgent,
tell him she wants to make a phone call. Jansen' – he flicked his
head towards the French windows – 'rustle up a WPC for a strip
search. You'll find Brownlow somewhere outside.' He waited till the
two men had left then turned to the mantelpiece and stood staring
at the open safe. After a moment he swung the door to and put his
hands on the mantelpiece, lowering his head to look into the unlit
fire. It was a gas replica of a real fire and the artificial coals were
peppered with cigarette ash and dog-ends. 'You should put them in
a bin,' he murmured. 'They'll leave marks when they burn.'

She craned her neck to see what he was looking at. 'Oh, those. I keep meaning to hoover them up.'

'I thought Mrs Phillips did the hoovering.'

'She does, but she discriminates against certain messes, or more accurately the makers of certain messes, and won't touch them with a barge pole.'

He turned to look at her, resting his elbow on the mantelpiece. He was shaking like a man with ague. 'I see.' He didn't, of course. What sort of discrimination did Molly go in for? Racial? Religious? Class?

'She discriminates on moral grounds,' Anne told him. Had he spoken his thoughts aloud? He couldn't remember, his head ached so much. 'She's a good old-fashioned Puritan, only truly happy when she's miserable. She can't understand why the rest of us don't feel the same way.'

'Like my mother,' he said.

She gave her throaty chuckle. 'Probably. Mine doesn't bother, thank God. I couldn't do battle with two of them.'

'Does she live near here?'

Anne shook her head. 'The last I heard of her she was in Bangkok. She remarried after my father died and set off round the world with husband mark two. I've rather lost track of them, to be honest.'

That hurt, he thought. 'When did you last see her?'

She didn't answer immediately. 'A long time ago.' She drummed her fingers impatiently on her desk. 'Give me one good reason why I should wait for the Inspector's permission to make this telephone call.'

Her voice vibrated with irritation. It made him laugh. Laughter swept over him like a kind of madness, wild, uncontrollable, joyous. He put a hand to his streaming eyes. 'I'm sorry,' he said. 'I'm so sorry. There is no good reason. Please. Be my guest.' The words, appallingly slurred, seemed to echo in his head and, even to his own ears, he sounded drunk. He clung to the mantelpiece and felt the hearth lurch beneath his feet.

'I suppose it hasn't occurred to you,' observed Anne at his shoulder, as she shoved a chair behind his legs and folded him neatly on to it with the pressure of one small hand on the nape of his neck, 'that it might be worth eating from time to time.' She abandoned him to rummage through her bottom drawer. 'Here,' she said, a moment later, pressing an unwrapped Mars bar into his hand. 'I'll get you something to drink.' She took a bottle of mineral water from a small drinks cabinet, poured a tumblerful and carried it back to him.

110

His hand, clasping the Mars bar, hung loosely between his knees. He made no attempt to eat it. He couldn't have moved, even if he'd wanted to.

'Oh, shit!' she said crossly, putting the glass on a table and squatting on the floor in front of him. 'Look, McLoughlin, you're a pain in the bloody arse, you really are. If you're trying to drink yourself into early retirement, fine, that's your choice – God knows why you joined the police force in the first place. You should be writing a biography of Francis Bacon or Rabbie Burns or something equally sensible. But if you're not trying for the chop, then do yourself a favour. Any minute now, that little toe-rag you sent off in search of the Inspector is going to come back through my door, and he'll wet himself when he sees you like this. Take my word for it, I know the type. And if there's anything left of you when Walsh has finished, then your friend the constable is going to piss all over it. He'll do it again and again and again, and he'll have an orgasm every time he does it. I promise you, you won't enjoy the experience.'

In her own way she was beautiful. He could drown quite happily in those soft brown eyes. He took a bite out of the Mars bar and chewed on it thoughtfully. 'You're a bloody awful liar, Cattrell.' He moved his head gently from side to side. 'You told me compassion was a frail thing, but I think you've just broken my neck.'

THIRTEEN

There was an atmosphere in the room. Walsh smelled it the minute he stepped inside. McLoughlin was by the window, hands resting on the sill, looking out over the terrace and the long sweep of lawn; Miss Cattrell sat at her desk, doodling, her boots propped on her open bottom drawer, her lower lip protruding aggressively. She looked up as he approached. 'Well, thank God for small mercies!' she snapped. 'I want to phone my solicitor, Inspector, I want to do it now, and I refuse to answer any more questions until he gets here.' She looked very cross.

Anger, thought Walsh with surprise. Somehow, it hadn't smelled like anger. 'I hear you,' he said equably, 'but why would you want to do that?'

McLoughlin opened the French windows to let in Jansen and WPC Brownlow. His legs, seeping sawdust, belonged to somebody else; his stomach, re-awakened by the Mars bar, was clawing at itself in a search for further nourishment; his heart was gambolling about his wilting frame like a healthy spring lamb. He felt rather pleased with himself. 'Miss Cattrell,' he said, his voice quite steady, 'would you agree to WPC Brownlow searching you now, while I explain the position to Inspector Walsh?'

'No,' she snapped again, 'I would not. I refuse to co-operate any further until my solicitor gets here.' She tapped a pencil angrily on the desk-top. 'And I'm bloody well not going to say any more in front of you, either, or those creeps you brought with you.' She glared at Walsh. 'I object to this very strongly. It's bad enough having your personal things mauled over, but to have them mauled over by men is the pits. You must have some women on your force. I refuse to talk to anyone but women.'

Walsh hid his excitement well but McLoughlin, with his new clarity of vision, could see the Inspector's scrawny tail wagging. 'Are you making a formal complaint against Sergeant McLoughlin and his team?' Walsh asked.

She glanced at Friar. 'I don't know. I'll wait until my solicitor gets

112

here.' She reached for her telephone and started dialling. 'But my objection stands, so, if you want my co-operation, I suggest you find me some women.'

The Chief Inspector jerked his head towards the door. 'Friar, Jansen, wait in the corridor. Sergeant McLoughlin, gather together what you've found and bring it outside. Brownlow, stay here.' He stood back, eyes narrowing, as he watched McLoughlin launch himself off the wall and plough firmly across the floor. There was something wrong, something he couldn't quite put his finger on. He darted sharp glances about the room.

Anne was murmuring into the telephone. 'Hold on a moment, Bill' – she cupped her hand over the receiver – 'I'd like to remind you, Sergeant,' she said icily, 'that you haven't given me a receipt for what's in my safe. The only receipt I have is the one for my diary.'

Jesus, woman, thought McLoughlin, give me a break. I'm not Charles Atlas, I'm the puny one who gets sand kicked in his face. He bowed ironically. 'I'll make one out now, Miss Cattrell.'

She ignored him and returned to her phone call, listening for a moment. 'Dammit, Bill,' she exploded angrily into the mouthpiece, 'considering how much you charge, you might make the effort to get here a bit sooner. Hell, I may not be one of your fancy London clients, but I always pay on the nail. For God's sake, you can make it in under two hours if you pull your finger out.'

Bill Stanley, long-time friend as well as solicitor, grinned at the other end of the line, He had just told her he'd drop everything to be with her in an hour. 'I could make it three hours,' he suggested.

'That's a bit more like it,' she growled. 'OK, I'll ask him.' She turned to the Inspector. 'Are you planning to take me down to the Police Station? My solicitor wants to know where to come.'

'That's entirely up to you, Miss Cattrell. Frankly, I'm a little puzzled at the moment as to why you want your solicitor present.' McLoughlin turned round with the carving-knife and rag neatly secured in a polythene bag. 'Ah!' said Walsh with ill-concealed glee. 'Well, that does rather suggest you can help us in our enquiries. As long as you understand there is no duress involved, I think it will be simpler for everyone if we pursue our questioning at the Station.'

'Silverborne Police Station,' she told her solicitor. 'No, don't worry, I won't say anything till you get there.' She hung up and snatched the second receipt from McLoughlin. 'And there'd better be nothing of mine hidden in that briefcase,' she said spitefully. 'I've yet to meet a policeman who didn't have sticky fingers.'

'That's enough, Miss Cattrell,' said Walsh sharply, wondering how

McLoughlin had managed to keep his temper with her. But perhaps he hadn't and perhaps that explained the tension in the air. 'I draw the line at unwarranted abuse against my officers. Constable Brownlow will wait with you while I have a couple of words with Sergeant McLoughlin in the corridor.' He walked stiffly from the room. 'Right,' he said, when the door had closed behind them, 'let's see what you've got.' He held out his hand for the polythene bag.

'It's like I told you, sir,' said Friar eagerly. 'She was hiding it in her safe. And then there's the diary, with talk about death and graves and God knows what else.'

'Andy?'

He supported himself against the wall. 'I'm not sure.' He shrugged.

'Not sure about what?' demanded Walsh impatiently.

'I suspect we're being had, sir.'

'Why?'

'A feeling. She's not a fool and it was very easy.'

'Friar?'

'That's balls, sir. The diary was easy, I grant you that, but the knife was well hidden. Jansen went all along that wall and missed the safe completely.' He threw a look of grudging acknowledgement in McLoughlin's direction. 'It was the Sergeant spotted it.'

Walsh thought deeply for several moments. 'Well, either way we're committed now, so if we're being had, let's find out why. Jansen, you take this back to the Station and get it fingerprinted before I bring Miss Cattrell in. Friar, cut along and give them a hand outside. Andy, I suggest you take over from me in Mrs Maybury's wing.'

'With respect, sir,' McLoughlin murmured, 'wouldn't it be a better idea if I went through her diary? Friar's right, there are some strange references in there.'

Walsh looked at him closely for a moment, then nodded. 'Perhaps you're right. Pick out anything you think relevant and have it on my desk before I talk to her.' He went back into the room, closing the door behind him.

Friar dogged McLoughlin's heels down the corridor. 'You jammy bastard!'

McLoughlin grinned evilly. 'Privilege has its perks, Friar.'

'You reckon she's going to make a complaint?'

'I doubt it.'

'Yeah.' Friar paused to light a cigarette. 'Jansen and me are clear, whichever way you look at it.' He called after McLoughlin: 'But I'd sure as hell like to know where those marks on her neck came from.'

114

McLoughlin drove straight to a transport café on the outskirts of Silverborne and ate and ate till he could eat no more. He kept his mind deliberately on his food and, when an errant thought popped in, he chased it out again. He was at peace with himself for the first time in months. When he'd finished, he went back to his car, reclined the seat and went to sleep.

Jonathan was hanging round the front door when Anne was ushered out by Walsh and WPC Brownlow. He moved aggressively into their path and Walsh had no difficulty recognising in him the gangling boy who had protected his mother so fiercely all those years ago.

'What's going on?' he demanded.

Anne laid a hand on his arm. 'I'll be back in two or three hours at the most, Jon. There's nothing to worry about, I promise. Tell your Ma I've phoned Bill Stanley and he's coming straight down.' She paused for a moment. 'And make sure she takes the phone off the hook and gets Fred to lock the front gates. The story's bound to be out by now and there'll be pressmen all over the place.' She gave him a long, straight look. 'It's a safe bet she'll be worrying, Jon, so try and take her mind off it. Play her some records or something.' She spoke over her shoulder as Walsh led her towards a car. 'Pat Boone and "Love Letters in the Sand". That's always a safe bet when you want to take Phoebe's mind off something. You know how she adores Pat Boone. And don't hang about, will you?'

He nodded. 'OK. Take care, Anne.'

He waved disconsolately as she was driven away, then retreated thoughtfully through the front door. As far as he was aware, his mother had never listened to a Pat Boone record in her life. *'Don't hang about, will you?'* He walked towards Anne's door, took a quick look about him, then turned the handle and trod softly down her corridor. He eased her living-room door open and peered around it. The room was empty. *'Safe bet,'* she had said that twice. *'Love Letters.'* It was the work of seconds to slip the hidden catches, take a firm grasp on the chromium handle and slide the whole safe out. It weighed virtually nothing, being made of aluminium. He rested it on one hip while he plunged his hand into the dark recess in the chimney breast and retrieved a large brown envelope. He flicked it on to the nearest easy chair, then carefully repositioned the safe and thrust it back into place. As he stuffed the envelope into the front of his jacket, it occurred to him that something or someone must have frightened Anne pretty badly to make that hiding place unsafe. And why on earth should she worry over some love letters? It was

115

odd. As he left by the French windows, he heard the door into Anne's wing open and close and the sound of footsteps in the corridor. He tip-toed across the terrace and out of sight.

He found Phoebe and Diana in the main drawing-room. They were murmuring quietly on the sofa, heads together, gold hair and red hair interwoven like threads in a tapestry. He was suddenly jealous of their intimacy. Why did his mother confide in Diana before him? Didn't she trust him? He had shouldered the guilt for ten years. Wasn't that long enough for her? Sometimes, he felt, it was only Anne who treated him like an adult.

'They've taken Anne,' he announced laconically.

They nodded, unsurprised. 'We were watching,' said Phoebe. She gave Jonathan a comforting smile. 'Don't worry, darling. I have more sympathy for the police than I do for her. They'll find that two hours in the ring with Mike Tyson would be preferable to half an hour in Anne's company when she's fighting her corner. She's phoned Bill, I hope.'

'Yes.' He went to the window and looked out on to the terrace. 'Where's Lizzie?' he asked them.

'She's gone with Molly,' said Diana. 'They're searching the Lodge now.'

'Is Fred there, too?'

'Fred's standing guard by the gates,' said Phoebe. 'It seems the press have arrived in force. He's keeping them at bay.'

'That reminds me. Anne said to take the phone off the hook.'

Diana stood up and walked over to the mantelpiece, retrieving a dog-end from behind a clock there. She struck a match and lit the crumpled tip. 'Already done.' She squinted at the pathetic half-inch of tube and puffed inexpertly.

Phoebe exchanged a glance with Jonathan and laughed. 'I'll go and get a decent one from Anne's room,' she said, pushing herself out of the sofa. 'She's bound to have some lying around and I do hate to see you suffer.' She left the room.

Diana dropped the dog-end into the fireplace. 'She's going to bring me one and I'm going to smoke it, and it'll be my second one today. Tomorrow it'll be three and so on till I'm hooked again. I must be mad. You're a doctor, Jon. Tell me not to.'

He walked over, mollified by her sudden need of him, and put an arm round her shoulders. 'Not a doctor yet and you wouldn't take any notice of me anyway. How does it go? "A prophet is not without honour, save in his own country and in his own house." Smoke, if it helps. I'd say stress is just as bad for you as nicotine.' It was like cuddling an older Elizabeth, he thought. They were so alike: in their

116

looks, in their constant search for reassurance, in the ironic twist they gave to everything. It explained so well why they didn't get on.

He squeezed her arm and let her go, moving back to the window. 'Have all the police gone?'

'Except for the ones at the Lodge, I think. Poor Molly. It'll take her months to get over having her long johns inspected by the fuzz. She'll probably wash them all several times before she wears them again.'

'Lizzie will calm her ruffled feathers,' he said.

She gave his back a speculative glance. 'Do you see much of Elizabeth in London?' she asked him.

He didn't turn round. 'On and off. We have lunch together sometimes. She works pretty anti-social hours, you know. She's in the casino till nearly dawn most nights.' It was tragic, he thought, how much there was about a daughter you could never tell her mother. You couldn't describe the exquisite pleasure of waking at four in the morning to find her warm naked body rhythmically arousing yours. You couldn't explain that just to think about her made you horny or that one of the reasons you loved her was because, whenever you slipped your hand between her thighs, she was wet with longing for you. Instead, you had to say you rarely saw her, pretend indifference, and the mother would never know of the fire her daughter could kindle. 'I should think I see more of her down here,' he said, turning round.

'She doesn't tell me anything about her life in London,' said Diana with regret. 'I assume she gets taken out but I don't know and I don't ask.'

'Is that because you don't want to know or you think she wouldn't tell you?'

'Oh, because she wouldn't tell me, of course,' she said. 'She knows I don't want her to repeat my mistake and marry too young. If she is serious about someone, I'll be the last to know, and by then it'll be too late for me to urge caution. My own fault entirely,' she said. 'I quite see that.'

Phoebe came back and tossed an opened packet of cigarettes at Diana. 'Would you believe they've left that child on guard in Anne's room? PC Williams, the one Molly's taken a shine to. He's had orders to stay there until further notice. Insisted on taking every one of these fags out to have a look at it.' She crossed to the telephone and replaced the receiver. 'I must have been out of my mind,' she went on. 'Jane's due in at Winchester some time this afternoon or evening. I told her to ring when she got there. We'll just have to put up with nuisance calls until we hear from her.'

117

With a grimace, Jonathan opened the French windows and stepped out on to the terrace. 'I'm going to take the dogs for a walk. I think I'll try and find Lizzie. See you later.' He put his fingers to his lips and gave a piercing whistle before setting off down the garden.

Just then the telephone rang. Phoebe picked it up and listened for a moment. 'No comment,' she said, replacing the receiver. A few seconds later it began to ring again.

Benson and Hedges cavorted around him, waggling their bottoms and barking, as if a walk was a rarity. He struck out towards the woodland between the Grange and Grange Farm, flinging a stick every now and then to please the scampering dogs. His direction took him past the ice house and he watched with distaste as they made a beeline for it, only to whine and scratch with frustration outside the sealed door. He went on, pausing regularly to turn and scan the way he had come, whistling to the dogs to keep up.

When he reached the two-hundred-year-old oak, standing majestically in its clearing in the middle of the wood, he took off his jacket and sat down, relaxing his back into a natural concave in the wrinkled bark. He remained there for half an hour, listening, watching, until he was satisfied that the only witnesses to what he was about to do were dogs and wild creatures.

He stood up, removed the envelope from inside his folded jacket and popped it through a narrow slit into a hollow in the oak's great trunk where a branch had died and been discarded in infancy. Only Jane, who had swarmed with him through the leafy panoply when they were children, knew the secrets of the hidey-hole.

He whistled up the straying dogs and went back to the house.

'Can I talk to you, darling?'

Elizabeth, halfway up the stairs to her bedroom, looked reluctantly at her mother. 'I suppose so.' She had just got back from the Lodge and was tired and irritable. Molly's unspoken distress over the police search had upset her.

'We'll leave it if it's not a good time.'

Elizabeth came slowly down the stairs. 'What's the matter?'

'Everything.' Diana gave a hollow laugh. 'What isn't the matter? I could answer that more easily.'

Elizabeth followed her into their sitting-room. It was a room like Anne's, but with a very different character, less startling, more conventional, with a gold carpet and classic floral prints in tones of russet and gold at the windows and on the chairs. A dwindling sun fingered the colours with a mellow glow.

'Tell me,' said Elizabeth as she watched Jonathan cross the terrace with Benson and Hedges and disappear through Phoebe's French windows.

Diana told her and, as the shadows lengthened, Elizabeth's distress grew.

Inspector Walsh glanced at his watch and, with an inward sigh, shouldered open the door of Interview Room Number Two. It was nine fifteen. He looked sourly from Anne to her solicitor.

Bill Stanley was a great bear of a man with ungroomed ginger hair sprouting everywhere, even on his knuckles, and an air of shabbiness. From his card he was with a top London firm, no doubt earning a packet, so the black pin-striped suit, crumpled and frayed at the cuffs, was presumably some sort of statement – equality with the huddled masses, perhaps – although why he chose to wear it over a yellowed string vest, Walsh couldn't imagine. He made a mental note to check up on him. In thirty years of rubbing shoulders with the legal profession, he had never seen the like of B.R. Stanley, LLB. The card was probably a forgery.

'You can go home now, Miss Cattrell. There's a car waiting for you.'

She gathered her bits and pieces together and stuffed them carelessly into her handbag. 'And my other things?' she asked him.

'They will be returned to you tomorrow.'

Bill unfolded himself from his chair, stretched his huge hands to the ceiling and yawned. 'I can take you home, if you'd prefer it, Anne.'

'No, it's late. You get back to Polly and the children.'

He straightened his shoulders and the snap as the bones locked into place was loud in the small room. 'This is going to cost you an arm and a leg, my girl – it's goodbye to fifty quid every time I draw breath, remember – so what do you say? Shall we sue? I'm game.' He beamed. 'We're embarrassed for choice really. Harassment, abuse of police powers, damage to your professional reputation, loss of self-esteem, loss of earnings. I always enjoy litigation cases when I've had a chance to see both teams in action.'

Her eyes gleamed. 'Would I win?'

'Good lord, yes. I've hit the opposition for six off far stickier wickets.'

Walsh, who had found Bill's wisecracks increasingly irritating, spluttered angrily. 'The law is not a joke, Mr Stanley. I regret any inconvenience Miss Cattrell may have suffered, but in the circumstances I don't see that we could have acted any differently. It was her choice to have you present while she answered questions and, frankly, had it not taken you three hours to get here, this could all have been dealt with very much more quickly.'

'Couldn't make it any sooner, old man,' said Bill, poking a finger through his string vest and scratching his bear-hairy chest. 'My day for child-minding. Can't abandon the brood to their own devices. They'd slaughter each other the minute I was out of the house. Mind you, you might have a point. Don't relish accusations of sloppincss floating around in open court.' He gave Anne's shoulder a friendly squeeze with his great paw. 'I'll give you a discount. It's less fun but probably more sensible.'

Walsh gobbled furiously. 'I've a damn good mind to charge you both with wasting police time.'

Laughter shook the solicitor's huge frame as he opened the door for Anne and ushered her out. 'No, no, Inspector. I do the charging. Indecent, isn't it? I win whichever way you look at it.' He escorted her to the front door where a police car was waiting, took her face in his hands and bent to whisper in her ear. 'That little farce is going to cost you fifty smackers to one of the AIDS charities, plus an explanation.'

She patted his cheek. 'I needed someone to hold my hand,' she told him.

He grunted his amusement. 'Bollocks! I'd have been angry if I hadn't wanted to find out what the hell was going on and if I hadn't been waiting for a chance to meet that bastard Walsh.' The smile faded from his voice. 'Give me a ring tomorrow and I'll come down and talk to the three of you. Murder is a dangerous game, Anne, even for the spectators. It's too easy to get dragged in. Phoebe knows that better than anyone.' He put his hand on her bottom and propelled her towards the car. 'Give her my love, and Diana too.' He waved goodbye, then walked to his own car and set off back to London and his weekly night-shift in a shelter for the homeless.

Andy McLoughlin lingered in his car on the other side of the road. It was parked in the twilight zone between two pools of orange lamplight and he had seen without being seen. His hands shook on the steering wheel. God, he needed a drink. Had she kissed him? It was difficult to be sure. Did it matter anyway? It was their easy understanding, the way their bodies had leant against each other in uncomplicated friendship that had rocked him. He didn't want her loved.

He eased himself out of the car and went inside in search of Walsh. 'How did it go?'

The Inspector was standing at his office window, glowering into the night. 'Did you see them? They've just gone.'

'No.'

'Damned solicitor took three hours to get here, arrived sporting a filthy string vest and looking like the hairy man of Borneo. Matter of fact, I'm highly doubtful about his credentials.' He took out his pipe. 'You were quite right, Andy. It was beef blood. We were being had. Why?'

McLoughlin lowered himself into a chair. 'A diversion. To draw you away from the rest of the house.'

Walsh walked back to his desk and sat down. 'Possibly. In that case it didn't work. There wasn't a stone left unturned by the time we'd finished.' There was a long silence before he tapped his pipe on a sheaf of letters in front of him. 'Jones found this little lot in Mrs Goode's studio.' He pushed the papers towards McLoughlin and waited while the Sergeant skimmed through them. 'Interesting, don't you think?'

'Did Jonesy question her about them?'

'Tried to. She said it was none of his business, that she'd got her fingers burnt and preferred to forget it, certainly had no intention of answering questions on the matter.' He fingered tobacco into the bowl of the pipe. 'When he told her he would have to take the letters, she lost her temper and tried to snatch them back.' There was a twinkle of amusement in his eye as he lit the tobacco and sucked in warm smoke. 'Two PCs had to restrain her while he removed them to his car.'

'And I thought she was the least volatile of the three. What about Mrs Maybury?'

'Good as gold. She took herself off to the greenhouse and spent most of the afternoon rooting Pelargonium cuttings while we turned her house inside out and found nothing.' Noises of succulent contentment puttered from his mouth. 'I've detailed a couple of lads to tout those shoes round the menders. It's a long shot but someone might remember re-heeling them. I don't care what Mrs Thompson says – let's face it, she's so damn cuckoo she wouldn't recognise her own reflection if it didn't have a halo round it – those shoes are the missing Daniel's. Size eight and brown. Too much of a coincidence.'

McLoughlin forced his pricking eyes to stay open as he re-read the top letter. It was undated and very brief. 'Monday. My dear Diana, Of course I regret what's happened, but my hands are tied. If it will help I can come out on Thursday to discuss the position with you. Yours ever, Daniel.' The address was Larkfield, East Deller, and scored across the page in angry writing was: 'Meeting

121

confirmed.' The previous letter, a carbon copy of a demand from Diana for an up-to-date statement of Daniel Thompson's business, was dated Friday, 20th May.

'So when did he go missing?'

'Thursday, twenty-fifth of May,' said Walsh with satisfaction, 'the very day he had arranged an appointment with Mrs Goode.'

'So why didn't you bring her in with Miss Cattrell?'

'I can only cope with one at a time, lad. She'll keep another twelve hours. At the moment I'm rather more interested in why Miss Cattrell went to such extraordinary lengths to get herself brought in for questioning. Any ideas?'

McLoughlin looked at the floor and shook his head.

FOURTEEN

Anne was dog-tired. Her body had been pumping adrenaline for several hours, exciting her brain, racing her heart, keeping her at a peak of almost intolerable stimulation. Her reaction when she sank into the back of the warm police car was immediate and total. She fell asleep, upright at first but ending in a flat ungainly sprawl along the length of the seat when the driver took a bend too fast. Thus, the photographers outside the unlit gates of Streech Grange missed the picture they had been waiting for: Murder Enquiry – Journalist In Questioning Drama. They had seen too many police cars come and go to be interested in one without a passenger. Fred, sitting doggedly on an old deckchair at the padlocked gates, was not so easily fooled. He let the car in, satisfied himself with a momentary flash of his torch that it contained Anne, then with a sigh of relief resumed his seat. His clutch was safely in the nest. When the police car had gone he could retire to bed.

Barely awake, Anne let herself in through the front door and staggered sleepily across the carpet. Outside, with a new passenger in the shape of PC Williams, now relieved from guard duty, the police car grated away across the gravel. Anne leaned against the wall for a moment to collect her scattered wits. Behind Phoebe's door, she heard the warning bark of the dogs. The next moment, Jane Maybury precipitated herself into the hall and flung herself on her godmother. Together, they collapsed in a heap on the floor where Anne lay, eyes closed, and trembling.

'My God,' said Jane, turning to her mother who had appeared in the doorway behind her, 'there's something wrong with her. Jon!' she shrilled with alarm. 'Come quick. Anne's ill.'

'I'm not ill,' said the shaking body, opening its eyes. 'I'm laughing.' She sat up. 'God, I am *knackered*. Get off me, you great dollop,' she said, giving the girl a kiss, 'and get me a brandy. I'm suffering severe post-interrogation trauma.'

Phoebe hauled her to her feet and marched her into the drawing-room while Jane fetched a brandy. Anne folded happily on to the sofa and beamed about her. 'What's the matter? You all look as if you've been sucking lemons.'

Diana pulled a face. 'We've been worried sick, you idiot.'

'You should have more faith,' said Anne sternly, accepting the brandy from Jane. 'And how's my god-daughter?' She examined the girl circumspectly while she warmed her glass.

Jane smiled. 'I'm fine.' She was still too thin but Anne was pleased to see that her face had filled out and lost some of its tension.

'You look it,' she agreed.

Phoebe turned to Jonathan. 'Shall we have that celebration we promised ourselves?'

'Sure thing. I'll raid the cellar. What does anyone fancy? Château Lafite '78 or those last bottles of the '75 Champagne? Anne, you choose.'

'The Lafite. Champagne on top of brandy will make me puke.'

He looked questioningly at his mother. 'Shall I drive down and get Fred and Molly to join us? It hasn't been much fun for them either.'

Phoebe nodded. 'Good idea.' She held out a hand to Elizabeth who was sitting slightly apart on the tapestry stool. 'You go too, Lizzie darling. Molly can say no to all of us, and does regularly, but she won't refuse you.' She looked pointedly at Jonathan.

'Come on,' he said. 'You, too, Jane.' They went out.

Phoebe walked over to the mantelpiece. 'I wish David had never used the cellar for storing his wretched imports.'

Anne sniffed her brandy. 'Why? I bless his memory for it regularly.'

'Exactly,' agreed Phoebe dryly, 'so do I. It's very upsetting.' She glanced at Diana. 'Lizzie's worried about something. Is it Molly and Fred?'

'No. I'm afraid it's me.'

'Why?'

Diana attempted a laugh which didn't work. 'Because I told her I'd be the next one in the police mincing machine.' She swung to face Anne. 'Why did they take you in?'

'They found the safe and it had some incriminating evidence in it.' Anne chuckled into her brandy. 'A bloody carving-knife, wrapped in a bloody rag.' She stirred her glass in her hands, warming it. 'It was straight out of Enid Blyton, but they all got very excited and I refused to answer any more questions till Bill arrived.'

'You're mad,' said Phoebe decidedly. 'What on earth were you up to?'

Mischief lit Anne's dark eyes. 'To tell you the truth, I didn't think they'd find the safe, and if it hadn't been for the Sergeant, they wouldn't have done.' She shrugged. 'Hell, you know me. I always put in an insurance policy, just in case.'

Diana groaned. 'You *are* mad. I do wish you'd take this whole thing a bit more seriously. God knows what they're thinking now. What was it you didn't want them to find?'

'Nothing too desperate,' said Anne easily. 'The odd document or two which probably oughtn't to be in my possession.'

'Well,' said Phoebe, 'I can't understand why you aren't still at the Police Station undergoing a grilling. That's more than Walsh ever had on me and he never let up for a minute.'

Anne sipped her brandy and looked from one to the other with laughter spilling out of her eyes. 'You didn't have my trump card. Bill did his stuff brilliantly. You should have seen him. Walsh damn nearly popped a blood vessel when he finally turned up. He was wearing his string vest.' She dabbed at her eyes and examined Diana's face through damp lashes. It was still very strained.

'It's a game with you, isn't it?' said Diana accusingly. 'I wouldn't mind so much, if I didn't think it was me they'll come down on. You are a fool, you know.'

Anne shook her head. 'What can they possibly have on you?'

Diana sighed. 'Nothing really, except that I've made a prize arse-hole of myself.' She smiled unhappily at the two women. 'I hoped you'd never find out. It makes me look such an idiot.'

'It *must* be bad then,' said Anne lightly.

Phoebe squatted on her haunches with her back to the fireplace. 'It can't be worse than Anne's toy-boy, can it?' She looked at her friend and giggled. 'Do you remember him? He still had adolescent acne. You thought he was the bee's knees for about a week.'

Anne, whose earlier hysteria was still perilously close to the surface, snorted stinging brandy through her nose. She gasped with pain and laughter. 'You mean Wayne Gibbons? A temporary aberration, I assure you. It was his whole-hearted commitment to the cause that attracted me.'

'Yes, but what cause? You looked worn out when he finally left.'

Anne mopped her running eyes. 'You know he's on a study course in Russia now? I had a letter from him not so long ago. It dwelt in extreme and tedious length on the subject of his constipation. I gather he hadn't had any green vegetables since Christmas.' She shuddered. 'God knows what it's done to his acne.' She turned to Diana with a grin. 'It can't be worse than Phoebe's wrestling match by the village pond with that ridiculous Dilys Barnes woman – the one whose daughter fornicates in our bushes. No question about that. Phoebe really looked a fool.'

In spite of herself, Diana laughed. 'Yes, that was funny.' She looked at Phoebe's smiling face. 'You should never have tackled her in a sarong.'

'How was I to know she was going to start a fight?' Phoebe protested. 'Also, it wasn't actually Mrs Barnes who pulled it off. It was Hedges. He got over-excited and did a runner with the damn thing between his teeth.'

Anne was shaking with tension-releasing laughter. 'It was the way you came stomping up the drive in your wellies, purple in the face, boobs bouncing all over the shop and with only a pair of knickers on. God, it was funny. I wish I'd seen the fight. And what were you doing wearing wellies with a sarong, anyway?'

Phoebe's eyes sparkled. 'It was hot, hence the sarong, and I wanted some pondweed from the village pond, hence the wellies. Absurd woman. She ran away screaming. I think she thought I'd taken the dress off myself in order to rape her.' She patted Diana's knee. 'If you've made a laughing-stock of yourself, it's hardly the end of the world.'

'Laughing-stock's right,' said Diana. 'Oh, hell! I'm never going to live it down. It's too bloody embarrassing. I wouldn't mind so much if I wasn't supposed to have good judgement in these things.'

Anne and Phoebe exchanged puzzled glances. 'Tell us,' prompted Phoebe.

Diana put her head between her hands. 'I was persuaded into parting with ten thousand quid,' she muttered. 'Half my savings straight down the drain, apart from anything else.'

Anne whistled sympathetically. 'That's rough. No chance of getting it back?'

'None. He's done a bunk.' She chewed her bottom lip. 'From the way they piled into my correspondence, I suspect the police think they've found him in our ice house.'

'Oh lord!' said Phoebe with feeling. 'No wonder Lizzie's worried. Who is this man?'

'Daniel Thompson. He got my name from that design consultant in Winchester, the one who helped me with the Council offices. He's an engineer, lives in East Deller. Have you come across him?'

Phoebe shook her head. 'You should have gone to the police yourself,' she said. 'It sounds to me as though you've been conned by this creep.'

'No,' said Diana tiredly, staring at her hands, 'it wasn't a con. I invested in a business he was running, all very legitimate and above board, but the bloody thing's gone bust and my money with it. Looking back, I must have been mad but it seemed like such a good idea at the time. It could have revolutionised interior design if it'd taken off.'

'Why on earth didn't you talk to us about it?'

'I would have done but it came up during that week in January when you were both away and I was holding the fort here. Another backer pulled out at the last minute and I had twenty-four hours to make up my mind. By the time you got back I'd rather forgotten about it, then things started to turn sour and I decided to keep mum. I wouldn't be telling you now if the police hadn't found out about it.'

'What business was it?'

Diana groaned. 'You'll laugh.'

'No, we won't.'

She gave them a ferocious glare. 'I'll throttle you if you do.'

'We won't.'

'See-through radiators,' she said.

The watcher in the garden was masturbating in an ecstasy of voyeuristic thrill. How many times had he spied on these cunts, preyed on them, seen them nude. Once he had creepy-crawled the house. His hand moved in mounting frenzy until, with convulsive shudders, he climaxed into his handkerchief. He held the sodden cloth to his face to muffle his giggles.

'I'm off to bed,' said Anne, putting her glass on a tray with the exaggerated care of the tipsy. 'Apart from anything else, I'm pissed. I happily volunteer to wash up in the morning, but tonight I'm off games. I'd break the lot,' she explained owlishly.

'Have you eaten anything this evening, Miss Cattrell?' scolded Molly.

'Not a thing.'

Molly muttered angrily. 'I'll have words with that Inspector in the morning. What a way to treat people.'

Anne paused on her way to the door. 'They brought me a corned beef sandwich,' she said, scrupulously fair. 'I didn't fancy it. There's something about corned beef.' She thought for a moment. 'It's the texture. Moist but crumbly. Reminds me of dog shit.' With a wave, she departed.

Diana, who was watching Molly's face, held her glass in front of her mouth to hide her smile. Even after eight years of Anne's careless bombardment, Molly's sensibilities were still so easily shocked.

Anne drank a pint of water in the kitchen, took a banana from the fruit bowl and wandered, eating it, through the hall and down the corridor. She switched on the lights in her sitting-room and collapsed gratefully into an armchair, tossing the banana skin into the waste-paper basket. She sat for some time, her weary brain in neutral, while the water slowly diluted the effects of the alcohol. After half an hour she began to feel better.

What a day! She had been shitting bricks at the Police Station, wondering if Jon had picked up her hint, and she thought now that she had probably panicked unnecessarily. Could McLoughlin be that sharp? Surely not. The room had been searched by experts – two, three years ago – when Special Branch suspected her of having a leaked MOD document in her possession. They had found the safe but not the secret cache behind it. She rubbed her eyes. Jon had whispered to her that he'd put the envelope somewhere outside where it would never be found. If that were true, she was tempted to let it stay there, wherever 'there' was. She hadn't asked for details. She ran hot and cold every time she thought of the contents of that envelope. God, she was a fool, but, at the time, a photographic record of that terrible brick tomb had made sense. She beat her fist against her head. Supposing Jon had opened it? But he hadn't, she told herself firmly. She could tell by the look in his eyes that he hadn't. But if he had? She thrust the thought away angrily.

McLoughlin held a fretful fascination for her. She kept going back to him, worrying at him, like a tongue against a loosening tooth. That business in front of the mantelpiece? Was it all a blind to cover his interest in the safe? She had looked into his face and seen only a deep, deep hurt, but an expression was only an expression, after all. She rubbed her eyes again. If only, she thought, if only, if only— There was a scream inside her, a scream that was as vast and as silent as the vast silence of space. Was her life always to be a series of *if onlys*?

There was a sharp tap on her French window.

She was so startled she flung her arm out and knocked her wrist on the occasional table beside her. She swung round, massaging the bruise, eyes straining into the night's blackness. A face was pressed against the window, eyes shielded from the bright glare of her lamps by a cupped hand. Fear flooded her mouth with sickly bile and the remembered stench of urine swamped her nostrils.

'Did I frighten you?' asked McLoughlin, easing open the unlocked window when she didn't get up.

'You gave me a shock.'

'I'm sorry.' Some shock, he thought.

128

'Why didn't you come to the front door?' Even her lips were bloodless.

'I didn't want to disturb Mrs Maybury.' He closed the glass doors behind him. 'The light's on in her bedroom. She'd have to have come downstairs to let me in.'

'We've each got a front doorbell. If you press the one with my name on, I'm the only one who hears it.' But he knew that already, didn't he?

'Can I sit down?'

'No,' she said sharply. He shrugged and walked towards the fireplace. 'All right, yes, sit down. What are you doing here?'

He didn't sit down. 'I wanted to talk to you.'

'What about?'

'Anything. Eternity. Rabbie Burns. Safes.' He paused. 'Why are you so frightened of me?'

He wouldn't have believed she had any more blood to lose from her face. She didn't answer. He gestured towards the mantelpiece. 'May I?' He took her silence for permission and slid back the oak panelling. 'Someone's been here before me,' he said conversationally. 'You?' He looked at her. 'No, not you. Someone else.' He grasped the chrome handle and gave a strong pull. Too strong. Jonathan had forgotten to snap home the catches and the safe came out in a rush, sending McLoughlin staggering backwards. With a small laugh he lowered it to the floor and peered into the empty hole. 'Are you going to tell me what was in here?'

'No.'

'Or who removed whatever it was?'

'No.'

He ran his fingers down the side of the safe and located the spring catches. 'Very neat.' He swung it back into position and shoved it home. 'But you've been taking it in and out far more often than it was ever designed for. You're wearing away the ledge.' He pointed to the bottom of the door. 'It isn't parallel with the mantelpiece any more. It should be resting on a concrete lintel. Bricks are no good, they're too soft, too easily crumbled.' He slid the oak panelling into place and folded himself into the chair opposite her. 'One of Mrs Maybury's building efforts?' he suggested.

She ignored that. 'How did you know it wasn't the mantelpiece that was out of true?' Some of the colour had trickled back into her lips.

'I didn't, not until I opened the panel just now, but whoever's been at it in the meantime put it back even more carelessly than you did. Judging by the unsecured catches, they were presumably in a hurry. What was in there?'

'Nothing. You're imagining things.' They sat in silence looking at each other. 'Well?' demanded Anne finally.

'Well what?'

'What are you planning to do about it?'

'Oh, I don't know. Find out who cleaned it out, I suppose, and ask them a few questions. It shouldn't be too hard. The field isn't very wide, is it?'

'You'll end up with egg on your face,' she said tartly. 'The Inspector phoned through for a constable to be in here all the time I was away.' He liked her better when she fought back. 'So in that case, how could anyone have tampered with the safe? It must have dropped of its own accord.'

'That explains the hurry,' was all he said. He sank deeper into his chair and rested his chin on steepled fingers.

'I've nothing to tell you. You're wasting your time.'

He closed his eyes. 'Oh, you've got lots to tell me,' he murmured. 'Why you came to Streech. Why Mrs Phillips calls this house a fortress. Why you have nightmares about death.' He opened his eyes a fraction to look at her. 'Why you panic every time your safe is mentioned and why you like to divert interest away from it.'

'Did Fred let you in?'

'No, I climbed the wall at the bottom.'

Her eyes were deeply wary. 'Why would you do that?'

He shrugged. 'There's a barrage of photographers at your gate. I didn't particularly want to be seen coming in.'

'Did Walsh send you?'

She was as taut as piano wire. He reached out and took her hand, playing with her fingers briefly before letting them drop. 'I'm not your enemy, Cattrell.'

A smile flickered. 'I'll bet that's what Brutus said as he stuck the knife into Caesar. I'm not your enemy, Caesar, and, hell, old chap, it's nothing personal, I just happen to love Rome more.' She stood up and walked to the window. 'If you're not my enemy, McLoughlin, then drop me, drop all of us, from the enquiry and look for your murderer somewhere else.' The moon was pouring herself in a shimmering libation about the garden. Anne pressed her forehead against the cold glass and stared out at the awesome beauty of what lay beyond. Black roses with coronas of silver; the lawn glittering like an inland sea; a weeping willow, its leaves and branches wrought in sparkling tracery. 'But you can't do that, can you? You're a policeman and you love justice more.'

'How can I answer that?' he teased her. 'It's based on so many false premises that it's entirely hypothetical. I sympathise with personal vengeance. I told you that this morning.'

She smiled cynically into the glass. 'Are you telling me you wouldn't have arrested Fred and Molly for murdering Donaghue?'

'No. I would have arrested them.'

She looked at him with surprise. 'That's a more honest answer than I expected.'

'I wouldn't have had any choice,' he said dispassionately. 'They wanted to be arrested. They sat there with the body, waiting for the police to come.'

'I see.' She smiled faintly. 'You make the arrest but you shed crocodile tears while you're doing it. That's a great way of salving your conscience, isn't it?'

He stood up and walked across to look down into her face. 'You helped me,' he said simply, putting his hands on her shoulders. 'I'd like to help you. But I can't if you won't trust me.'

He was so damn transparent, she thought, with his state-of-the-art cunning. She chuckled amiably. Two could play at this game. 'Trust *me*, McLoughlin. I don't need your help. I am as innocent of personal revenge and murder as a newborn baby.'

Abruptly, as if she were no more than a rag doll, he lifted her off her feet and twisted her towards the light, examining every inch of her face. As a face, it wasn't that special. She had laughter lines etched deeply round her eyes and mouth, frown lines on her forehead, but there was no menace lurking in her dark eyes, no shutters closed on nefandous secrets. Her skin gave off a faint scent of roses. He let go with one hand and ran the tips of his fingers along the curve of her jaw and down the soft line of her neck before, as abruptly, releasing her. 'Did you cut his balls off?'

She hadn't expected that. She straightened her sleeves. 'No.'

'You could be lying through your teeth,' he murmured, 'and I can't see it.'

'That's probably because I'm telling the truth. Why do you find that so hard to believe?'

'Because,' he growled angrily, 'my damn crotch is ruling my brain at the moment and lust is hardly an indicator of innocence.'

Anne glanced down and gave a gurgle of laughter. 'I see your problem. What do you plan to do about it?'

'You tell me. Cold showers?'

'God no. That would be Molly's choice. My advice is, when you've got an itch, scratch it.'

'I'd enjoy it a little more if you scratched it.'

Her black eyes danced. 'Did you have the sense to eat something?'

'Sausage and chips about five hours ago.'

'Well, I'm starving. I haven't eaten since lunchtime. There's an Indian take-away a couple of miles down the road. How do you fancy discussing your options over a Vindaloo?'

He lifted his hand to caress the curls round the base of her neck. The need to touch her was like an addiction. He was crazy, he didn't believe a damn word she said, but he couldn't help himself.

She saw the look in his eyes. 'I'm not your type, McLoughlin,' she warned. 'I am selfish, self-opinionated and entirely self-centred. I am independent, incapable of sustaining relationships and am often unfaithful. I dislike babies and housework and I can't cook. I am an intellectual snob with unconventional philosophies and left-wing politics. I don't conform, so I'm an embarrassment. I smoke like a chimney, am often rude, loathe getting tarted up and I fart very loudly in bed.'

He dropped his hand and grinned down at her. 'And on the plus side?'

'There isn't a plus side,' she said, suddenly serious, 'not for you. I'll get bored, I always do, and when something better comes along, as it surely will, I'll dump you just as I've dumped everyone else. We'll have a half way decent bonk from time to time, but you'll pay heavily in emotion for what you can buy free of strings in Southampton. Is that what you want?'

He regarded her thoughtfully. 'Is this a regular turn-off, or am I privileged?'

She smiled. 'Regular. I like to be fair.'

'And what's the drop-out rate at this stage?'

'Low,' she said ruefully. 'A few sensible ones leg it. The rest plunge in thinking they're going to change me. They don't. You won't. ' She watched his expression. 'Getting cold feet?'

'Well, I can't say I fancy it much,' he admitted. 'It sounds horribly like the relationship I had with my wife, dull, stifling and leading nowhere. I had no idea you were so narrow-minded. Put in "frightened to explore" after "selfish, self-opinionated and self-centred", and I guarantee the drop-out rate, pre-copulation, will astonish you.'

He took her arm and steered her towards the window.

'Let's eat,' he said. 'My judgement's better on a full stomach. I'll decide then whether I want to sow my seed in sterile ground.'

She pulled away. 'Go fuck yourself, McLoughlin.'

'Getting cold feet, Cattrell?'

She laughed. 'I'll turn off the lights.' She slipped back to the door and plunged the room into darkness. He took out his torch and waited by the windows. As she approached, she neatly avoided a small table with a bronze statuette of a naked woman on it. 'Me,' she said. 'When I was a nubile seventeen-year-old. I had a bit of a thing going with the sculptor during one school holidays.'

He lit it with the torch and studied it with interest. 'Nice,' he said appreciatively.

She chuckled as she followed him out. 'The figure or the sculpture?'

'Both. Do you lock these doors?' he asked, sliding them to behind him.

'I can't, not from the outside. They'll be all right.'

He put a hand on the back of her neck and walked her across the terrace on to the lawn. An owl hooted in the distance. He looked back at the house to get his bearings and half-turned her to the left. 'This way,' he said, flashing the torch ahead of them. 'I parked the car in a lane that runs along the corner.' Beneath his fingers he could feel the tightness of her skin. They walked in silence until they entered the woodland bordering the lawn. Away to their left, something scuttered noisily through the undergrowth. Her skin leapt with fear, jolting him as violently as it jolted her. 'For God's sake, woman,' McLoughlin growled, swinging his torch beam among the trees. 'What's the matter with you?'

'Nothing.'

'Nothing?' He shone the torch into her eyes, suddenly angry. 'You've buried yourself alive, erected a mountain of barbed wire over the mound, and you call it nothing. She's not worth it. Can't you see that? What the hell can she ever have done for you that you have to sacrifice your whole life in exchange? For Christ's sake, do you enjoy dying by inches? What happened to the Anne Cattrell who seduced sculptors in her school holidays? Where's the thorn in the Establishment's flesh who stormed citadels single-handed?'

She pushed the torch away and her teeth gleamed momentarily as she smiled. 'It was fun while it lasted, McLoughlin, but I did tell you not to try and change me.'

She was gone so fast that even his torch beam couldn't follow her.

FIFTEEN

He let her go and set off back to his car. He knew that if he went after her, her windows would be locked. He felt regret and relief in equal measure, like the suicide playing Russian roulette who hears the hammer click against an empty chamber. The Station was lousy with women wanting to console him. To hold a loaded gun to his temple by seeking his consolation with her was madness. He swiped in angry frustration at the branches of a tree and ripped the flesh on the side of his hand. He sucked the blood and swore profusely. He was in a mess, and he knew it. He needed a drink.

An owl screeched. Somewhere, far away, he thought he heard voices. He turned his head to listen but the silence only thickened about him. He shrugged and walked on, and it came again, a thread of sound, insubstantial – imagined? The skin on his scalp prickled uneasily. Damn the woman, he thought. If he went back, she would laugh at him.

He was cursing himself for a fool by the time he reached the terrace. He had seen no one, the house was in darkness and Anne was obviously already tucked up in bed. He flashed his torch across the flagstones and lit up her half-opened French window. With a frown, he walked over to it and shone his torch round the interior. He found her almost immediately. He thought she was asleep until he saw the blood glistening in her velvet cap of hair.

After the first paralysing moment of shock, he set to with such speed that time became elastic. In ten seconds he had worked up a sweat that would be rare after an hour's strenuous effort. His torch beam found a table lamp which he switched on as he sank to his knees beside the crumpled heap of clothes. He felt for a pulse in her neck, couldn't find one; laid his head on her chest, no heartbeat. With one fluid movement he rolled the tiny body over, shoved a hand under her neck, pinched her nostrils closed and began mouth-to-mouth respiration. He needed help. The part of his brain that wasn't directly concerned with the resuscitation directed him backwards, drawing the lifeless body with him, feeling with his feet for

134

the table with the bronze statuette. He found it. While he continued the regular in-flows of air, he gave a vicious backward kick and sent the heavy bronze smashing through the plate–glass window. The glass exploded outwards on to the terrace, shattering the silence of the night and sending Benson and Hedges into a frenzy of alarm in another part of the house. He realised with a sense of desperation that he was getting no response. Her face was grey, her lips blue. He placed the heel of his right hand over her breast bone and with the heel of his left hand pressed down, rocking forward, arms straight. While his mouth was free, he shouted for help. After five compressions, he gave her another mouth-to-mouth respiration, before returning to the heart massage. As he rocked forward on the third compression, he saw Jonathan press his fingers against the colourless neck and feel for the pulse.

'Give her another breath,' said Jonathan. 'There's a very faint pulse. My bag, Mum. It's in the hall.'

McLoughlin breathed again into her lungs and, this time, when he turned his head to look at her chest it fluttered weakly. 'Keep going,' said Jonathan, 'one breath every five seconds until she's breathing normally. You're doing great.' He took his bag from a white-faced Phoebe. 'Get some blankets,' he told her. 'Hot-water bottles, anything to keep her warm. And get an ambulance.' He took out his stethoscope, pulled open Anne's shirt and listened for the heartbeat. 'Brilliant,' he said warmly. 'It's weak, but there.' He pinched her cheek and watched with relief as the sluggish blood tinged it faintly pink. Her breathing began to take on a regular rhythm. Gently, he pushed McLoughlin off. 'OK,' he said. 'I think she's under her own steam now. We'll put her in the recovery position.' With the Sergeant's help he pulled her arm across her midriff, then rolled her on to her front, turning her face gently to one side and bending her nearest arm and leg at the elbow and knee. Her breathing was slow but even. She muttered something into the carpet and opened her eyes.

'Hey, McLoughlin,' she said distinctly before giving a huge yawn and falling asleep.

McLoughlin's face was running with sweat. He sat back and wiped it with his shirt sleeve. 'Can't you give her something?'

'Nothing to give. I'm not qualified yet. Don't worry. She's doing all right.'

McLoughlin pointed to the bloody hair. 'She may have a fractured skull.'

Phoebe had come in quietly with a pile of blankets which she spread over the prone figure. She popped her own hot-water bottle at the feet. 'Diana's on the phone for an ambulance. Jane's run down to wake Fred and get the gates open.' She squatted by Anne's head. 'Is she going to be all right?'

'I don't— ' Jonathan began.

'Your daughter's outside?' McLoughlin interrupted, staggering to his feet.

Phoebe stared at him. 'She's gone to the Lodge. They're not on the phone.'

'Is anyone with her?'

Phoebe's face turned pale. 'No.'

'Jesus!' swore McLoughlin, thrusting past her. 'Ring the police for God's sake, get some cars up here. I don't want to tackle a bloody maniac on my own.' He shouted back to them as he ran down Anne's corridor: 'Tell them someone's tried to murder your friend and may have a go at your daughter. Tell them to get a fucking move on.'

He ran past Diana and burst out of the front door, his sweat turning ice-cold in the night air. It was four hundred yards to the gates and he reckoned Jane was a couple of minutes ahead of him. He set off at a blistering pace. Two minutes was an eternity to kill a woman, he thought, when a second was all it needed to smash an unsuspecting skull. The drive was in pitch darkness with the overhanging trees and bushes blocking out even the weak light of a shrouded moon. He swore at himself for not bringing his torch as he blundered unseeingly into the stinging branches at the edge of the way. He set off again, this time using the crown of the road for his guide, eyes straining to adjust themselves to the night. It was several seconds before he realised that the bobbing yellow pin-point in the distance ahead of him was a torch beam. The drive had straightened out.

'Jane!' he yelled. 'Stop! Wait there.' He pounded on.

The torch swung round to point in his direction. The beam wobbled as if the hand that held it was unsteady.

'I'm a police officer,' he called, his lungs straining. 'Stay there.'

He slowed to a walk as he approached her, hands held placatingly in front of him, chest heaving. The torchlight, wavering frantically now, danced across his face and dazzled him. He fished for his warrant card in his trouser pocket, holding it in front of him like a talisman. With a groan he put his hands on his knees, bent forward and whooped for breath.

'What's the m-matter?' she stammered in a shrill, frightened voice.

'Nothing,' he said, straightening. 'I didn't think you should come alone, that's all. Could you shine the torch on the ground? You're blinding me.'

'Sorry.' She dropped her hand to her side and he saw she was wearing a dressing-gown and carpet slippers.

'Let's go,' he suggested. 'It can't be far now. Shall I take the torch?'

She passed it to him and he caught a brief glimpse of her in its gleam as he turned to light the way ahead. She was like a bloodless ghost, white-faced and insubstantial with a cloud of dark hair. She looked absolutely terrified.

'Please don't be frightened. Your mother knows me,' he said inadequately as they went on. 'She agreed I should come after you.' They could see the black mass of the Lodge in the distance.

She tried to speak but it was a second or two before the sound came. 'I could hear b-breathing,' she wobbled out.

'That was my lungs gasping,' he said, attempting a joke.

'No,' she whispered, 'it wasn't you.' Her step faltered and he swung the beam towards her. She plucked pathetically at her dressing-gown. 'I've got my nightie on.' Her lips were trembling uncontrollably. 'I thought it was my father.'

McLoughlin caught her as she slumped in a dead faint. In the distance, carried on the wind, came the faint sough of a siren.

'What did she mean, Mrs Maybury?' McLoughlin was leaning wearily against the Aga, watching Phoebe make tea.

Anne had been rushed to hospital with Jonathan and Diana in attendance. Jane was asleep in bed with Elizabeth watching over her. Police were swarming all over the garden in search of a suspect. Phoebe, under pressure from McLoughlin, was answering questions in the kitchen.

She had her back to him. 'She was frightened. I don't suppose she meant anything by it.'

'She wasn't frightened, Mrs Maybury, she was terrified, and not of me. She said: "I've got my nightie on. I thought it was my father." ' He moved round so that he was facing her. 'Forgetting for the moment that she hasn't seen her father for ten years, why should she associate him with the fact that she was wearing a nightie? And why should it terrify her? She said she heard breathing.'

Phoebe refused to meet his eyes. 'She was upset,' she said.

'Are you going to make me ask Jane when she wakes up?' he demanded brutally.

She raised her lovely face. 'You'd do that, I suppose.' She made as if to push her spectacles up her nose, then realised she hadn't got them on and dropped her hand to the table.

'Yes,' he said firmly.

With a sigh, she poured two cups of tea. 'Sit down, Sergeant. You may not know it but you look dreadful. Your face is covered in scratches and your shirt's torn.'

'I couldn't see where I was going,' he explained, taking a chair and straddling it.

'I gathered that.' She was silent for a moment. 'I don't want you asking Jane questions,' she said quietly, taking the other chair, 'even less so after tonight. She couldn't cope. You'll understand that because I think you've guessed already what she meant by her remark.' She looked at him enquiringly.

'Your husband abused her sexually,' he said.

She nodded. 'I blame myself because I had no idea what he was doing. I found out one night when I came home early from work. I was the evening receptionist at the doctor's surgery,' she explained. 'We needed the money. David had sent Johnny to a boarding prep-school. That day I had flu and Dr Penny sent me home and told me to go to bed. I walked in on my poor little Jane's rape.' Her face was quite impassive as if, long ago, she had realised the futility of nurtured anger. 'His violence had always been directed at me,' she went on, 'and in a way I asked for it. While he was beating me, I could be certain he wasn't touching the children. Or I thought I could.' She gave a mirthless laugh. 'He took full advantage of my naivety and Jane's terror of him. He had been raping her systematically since she was seven years old and he kept her quiet by telling her he would kill me if she ever said anything. She believed him.' She fell silent.

'Did you kill him?'

'No.' She raised her eyes to his. 'I could have done quite easily. I would have, if I'd had anything to kill him with. A child's bedroom doesn't lend itself to murder weapons.'

'What happened?'

'He ran away,' she said unemotionally. 'We never saw him again. I reported him missing three days later after several people had phoned to say he hadn't kept appointments. I thought it might look odd if I didn't.'

'Why didn't you tell the police the truth about him?'

'Would you, Sergeant, with a severely disturbed child your only witness? I wasn't going to let her be questioned, nor was I going to give the police a motive for a murder I didn't commit. She was under a psychiatrist for years because of what happened. When she became anorexic, we thought she was going to die. I'm only telling you now to protect her from further distress.'

'Have you any idea what happened to your husband?'

'None. I've always hoped he killed himself but, frankly, I doubt he had the guts. He loved inflicting pain on others but couldn't take it himself.'

'Why did he run away?'

She didn't answer immediately. 'I honestly don't know,' she said at last. 'I've thought about it often. I think, perhaps, for the first time in his life he was afraid.'

'Of what? The police? Prosecution?'

She smiled grimly, but didn't answer.

McLoughlin toyed with his teacup. 'Someone tried to murder Miss Cattrell,' he said. 'Your daughter thought she heard her father. Could he have come back?'

She shook her head. 'No, Sergeant, David would never come back.' She looked him straight in the eye as she brushed a strand of red hair from her forehead. 'He knows if he did, I'd kill him. I'm the one he's afraid of.'

A very irritable Walsh sat in Anne's armchair and watched a policeman photographing prints on the outside of what was left of the French windows. It was a job that couldn't be put off till the morning in case it rained. The broken slivers of glass on the flagstones had been covered with weighted-down polythene. 'There are going to be dozens of prints,' he muttered to McLoughlin. 'Apart from anything else, half the Hampshire police force have left their grubby paw marks round the shop.' McLoughlin was examining the carpet by the French windows, looking for blood spots. He moved across to the desk. 'Anything?' Walsh demanded.

'Nothing.' His eyes were red-rimmed with exhaustion.

'So what happened here, Andy?' Walsh cast a speculative eye over his Sergeant, before glancing at his watch. 'You say you found her at eleven forty or thereabouts. It is now one thirty and we have come up with some vague sounds in the distance and a woman with a fractured skull. What's your guess?'

McLoughlin shook his head. 'I haven't got one, sir. I wouldn't even know where to start. We'd better pray she comes round soon and can tell us something.'

Walsh levered himself out of the chair and shuffled over to the window. 'Haven't you finished yet?' he demanded of the man outside.

'Just about, sir.' He took a last photograph and lowered his camera.

'I'll leave someone here overnight and you can do the inside tomorrow.' Walsh watched while the man packed up his equipment and left, carefully skirting the broken glass, then he shuffled back to the chair, playing up his age. He took out his pipe and began the process of filling it, watching McLoughlin closely from beneath the angry jut of his brows. 'All right, Sergeant,' he snapped, 'now you can tell me just what the hell you've been up to. I don't like the smell of this one little bit. If I find you've been getting your priorities mixed, by God you'll be for the high jump.'

Exhaustion and jangling nerves combined in a prolonged yawn. 'I was trying to steal a bit of a march, sir. I thought there might be promotion in it.' Bold, bare-faced lies, he thought, nothing too concrete, not even a half-truth that Walsh could check up on. If Phoebe could get away with it, then so could he.

Walsh's frown deepened. 'Go on.'

'I came over the wall at the bottom to see what happened when she came back from the Station. I must have got here by about ten forty-five. The others had all gone to bed but Miss Cattrell was sitting in that chair you're sitting in. She finally switched off her downstairs light at about eleven fifteen. I hung around for another ten minutes then set off for the car. I hadn't gone far when I thought I heard voices, so I came back to investigate. Her window was slightly open. I shone my torch round inside and found her there.' He jerked his head towards the middle of the room.

Walsh champed thoughtfully on the stem of the pipe. 'It was lucky you did. Mrs Maybury said you were giving her heart massage when she came in. You probably saved her life.' He lit the pipe and studied the Sergeant through the smoke. 'Is this the truth?'

McLoughlin gave another huge yawn. He couldn't control them. 'It's the truth, sir,' he said wearily. Why was he trying to protect himself? This morning he would have welcomed an excuse to go. Perhaps he just wanted to know the end of the story, or perhaps he wanted vengeance.

Walsh was deeply suspicious. 'If I find there's something been going on between the two of you, you'll be up on a discipline charge so damned fast you'll wonder what happened. She's a suspect in a murder enquiry.'

The dark face cracked into a grin. 'Do me a favour, sir, she's been treating me like Vlad the Impaler since I called her a dyke.' He yawned again. 'But I appreciate the compliment. In view of the bashing it's taken in the past couple of weeks, it does my ego good that you think I can pull a reluctant bird after twenty-four hours. Kelly wouldn't agree with you,' he finished bitterly.

Walsh grunted. 'Was it you who hit her?'

140

McLoughlin didn't have to feign surprise. 'Me? Why would *I* want to hit her?'

'To get even. You're in the mood for it.'

He stared at Walsh for a moment, then shook his head. 'That's not the way I'd choose,' he said. 'But if Jack Booth ever turns up with a hole in his head, that might be down to me.'

The Inspector nodded. 'So what was Miss Cattrell doing for the half hour you watched her?'

'She sat in that armchair, sir.'

'And did what?'

'Nothing. I presume she was thinking.'

'You say the Maybury woman made no bones about wanting to kill her husband. Would she kill her friend too?'

'Possibly. If she was angry enough. But what was her motive?'

'Revenge? Perhaps she thought Miss Cattrell had talked to us.'

McLoughlin shook his head slowly. 'I imagine she knows Miss Cattrell better than that.'

'Mrs Goode? The Phillipses? The children?'

'Same question, sir. What was the motive?'

Walsh stood up. 'I suggest we start looking,' he said acidly, 'before we all end up on point-duty. A weapon would be helpful. I want this entire house turned upside down, Sergeant. You can lead the search till Nick Robinson gets here. He'll be my number two in this investigation.' He looked at his watch. 'You'll be concentrating on the Maybury file. Be in my office at ten tomorrow morning. There's a pattern to all of this and I want it found.'

'With respect, sir, I believe I can make a more valuable contribution here.'

'You'll do as you're told in future, Sergeant,' the older man snapped angrily. 'I'm not sure what your game is, but I don't like people who try to steal a march over me.'

McLoughlin shrugged. 'Then I urge you not to get too sold on a pattern, sir. Mrs Maybury has told you what she thinks happened and, as I pointed out this morning, Mrs Phillips describes this house as a fortress. Why?'

Walsh eyed him thoughtfully for a moment then walked to the door. 'You're being conned by some very professional liars, lad. If you don't sharpen up, you're going to look very foolish indeed.'

SIXTEEN

There was a new sense of urgency about police activities. They moved into top gear with alacrity, demonstrating all too clearly that there was another gear to move into. It was as if the attempted murder of a known woman was on a different scale from the murder of an anonymous male stiff in the garden. Anne would have found it disquieting, except that she was in a coma in Intensive Care and knew nothing about it. Walsh would have denied it vigorously, but his irascible temper flayed his men instead when, after a thorough search of the house and grounds, they failed to come up with anything.

In the press, Streech Grange was likened, quite inappropriately, to 10 Rillington Place, as a setting for mass murder and decomposing remains. To Anne's friends, the burden of their association with it was heavy. In retrospect, their previous interrogations had the relaxed air of a social gathering. After the assault on Anne, the gloves came off and they were grilled dry. Walsh was looking for a pattern. Logic told him there was one. The odds against three unconnected mysteries in one house were so incalculable as to be beyond consideration.

For the children, it was a new experience altogether. As yet none of them had been questioned and it came like a baptism of fire. Jonathan hated his sense of impotence, of being involved in something over which he had no control. He was surly and uncooperative and treated the police with a sort of weary disdain. Walsh wanted nothing so much as to kick him up the backside, but after two hours of questioning he was satisfied there was nothing more he could get out of him. Jonathan had vindicated the three youngsters of the assault on Anne. According to him, they had changed into their nightclothes after the impromptu Lafite party, wrapped themselves in duvets and curled up in Jane's room to watch the late film on her television. The shattering glass, followed by McLoughlin's shouts for help, had startled them. No, they had heard nothing before that, but then the television had been quite loud. Walsh questioned Elizabeth. She was nervous but helpful. When asked for her movements on the previous evening, her account tallied exactly with Jonathan's, down to the most trivial detail. Jane, after a day's respite, gave a similar story. Unless they were in some fantastic and well-organised conspiracy, they had had nothing to do with the attempt on Anne's life.

For Phoebe it was a case of déjà vu. The only difference this time was that her interrogators now had information she had withheld from them ten years previously. She answered them with the same stolid patience she had shown before, annoyed them with her unshakable composure and refused to be drawn when they needled her on the subject of her husband's perversions.

'You say you blame yourself for not knowing what he was doing to your daughter,' said Walsh on more than one occasion.

'Yes, I do,' she answered. 'If I had known earlier, perhaps I could have minimised the damage.'

He got into the habit of leaning forward for the next question, waiting for the tell-tale flicker of weakening resolve. 'Weren't you jealous, Mrs Maybury? Didn't it madden you that your husband preferred sex with your daughter? Didn't you feel degraded?'

She always paused before she answered, as if she were about to agree with him. 'No, Inspector,' she would say. 'I had no such feelings.'

'But you've said you could easily have murdered him.'

'Yes.'

'Why did you want to murder him?'

She smiled faintly at this. 'I should have thought it was obvious, Inspector. If I had to, I'd kill any animal I found savaging my children.'

'Yet you say you didn't kill your husband.'

'I didn't have to. He ran away.'

'Did he come back?'

She laughed. 'No, he didn't come back.'

'Did you kill him and leave him to rot in the ice house?'

'No.'

'It would have been a sort of justice, wouldn't it?'

'It certainly would.'

'The Phillipses, or should I say Jeffersons, believe in that kind of justice, don't they? Did they do it for you, Mrs Maybury? Are they your avenging arm?'

It was always at this point that Phoebe's anger threatened to spill over. The first time he put the question it had come like a blow to the solar plexus. Afterwards, she was better prepared, though it still required iron self-control to keep from tearing and gouging at his hated face. 'I suggest you ask Mr and Mrs Phillips that,' she always said. 'I wouldn't be so presumptuous as to answer anything on their behalf.'

'I'm asking you for an opinion, Mrs Maybury. Are they capable of exacting vengeance for you and your daughter?'

A pitying smile would curl her lips. 'No, Inspector.'

'Was it you who struck down Miss Cattrell? You say you were in bed, but we only have your word for it. Was she going to reveal something you didn't want revealed?'

'Who was she going to reveal it to? The police?'

'Perhaps.'

'You're such a fool, Inspector.' She smiled humourlessly. 'I've told you what I think happened to Anne.'

'Guesswork, Mrs Maybury.'

'Perhaps, but in view of what happened to me nine years ago, not unlikely.'

'You never reported it.'

'You wouldn't have believed me if I had. You'd have accused me of doing it to myself. In any case, nothing would have induced me to have you back in the house, not once I'd got rid of you. In some ways I was luckier than Anne. My scars were all internal.'

'It's too convenient. You must think me very gullible.'

'No,' she said honestly, 'narrow-minded and vindictive.'

'Because I don't share your taste for melodrama? Your daughter is very vague about what frightened her. Even Sergeant McLoughlin only *thinks* he heard someone. I'm a realist. I prefer to deal in fact, not female neurosis.'

She studied him with a new awareness. 'I never realised how much you dislike women. Or is it just me, Inspector? The idea that I might be getting my just deserts really appeals to you, doesn't it? Would I have saved myself all this misery if I'd said "yes" ten years ago?'

Invariably it was Walsh who became angry. Invariably, after a bout of questioning, Phoebe would get in her car and drive to the hospital to sit at Anne's bedside, massaging her hands and talking to her, willing her back to consciousness.

Diana's interrogations probed and prodded her connection with Daniel Thompson. She couldn't control her anger against Walsh in the way that Phoebe did and she frequently lost her temper. Even so, after two days, he could still detect no flaws in her story.

He tapped the pile of correspondence. 'It's perfectly clear from your letters that you were furious with him.'

'Of course I was furious,' she snapped. 'He had squandered ten thousand pounds of my money.'

'Squandered?' he repeated. 'But he was doing his best, wasn't he?'

'Not in my view.'

'Didn't you have the business checked before you agreed to invest in it?'

'We've already been through all this, for God's sake. Don't you listen to anything?'

'Answer the question, please, Mrs Goode.'

She sighed. 'I wasn't given much time. I spent a day going through the company books. They seemed in order, so I made over the cheque for ten thousand. Satisfied?'

'So why do you say he squandered your money?'

'Because as I got to know him, I realised he was supremely incompetent, may even have been an out-and-out rogue. The figures I saw had been heavily massaged. For example, I now think he inflated the company's assets by overvaluing his stock and I have discovered he was also using his employees' National Insurance contributions to keep the business afloat. The order books I saw were full, yet after three months he had sold virtually nothing and the little stock he had at his factory apparently had nowhere to go. His PR was a joke. He kept saying that word-of-mouth would spread and the thing would take off.'

'And that made you angry?'

'God give me strength,' she said, raising her hands to heaven. 'Do you need it spelled out? It made me livid. I was conned.'

'Do you know anything about Mr Thompson's disappearance?'

'For the last time, no. N-O, no.'

'But you knew he'd disappeared before we told you.'

'Yes, Inspector, I knew. He was supposed to come here to explain what was going on.' She leaned forward and banged her fist on the letters. 'You've got the date and the time in front of you. He never turned up. I rang his office and was told he wasn't there. I rang his home and was given a flea in my ear by his wife. I rang his office again a couple of days later and was told Mrs Thompson had reported him missing. I went to the office the next day to find some very angry employees who had not been paid for three weeks and had just discovered that their insurance contributions had not been paid for nearly a year. There has been no sign of Daniel Thompson since. The business is bankrupt and a lot of people, not just me, are owed a considerable amount of money.'

'Frankly, Mrs Goode, anyone who invests money in see-through radiators should expect to lose it.'

Ice-blue eyes, he thought, had a capacity for murderous dislike that the greens and browns lacked. The epithets she now applied to him were unprintable.

'It's your pride that's hurt, isn't it?' he said with interest. 'Your amour-propre. I can easily imagine you killing someone who made a fool of you.'

'Can you?' she snapped. 'Then you've an over-active imagination. No wonder the police have such a poor detection record.'

'I think Mr Thompson did come here, Mrs Goode, and I think you got as angry with him as you are with me, and you hit out at him.'

She laughed. 'Have you ever seen him? No? Well, take it from me, he's built like a tank. Ask his silly wife if you don't believe me. If I'd hit him, he'd have hit me back and I'd still be sporting the bruises.'

'Were you sleeping with him?'

'I'll make a confession,' she conceded. 'I found Daniel even less fanciable than I find you. He had wet lips, very like yours. I don't like wet lips. Does that answer your question?'

'His wife denied any connection between him and the Grange.'

'That doesn't surprise me. I've only met her once. She didn't approve of me.'

'Did Fred and Molly know about this investment of yours?'

'No one here knew.'

'Why not?'

'You know bloody well.'

'You didn't want to look a fool.'

She didn't bother to answer.

'Perhaps Fred and Molly did your dirty work for you, Mrs Goode?'

She massaged the beginnings of a headache. 'What a nasty manipulative man you are.'

'Did they, Mrs Goode?'

She studied him thoughtfully. 'No,' she said. 'And if you ever dare ask me that question again, I'll hit you.'

'And be arrested for assault?'

'It would be worth it,' she said.

'You're a very aggressive woman, aren't you? Did you take out your aggressions on Miss Cattrell?'

She punched him on the nose.

Jonathan tapped his mother on the shoulder, then bent forward and looked at Anne. 'How is she?' She was off the critical list and had been removed from Intensive Care to a side room on a surgical ward. She was attached via a catheter and a plastic tube to an intravenous drip.

'I don't know. She's very restless. She's opened her eyes once or twice, but she's not seeing anything.'

He squatted on the floor beside her. 'You're going to have to leave her for a bit, I'm afraid. Diana needs you.'

'Surely not.' Phoebe frowned.

'"Fraid so. She's been arrested.'

She was visibly surprised. 'Diana? Whatever for?'

'Assault on a police officer. She punched Inspector Walsh and gave him a nose bleed. She's been carted off to the nick.'

Phoebe's mouth dropped open. 'Oh, lord, how funny,' she said, beginning to laugh. 'Is he all right?'

'Bloody but unbowed.'

'I'll come. We'd better get hold of poor Bill again.' She looked down at Anne. 'Nothing I can do for you at the moment, old girl. Keep fighting. We're all rooting for you.'

'I'll bring Jane in later,' said Jonathan. 'She wants to come.'

They walked into the corridor. 'Is she up to it?'

'I'd say so. She's coped fantastically since it happened. We had a long chat this afternoon. She was more objective than I've ever known her. Ironically, the whole thing may have done her some good, silver linings and all that, made her realise she's tougher than she thought she was. She likes the Sergeant, by the way. If they want to question her again, we should press for him to do it.'

'Yes,' said Phoebe. 'Apart from anything else, he saved Anne's life. That would always commend him to Jane. She dotes on her godma.'

Jonathan linked his arm through his mother's. 'She dotes on you, too. We all do.'

Phoebe gave her rich laugh. 'Only because you haven't discovered my clay feet yet.'

'No,' he said seriously. 'It's because you've never pretended they were anything else.'

They walked on and disappeared round a bend in the corridor. Behind them, Andy McLoughlin inched with the embarrassment of the eavesdropper from where he had been hiding in a recessed doorway.

Damn Walsh and his bloody pattern, he thought. Logic was fallible. It had to be.

He showed his warrant card to the Sister. 'Miss Cattrell?' he asked. 'Any change?'

'Not really. She's getting restless and opening her eyes which is a good sign but, as I told the Inspector, you'll be wasting your time if you want to interview her. She could come out of it any moment or she could be like this for a day or two. We'll let you know as soon as she's up to talking.'

'I'll stay for a few minutes, if that's all right. You never know.'

'She's in side ward two. Chat to her,' the Sister encouraged. 'Might as well make yourself useful while you're here.'

He hadn't seen her since she had been taken away in the ambulance and he was shocked. She was even smaller than he remembered, a tiny, shrunken thing with bandaged head and ugly, sallow skin. But, even unconscious, she seemed to be smiling at some private joke of her own. He felt no lust – how could he? – but his heart warmed with a sense of recognition as if he had known her a long time. He pulled the chair close to her pillows and started to speak. There was no hesitation for he knew, without thinking, just what would give her pleasure. After half an hour he ran dry and looked at his watch. She had moved once or twice, like a child in her sleep, but her eyes had stayed firmly closed. He pushed his chair back. 'That's it, Cattrell. Time's up, I'm afraid. I'll see if I can get you alone again tomorrow.' He touched her cheek with his fingertips.

'You're a mean sod,' she mumbled. 'Give me "Tam o' Shanter".' She opened one eye and glared at him. 'I'm dying.'

'You've been awake all the time,' he accused her.

She opened the other eye and there was a twinkle amidst the confusion. 'Was Phoebe here?'

He nodded.

'I remember Phoebe being here. Am I at home?'

'You're in hospital,' he told her.

'Oh, shit. I hate hospitals. What day is it?'

'Friday. You've had a two-day snooze.'

That worried her. 'What happened?'

'I'll find a nurse.' He started to get up.

'You bloody well won't,' she growled. 'I hate nurses too. What happened?'

'Someone hit you. Tell me what you remember.'

She knit her brows into a deep furrow. 'Curry,' she said experimentally.

He gripped her hand tightly. 'Can we forget the curry, Cattrell?' he asked her. 'It'll be easier all round if you never saw me that evening.'

She wrinkled her forehead. 'But what happened? Who found me?'
He rubbed her fingers. 'I found you, but I've had the devil's own job explaining to Walsh what I was doing there. I can hardly admit to carnal designs on a suspect.' He searched her face. 'Do you understand what I'm saying? I want to stay on the case, Anne. I want justice.'

'Of course I bloody understand.' Humour danced in the dark eyes and he wanted to hug her. 'I can chew gum and walk at the same time, you know.' She thought deeply. 'I remember now. You were telling me how to live my life.' She looked at him accusingly. 'You had no right, McLoughlin. As long as I can live with myself, that's all that matters.'

He raised her fingertips and brushed them softly across his lips. 'I'm learning. Give me time. Tell me what else you remember?'

'I ran all the way back,' she said with an effort of concentration. 'I opened the window, I remember that. And then' – she frowned – 'I heard something, I think.'

'Where?'

'I don't remember.' She looked worried. 'What happened then?'

'Someone hit you on the back of the head.'

She looked dazed. 'I don't remember.'

'I found you inside your room.'

A heavy hand descended on his shoulder and made him jump. 'You've no business to be asking her questions, Sergeant,' said the Sister angrily. 'Get me Dr Renfrew,' she called to a nurse in the corridor. 'Out,' she told McLoughlin.

Anne looked at her with unalloyed horror and clung to his hand. 'Don't you dare go,' she whispered. 'I've seen her picture on *World at War* and she wasn't fighting for the Allies.'

He turned and raised his hands in helpless resignation.

'Is there anything I should remember?' she asked him. 'I wouldn't want to confuse the Inspector.'

His eyes softened. 'No, Miss Cattrell. You just concentrate on getting better and leave the remembering to me.'

She winked sleepily. 'I'll do that.'

DS Robinson was after promotion. He had gone diligently door-to-door again, looking for leads to Anne's assailant, but he had come up against the proverbial brick wall. No one had seen or heard anything on that night, except the ambulance, and they'd all heard that. He had had another pint with Paddy Clarke, this time under the beady eye of Mrs Clarke. He had found her immensely intimidating, more so since Anne's revelation that she had once been a nun.

149

Paddy assured him they had looked for the map of the grounds but hadn't found it and, with Mrs Clarke breathing over his shoulder, he expressed complete ignorance of Streech Grange and its inhabitants. In particular, he knew nothing at all about Anne Cattrell. Nick Robinson didn't press him. Frankly, he didn't rate his chances if he got caught up between Mr and Mrs Clarke and he was unashamedly attached to his balls.

There was nothing to stop him going home now. By rights, he was off-duty. Instead, he turned his car in the direction of Bywater Farm and one Eddie Staines. So far, Mrs Ledbetter's information had paid dividends. No harm in giving her another whirl.

The farmer pointed him to the cow-sheds where Eddie was cleaning up after the evening's milking. He found Eddie leaning on a rake and carelessly chatting up an apple-cheeked girl who giggled inanely at everything he said. They fell silent as Nick Robinson approached and looked at him curiously.

'Mr Staines?' he asked, producing his warrant card. 'Can I have a word?'

Eddie winked at the girl. 'Sure,' he said. 'Would bollocks do?'

The girl shrieked her mirth. 'Ooh, Eddie! You are funny!'

'Preferably in private,' continued Robinson, making a mental note of Eddie's riposte for his own future use.

'Buzz off, Suzie. I'll see you later in the pub.'

She went reluctantly, scuffing her boots through the muck in the yard, looking over her shoulder in the hopes of being invited back. For Eddie, it was clearly a case of out of sight out of mind. 'What do you want?' he asked, raking soiled straw into a heap while he spoke. He was wearing a sleeveless tee-shirt which gave full expression to the muscles of his shoulders.

'You've heard about the murder at the Grange?'

'Who hasn't?' said Staines, uninterestedly.

'I'd like to ask you a few questions about it.'

Staines leant on his rake and eyed the detective. 'Listen, mate, I've already told your lot all I know and that's nothing. I'm a farmhand, a salt-of-the-earth prole. The likes of me don't mix with the people at the Grange.'

'No one said you did.'

'Then what's the point of asking me questions?'

'We're interested in anyone who's been into the grounds in the last couple of months.'

Staines resumed his raking. 'Not guilty.'

'That's not what I've heard.'

The young man's eyes narrowed. 'Oh, yeah? Who's been blabbing?'

'It's common knowledge you take your girlfriends up there.'

'You trying to pin something on me?'

'No, but there's a chance you may have seen or heard something that could help us.' He offered the man a cigarette.

Eddie accepted a light. He appeared to be thinking deeply for several minutes. 'Happen I did then,' he said surprisingly.

'Go on.'

'Seems you've been asking my sister questions about a woman crying one night. Seems you've been back a couple of times.'

'The farm cottages on the East Deller road?'

'That's right. Maggie Trewin's my sister, lives in number two. Her man works up at Grange Farm. She tells me you want to know which night this – woman' – he put a derisory emphasis on the word – 'was crying.'

Robinson nodded.

'Well, now,' said Staines, blowing perfect smoke rings into the air above his head, 'I can probably tell you, but I'd want a guarantee my brother-in-law'll never know where you got it from. No court appearances, nothing like that. He'd skin me alive if he knew I'd been up there and he'd not give up till he found out who I was with.' He shook his head morosely. 'It's more'n my life's worth.' His brother-in-law's young sister was the apple of his eye.

'I can't guarantee no court appearances,' said Robinson. 'If the prosecution serves a writ on you, you'll have to attend. But it may never happen. The woman may have no bearing on the case.'

'You reckon?' Staines snorted. 'More'n I do.'

'I could take you in for questioning,' said Robinson mildly.

'Wouldn't get you nowhere. I won't say nothing till I'm certain Bob Trewin won't find out. He'd kill me, no mistake.' He flexed his muscles and returned to his raking.

Nick Robinson wrote his name and the address of the Police Station on a page of his notebook. He tore it out and handed it to Staines. 'Write down what happened and when, and send it to me unsigned,' he suggested. 'I'll treat it as an anonymous tip-off. That way no one will know where it came from.'

'You'll know.'

'If you don't,' Robinson warned, 'I'll come back and next time I'll bring the Inspector. He won't take no for an answer.'

'I'll think on it.'

'You do that.' He started to leave. 'I suppose you weren't up there three nights ago?'

Staines hefted a lump of dung to the top of his straw pile. 'You suppose right.'

'One of the women was attacked.'

'Oh, yeah?'

'You hadn't heard?'

Staines shrugged. 'Maybe.' He cast a sideways glance at the detective. 'One of her girlfriends did it, bound to be. Bitches fight like the devil when they're roused.'

'So you didn't hear or see anything that night?'

Eddie turned his back to attack the farthest corner of the shed. 'Like I just said, I wasn't there.'

Now, why don't I believe you, Robinson wondered, as he picked his way with distaste through the cow dung in the yard. The apple-cheeked girl giggled as he passed her by the gate then, like a moth to the flame, she dashed back to the cow-sheds and the arms of her philanderer.

SEVENTEEN

Walsh was still nursing a bloody nose when McLoughlin got back to the Station. It had long since stopped bleeding but he persisted in holding his blood-stained handkerchief to it. McLoughlin, who hadn't overheard that part of Phoebe's and Jonathan's conversation, looked at him in surprise.

'What happened?' he asked.

'Mrs Goode hit me, so I arrested her for assault,' said Walsh maliciously. 'That soon wiped the smile off her face.'

McLoughlin sat down. 'Is she still here?'

'No, dammit. Mrs Maybury persuaded her to apologise and I let her go with a caution. Bloody women,' he said. He stuffed the handkerchief into his pocket. 'We've had a result on the shoes. Young Gavin Williams turned up an old cobbler in East Deller who does it for pin money.'

McLoughlin whistled. 'And?'

'Daniel Thompson's for sure. The old boy keeps records, bless him. Writes a description of the shoes – in this case, made a special note of the different coloured laces – what needs to be done, name of owner and the dates they come in and go out. Thompson collected them a week before he went missing.' Walsh fingered his nose tenderly. 'The timescale's perfect. It's not looking good for Mrs Goode.' He chuckled at his witticism. 'If we can find just one person who saw him going into the Grange— ' He let the thought hang in the air while he took out his pipe and started to clean it with cheerful industry. 'How do you fancy Miss Cattrell for that part? She went through the little pantomime with her solicitor to steer us away from her friend, then panicked her friend by letting on how much she knew.' He tapped the pipe against his head. 'Goodbye Miss Cattrell.'

'No chance,' said McLoughlin decidedly, watching the pipe-cleaner turn black with tar. 'I dropped into the hospital on my way here. She's come round. I've sent Brownlow down to sit with her.'

'Has she now? Did you speak to her?'

'Briefly, before I was booted out by the Sister. She needs a good sleep, apparently, before she can answer questions.'

'Well?' demanded Walsh sharply. 'What did she say?'

'Nothing much. The whole thing's a complete blank to her.' He examined his nails. 'She did say she thought she heard something outside.'

Walsh grunted suspiciously. 'Suits your case rather neatly, doesn't it?'

McLoughlin shrugged. 'You're barking up the wrong tree, sir, and if you hadn't tied my hands I'd have proved it by now.'

There was malice in the older man's voice. 'Jones has taken his team over the ground twice and they haven't found anything.'

'Then let me have a look. I'm wasting my time on the Maybury file. No one I've spoken to so far knew anything about his penchant for little girls. Jane appears to be the only one. It's a dead end, sir.'

Walsh dropped the fouled pipe-cleaner into his waste-paper basket and glared at his Sergeant with open dislike. McLoughlin's admission that he had been trying to steal a march rankled with him, all the more because his own grip on the case was so tenuous. He was deeply suspicious of the man in front of him. What did McLoughlin know that *he* didn't? Had he found the pattern? 'You'll stick with that file till you've talked to everyone who knew Maybury,' he said angrily. 'It's a whole new line of enquiry and I want it thoroughly explored.'

'Why?'

Walsh's brows snapped together. 'What do you mean, why?'

'Where will it lead us?'

'To Maybury's murderer.'

McLoughlin looked at him with amusement. 'She's got the better of you, sir, and there's damned all you can do about it. Raking over dead ashes isn't going to produce a prosecution. He terrorised one child and that was his own daughter, and now he's dead. My guess is he's buried in that garden somewhere, possibly in one of the flowerbeds at the front. She does those herself. Fred is never allowed near them. I think you were right and she hid the body in the ice house till the coast was clear and I doubt very much if, after ten years, there's anything left for us to find. Those dogs of hers are rather partial to human remains.'

Walsh plucked at his lips. 'I'm keeping an open mind. Webster still hasn't proved to my satisfaction that it wasn't Maybury in the ice house.'

McLoughlin gave a derisive snort. 'A minute ago you were convinced it was Daniel Thompson. For God's sake, sir, face up to the fact that you've got a *closed* mind on this whole thing. Result, we're all working with one hand behind our backs.' He leaned forward. 'There is no pattern, or not the sort you're looking for. You're trying to force unrelated facts to fit and you're making a mess of it.'

A panic of indecision gripped Walsh's belly. It was true, he thought. There was too much pressure. Pressure from within him to close the Maybury case once and for all, pressure from the media for eye-catching headlines, pressure from above to find quick solutions. And, always, the unrelenting pressure from below as the new bloods challenged for his job. He eyed McLoughlin covertly as he fingered tobacco into his pipe bowl. He had liked and trusted this devil once, he reminded himself, when the devil was shackled to a tiresome wife and troubled by his inadequacies. 'What do you suggest?'

McLoughlin, who had been up for three nights in a row, rubbed his tired eyes vigorously. 'A constant watch on Streech Grange. I'd suggest a minimum of two in each shift. Another thorough search of the grounds, but concentrated up near the Lodge. And, finally, let's be done with Maybury and put our energies into pursuing the Thompson angle.'

'With Mrs Goode as chief suspect?'

McLoughlin pondered for a moment or two. 'We can't ignore her certainly, but it doesn't feel right.'

Walsh touched his sore nose tenderly. 'It feels very right to me, lad.'

Mrs Thompson greeted them with her look of long-suffering martyrdom and showed them into the pristine but characterless room. McLoughlin had a sense of going back in time, as if the intervening days hadn't happened and they were about to explore the same conversation in the same way and with the same results. Walsh produced the shoes, no longer in their polythene bag, but with the odd meagre dusting of powder where an attempt had been made to bring up fingerprints and had failed. He put them on a low coffee table for her to look at.

'You said these weren't your husband's shoes, Mrs Thompson,' he accused her mildly.

Her hands fluttered to the cross on her bosom. 'Did I? But of course they're Daniel's.'

Walsh sighed. 'Why did you tell us they weren't?'

The awful tears swam into her eyes and drizzled over her cheeks. 'The devil whispers in my ear.' Her fingers fumbled at her shirt buttons.

'Give me strength,' muttered Walsh.

McLoughlin stood up abruptly and walked to a telephone in one corner. 'Pull yourself together, Mrs Thompson,' he ordered sharply. 'If you don't, I shall call for an ambulance and have you taken into hospital.'

She shrank into her chair as if he had slapped her.

Walsh frowned angrily at his Sergeant. 'Are these the shoes Mr Thompson was wearing when he disappeared?' he asked the woman gently.

She examined them closely. 'No,' she said.

'Are you sure? You told us the other day he had only one pair of brown shoes and he was wearing them the day he went.'

Her eyelids fluttered uncontrollably. 'Did I?' she gasped. 'How very odd. I don't believe I was feeling quite well the last time you came. Daniel loved brown shoes. You can have a look in his cupboard if you like. He had pairs and pairs.' She waved her hand at the table. 'No, these are the ones Daniel gave to the tramp.'

Walsh closed his eyes. His threadbare case against Diana was disintegrating. 'What tramp?' he demanded.

'We didn't ask his name,' she said. 'He came to the door, begging. The shoes were on the stairs to go up and Daniel said he could have them.'

'When was this?'

She produced the lace handkerchief and touched it to her eyes. 'The day before he left. I remember it very clearly. Daniel was a saint, you know. In spite of all his troubles he had time for a poor beggarman.'

Walsh took some papers from his briefcase and flicked through them. 'You reported your husband missing on the night of the twenty-fifth of May,' he said. 'So this tramp came on the twenty-fourth.'

'He must have done,' she said through her tears.

'What time was it?'

She looked helpless. 'Oh, I couldn't remember that. Some time during the day.'

'Why was your husband at home during the day, Mrs Thompson?' asked McLoughlin, looking at his diary. 'The twenty-fourth was a Wednesday. Shouldn't he have been at work?'

She pouted. 'His beastly business,' she said viciously. 'All his worries came from that. It wasn't his fault, you know. People expected too much of him. He stopped going in towards the end,' she admitted lamely.

'Can you give me a description of this tramp?' asked Walsh.

156

'Oh, yes,' she said. 'He'll be able to help you, I'm sure. He was wearing a pair of pink trousers and an old brown hat.' She thought back. 'He was about sixty, I suppose, not much hair and he smelled terribly. He was very drunk.' She paused, a thought suddenly occurring to her. 'But you must have found him already,' she said, 'or why would you have the shoes?'

Walsh picked them up and turned them over. 'You said your husband had no connection with the women at Streech Grange, yet one of them, Mrs Goode, invested money in his business.'

A shadow crossed her face. 'I didn't know.'

'Mrs Goode claims to have met you,' Walsh went on.

There was a long silence. 'Possibly. I do recall talking to someone of that name three or four months ago in the street. Daniel told me she was a client.' A glint sharpened in her eye. 'Brassy blonde woman, over-dressed, with a come-hither look.'

'Yes,' said Walsh who found the description inept but entertaining.

'She rang me,' said Mrs Thompson, pursing her lips in disapproval, 'wanting to know where Daniel was. I told her to mind her own business.' She pinioned the Inspector with a basilisk's glare. 'Did she have something to do with Daniel's disappearance?'

'We've been going through your husband's books,' said McLoughlin glibly from his corner. 'We noted the discrepancy. It puzzled us.'

'I didn't know she was one of them.' She held her handkerchief to dry eyes. 'Now you tell me she invested money in his company?' The floodgates opened and this time her tears were of real distress. 'How could he?' she sobbed. 'How could he? Such terrible women.'

Walsh looked at McLoughlin and stood up. 'We'll be off now, Mrs Thompson. Thank you for your help.'

She tried without success to stem the flood.

'Have you thought about going away at all?' the younger man asked.

She gave a long shuddering sigh. 'The Vicar's arranged a holiday,' she said. 'I'm going to a hotel by the seaside at the end of the week, just for a few days' rest. It won't do any good though, not without Daniel.'

McLoughlin looked very thoughtful as he closed the door behind him.

Chief Inspector Walsh ground his teeth with fury as he jerked the clutch on his brand new Rover and promptly stalled. 'What are you looking so damned cheerful about? We've just lost our only promising lead.'

McLoughlin waited until the car was moving. 'Who was in charge of the case at the beginning?'

'If you mean Thompson's disappearance, it was Staley.'

'Did he do a thorough job? Did he check Mrs Thompson?'

'Checked everything. I've been through the file.'

'Does he know about our body?'

'He does.'

'And it hasn't made him suspicious?'

'No. Her alibi's too good. She took Mr T. to Winchester station where he boarded a train to London. Various people remember seeing him during the journey and one remembers seeing him on the platform at Waterloo. After dropping him off, Mrs T. went straight to East Deller Church where she took part in a twenty-four-hour fast with other members of the congregation. The saintly Daniel was due to join her there at six o'clock on his return from London where, incidentally, he was supposed to be raising a loan to keep the business afloat. He never came back. At ten o'clock, the Vicar's wife took Mrs T. home to Larkfield and waited with her while she telephoned office, friends and acquaintances. At nearly midnight, Mrs Vicar rang the police and stayed with Mrs T. who was by then quite hysterical, through the night and most of the following day. Daniel has not been since he got off the train in London.'

'But her alibi's only good for the twenty-fifth and twenty-sixth. Supposing he came back later?'

Walsh manoeuvred his way into the traffic on a roundabout. 'Why would he, if he'd gone to the lengths of doing the bunk in the first place? Staley reckons he planned to kill two birds with one stone – get shot of the awful wife and duck out of the bankruptcy. He hopped into the bog at Waterloo, reversed his mac, stuck on a false moustache and went to ground with whatever he'd managed to stash away from the business. For what it's worth, Thompson's number two at the radiator firm said he wasn't in the least surprised Thompson legged it, he only wondered why it had taken him so long. According to him, Thompson had no balls and less bottle and from the moment things began to get dicey, he looked like running.'

McLoughlin picked at a fingernail. 'You must have thought he had a good reason for coming back, sir. Otherwise, how could Mrs Goode have killed him?'

'Yes, well, Mrs Goode's a damn sight more attractive than that silly bitch back there. I felt there was a good chance he staged his disappearance in order to throw in his lot with a blonde bombshell.'

'But when he turned up on her doorstep, Mrs Goode, who was

down by ten thousand, found she didn't fancy him as much as she thought she did and stuck a knife into him?'

'Something like that.'

McLoughlin laughed out loud. 'Sorry, sir.' He thought for a moment. 'The Thompsons don't have any children do they?'

'No.'

'OK, let's say you've been married to a man for thirty-odd years. He's been the be-all and end-all of your existence and he suddenly deserts you.' He paused for further thought.

'Go on.'

'I'll need to think it through properly but something along these lines. Daniel does a runner because the business has gone down the chute and he can't cope. He hangs around in London for a bit but finds that living off his wits there is worse than facing the music at home, so he comes back. Meanwhile, Mrs Thompson has discovered, because Mrs Goode telephones and tells her that Daniel was supposed to have gone to Streech Grange, that her husband has been seeing another woman, worse, a woman steeped in sin. She's very near the edge already and this sends her right over. Bear in mind she's a religious fanatic, her marriage has been a sham and she's had several days to sit and brood. What's she going to do when Daniel comes home unexpectedly?'

'Yes,' agreed Walsh thoughtfully. 'That works quite nicely. But how did she get the body to the ice house?'

'I don't know. Perhaps she persuaded him to go there when he was alive. But it's entirely logical for her to leave the body somewhere in Streech Grange, the site of Daniel's sin, and it's logical for her to have stripped him and chopped him about a bit so that we'd think it was David Maybury. She'd see that as retribution against the evil women – she probably thought they were all in it – who'd ruined her life. Do we have a follow-up on that report of someone crying near the Grange Farm cottages?'

'We do, but it's not very helpful. Both sets of occupants agreed it was after midnight because they were in bed, and they both agreed it was during the spell of hot weather that spanned the last week in May and the first two weeks in June. One lot said it was May, the other lot said it was the second week in June. Yer pays yer money and takes yer choice.'

'It's all too nebulous. We need a fix on some dates. Did Staley search the Thompsons' house?'

'Twice, once on the night of his disappearance and again about two weeks later.'

McLoughlin frowned. 'Why the second time?'

159

'Well, it's interesting that. He had an anonymous tip-off that Mrs T. had lost her marbles, butchered Daniel and hidden him under the floorboards. He turned up out of the blue one day, a couple of weeks into June, and went through the house with a magnifying glass. He found nothing except one sex-starved little woman who kept following him from room to room and making advances. He's convinced it was Mrs Thompson who made the tip-off.'

'Why?'

Walsh chuckled. 'He reckons she fancied him.'

'Perhaps her conscience was troubling her.'

Walsh pulled into the kerb outside the Police Station. 'It's all very well, Andy, but where do those blasted shoes fit in? If Daniel was wearing them, why did she leave them in the grounds? And if he wasn't, how did they get there?'

'Yes,' mused McLoughlin. 'I've been wondering about that. I can't help feeling she's telling the truth about the shoes. There must have been a tramp, you know. The description was too fluent and it matches the one Nick Robinson came up with. I remember the pink trousers.' He raised an enquiring eyebrow. 'I could try and trace him.'

'Waste of time,' muttered Walsh. 'Even if you found him, what could he tell you?'

'Whether or not Mrs Thompson's telling lies.'

'Hmm.' He hunched his shoulders over the steering wheel. 'I've had an awful thought.' He looked sick.

McLoughlin glanced at him.

'You don't suppose those damn women have been right all along, do you? You don't suppose this miserable tramp went into the ice house and had a heart attack?'

'What happened to his pink trousers?'

Walsh's face cleared. 'Yes, yes, of course. All right, then, see if you can find him.'

'I'll have to give up on the Maybury file.'

'Temporarily,' growled Walsh.

'And I want to take a team to search Streech grounds again.' He saw thunder clouds gathering across the Inspector's face. 'With a view to linking Mrs Thompson with the ice house,' he finished dispassionately.

Elizabeth stood in her favourite position, by the long window in her mother's room, watching the shadows lengthen on the terrace. She wondered how many times she had stood just so in just that place, watching. 'I shall have to go back,' she said at last. 'They won't keep the job open indefinitely.'

'You haven't any holiday owing?' asked Diana, glad that the silence was finally broken.

'Not spare. I'm going to the States for two weeks at the end of September. It leaves me with nothing to play with.' She turned round. 'I'm sorry, Mum.'

Diana shook her head. 'No need to be. Will you be staying with your father?'

Elizabeth nodded. 'It's three years since I've seen him,' she excused herself, 'and the flight's booked.'

What a gulf of misunderstanding lay between them, Diana thought, and all because they found each other so hard to talk to. When she thought back over the years, she realised their conversations had been polite but safe, never touching on anything that might lead to embarrassment. In one way, Phoebe had been lucky. There had been no division of loyalties for her children, no lingering love for their father, no need for her to justify why he had deserted them.

'Would you like a drink?' She walked over to a mahogany cabinet.

'Are you having one?'

'Yes.'

'OK. I'll have a gin and tonic.'

Diana poured the drinks and took the glasses over to the window. 'Cheers.' She perched on the back of a chair and joined her daughter's contemplation of the terrace. It was easier, on the whole, not to look at her. 'For years I couldn't think about your father without getting angry. When his letters arrived for you and I saw his handwriting, I used to get so tensed up my jaw would ache for hours. I kept wondering what Miranda had that I hadn't.' She gave a short laugh. 'That's when I first understood what "grinding your teeth" meant.' She paused. 'It took me a while but I've got over it. Now I try to remember the good times. Is she nice? I never met her, you know.'

Elizabeth's attention was riveted on the antics of a sparrow on the flagstones outside, as if in its small person it was about to provide an answer to the mysteries of the universe. 'It wasn't all his fault,' she said defensively.

'No, it wasn't. Actually, in many ways it was more my fault. I took him for granted. I assumed he was the sort of man who could cope with a working wife, and he wasn't. He particularly disliked competing with me as a business partner. I don't blame him. He couldn't help that, any more than I could help wanting a career after

161

you were born. The truth is, we should never have married. We were far too young and neither of us knew what we were doing. Phoebe feels the same. She married David because she was pregnant with Jonathan, and propriety amongst the middle classes twenty years ago dictated marriage. I married your father for virtually the same reasons. I wanted to go to the States with him and my parents wouldn't hear of my going as his mistress.' She sighed. 'God knows, Lizzie, we've all lived to regret it. We made a mess of each other's lives because we didn't have the courage to raise two fingers to convention.'

The girl stared at the sparrow. 'If you regret the marriage, do you also regret its consequence?'

'Do you mean, do I regret you?'

'Of course,' she snapped angrily. 'The two are rather closely linked, wouldn't you say?' The hurt ran deep.

Diana sought carefully for the right words. 'When you were born, I used to be driven mad by people asking: Who does she take after? Is she like you or Steven? My answer was always the same: Neither. I couldn't understand why they needed to tie you to one or other of us. To me, from the moment you drew breath, you were an individual with your own character, your own looks, your own way of doing things. I love you because you're my daughter and we've grown up together, but much more than that I actually like you. I like Elizabeth Goode.' She brushed a speck of dust from the girl's sleeve where it rested on the chair beside her. 'You exist in your own right. You're not a consequence of a marriage.'

'But I *am*,' the girl cried. 'Don't you see that? I am what you and Dad have made me.'

Diana looked at her. 'No, you were bolshy as a baby. I had to put you on solids when you were about eight weeks old because you wouldn't stop yelling for food. Steven always called you "The Despotic Diaper" because you had us both so well trained. Whatever makes you think now that you were born without personality and had to be fashioned by two untrained people? God knows, you've a horrible shock coming if you think babies don't have minds of their own.'

Elizabeth smiled. 'You know what I mean.'

'Yes,' her mother conceded, 'I know what you mean.' She was silent for a moment. 'The truth is, I should have thought this one out before. On the one hand, I've been patting myself on the back for having a strong-minded, independent daughter even if she is a bit wilful; on the other, I've been nagging at you not to make my

162

mistakes.' She smiled ruefully. 'Sorry, darling. Hardly a consistent position.'

'Phoebe's just the same,' said Elizabeth. 'It must be a common maternal weakness.'

Diana laughed. 'What does Phoebe do?'

'Haven't you noticed? Whenever Jonathan takes a drink she quietly marks the level in the bottle with a felt-tip pen. She thinks he's never noticed.'

'Well, I haven't,' said Diana in some surprise. 'How extraordinary. Why does she do it?'

'Because his father drank too much. She's watching like a hawk to make sure Jonathan doesn't do the same.'

God, and I can't blame her, thought Diana, yet how foolish her actions seemed when looked at objectively. 'Does Jonathan understand?' she asked curiously.

'I think so.'

'Do you understand?'

'Yes, but that's not to say you or Phoebe are right. My own view is you're both getting your knickers in a twist over something that may never happen.'

'I'll drink to that,' said Diana, clinking her glass against her daughter's, but if she hoped this new fragile accord would lead to confidences, she was disappointed. Elizabeth had kept her own counsel too long to give it free expression on such tenuous beginnings.

'She *is* nice,' said Elizabeth unexpectedly. 'Very different from you. She's short and rather dumpy and she wears pinafore dresses all the time. She cooks very well. Dad's put on about two stone since he married her.' She smiled. 'None of his shirts do up any more, or they didn't three years ago.'

Good lord, thought Diana, so that's what he wanted. She thought of the slim young man she had married with the cadaverous good looks and the designer clothes, and she chuckled. 'Poor old Steven.'

'He's very happy,' her daughter protested, quick to see a criticism.

Diana held up her hands in mock surrender. 'I'm sure he is and I'm glad. Very glad,' she said, and she was.

'I suppose I'll have to ask the police if it's all right for me to go back to London,' Elizabeth hazarded after a moment.

'When do you want to go?'

'Straight after lunch tomorrow. Jon said he'd drive me to the station.'

'We'll ask Walsh in the morning,' said Diana. 'He's sure to be up here bright and early to rap me over the knuckles for this afternoon's little naughtiness.'

'Oh, Mum,' scolded Elizabeth as if she were speaking to a child, 'you will be careful, won't you? You've got such a temper when you're angry. Frankly, I think you're damn lucky to have got off as lightly as you did.'

'Yes,' agreed Diana meekly, marvelling at how rapidly roles reversed.

Elizabeth pursed her lips. 'Jon got into a fight today,' she announced surprisingly, 'but don't tell Phoebe. She'll have a fit.'

'Where?'

'Silverborne. Some yobbos recognised him from that photo in the local newspaper, the one taken outside the hospital the night Anne was attacked. They called him a lessies' pimp, so he bopped one of them in the eye and took to his heels.' She smiled. 'I was rather impressed when he told me. I didn't think he had it in him.'

Diana thought of David Maybury. Jonathan had it in him all right.

EIGHTEEN

Within twenty-four hours Anne had made such a rapid recovery that she was suffering severe nicotine withdrawal symptoms and announced her intention of discharging herself. Jonathan told her not to be such a fool. 'You nearly died. If it hadn't been for the Sergeant, you probably would have done. Your body needs time to recover and get over the shock.'

'Damn,' she said roundly, 'and I can't remember a thing about it. No near-death experiences, no free-floating on the ceiling, no tunnels with shining lights at the end. What an absolute bugger. I could have written it all up. That's what comes of being an atheist.'

Jonathan, who for various reasons had come to view McLoughlin as a bit of a hero, certainly not all to do with coming to Anne's rescue, took her to task. 'Have you thanked him?'

She scowled from him to the WPC beside her bed. 'What for? He was only doing his job.'

'Saving your life.'

She glowered. 'Frankly, the way I feel at the moment, it wasn't worth saving. Life should be effortless, painless and fun. None of those apply here. It's a gulag, run by sadists.' She nodded in the direction of the ward. 'That Sister should be locked up. She laughs every time she sticks the needles into me and trills that she's doing it for my own good. God, I need a fag. Smuggle some in for me, Jonny. I'll puff away under the sheets. No one will know.'

He grinned. 'Until the bed goes up in flames.'

'There you are, you're laughing,' she accused. 'What's the matter with everyone? Why do you all find it so hilarious?'

WPC Brownlow, on duty on the other side of the bed, sniggered.

Anne cast a baleful eye upon her. 'I don't even know what you're doing here,' she snapped. 'I've told you all I can remember, which is absolutely zero.' She had been unable to talk freely to anyone, which was undoubtedly why the bloody woman had been stationed there, and it was driving her mad.

'Orders,' said the WPC calmly. 'The Inspector wants someone on hand when your memory comes back.'

Anne closed her eyes and thought of all the ways she could murder McLoughlin the minute she got her hands on him again.

He for his part had collated the information on the tramp and relayed his description through the county. He rang a colleague in Southampton and asked him, for a favour, to check round the hostels there.

'What makes you think he came here?'

'Logic,' said McLoughlin. 'He was heading your way and your Council's more sympathetic to the homeless than most in this area.'

'But two months, Andy. He'll have been on his way weeks ago.'

'I know. It's a good description though. Someone might remember him. If we had a name, it'd make things easier. See what you can do.'

'I'm pretty busy at the moment.'

'Aren't we all. Cheers.' He put an end to the grumbles by the simple expedient of replacing the receiver, abandoned a cup of congealing plastic coffee and left in a hurry before his friend could ring back with a string of excuses. With a light conscience, he set off for the Grange and a chat with Jane Maybury who had announced herself ready to answer questions.

He asked her if she would prefer to have her mother present, but she shook her head and said no, it wasn't necessary. Phoebe, with a faintly troubled smile, showed them into her drawing-room and closed the door. They sat by the French windows. The girl was very pale, with a skin like creamy alabaster, but McLoughlin guessed this was her natural colouring. She was wearing a pair of faded jeans and a baggy tee-shirt with BRISTOL CITY emblazoned across the chest. He thought how incongruous it looked on the waif-like body.

She read his mind. 'It's the triumph of hope over experience,' she said. 'I go in for a lot of that.'

He smiled. 'I suppose everyone does, one way or another. If at first you don't succeed and all that.'

She settled herself a little nervously. 'What do you want to ask me?'

'Just a few things but, first, I want you to understand that I have no desire to distress you. If you find my questions upsetting, please say so and we'll stop. If at any point you decide you'd rather talk to a policewoman, again just tell me and I'll arrange it.'

She nodded. 'I understand.'

He took her back to the night of the assault and quickly ran through her account of watching television and hearing the sound of

166

the breaking glass. 'Your brother was the first to go downstairs, I think you said.'

'Yes. He decided it was a burglar and told Lizzie and me to stay where we were until he called for us.'

'But did you stay?'

'No. Lizzie insisted on going downstairs after him to get through to Diana's wing. We didn't know at that stage which window had been broken. I said I'd check Mum's rooms and Jon ran through to where you were.'

'What happened then?'

'Mum and Diana arrived in the hall at the same time as us. Mum followed Jonathan. I checked this room, Diana checked the library and Lizzie the kitchen. When I got back to the hall, Mum was running downstairs with some blankets and a hot-water bottle and yelling at Diana to call an ambulance. I said, someone ought to warn Fred to open the gate and Mum said, of course, she hadn't thought of that.' She spread her hands in her lap. 'So I took the torch from the hall table and left.'

'Why you? Why didn't Mrs Goode's daughter go?'

She shrugged. 'It was my idea. Anyway, Lizzie hadn't come back from the kitchen.'

'You weren't frightened? You didn't think of waiting for her to go with you?'

'No,' she said, 'it never occurred to me.' She was surprised now that it hadn't. She thought about it. 'To be honest, there was nothing to be frightened of. Mum just said Anne was ill. I suppose I thought she'd got an appendix or something. I just kept thinking what a nuisance it was that we had to keep the reporters at bay by locking the gates.' Her voice rose. 'And it's not as if I've never been up the drive before on my own. I've done it hundreds of times, and in the dark. I sometimes go and chat to Molly when Fred goes to the pub.'

'Fine,' he said unemotionally. 'That's all very logical.' He smiled encouragement. 'You're a fast runner. I had the devil's own job to catch you and I was going like a train.'

She unknit her fingers from the tangled bottom of her tee-shirt. 'I was worried about Anne,' she admitted. 'I keep telling her she's going to drop dead of cancer any minute. I had this ghastly thought that that was exactly what she'd done. So I put a spurt on.'

'You're fond of her, aren't you?'

'Anne's good news,' she said. 'Live and let live, that's her motto. She never interferes or criticises, but I suppose it's easier for her. She doesn't have children to worry about.'

'My mother's a worrier,' lied McLoughlin, thinking the only thing

167

Mrs McLoughlin Snr ever worried about was whether she was going to be late for Bingo.

Jane put her chin on her hands. 'Mum's an absolute darling,' she confided naively, 'but she still thinks I need protection. Anne keeps telling her to let me fight my own battles.' She twisted a lock of the long dark hair round her finger.

He crossed his legs and pushed himself down into the chair, deliberately relaxed. 'Battles?' he teased gently. 'What battles do you have?'

'Silly things,' she assured him. 'Molehills to you, mountains to me. They'd make you laugh.'

'I shouldn't think so. You're just as likely to laugh at some of my battles.'

'Tell me,' she demanded.

'All right.' He looked at her smiling, trusting face and he thought, pray God there is nothing you can tell me or that smile will never come again. 'The worst battle I ever had was with my mother when I was about your age,' he told her. 'I'd sneaked my girlfriend into my bedroom for a night of passion. Ma walked in on us in the middle.'

'Golly,' she breathed. 'Why didn't you lock the door?'

'No key.'

'How embarrassing,' said Jane with feeling.

'Yes, it was,' he said reminiscently. 'My girlfriend hopped it and I had to do battle with the old dragon in the nuddy. She gave me two choices: if I swore on oath I'd never do it again, I'd be allowed to stay; if I refused to swear, then she'd boot me out just as I was.'

'What did you do?'

'Guess,' he invited.

'You left, starkers.'

He pointed his finger at her with thumb cocked. 'Got it in one.'

She was like a wide-eyed child. 'But where did you get clothes from? What did you do?'

He grinned. 'I hid in the bushes until all the lights went out, then I took a ladder from the shed and climbed up to my bedroom. The window was open. It was very easy. I crept back into bed, had a decent night's kip and scarpered with a suitcase before she got up in the morning.'

'Do you still see her?'

'Oh, yes,' he said, 'I do my duty Sunday lunches. To tell you the truth, I think she regretted it afterwards. The house became very quiet when I left.' He was silent for a moment. 'Your turn now,' he said.

She giggled. 'That's not fair. Your battle was funny, mine are all pathetic. Things like: Will I or will I not eat my mashed potato? Am I working too hard? Shouldn't I go out and enjoy myself?'

'And do you?'

'Go out and enjoy myself?' He nodded. 'Not much.' Her lips twisted cynically and made her look older. 'Mum's idea of my enjoying myself is to go out with boys. I don't find that enjoyable.' Her eyes narrowed. 'I don't like men touching me. Mum hates that.'

'It's not surprising,' he said. 'She must feel it's her fault.'

'Well, it's not,' she said dismissively, 'and I wish she'd realise it. The hardest thing in the world is to cope with someone else's guilt.'

'What do you think happened to your father, Jane?'

The question hung in the air between them like a bad smell. She turned away and looked out of the window and he wondered if he had pushed too fast and lost her. He hoped not, as much for her own sake as for the sake of the enquiry.

'I'll tell you what happened the night he left,' she said at last, speaking to the window. 'I remember it very clearly but even my psychiatrist doesn't know all of it. There are bits I kept back, bits that at the time didn't fit the pattern and which I left out.' She paused for a moment. 'I hadn't thought about it for ages until the other night. Since then I've thought of nothing else, and I think now that what I left out may be important.'

She spoke slowly and clearly as though, having geared herself to tell the story, she saw no point in making it garbled. She told him how, after her mother had left for work, her father had run her bath. That was the signal, she said, that he intended to have sex with her. It was a routine he had established and which she had learned to accept. She described the entire process without a flicker of emotion and McLoughlin guessed she had rehearsed it many times on the psychiatrist's couch. She spoke of her father's approaches and her removal to her bedroom as if she were commentating on a chess game.

'But he did something different that night,' she said, turning her dark gaze on the Sergeant.

He found his voice. 'What was it?'

'He told me he loved me. He'd never done that before.'

McLoughlin was shocked. So much pain and without a word of love. Yet, after all, what good would kind words have done except make the man a hypocrite? 'Why do you think that's important?' he asked dispassionately.

'Let me finish the story,' she suggested, 'and perhaps it will strike you, too.' Before raping her this time, he had given her a present, carefully wrapped in tissue paper. 'He'd never done that before either.'

'What was it?'

'A little teddy-bear. I used to collect them. When he had finished,' she said, dismissing the entire incident in four words, 'he stroked my hair and said he was sorry. I asked him why because he'd never apologised before, but my mother came in and he never answered.' She fell silent and stared at her hands.

He waited but she didn't go on. 'What happened then?' he asked after several minutes.

She gave a mirthless laugh. 'Nothing really. They just looked at each other for what seemed like hours. In the end, he got off the bed and pulled up his trousers.' Her voice was brittle. 'It was like one of those awful Whitehall farces. I do remember my mother's face. It was frozen, like a statue's. She was very pale except for the bruise on her face where he hit her the day before. She only moved after he'd left the room, then she lay beside me on the bed and hugged me. We stayed like that all night and in the morning he'd gone.' She shrugged. 'We've never seen him again.'

'Did she say anything to him?' he asked.

'No. She didn't need to.'

'Why not?'

'You know that expression "if looks could kill".' He nodded. 'That was what was frozen on her face.' She bit her lip. 'What do you think?'

She caught him off guard. He so nearly said, I think your mother killed him. 'About what?' he asked her.

She showed her disappointment. 'It seems so obvious to me. I hoped it would strike you, too.' There was a hunger in the thin face, a yearning for something that he didn't understand.

'Hang on,' he said firmly. 'Give me a minute to think about it. You know the story backwards. This is the first time I've heard it, remember.' He looked at the notes he had been taking and cudgelled his brain to find what she wanted him to find. He had ringed the three things she said her father had never done before: love, present, apology. What was their significance? Why did she think he had done them? Why *had* he done them? Why would any father tell his daughter he loved her, give her a present and regret his unkindnesses? He looked up and laughed. It was stunningly obvious, after all. 'He was planning to leave anyway. He was saying goodbye. That's why he disappeared without trace. He'd arranged it all beforehand.'

She let out a long sigh. 'Yes, I think so.'

He leaned forward excitedly. 'But do you know why he would want to disappear?'

'No, I don't.' She sat up straight and pushed the hair back off her face. 'All I do know, Sergeant, is that it wasn't my fault.' A slow smile curved her lips. 'You can't imagine how good that makes me feel.'

'But surely no one's ever suggested it was?' The idea appalled him.

'When I was eight years old, my mother caught me in bed with my father. My father ran away because of it and my mother was labelled a murderess. At the age of ten, my brother's personality changed. He stopped being a child and took his father's place. He was sworn to secrecy about what had happened and has never mentioned his father again.' She played with her fingers. 'My mother's guilt has been an irrelevancy beside mine.' She raised her eyes. 'What happened the other night was a blessing in disguise. For years I've sat with a psychiatrist who has done his level best to intellectualise me out of my feelings of guilt. To a certain extent he succeeded and I pushed it all to the back of my mind. I was the victim, not the culprit. I was manipulated by someone I had been taught to respect. I played the role that was demanded of me because I was too young to understand I had a choice.' She paused briefly. 'But the other night, perhaps because I was so frightened, it all came back to me with amazing clarity. For the first time, I realised how the pattern had changed the night he left. For the first time, I didn't need to consciously justify my innocence, because I saw that the misery and uncertainty of the last ten years would have happened anyway, whether my mother had found us or not.'

'Have you told her all this?'

'Not yet. I will after you've gone. I wanted someone else to reach the same conclusion I had.'

'Tell me what happened when you were going to the Lodge,' he encouraged. 'You said you heard breathing.'

She compressed her lips in thought. 'It's a bit of a blur now,' she admitted. 'I was fine till I came to the beginning of the long straight bit leading to the gates. I slowed down as I came round the bend because I was getting a stitch and I heard what sounded like someone letting out a long breath, the sort of sound you make when you've been holding your breath for hiccups. It seemed to be very close. I was so frightened, I started to run again. Then I heard running footsteps and someone shouting.' She looked at him sheepishly. 'That was you. You scared me out of my wits. Now I'm not sure I heard breathing at all.'

171

'OK,' he said. 'It's not important. And when you said you thought it was your father, that was just because you were frightened? There wasn't anything about the breathing that reminded you of him?'

'No,' she said. 'I can't even remember what he looked like. It was so long ago and Mum's burnt all his photos. I couldn't possibly recognise his breathing.' She watched him gather his bits and pieces together. 'Have I been any good?'

'Good?' On impulse, he reached forward and gave her hands a quick impersonal squeeze. 'I'd say your godma's going to be pretty pleased with you, young lady. Forget about fighting battles, you've just scaled your own Mount Everest. And it's all downhill from now on.'

Phoebe was sitting on a garden seat beside the front door, chin on hands, staring unseeingly at the flowerbeds which bordered the gravel drive. 'May I join you?' he asked her.

She nodded.

They sat in silence for some minutes. 'The dividing line between a fortress and a prison is a fine one,' he remarked softly. 'And ten years is a long time. Do you not think, Mrs Maybury, that you've served your sentence?'

She sat up straight and gestured bitterly in the direction of Streech Village and beyond. 'Ask them,' she said. 'It was they who put up the barbed wire.'

'Was it?'

Instinctively, defensively, she pressed her glasses up her nose. 'Of course. It was never my choice to live like this. But what do you do when people turn against you? Beg them to be kind?' She gave a harsh laugh. 'I wouldn't do it.'

He stared at his hands. 'It wasn't your fault,' he said quietly. 'Jane understands that. He was what he was. Nothing you did or didn't do would have made any difference.'

She withdrew into herself and let the silence lengthen. Above them swallows and house martens dipped and darted and a lark swelled its little throat and sang. At long last she took a handkerchief from her sleeve and held it to her eyes. 'I don't think I like you very much,' she said.

He looked at her. 'We all carry our burden of guilt – it's human nature. Listen to anyone newly bereaved or divorced and you'll hear the same story – if only I had done this . . . if only I hadn't done that . . . if only I had been kinder . . . if only I had realised. Our capacity for self-punishment is enormous. The trick is to know when

172

to stop.' He rested a light hand on her shoulder. 'You've been punishing yourself for far too long. Can you not see that?'

She turned her face away from him. 'I should have known,' she said into her handkerchief. 'He was hurting her and I should have known.'

'How could you have known? You're no different from the rest of us,' he told her brutally. 'Jane loved you, she wanted to protect you. If you blame yourself, you take away everything she tried to do for you.'

There was another long silence while she fought to control her tears. 'I'm her mother. There was only me to save her, but when she needed me I never came. I can't bear to think about it.' A convulsive tremor rocked the shoulder beneath his hand.

He didn't stop to consider whether it was a good idea but reacted instinctively, drawing her into the fold of his arm and letting her weep. They were not the first tears she had shed, he guessed, but they were the first she had shed for her lost self, that self who had come into an enchanted world, wide-eyed and sure that she could do anything. The triumph of the human condition was to face one small defeat after another and to survive them relatively intact. The tragedy, as for Phoebe, was to face the worst defeat too soon and never to recover. His heart, still bruised and battered, ached for her.

He stopped his car on the bend before the straight stretch of drive and got out. Close, Jane had said, which meant in all probability crouched among the rhododendron bushes along the edge of the way. His searches so far had been disappointing. While he had set a team to scour the ice house for a link with Mrs Thompson, he himself had gone on hands and knees about the terrace for signs of Anne's attacker. If what he believed had happened, there would have been ample evidence of it. But Walsh was right. Bar some dislodged bricks and a cigarette end which was a brand that neither Fred nor Anne smoked, there was nothing. No weapon – he'd examined every brick and stone minutely for bloodstains; no footprints – the lawn was too hard from lack of rain and the flagstones too clean from Molly's regular sweepings; no blood, not even the tiniest speck, to prove that Anne had been hit outside and not inside. He had begun to wonder if he'd put too much faith in Phoebe's certainty – ten years was a long time and people changed – and she admitted herself it had only happened the once. But if she were wrong or if she were lying? He couldn't bring himself to explore either alternative. Not yet.

He sank to hands and knees again and began to inch along the

173

drive. If there *was* anything, it wouldn't be easy to find. A team had been over here once without success but then he had told them to concentrate further down, near where he had caught her and where, for one brief moment, he had had the feeling that he and Jane were being watched. He crawled along the left-hand side, knees aching, eyes constantly alert, but after half an hour he had found nothing.

He sat back wearily on his heels and swore at the injustice of it. Just once, he thought, let me be lucky. Just once, let something come my way that I haven't had to work my bloody butt off for.

He moved to the right-hand side of the drive and inched back towards the bend. Predictably, he was almost at the car before he found it. He took a deep breath and thumped his fist on the tarmac, growling and shaking his head from side to side like a mad dog. Had he only started on the right-hand side, he would have found the damn thing over an hour ago and saved himself a lot of trouble.

'You all right, son?' asked a voice.

McLoughlin looked over his shoulder to find Fred staring at him. He grinned self-consciously and stood up. 'Fine,' he assured him. 'I've just found the bastard who did for Miss Cattrell.'

'I don't see him,' muttered Fred, eyeing McLoughlin doubtfully.

McLoughlin crouched down and parted the bushes, sweeping leaves away from something on the ground. 'Look at that. The forensic boys are going to have a field day.'

With much panting and heaving Fred squatted beside him. 'Well, I'll be blowed,' he said, 'it's a Paddy Clarke Special.'

Nestling in the débris under the rhododendron, beautifully camouflaged, was an old-fashioned stone beer bottle with a dark brown crust clinging to its bottom. McLoughlin, who had been thinking only in terms of some decent fingerprints and what looked like the imprint of a trainer in the soft damp earth beneath the dense bushes, flicked him a curious glance. 'What on earth is a Paddy Clarke Special?'

Fred lumbered unhappily to his feet. 'There's no harm in it, not really. It's more of a hobby than a business, though I don't s'pose the tax man would agree. He's got a room at the back of his garage where he makes it. Uses only traditional materials and leaves it to mature till it has the kick of a horse and tastes like nectar. There's not a beer to touch Paddy's Special.' He stared glumly at the rhododendron. 'You have to drink it on the premises. He sets great store by those bottles, says they breathe flavour in a way glass never does.' He looked immensely troubled. 'I've never known him let one out of the pub.'

'What's he like? The type to beat up women?'

174

The old man shuffled his feet. 'No, never that. He's a good sort. Mind you, the wife's got little time for him on account of he's married and not too particular about his vows, but – hit Miss Cattrell?' He shook his head. 'No, he'd not do that. He and she are' – he looked away – 'friends, as you might say.'

An entry in Anne's diary swam before his eyes. *'P. is a mystery. He tells me he screws fifty women a year, and I believe him, yet he remains the most considerate of lovers.'* 'Does he smoke?'

Fred, who had supplied Paddy with many a cigarette over the years, thought the question odd. 'Other people's,' he said warily. 'His wife's a bit of a tyrant, doesn't approve of smoking.'

McLoughlin pictured her fireplace awash with cigarette ends. 'Don't tell me,' he said gloomily, 'let me guess. He looks like Rudolph Valentino, Paul Newman and Laurence Olivier, all rolled into one.' He opened his car door and reached for his radio.

'Tut, tut, tut,' clicked Fred impatiently. 'He's a big man, dark, full of life, clever in his way. Always reminds me of the one who plays *Magnum*.'

Tom Selleck! I hate him, thought McLoughlin.

Sergeant Jones was leaving the Station as McLoughlin came in. 'You know that tramp you're after, Andy?'

'Mm.'

'Got a sighting from your friend the Vicar in East Deller. Wife claims she gave him a cup of tea.'

'Any idea of a date?'

'No, but the Vicar remembers he was writing a sermon at the time and was annoyed by the disturbance, found himself praying to the Good Lord for deliverance from tramps, then had to reprimand himself for his lack of charity.'

McLoughlin chuckled. 'That sounds like the Vicar all right.'

'Apparently he always writes his sermons on a Saturday while he's watching the sport on telly. Any good?'

'Could be, Nick, could be.'

NINETEEN

The phone rang on McLoughlin's desk the following morning.
'You're a jammy bastard, Andy. I've got a lead on that tramp of
yours,' said his mate in Southampton. 'One of the uniformed sergeants recognised the description. Seems he picked up the old boy
about a week ago and took him to a new hostel out Shirley way. No
guarantee he's still there but I'll give you the address. You can check
it out for yourself. He's called Wally Ferris and he's a regular down
here during the summer. Sergeant Jordan's known him for years.'
McLoughlin wrote down the address, Heaven's Gate Hostel, and
thanked him. 'You owe me one,' said the other cheerfully and hung
up.

Heaven's Gate was a large detached Victorian house, probably
much sought after in the days before motor cars, but its appeal was
diminished now by the busy thoroughfare which mewled and milled
about its front door.

Wally Ferris bore no resemblance to the description McLoughlin
had circulated, except in age and height. He was clean. Scrubbed
rosy cheeks and gleaming pate with frill of washed hair dazzled
above a white shirt, black slacks and highly polished shoes. He
looked, for all the world, like an elderly schoolboy on his first day
in class. They met in the sitting-room and Wally gestured to a chair.
'Take a pew,' he invited.

McLoughlin showed his disappointment. 'No point,' he said. 'To
be honest, I don't think you're the person I'm looking for.'

Wally did a rapid about-turn and beetled for the door. 'Suits me,
son. I'm not comfortable wiv bluebottles and that's a fact.'

'Hold on,' said McLoughlin. 'At least, let's establish it.'

Wally turned and glowered at him. 'Make yer bleeding mind up.
I'm only 'ere because the lady of the 'ouse arst me. She's scratched
my back, in a manner o' speaking, so I'm scratching 'ers. What you
after?'

McLoughlin sat down. 'Take a pew,' he said, echoing Wally.

'Gawd, you're a shilly-shallyer and no mistake. Can't make yer mind up, can yer.' He perched on a distant chair.

'What were you wearing when you came here?' asked McLoughlin.

'None of your effing business.'

'I can ask the lady of the house,' said McLoughlin.

'What's it to you, anyway?'

'Just answer. The sooner you do, the sooner I'll leave you in peace.'

Wally sucked his teeth noisily. 'Green jacket, brown 'at, black shoes, blue jumper and pink trews,' he reeled off.

'Did you have them long?'

'Long enough.'

'How long?'

'All different. 'Ad the 'at and jacket near on five years, I'd say.'

'The trousers?'

'Twelve monfs or so. Bit on the bright side but a good fit. 'Ere, you're not finking I nicked 'em, are you? I was give 'em.' He looked thoroughly indignant.

'No, no,' said McLoughlin soothingly. 'Nothing like that. The truth is, Wally, we're trying to trace a man who's disappeared and we think you may be able to help us.'

Wally planted his feet firmly on the ground, one in front of the other beneath his chair, poised to take flight. 'I don't know nuffink about nuffink,' he said with absolute conviction.

McLoughlin raised his hands in a conciliatory gesture. 'Don't panic, Wally. As far as we know, there's no crime involved. The man's wife asked us to find him. She says you came to the house the day before he disappeared. All we're wondering is if you remember going there, and if you saw or heard anything that might help us find out why he went.'

Wally's rheumy eyes looked his suspicion. 'I go to a lot of 'ouses.'

'These two gave you a pair of brown shoes.'

Something like relief flickered across the wizened features. 'If the wife was there, why can't she tell you why 'er old man went?' he asked reasonably.

'She's become very ill since her husband went,' said McLoughlin, stretching the truth like a rubber band. 'She hasn't been able to tell us much at all.'

'What's this chap done?'

'Nothing, except lose all his money and run away.'

That struck a chord with Wally. 'Poor bastard. Does 'e want to be found?'

'I don't know. What do you think? His wife certainly wants him back.'

Wally considered for several minutes. 'No one bovvered to come looking for me,' he said in the end. 'Sometimes I wished they 'ad 'ave done. They was glad to see the back of me, and that's the trufe. Go on then. Arst yer questions.'

It took over an hour, but in the end McLoughlin had a clear picture of Wally's movements during the last week in May, or as clear as the old man could make it, bearing in mind he had been tight most of the time. 'I was give a fiver,' he explained. 'Some old geezer in the middle of Winchester popped it in me 'and. Put the lot on a gee-gee called Vagrant, didn't I. Came up eleven to one. Ain't 'ad so much cash for years. Kept me plastered for free weeks 'fore it ran out.'

He had hung around Winchester for most of the three weeks, then, when he was down to his last few quid, he'd made his way along the back roads to Southampton in search of new pickings. 'I like the villages,' he said. 'Reminds me of cycling holidays in my youf.' He remembered stopping at the pub in Streech. 'It was pissing down,' he explained. 'Landlord was a decent sort, gave me no bovver.' Paddy's wife, by contrast, was a fat old cow whom, for unspecified reasons, Wally didn't take to, but he winked ferociously a couple of times as he mentioned her. At three o'clock, they turned him out into the rain. 'Ain't no fun when it's wet,' he said lugubriously, 'so I took meself off to a little shelter I know of and spent the afternoon and night there.'

'Where?' asked McLoughlin when the old man fell silent.

'Never did no 'arm,' said Wally defensively. 'No call for anyone to complain.'

'There haven't been any complaints,' said McLoughlin encouragingly. 'I won't rat on you, Wally. As far as I'm concerned, if you behave yourself, you can use it as often as you like.'

Wally pursed his lips into a pink rosette. 'There's a big 'ouse there. Easy as winking to pop over the wall. Been in the garden a few times, never seen no one.' He gave McLoughlin a speculative look to see if he was interested. He was. 'There's a sort of man-made cave near the woods,' he went on. 'Can't fink what it's for but it's got some bricks stacked in it. The door's 'idden by a big bramble but it's a doddle to creep in be'ind it. I always take bracken in wiv me to give me a good kip. 'Ere, why you looking like that?'

McLoughlin shook his head. 'No reason. I'm just interested. Have you any idea what day this was, Wally?'

'Gawd knows, son.'

178

'And you didn't see anyone when you were in the garden?'

'Not a soul.'

'Was this cave in darkness?'

'Well, there ain't no electricity, if that's what you mean, but while it's light you can see. If the door's ajar, of course,' he added.

McLoughlin wondered how to put the next question. 'And the place was empty except for this stack of bricks you mentioned?'

'What you getting at?'

'Nothing. I'm just trying to get a clear picture.'

'Then yes. It was empty.'

'And what happened the next morning?'

'Hung around till lunchtime, didn't I?'

'In the cave?'

'No. In the woods. Nice and peaceful, it was. Then I got to feeling peckish, so I 'opped over the wall and looked about for somefing to eat.' He had knocked on several doors, without much success.

'Why didn't you buy something with your winnings?' asked McLoughlin, fascinated.

Wally was intensely scornful. 'Do me a favour,' he admonished. 'Why pay for somefink you can get free? It's booze they won't give away. Anyway, I 'adn't much winnings left and that's a fact.'

He had found a group of houses on the outskirts of Streech where 'an old bat' had given him a sandwich. The council houses, McLoughlin thought. 'Did you try anyone else?' he asked.

'Young lass told me to push off. Gawd knows, I sympathised wiv 'er. There was a dozen nippers yelling their 'eads off in 'er front room.' He abandoned Streech as a dead duck at that point and set off down the road. After about an hour, he came to another village. 'Don't recall the name, son, but there was a vicarage. Always good for a touch, they are.' He had roused the Vicar's wife and persuaded her out of a cup of tea and some cake. 'Nice little woman, but she came over sanctimonious. That's the trouble wiv vicarages. You can always get a bite but you has to take the lecture wiv it. I scarpered sharpish.' It had begun to rain again. 'Strange wevver, I can tell yer. 'Ot as blazes most of the time, but every now and then there was a funder storm. You know the sort. Fat rain, I calls it. Flashes of lightning and great claps of funder.' He had looked around for shelter. 'Not a blooming fing. Nice little boxes wiv neat garages. No help to me. Then I comes to this bigger house, set back a bit. I fought I'd explore the back, see if there was a shed. I sneaks down the side and lo and be'old there's just what I'm looking for, nice little shed wiv no one in sight. I opens the door and pops inside.' He stopped.

'And?' prompted McLoughlin.

A cunning gleam had appeared in the old man's eyes. 'Seems like I'm giving you a lot of information for nuffink, son. What's in it for me?'

'A fiver,' said McLoughlin, 'if what you tell me's worth it.'

'Ten,' said Wally. He glanced behind him at the closed door then leaned forward confidentially. 'To tell you the trufe, son, it's a bit claustrophobic this place. The lady of the 'ouse does 'er best but there's no fun. Know what I mean. A tenner'd give me a day out. I've been 'ere a week for Gawd's sake. I've 'ad more fun in prison.'

McLoughlin considered the morality of giving Wally the where-withal to turn his back on Heaven's Gate and concluded that Wally was on the point of scarpering whatever happened. You can't teach an old dog new tricks. Ten pounds would give him a start at least. 'Done,' he said. 'What happened when you went into this shed?'

'Looked around for somefink to sit on, didn't I, make meself comfortable while I was there. Found this feller 'iding at the back be'ind some boxes. When 'e realised I'd seen 'im, 'e came over all 'oity-toity and ordered me off 'is property. I arst, reasonable like, why I should imagine 'e was the owner when 'e was skulking in the shed same as me. 'E got properly riled and called me a few names. In the middle of it, this woman comes out of the kitchen door to see what the noise is. I explains the situation and she tells me the geezer's 'er 'usband and 'e's in the shed looking for a paintbrush.' Wally pulled a wry face. 'They must've fought I was born yesterday. The paintbrushes was all laid out neat and tidy on a workbench at the side. The geezer was 'iding, no mistake. Anyway, I sees my opportunity. They wants rid of me and they'd pay up to see me go. I got a bottle of whisky, a decent pair of shoes and twenty quid out of it. Tried for more but they turned nasty and I reckoned it was time to skedaddle. This the feller you're looking for?'

McLoughlin nodded. 'Sounds like it. Can you describe him?'

Wally's brow wrinkled. 'Five tennish, fat, grey 'air. 'E 'ad nancy feet for a man. The shoes they gave me didn't 'alf pinch.'

'What did the woman look like?'

'Mousey little fing, sorrowful eyes, but Gawd she 'ad a temper. Lammed into me and 'er old man somefink rotten for making a noise.' He looked suddenly thoughtful. 'Not that we was, mind you. Froughout the 'ole fing, we spoke in whispers.' He shook his head. 'Bats the pair of 'em.'

McLoughlin was jubilant. Got you, Mrs T., he thought. 'Where did you go then?'

A thoughtful expressiom crossed Wally's face. 'There's a saying, son. A bird in the 'and is worf two in the bush. It had stopped raining but I 'ad this feeling we was in for anover funder storm. I fought to meself I've a bottle o' whisky and nowhere cosy to drink it. If I push on, 'oo's to say if I'll find a dry place for the night. So I 'ightailed it back to the cave at the big 'ouse and passed a 'alfway decent night.' He considered McLoughlin out of the corner of his eyes. 'The next day, I finks to myself, I've a few quid in me pocket and I've 'ad nuffink decent to eat for days, so I 'eaded off towards Silverborne. There's a nice café on the road— '

'Did you leave anything behind?' McLoughlin cut in.

'Like what?' asked the old man sharply.

'Like the shoes?'

'Dumped 'em in the woods,' said Wally scornfully. 'Damn fings gave me corns a right drubbing. That's where experience comes in. A young bloke would've chucked the old pair out before 'e'd properly tried the new. Then 'e'd've been in agony till 'e found some more.'

McLoughlin tucked his notebook into his pocket. 'You've been a great help, Wally.'

'That it?'

McLoughlin nodded.

'Where's my tenner?'

McLoughlin took a ten-pound note out of his wallet and stretched it between his fingers. 'Listen to me, Wally. I'm going to give you ten pounds now as a token of good faith, but I want you to stay here another night because I may want to talk to you again. If you do, I'll come back tomorrow morning with another ten, making twenty in all.' He held out the tenner. 'Is it a deal?'

Wally got up and pounced on the note, secreting it in the depths of his shirt. 'Are you on the level, son?'

'I'll give you an IOU if you like.'

Wally made as if to spit on the carpet, then thought better of it. 'Be about as much use to me as a mug of water,' he said. 'OK, son, it's a deal. But if you don't come back first fing, I'm off.' His eyes narrowed. 'Don't you go telling the lady of the 'ouse, mind. I've 'ad my fill of good works this week. They don't know when to leave a bloke alone in this place.'

McLoughlin chuckled. 'Your secret's safe with me, Wally.'

'I spotted the *pattern*,' said McLoughlin to Walsh, with a tinge of irony which brought a glitter to the older man's eyes, 'when I marked the houses which reported seeing the tramp.' He pointed to small red crosses on the map in front of them. 'If you remember, Nick

Robinson had two reports. One from a woman in Clementine Cottage who said the tramp passed her house and went into the pub, which meant he was coming from the direction of Winchester. The next from the landlord at the pub who said he stayed until closing time then ambled off in the lee of the wall round the Grange estate, in other words heading towards East Deller.' He traced his finger along the printed road. 'The next reports we had of him were PC Williams's. He said an elderly woman had given the tramp a sandwich and a young woman had turned him away because it was her son's birthday. They both live on the council estate which is to the west of Streech and on the East Deller road. The date the young woman gave was May twenty-seventh. But when we spoke to Mrs Thompson she told us he'd visited them in East Deller on the twenty-fourth. That would have meant he had doubled back on himself for some reason to come through Streech three days later from the direction of Winchester.'

Walsh gathered together the remnants of his authority and buttoned them about himself with as much dignity as he could muster. 'I went into all this myself,' he lied. 'The fact that we found the shoes at the Grange implies he did just that.'

'I agree, so we needed another sighting in East Deller, with a date, if possible. Jonesy went out there to see what he could dig up. He had a chat with our friend the Vicar who told Jonesy he was writing a sermon when the tramp called at the vicarage. The Vicar couldn't give a date but he always writes his sermons on a Saturday. OK, now only two people have offered a definite date, May twenty-fourth, supplied by Mrs Thompson, a Wednesday, and May twenty-seventh, the day of the birthday party, a Saturday. Wally is adamant he went from the council estate in Streech to the vicarage and the Thompsons at East Deller which puts him there on Saturday, May twenty-seventh. So why did Mrs T. lie about the date?'

'Get on with it,' ordered Walsh impatiently.

'Because, in face of her blatant lie, we had proved the shoes were her husband's and she had to explain why they were no longer in her possession. She opted for the truth this time, or as near the truth as damn it, and invited us to corroborate the story by giving us a description of the tramp. Remember, we never told her where we found the shoes. For all she knew we got them from the tramp himself.' He collected his thoughts. 'Now she could be sure, if we had the tramp, that he would say he'd seen her husband. So to give us the actual day of his visit would be tantamount to telling us her husband was alive and well and living in East Deller after she'd reported him missing. Bang would go her alibi. So she advanced the

182

tramp's visit by three days. It was a gamble but it damn nearly paid off. Wally hasn't a clue when he went through, and if it wasn't for the child's birthday, neither would we. No one else can remember the date.' He paused for a moment. 'It's going to come as a nasty shock when we tell her where Wally dumped the shoes. In her wildest nightmares she couldn't believe it would be at the scene of her proposed crime.'

Walsh stood up. 'Poetic justice, I say. But I'd like to know how she persuaded him to lie low and how she got him to the ice house.'

'Use your charm and she'll probably tell us,' said McLoughlin.

TWENTY

Mrs Thompson opened the door with a smile of welcome. She was dressed to go out in a neat blue suit and white gloves but there was a sad, rather dated air about her as if her fashion sense had expired with the '50s. Two suitcases stood behind her in the hall. Splashes of rouge on her cheeks and a touch of lipstick gave her face a bogus gaiety but when she saw the gathered policemen her mouth drooped tragically.

'O-oh.' She breathed her disappointment. 'I thought it was the Vicar.'

'May we come in?' asked Walsh. Her inadequacies repulsed as effectively as cheap perfume.

'So many of you,' she whispered. 'Has the devil sent you?'

Walsh took her arm and eased her backwards, allowing his men in behind. 'Shall we go into the sitting-room, Mrs Thompson? No point in standing around on the doorstep.'

She put up a feeble resistance. 'What is this?' she beseeched, eyes welling, little heels digging into the hall carpet. 'Please don't touch me.'

McLoughlin slipped his hand under her other arm and, together, they whisked her through the sitting-room door and into a chair. While McLoughlin kept her seated with a firm hand on her shoulder, Walsh directed his men to a thorough search of the house and garden. He flashed the warrant under her eyes before tucking it back into his jacket pocket and sitting in the chair opposite her.

'Well, now, Mrs Thompson,' he said genially. 'Off for your little rest by the sea?'

She shook McLoughlin's hand from her shoulder but remained seated. 'I'm expecting the Vicar at any moment to take me to the station,' she announced with dignity. McLoughlin noticed a thinning patch in her hair. He found it oddly embarrassing as if she had taken off part of her clothing and revealed something best kept hidden.

'Then I suggest we don't beat around the bush,' announced Walsh. 'We wouldn't want to keep him waiting.'

'Why are you here? Why are your men searching my house?'

Walsh steepled his fingers in his lap. 'You remember that tramp you told us about, Mrs Thompson?' She gave a brief nod. 'We've found him.'

'Good. Then you'll know I was telling you the truth about dear Daniel's generosity.'

'Indeed, yes. He also mentioned that Mr Thompson gave him a bottle of whisky and twenty pounds.'

The sad eyes lit with pleasure. 'I told you Daniel was a saint. He would have given the shirt off his back if the man had asked for it.'

McLoughlin took the chair next to Walsh and leaned forward aggressively. 'The tramp's name is Wally Ferris. I've had a long talk with him. He says you and Mr Thompson wanted rid of him, that's why you were so generous.'

'The ingratitude,' she gasped, her lips parting on a tremor. 'What did our Lord say? "Give to the poor and you shall have treasure in Heaven." My poor Daniel has earned his place there by his kindness. The same cannot be said of this tramp.'

'He also said,' continued McLoughlin doggedly, 'that he found your husband hiding in the shed outside.'

She tittered behind her hand like a teenager. 'Actually,' she said, looking directly at him, 'it was the other way round. Daniel found the tramp hiding in the shed. He went out to look for a paintbrush and tripped over a bundle of old clothes behind some boxes at the back. Imagine his surprise when the bundle spoke.'

Her words carried conviction and McLoughlin knew a sudden doubt. Had he relied too heavily on an old man who, by his own admission, lived in an alcoholic haze? 'Wally claims it was raining while he was in your shed. I've checked with the local meteorological office and they have no record of any rainfall on Wednesday, twenty-fourth May. The storms began two days later and lasted on and off for the next three days.'

'Poor man,' she murmured. 'I told Daniel at the time we should have tried to get him to a doctor. He was drunk and very confused. You know, he asked me if I was his sister. He thought I'd come looking for him at last.'

'But, Mrs Thompson,' said Walsh, allowing surprise into his voice, 'if he was as drunk as you say, why did you give him a bottle of whisky? Were you not compounding his already severe problems?'

She cast her eyes to the ceiling. 'He begged us in tears, Inspector. Who were we to refuse? Judge not and you shall not be judged. If the poor man chooses to kill himself with demon alcohol, I have no right to condemn him.'

185

'But you do have the right to speed up the process, I suppose,' said McLoughlin sarcastically.

'He's a sad little man whose only comfort lies in a whisky bottle,' she said quietly. 'It would have been cruel to deny him his comfort. We gave him money to spend on food, shoes for his feet and we urged him to seek help for his addiction. There was not much more we could do. My conscience is clear, Sergeant.'

'Wally claims he came here on Saturday, May twenty-seventh.' Walsh spoke casually.

She wrinkled her forehead and thought for a moment. 'But it can't have been,' she said with genuine puzzlement. 'Daniel was here. Didn't we decide it was the twenty-fourth?'

McLoughlin was fascinated by her performance. It occurred to him that she had expunged the memory of murder from her mind and had convinced herself that the story she told was the real one. If that was so, they were going to have the devil's own job bringing a prosecution. With only Wally's testimony, backed by the woman in the council house, they wouldn't stand a chance. They needed a confession.

'The date is corroborated by an independent witness,' he told her.

'Really?' she breathed. 'How extraordinary. I don't remember seeing anyone with him and we are so secluded here.' She fingered her cross and gazed at him with reproachful eyes. 'Who could it be, I wonder?'

Walsh cleared his throat noisily. 'Would it interest you to know where we found your husband's shoes, Mrs Thompson?'

'Not really,' she assured him. 'I assume from the things you've said that the tramp – Wally – discarded them as useless. I find that hurtful to my dear Daniel's memory.'

'You're very sure he's dead, aren't you?' said McLoughlin.

She produced her lace hankie like a magician and dabbed at the inevitable tears. 'He would never leave me,' came the refrain.

'We found the shoes in the woods at Streech Grange, not far from the ice house,' said Walsh, watching her closely.

'Did you?' she asked politely.

'Wally spent the night of the twenty-seventh of May in the ice house and abandoned the shoes in the woods the next morning as he left.'

She lowered the handkerchief and looked with curiosity from one to the other. 'Really,' she commented. Her expression was one of bafflement. 'Is that significant?'

'You do know we've found a corpse in Streech Grange ice house, don't you?' McLoughlin remarked brutally. 'It is male, aged between fifty and sixty, broad build, grey hair and five feet ten inches tall. He was murdered two months ago, around the time your husband went missing.'

Her amazement was utter. For several seconds a kaleidoscope of emotions transformed her face. The two men watched closely, but if guilt was there, it was impossible to isolate. To the forefront was surprise. 'I had no idea,' she said, 'no idea at all. No one's said anything to me. Whose corpse is it?'

McLoughlin turned to Walsh and raised a despairing eyebrow. 'It's been in all the newspapers, Mrs Thompson,' said the Inspector, 'and on the local television news. You could hardly have missed it. The body has decomposed to such an extent that we have not yet been able to identify it. We have our suspicions, however.' He studied her pointedly.

She was taking deep breaths as though breathing were difficult. The rouge stood out on her cheeks in bright spots. 'I don't have a television,' she told them. 'Daniel used to get a paper at work and tell me all the news when he came home.' She struggled for air. 'God,' she said surprisingly, holding a hand to her chest, 'they've all been keeping it from me, protecting me. I had no idea. No one's said a word.'

'No idea we'd found the body, or no idea there was a body to find?' asked McLoughlin.

She digested the implications of this for a moment. 'No idea there was one, of course,' she snapped, eyeing him with dislike. She calmed her breathing with a conscious effort and tightened her lips into their customary thin lines. She addressed herself to Walsh. 'I now understand your interest in Daniel's shoes,' she told him. A small tic had started above her lip. 'You are assuming they are connected in some way with this body you've found.'

'Perhaps,' he said guardedly.

A gleam of triumph showed in her eyes. 'Yet this tramp you've found has proved they can't be. You say he spent the night of the twenty-seventh in the – what did you call it?'

'Ice house.'

'In the ice house. I assume he wouldn't have stayed if the dead body had been there, too, so he must have abandoned the shoes before the body ever got there.' She seemed to relax slightly. 'I cannot see a connection, merely a bizarre coincidence.'

'You're absolutely right,' agreed Walsh. 'In that sense, there is no connection.'

'Then why have you been asking me questions?'

'The bizarre coincidence led us to the tramp, Mrs Thompson, and to some interesting facts about you and your husband. We can prove he was alive in this house two days after you reported him missing and well outside the time for which you'd provided yourself with an alibi. Mr Thompson has not been seen since, and a week ago we were presented with an unidentifiable body, corresponding to his description and less than four miles away. Frankly, we can make out an excellent case against you for the murder of your husband on or after the twenty-eighth of May.'

The tic came faster. 'It can't be Daniel's body.'

'Why not?' demanded McLoughlin.

She was silent, gathering her thoughts.

'Why not?' he pressed.

'Because I had a letter from him about two weeks ago.' Her shoulders slumped and she started to weep again. 'It was a beastly letter, telling me how much he hated me and what a bad wife I'd— '

McLoughlin cut her short. 'Will you show us the letter, please?'

'I can't,' she sobbed. 'I burnt it. He'd written such vile things.'

There was a knock on the door and one of the uniformed policemen came in. 'We've been through the house and garden, sir.' He shook his head at Walsh's questioning look. 'Nothing yet. There's still this room to do and Mrs Thompson's cases. They're locked. We'll need the keys.'

The little woman grabbed her handbag and held it to her middle. 'I will not give you the keys. You will not search my cases. They contain my underwear.'

'Fetch me a WPC,' instructed the Inspector. He leaned towards Mrs Thompson. 'I'm sorry, but you've no choice in the matter. If you prefer it, I will ask the WPC to bring the cases in here and you may watch while she examines the contents.' He held out his hand. 'The keys, please.'

'Oh, very well,' she said crossly, delving into her handbag and producing two small keys tied together with a white ribbon. 'Personally, I think the whole thing's outrageous. I intend to make a strong complaint to the Chief Constable.'

Walsh wasn't surprised she objected to having her underwear scrutinised. Pieces of filmy black lacework, more at home in a brothel, he would have thought, than in the luggage of this drab, boring woman, were held up for inspection. But a truth he had discovered during his career was that some of the unlikeliest women possessed attractive lingerie. His own wife was a case in point. She had come to bed every night of their married lives in silks or soft satins, with only him to appreciate the effect. And for a long time he *had* appreciated it and done his best to show it, before years of indignant rejection had taught him that Mrs Walsh did not don her lingerie for his benefit but for some private delight of her own. And he had long since given up trying to discover what that was.

The WPC shook her head as she re-locked the cases. 'Nothing there, sir.'

'I did tell you,' said Mrs Thompson. 'Heaven knows what you think you're looking for.'

'Your handbag, please.'

She relinquished it with a moue of disgust. The constable emptied the contents carefully on to the coffee table, felt the soft leather bag for anything hidden in the lining, then sorted through the various objects. She glanced enquiringly at Walsh. 'Seems OK, sir.'

He gestured to her to return everything to the bag. 'Would you rather wait outside while we search this room?' he asked Mrs Thompson.

She settled herself deeply into her chair, gripping the cushion beneath her as if she expected to be wrestled from it. 'I would not, Inspector.'

As the search got under way, Walsh returned to the questioning. 'You say you've had a letter from your husband. Why haven't you mentioned this before?'

She cringed away from him, tucking herself sideways into a tight ball in the chair. 'Because I have only my pride left. I didn't want anyone to know how shamefully he's treated me.' She dabbed at her dry eyes.

'What was the postmark?' asked McLoughlin.

'London, I think.'

'Presumably the letter was handwritten,' he mused. 'He wouldn't have access to a typewriter.'

She nodded. 'It was.'

'What sort of envelope?'

She thought for a moment. 'White,' she told him.

McLoughlin laughed. 'It won't wash, you know. You can't just keep pulling lies out of the hat and expect us to applaud your ingenuity. We'll check with your postman. In a place like this you'll have had the same postman for years, it's probably the chap who runs the little shop-cum-post-office near the church. Your letters will have been a source of great interest to him in the last couple of months. He's probably scrutinised every one carefully in the hopes of being first with news of the errant Daniel. You won't persuade us your husband's still alive by dreaming up letters, Mrs Thompson.'

She glanced beyond him to where the woman constable was going through the sideboard. 'Ask the postman, Sergeant. You'll find I'm telling you the truth.' She spoke with sincerity, but the look in her eyes was as level and calculating as any he'd seen. 'If only I'd known what was in your mind, I'd have told you about the letter the first time you came.'

McLoughlin stood up and leaned over her, resting his hands on the arms of her chair. 'Why were you so shocked to hear about the body at the ice house? If you know your husband's alive, it couldn't mean anything to you.'

'This man's threatening me,' she snapped at Walsh. 'I don't like it.' She cringed, deep into the chair.

'Back off, Andy.'

'With pleasure.' Without warning, he hooked his hand under her arm and stepped back sharply. She popped out of the chair like a champagne cork, then wriggled and spat with ferocity. He clung on to a flailing arm, dodged a swipe from the other and felt warm spittle smear his cheek. 'The chair, sir,' he called. 'She's hiding something.'

'Got it.'

McLoughlin took a grip on both her arms, arching his body away to avoid the kicking points of her shoes. 'Come on, you sods,' he shouted angrily at the two constables. 'She's pulverising me. Who's got the handcuffs, for God's sake?'

'Bastard!' she screamed. 'Bloody fucking bastard!' She rolled another ball of spittle into her mouth and launched it at him. To his immense disgust, it caught his lip and dribbled inside.

The constables, galvanised out of frozen inactivity, snapped on the handcuffs and pushed the woman on to the sofa. She looked at McLoughlin's vain attempts to get rid of the venom and laughed. 'Serves you bloody right. I hope you catch something.'

'Looks like I've caught you,' he said grimly. He turned to Walsh. 'What is it?'

Walsh handed him a thin envelope. 'She must have slipped it out of her bag when we were gawping at her blasted knickers.' He chuckled good-humouredly. 'Waste of time, dear lady. We'd have found it eventually.'

McLoughlin opened the envelope. Inside were two aeroplane tickets, made out to Mr and Mrs Thompson, for a flight to Marbella that evening. 'Where's he been hiding all this time?' he asked her.

'Go to hell!'

'Mrs Thompson! Mrs Thompson!' exclaimed a shocked voice from the doorway. 'Some control, I beg you.'

She laughed. 'Go and play with yourself, you silly little man.'

'Is she mad?' asked the horrified Vicar.

'In a manner of speaking,' said Inspector Walsh cheerfully.

TWENTY-ONE

Anne laughed as McLoughlin told the story. Colour had returned to her face and lively enjoyment sparkled in her eyes. The only visible reminder that she'd been attacked was the brilliant red and white spotted scarf that she had tied, bandit-style, over her bandage. Against medical advice, she had discharged herself the day before, maintaining that five days in hospital was the absolute maximum that a sentient drug addict could tolerate. Bowing to the inevitable, Phoebe had brought her home after extracting a promise that she would do precisely as she was told. Anne gave the promise readily. 'Just lead me to a cigarette,' she said, 'and I'll do anything you say.'

What she didn't know was that Phoebe had also assumed responsibility for her safety. 'If she leaves hospital, Mrs Maybury, we won't be able to protect her,' Walsh had pointed out, 'any more than we can protect you. We simply haven't enough men to patrol Streech Grange. I shall be advising her to stay put in hospital, just as I've advised you to move out.'

'Don't waste your breath, Inspector,' Phoebe told him contemptuously. 'Streech is our home. If we had to rely on you to protect us it wouldn't be worth living in.'

Walsh shrugged. 'You're a very foolish woman, Mrs Maybury.'

Diana, who was in the room with them, was incensed. 'My God, you really are the pits,' she snapped. 'Two days ago you didn't believe a word Phoebe told you. Now, because Sergeant McLoughlin took the trouble to find some evidence, you tell her she's a fool for not running away on your bloody say-so. Well, let me tell you this, the only thing that's changed in the last two days is your mind.' She stamped her foot in exasperation. 'Why the hell should we run away today when we didn't run away yesterday or the day before that? The danger's the same for God's sake. And who do you imagine has been protecting us all this time?'

'Who, Mrs Goode?'

She turned her back on him.

'We've been protecting ourselves of course,' said Phoebe coolly, 'and we'll go on doing it. The dogs are the best safeguard we've got.'

Anne was propped on pillows in her favourite armchair, her feet resting on Phoebe's tapestry stool, an old donkey jacket which passed for a dressing-gown round her shoulders, a pencil stuck behind one ear. She was, McLoughlin thought, completely careless of other people's opinions. The message was simple: I am what you see; take it or leave it. He wondered if it came from supreme self-confidence or total indifference. Whatever it was, he wished he shared it. For his own part, he still felt the need of others' approval.

'So where was Mr Thompson hiding?' she asked him.

'She wouldn't tell us, but it wasn't very difficult to find him. He turned up like a lamb, for the seven-thirty flight to Marbella.'

'Skedaddling with the loot?'

McLoughlin nodded. Once caught and identified by Wally as the man in the shed, Daniel Thompson had offered to co-operate. The idea had come to them, he said, when they had found a book in the library describing the life of luxury enjoyed by British embezzlers on the Spanish riviera. Thompson's engineering business was on the decline and he had complained to his wife about the injustice of having to work his balls off to keep it alive when other men, faced with the same problem, simply absconded with the capital and lived it up in the sun. The answer was simple, announced Mrs T., they too would follow the sun. They had no dependants, she had never liked England, positively loathed East Deller where the community was worthy and stultifying, and she had no intention of spending the next ten years scrimping and saving to keep Daniel's business from going broke. 'The most extraordinary thing,' said Thompson reminiscently, 'was how easy it was to persuade people to invest in transparent radiators. It just proved to me how much money and how little sense there is floating around in the South.' He reminded McLoughlin of Arthur Daley.

'What do you make transparent radiators from?' he'd asked him curiously.

'Toughened, heatproof glass,' said Thompson, 'the same sort of stuff they use for those saucepans. The idea was to add dyes to the water in the expansion tank and watch them flow through the system.'

'Mrs Goode said it could have revolutionised interior design.'

The saintly Daniel sighed. 'That was the terrible irony of it all. I think she may have been right. I opted for the idea because while it was feasible to make the things, it was also absurd enough to make bankruptcy a likely possibility. Imagine my surprise when, without

193

any publicity, it started to take off. By that time, of course, it was too late. To turn the business into a success then would have presented enormous difficulties. On top of which, Maisie – the wife' – he explained helpfully – 'had set her heart on the Costa del Sol. Sad, really,' he mused with a faraway look in his eyes. 'They might well have made my fortune and we could have retired to the sun anyway.'

'Why did you bother with the disappearing act? Why not simply pack up, both of you, and go?'

Mr Thompson beamed. 'Moonlight flits worry people,' he said, 'make them suspicious, and we didn't want the Spanish to take against us. They're not as easy-going as they used to be. While Maisie remained, everyone merely felt sorry for her for having married so weak and inept a man.'

'So where have you been for the last two months?'

'East Deller,' he said, as if surprised by the question, 'until two nights ago when I went to a B & B so Maisie could pack up. Your visits were becoming a little too frequent for comfort.'

'You were hiding in your own house?'

He nodded. 'It was quite safe. Maisie phoned me at my hotel in London after the police had searched the house and garden the first time. I came home during the night of the twenty-sixth and lay low in the attic. We reckoned that was safer than my being on the loose with my description floating about.'

'Wally saw you in the shed,' McLoughlin pointed out.

'That was a mistake,' he admitted. 'We thought the shed would be the best hiding place because it would be easier to escape from if the police turned up unexpectedly. Of course it was also the easiest place for someone to walk into. Not that any normal person walking in would have mattered,' he said without rancour. 'Maisie had hidden me behind a stack of old boxes, no way I'd have been seen by a casual visitor.' He tapped two pudgy forefingers together. 'But the silly old fool was looking for a place to hide himself. I don't know who got the worse shock when he pulled the boxes aside, him or me.'

'The police made two searches,' McLoughlin said. 'How did they miss you the second time?'

'Because we were expecting it. We worked out if the police made a surprise search and found nothing, they'd conclude I really had run away because of my business problems and abandoned Maisie to fend for herself. So Maisie made an anonymous phone call to stimulate another search. It was a nerve-racking two days waiting for it, but we were ready when it came. I simply hopped over the fence at the bottom of the garden and crouched in a bush in our neighbours' orchard until Maisie gave me the all-clear.' He smiled amiably. He was, as Diana had described him, built like a tank. The smile split his chubby face into two half moons, the lower half pendulous with double chins. 'After that we had no more trouble till you turned up with those shoes. Until then my disappearance had been a nine-day wonder.'

McLoughlin acknowledged he was right. 'You were taking a gamble, though. Neighbours must have been popping in all the time.'

'Not after Maisie developed her wonderfully outrageous sex mania,' said Thompson. 'The women kept coming for a few days out of kindness, but it's amazing how rapidly embarrassment alienates people. Maisie should have gone on the stage, I've always said it. We got the idea of the attic from Anne Frank's diary,' he volunteered.

'And she really didn't know about the body in the ice house? I find that extraordinary.'

'It was a damn nuisance,' said Thompson, showing annoyance for the first time. 'She couldn't be seen to change her habits. If she had rented a telly or started buying papers, people might have thought she was taking an interest again. Wrong image, do you see?'

McLoughlin nodded. 'And no one told her because they were afraid the body was yours.'

Daniel sighed. 'Hoist with our own petard.'

'Why did you leave it so long to fly out? You could have gone weeks ago.'

'We were greedy,' confessed Thompson. 'We wanted the money from selling the house. You're talking over a quarter of a million pounds for a property like that. It was the icing on the gingerbread. The plan was for Maisie to become more and more depressed until the obvious solution was to sell the house and move somewhere smaller which had no memories for her. No one would have questioned it. If the truth be told, they'd have been relieved to see the back of her. Then, with the money safely under our belts, we were off on a ferry to France and from there to sunny Spain.'

'And you were intending to use your own passports?'

The other man nodded.

'You'd been reported missing, Mr Thompson. You'd have been stopped.'

'Oh, I don't think so, Sergeant,' he said comfortably. 'Six months on, brouhaha died down, hundreds of people on day trips, a middle-aged couple with a common name. What would they have against me anyway? My wife could testify I was no longer missing. And it's not as though there's a warrant out for my arrest, is there?' He cocked his head on one side and considered the Sergeant with amusement.

'No,' McLoughlin admitted.

'I was incompetent,' said Thompson. 'I admit it freely. But no one person lost very much money through my failure.' He folded his hands across his plump stomach. 'My employees have all found other jobs and the Inland Revenue has agreed to honour their National Insurance contributions which I so rashly – how shall I put it – "borrowed" to keep the business afloat.' He winked outrageously. 'I give credit to my number two for that. He's done all the negotiations on their behalf, or so Maisie tells me. Splendid chap, great organisational flair, full of integrity. He's sorted out the mess I made and wound up the business. Mind you, he's said some harsh words to Maisie on the phone, called me an amateurish bungler, but I don't hold it against him.' He flicked a speck of dust from his jumper. 'My investors took a gamble on me which was sadly misplaced, but they have cheerfully cut their losses and moved on to more lucrative ventures. I'm delighted. It saddened me to have failed them.'

'Hang on,' said McLoughlin sharply. 'You didn't fail them, Mr Thompson. You embezzled their money.'

'Who says so?'

'You admitted it yourself.'

'When?'

McLoughlin turned to WPC Brownlow who had been taking shorthand notes. 'Find that bit where he said he got the idea from British embezzlers living in Spain.'

She flicked back through her notebook. 'He didn't actually say *he* was an embezzler,' she admitted after a couple of minutes, 'only that his business was in decline.'

'Skip on a few pages,' said McLoughlin. 'He said it was ridiculously easy to get people to invest in the radiator idea.'

'It was,' said Thompson. 'It was a good idea.'

'Dammit all,' exploded McLoughlin. 'You said it was absurd enough to make bankruptcy likely.'

'And I was proved right. That's just what happened.'

'You didn't go bankrupt because it wouldn't work. You salted the money away. You said yourself it could have been a great success.'

Thompson sighed. 'I'm sure it would have been, too, if I'd had more business sense. My problem, as I've tried to explain to you, is incompetence. Are you going to arrest us, Sergeant?'

'Yes, Mr Thompson, I bloody well am.'

'On what charge?'

'Wasting police time, for a kick-off, while I find someone who's willing to press a more serious charge.'

'Who?'

'One of your creditors, Mrs Goode.'

'I'll get my solicitor to discuss an out-of-court settlement with her,' he said comfortably. 'Much more satisfactory than pursuing me through the courts.'

'I'll get your wife on an assault charge.'

'Poor Maisie. She's demented, you know.' He winked with enormous enjoyment. 'Doesn't know what she's doing half the time. A short spell of treatment with a sympathetic doctor will do her far more good than a police prosecution. The Vicar will agree with me on that.'

'You're a pair of rogues.'

'Harsh words, Sergeant. The truth is I'm a coward who couldn't face the disappointment of those who'd put their trust in me. I ran away and hid. Contemptible, I agree, but hardly criminal.' His gaze was level and sincere, but his double chins wobbled. Whether from mirth or contrition, McLoughlin couldn't say.

By the end of his account, Anne was laughing so much it hurt. 'Did you let them go?'

He grinned sheepishly. 'It was like trying to hold on to a couple of eels. Every time you thought you'd got a grip, they wriggled out of it. They're back home now, but due to answer a charge of obstruction in a couple of weeks' time. Meanwhile, I've got on to his number two, who's hopping mad at being taken for a ride, and told him to go through the books with an accountant and look for straightforward embezzlement.'

'He won't find it,' said Anne, mopping her eyes. 'Mr Thompson sounds like a real pro. It'll all be neatly tied up in a villa in Spain by now.'

'Perhaps.' McLoughlin stretched his arms above his head, then subsided comfortably into his chair. He had been up all night again and he was tired.

Jane had told Anne that McLoughlin was in the wrong job. Why? Anne had asked. Because he was over-sensitive to other people's problems. Anne watched him through the smoke from her cigarette. She had none of her god-daughter's naivety so her appraisal was untinged by sentiment. Lust after him she might, but it in no way affected her objectivity. He was not troubled by over-sensitivity towards others, she concluded, but by over-sensitivity towards himself, a trap, in Anne's view, that far too many men fell into. To

197

burden oneself with a socially acceptable image was to put oneself in a strait-jacket. She wondered when McLoughlin had last had a good laugh at himself – if ever. Life for him, she thought, was a series of hurdles which had to be taken cleanly. To touch one would represent failure.

'What are you thinking?' he asked.

'I was wondering why men take themselves so seriously.'

'I didn't know they did.'

'I'm trying to think if I've ever met one who doesn't. Your Mr Thompson sounds a likely candidate.' She waggled her toes on the tapestry stool. 'A woman's problems centre round her biological programming. Without her willingness to reproduce and nurture a new generation, the species would die out. Her frustrations come from the species' unwillingness to recognise the sacrifices she makes for the general good. You don't get paid by a grateful government for being on duty twenty-four hours a day to raise a family; you don't get an MBE for training your children to be good citizens; nine times out of ten even your children don't thank you for your efforts, but chuck in your face that they didn't ask to be born anyway.' She tapped the end of her cigarette against the ashtray and chuckled. 'It's a dog's life being a mother. There's no management structure to speak of, no independent arbitrator, no dismissal procedure for repeated offences and no promotion prospects. Emotional blackmail and sexual harassment are rampant and backhanders commonplace.' Her eyes gleamed as she leant forward. 'No man would tolerate it. His self-esteem would suffer.'

McLoughlin cursed himself silently for being a fool. He should have trusted his first impressions and steered clear. She would have to be very special in bed to make it worth his while to sit through feminist clap-trap to get her there. After all, he thought, was there really so much difference between her and his absent wife? The complaints were the same, merely more fluent and better articulated from Anne. He vowed to become celibate. He had neither the inclination nor the energy to wage war every time he felt randy. If the price of pleasure was capitulation, he could do without it. He'd had to grovel past his wife's headaches and stay awake through low-budget late films for Saturday night sex. He was damned if he'd do it for a woman he wasn't tied to.

He stood up abruptly and unleashed his pent-up rage and disappointment. 'Let me tell you something, *Ms* Cattrell. I'm sick to death of hearing women complain about their lot. You're all so bloody strident about what a grand time men have and how badly we treat you.' He walked to the fireplace and leaned both hands on the mantelpiece, staring into the unlit fire. 'Do you think yours is the only sex to suffer from biological programming? The burden on men to perform is infinitely greater. If we weren't programmed to sow our seed, female disinclination would have wiped out the human race centuries ago. You try persuading a woman to have sex. It costs money, effort, emotional commitment and the trauma of regular rejection. If a man wants to do his bit by society, he has to spend a lifetime in chains flogging his guts out to keep his woman content and well-fed so that she first agrees to have his offspring and then looks after them properly when she's got them.' He turned to look at her. 'It's humiliating and degrading,' he said with bitterness.'My procreative chemistry is no different from a dog's. Nature compels us both to eject sperm into a fertile female, the difference is that he doesn't have to justify why he wants to do it whereas I do. Think about that next time you feel like sneering at male self-esteem. It's fragile in the extreme. You're damn right I take myself seriously. I bloody well have to. I've only my office left where rules of behaviour still apply and where I don't have to tie myself in knots to achieve the goals set for me.'

She took an apple from the bowl beside her and tossed it to him. 'You're doing great, McLoughlin. In a minute you'll be telling me you'd rather be a woman.'

He looked at her, saw the amused lift of her lips and laughed. 'I damn nearly did. You're winding me up.'

'No,' she said with a smile, 'I'm winding you down. Life is pure farce from beginning to end, with a little black comedy thrown in for shade. If it was anything else, mankind would have stuck his collective head in the gas oven years ago. No one could tolerate seventy years of tragedy. When I die – probably of cancer – Jane has promised to put on my tombstone: "Here lies Anne Cattrell who laughed her way through it. The joke was on her but at least she knew it." ' She tossed another apple into the air and caught it. 'In a couple of weeks, if you last the pace, you could be as cynical as I am, McLoughlin. You'll be a happy man, my son.'

He sat down with the apple clenched between his teeth and drew his briefcase towards him. 'You're not all cynic,' he said, speaking round the apple.

She smiled. 'What makes you say that?'

'I've read your diary.' He snapped the locks on the briefcase, half-opened it and withdrew the slim volume.

She watched him curiously. 'Did you enjoy it?'

'Was I supposed to?'

'No,' she said tartly. 'I didn't write it for publication.'

'Good thing too,' he said frankly. 'It needs editing to make it readable.'

She glared at him. 'You would know, I suppose?' She was incredibly hurt. Her writing, even the writing she did for herself, mattered to her.

'I can read.'

'I can hold a paintbrush. That doesn't make me an expert on art.' She looked pointedly at her watch. 'Shouldn't you be trying to solve a murder? As far as I can see you're still no nearer finding out who the body belongs to or, for that matter, who hit me on the head.' She couldn't give a damn what he thought, he was only a policeman, so why did her stomach feel as if it had just bounced off the floor?

He munched on his apple. 'P. needs editing out,' he told her. 'P. ruins it.' He flicked the diary into her lap. 'The carving-knife is still at the Station, awaiting your signature. I rescued this early on to prevent Friar sneaking it out to photocopy the rude bits.' He was sitting with his back to the windows and his eyes, shadowed, gave nothing away. She couldn't tell if he was joking.

'Pity. Friar might have appreciated it.'

'Tell me about P., Anne.'

She eyed him cautiously. 'What do you want to know?'

'Would he have attacked you?'

'No.'

'Sure? Perhaps he's the jealous type. It was one of his Special Brew bottles that was used to hit you, and I'm told he never lets them out of the pub.'

She could deny that P. and Paddy were one – the prospect of McLoughlin meeting the P. he had read about rather appalled her – but that would be coy, and Anne was never coy. 'I'm positive,' she said. 'Have you spoken to him?'

'Not yet. We only got confirmation of the forensic results this morning.' The match on Anne's blood and hair proved the bottle was the weapon, but the other results were disappointing. A smudged set of fingerprints round the neck and an incomplete footprint built up from barely seen depressions in the ground. It wasn't enough to take them any further.

Anne wished she knew what he was thinking. Was he a harsh judge? Would he ever understand how Paddy, just because he always came back, however irregularly, made Streech bearable? Somehow she doubted it, for, in spite of his strange attraction to her, McLoughlin was a conventional man. The attraction wouldn't last, she knew that. Sooner or later he would snap back into character and then she would be remembered only as a brief madness. And for Anne, there would be just Paddy, once again, to remind her that the walls of Streech Grange were not totally impenetrable. Tired tears pricked at the back of her eyes. 'He's a kind man,' she said, 'and he understands everything.'

If McLoughlin understood, he didn't show it. He left without saying goodbye.

Paddy was hefting empty beer barrels at the rear of the pub. He eyed McLoughlin thoughtfully as he swung another barrel effortlessly atop the pile. 'Can I help you?'

'Detective Sergeant McLoughlin, Silverborne Police.' Imagination had created in McLoughlin's mind a huge, muscular Adonis with the magnetic attraction of the North Pole and the brain of Einstein. The reality was a big, rather overweight, hairy man in a tatty jumper and seated trousers. The jealous fire dimmed perceptibly in McLoughlin's belly. He showed Paddy a photograph of the stone beer bottle, taken after its removal from the undergrowth. 'Do you recognise it?'

Paddy squinted briefly at the picture. 'Maybe.'

'I'm told you bottle your Special in it.'

For a moment they scented the air suspiciously like two powerful mongrels poised to defend their territory. Then Paddy chose to back off. He shrugged good-humouredly. 'OK, yes, it looks like one of mine,' he said, 'but it's a hobby. I'm writing a book on traditional beer-making methods to make damn sure the old ways aren't forgotten.' His gaze was level and without guile. 'I host the odd tasting session where I give it away to the locals to get their opinions.' He studied the other's dark face, looking for a reaction. 'All right, so I may have asked for a donation from time to time towards my costs. That's not unreasonable, it's an expensive hobby.' He found the other's silence irritating. 'Dammit, man, haven't your lot got more important things to exercise your minds at the moment? Who gave it to you anyway? I'll skin the bastard.'

'Is it true you never let these bottles out of the pub, Mr Clarke?' McLoughlin asked coldly.

'Yes, it's true, and I'd bloody well like to get my hands on the bugger who took it. Who was it?'

McLoughlin tapped the black stain round the bottom of the monochrome bottle. 'That's blood, Mr Clarke, Miss Cattrell's blood.'

The big man became very still. 'What the hell is this?'

'It's the weapon that was used to beat a woman's skull in. I thought you might know how it found its way into her garden.'

Paddy opened his mouth to say something, then sank abruptly on

201

to the nearest barrel. 'Jesus Christ! Those bottles weigh a ton. I heard she was all right, but Jesus!'

'How did the bottle get into her garden, Mr Clarke?'

Paddy took no notice. 'Robinson said she'd had a knock on the head. I thought it was concussion. Those bloody wankers keep calling it concussion.'

'What wankers?'

'Journalists.'

'Someone fractured her skull.'

Paddy stared at the ground. 'Is she all right?'

'They used one of your bottles to do it.'

'Goddammit, man, I asked you a question.' He surged to his feet and stared angrily into McLoughlin's face. 'Is she all right?'

'Yes. But why are you so interested? Did you hit her harder than you meant to?'

Anger flared briefly in Paddy's face. He glanced towards the kitchen door to make sure it was closed. He lowered his voice. 'You're on the wrong track. Anne's a friend of mine. We go back a long way. She'll tell you I wouldn't hurt her.'

'It was dark. Perhaps you thought it was Mrs Goode or Mrs Maybury.'

'Don't be a fool, man. I go back a long way with them, too. Hell, they're all friends of mine.'

McLoughlin's mouth dropped open. 'All three of them?'

'Yes.'

'You're telling me you sleep with all three of them?'

Paddy made damping gestures with his hands. 'Keep your voice down for God's sake. Who said anything about sleeping with anybody? It's damn lonely up there. I keep each one company from time to time, that's all.'

McLoughlin shook with laughter as the jealous flame spluttered and died. 'Do they know?'

Paddy sensed the lack of hostility and grinned. 'I don't know. It's not the sort of thing you ask, is it?' He made a snap judgement. 'Will your conscience allow you a bottle of Special? We might as well drink it before Customs and Excise get their miserable paws on it. And while we're enjoying it, I'll give you a list of all my Special customers. I never let strangers near it, so I know each customer personally. The bastard you're looking for has to be one of them, and I rather think I know who it is. There's only one person in this village who's stupid enough and vindictive enough.' He led McLoughlin across the yard and into the room behind the garage where the rich smell of fermenting malt tingled in the nose. 'To tell you the truth, I've often toyed with the idea of doing the thing properly and going into full legal production. Maybe this is the push I needed. The wife can take over the pub licence, she's a far better landlord than I am.' He took two unopened bottles, removed the clamped rubber stoppers and with immense care poured a deep amber liquid with a foaming white head into two straight-sided glasses. He handed one to McLoughlin. 'Be advised by me, Sergeant.' There was a twinkle in his eye. 'You have all the time in the world, so approach it the way you approach your women. Slowly, lovingly, patiently, and with infinite respect. Because if you don't, you'll be flat on the floor within three mouthfuls, wondering what hit you.'

'Is that your secret?'

'It is.'

McLoughlin raised his glass. 'Cheers.'

The letter was waiting on Detective Sergeant Robinson's desk when he arrived that morning. The handwriting on the envelope was childish and unformed, the postmark local. He ripped it open eagerly and spread the lined paper flat on the desk in front of him. The lines were covered in the same unformed script, a rambling, hard-to-read account of a bizarre happening one night in the middle of May. Eddie Staines, anonymously, had come up trumps.

You been asking about a woman when and so forth. It were a Sunday. Know that becos my girls relijus and took some purswading becos she'd been to comunion. Must of been May 14 as May 12 is my birthday and it was by way of a late pressent. We did it in Grange woods as per normal. We left after 12 and wolked along the wall by the farm. We heard this waleing and weeping on the other side. My girl wanted to beet it but I hopped up for a look. Well you got it rong see. It was a man not a woman and he was rocking about and banging his head. Mad as a hatter if you ask me. I shone the torch on him and said was he all write. He said fuck off so I did. I seen the descripshun of the dead bloke. Sounds write to me. He had long grey hair anyways. Forgot about it till reesently. Thing is I knew him. Couldn't put a name to him mind just knew his face from sumwere. But it weren't no one reglar if you follow. Reckon now it was Mayberry. Thats all.

With promotion signs flickering in his eyes, Sergeant Robinson rang through to Walsh. He had a momentary qualm about his promise of anonymity – there was no way he could keep Eddie's identity secret now – but it was only momentary. When all was said and done, Eddie had not threatened to string him up by his balls.

TWENTY-TWO

McLoughlin threw open the glass doors of the Police Station and let the heat from outside billow in behind him like a swelling spinnaker. Paddy's Special, taken slowly, lovingly and with immense respect, was swirling nicely in his brain. ' "Now's the day and now's the hour," ' he roared. ' "See the front of battle lour." Where's Monty? I need troops.'

The Desk Sergeant gave a grunt of amusement. There *was* a certain skinny similarity between Walsh and Montgomery. 'On manoeuvres.'

'Hell!'

'Someone's identified the body.'

'And?'

'David Maybury. The Inspector's wetting himself.'

Shock waves drove the alcohol from McLoughlin's brain. Godammit, he thought, it couldn't be. He'd come to love those women. The pain of loving them gnawed at his insides like a half-starved rat. 'Where's he gone?'

The other shook his head. 'No idea. Presumably questioning the witness. He and Nick took off like scalded cats about two hours ago.'

'Well, he's wrong.' His voice was harsh. 'It's not Maybury. Tell him that if he gets back before I do, will you?'

Not bloody likely, thought the Desk Sergeant, watching the angry young man shoulder open the doors and surge out on to the pavement. If McLoughlin was intent on self-destruction, he had no plans to go with him. He glanced at his watch and saw with relief that his shift was nearly over.

McLoughlin pulled Anne bodily out of her chair and shook her till her teeth rattled. 'Was it David Maybury?' he shouted at her. 'Was it?' he spat.

She didn't say anything and, with a groan, he pushed her from him. The donkey jacket slipped from her shoulders, leaving her clad

204

only in a pair of men's pyjamas that were far too big for her. She looked oddly pathetic, like a child playing at being an adult. 'I don't know,' she said with dignity. 'The body was unrecognisable, but I shouldn't think it was David. He's not likely to have come back here after ten years, assuming he was still alive.'

'Don't play games, Anne,' he said angrily. 'You saw the body before it rotted. Who was it?'

She shook her head.

'Someone's ID'd it. They say it's David Maybury.'

She licked her lips but didn't answer.

'Help me.'

'I can't.'

'Can't or won't?'

'Does it matter?'

'Yes,' he said bitterly, 'it matters to me. I believed in you. I believed in all of you.'

Her face twisted. 'I'm sorry.'

He gave a savage laugh. 'You're sorry? Jesus Christ!' He gripped her arms again, his long fingers curling into the flesh. 'Don't you understand, you little bitch? I trusted you. I've put my head on the line for you. Dammit, you owe me.'

There was a long silence. When she spoke, her voice was brittle. 'Well, hey, McLoughlin, never let it be said that Cattrell doesn't pay her debts.' She pulled the cord on her pyjama trousers and let them slither to the floor. 'Go ahead. Screw me. That's all you were ever interested in, wasn't it? A good fuck. Just like your precious boss ten years ago.'

The sands shifted under his feet. He raised his hands to her throat and stroked the soft white flesh of her neck.

'You didn't know?' Her eyes glittered as she put her hands between his wrists and thrust them apart to break his grip. 'The horny little bastard made Phoebe a proposition – a nice clean line drawn under the investigation in return for a weekly screw. Oh, he wasn't quite so vulgar. He dressed it up a bit.' She mimicked Walsh's voice. 'She was alone and vulnerable. He wanted to protect her. Her beauty had touched him. She deserved something better after her husband's brutal treatment.' Her lip curled in derision. 'She turned him down and told him where to stick his protection.' A strident note made her voice unattractive. 'My God, but she was naive. She never considered for one moment that the man held her future in his hands.'

'I don't believe this.'

She walked across to her armchair and took a cigarette from the packet on the arm. 'Why not?' she asked coolly, flicking her lighter. 'What makes you think you have a monopoly on wanting to ball murder suspects?' Her eyes mocked him. 'God knows what it is, but there's something very attractive about us. Perhaps it's the uncertainty.'

He shook his head. 'What did you mean when you said he held her future in his hands? You said she was naive.'

'Oh, for pity's sake,' she countered scornfully. 'Who told the world and his wife that Phoebe killed her husband? Who briefed the press, McLoughlin?'

He looked very thoughtful. 'She could have sued.'

'Who?'

'The newspapers.'

'She was never libelled. They weren't so crude as to call her a murderess. They referred to her as "an avid gardener" in one sentence, then in the next revealed that the police were digging up the flowerbeds. And all neatly sign-posted for them by your boss.'

'Why didn't she put in a complaint?' He saw the expression on her face and held up his hands. 'Don't say it. Her word against his and he was a detective inspector.' He lapsed into silence. 'So what happened?'

She drew on her cigarette and raked him with angry eyes. 'Walsh couldn't produce the goods because of course David had never been murdered, so the investigation was eventually stopped. It was then the fun started. She found herself on the wrong end of a malicious smear campaign and there wasn't a soul in this bloody place who would give her the time of day. She was on the verge of a nervous breakdown by the time I moved in. Jonny, at the age of eleven, had started to wet his bed and Jane— ' She searched his face. 'It's going to happen again. That bastard is going to throw Phoebe to the wolves a second time.' She looked pale beneath the scarlet bandanna.

'Why didn't you tell me all this at the beginning?'

'Would you have believed me?'

'No.'

'And now?'

'Maybe.' He eyed her for a long time, rubbing his jaw in thoughtful silence. 'You're a good journalist, Anne. Couldn't you have written Phoebe's side of it and got her off the hook?'

'You tell me how I can do that without giving Jane as her alibi and I'll write it. Phoebe would burn at the stake before she let her daughter become a sideshow for ghouls. Me, too, if it ccmes to that.' She inhaled deeply. 'It's not an alibi anyway. Jane might have fallen asleep.'

He nodded. 'In that case, why are you so sure he left this house alive?'

She turned away to stub out her cigarette. 'Why are *you* so sure?' She looked back at him. 'You are, aren't you?'

'Yes.'

'Because someone claims now it was David in the ice house?'

'No.'

'Why then?'

He looked at her for a long moment. 'Because you chose to bury yourself in Streech Grange. That's how I know he walked out of here alive.'

'I don't know what you're talking about.'

'You're a bloody awful liar, Cattrell.'

'I wish you wouldn't keep saying that,' she said crossly, stamping her foot, 'and I'm freezing.'

'So, stop waggling your fanny at me and put some clothes on,' he said reasonably, reaching down for her pyjama trousers and tossing them across to her. He watched while she put them on. 'It's a nice fanny, Cattrell,' he murmured, 'but I only came for the truth. I got rather more than I bargained for.'

He drove to the forensic laboratories and searched out Dr Webster in his office. 'I was passing,' he said. 'I wondered if you'd had any new ideas on that corpse of ours.'

If Dr Webster found this approach a little unorthodox, he didn't remark on it. 'I've the full report here,' he said, tapping a folder on the desk beside him. 'The typist finished this morning. You can take a copy back with you if you like.' He chuckled. 'Mind you, I don't think it's going to please George much, but there we are, he will push for instant opinions and they're not always accurate. Made any progress?'

McLoughlin made a see-saw motion with his hand. 'Not much. Our most promising lead turned up alive. Now we're in the dark again.'

'In that case I doubt that anything I've managed to piece together is going to help you much. Give me a description, better still a photograph, and I'll say yea or nay to whether he's on my slab. But I can't tell you who he is. George is on the phone every day, yelling for results, but miracles take time. Fresh bodies are one thing, bits of old shoe leather need patience to sort out.'

'What about Maybury?'

The pathologist grunted impatiently. 'You're all obsessed with that wretched man. Of course it's not Maybury. And you can tell George

I've taken a second opinion and it agrees with mine. Facts are facts,' he grumbled, 'and in this case they are not open to interpretation.'

McLoughlin breathed deeply through his nose. 'How do you know?'

'Too old. I've done a lot of work on the X-rays and the fusion's more advanced than I thought. I'm sure now we're looking at a sixty-five to seventy-year-old. The bottom line's sixty. Maybury would be what? Fifty-four, fifty-five?'

'Fifty-four.'

Webster reached for the folder and removed some photographs. 'In the report, I've come down against mutilation but it's only an opinion and I'm prepared to be proved wrong. There *are* some scratches on the bone that might have been made with a sharp knife, but my own view is it wasn't.' He pointed to one of the photographs. 'Clearly rat droppings.'

McLoughlin nodded. 'Anything else?'

'I'm in two minds about how he died. It really depends on whether he was wearing any clothes at the time of his death. Have you sorted that one out yet?'

'No.'

'I scraped up a lot of earth from the floor round the body. We've analysed it but, frankly, there's a negligible amount of blood in it.'

McLoughlin frowned. 'Go on.'

'Well, that makes it very difficult for me to say with any certainty how he died. If he was nude and he was stabbed, the ground would have been saturated with blood. If he was fully clothed and stabbed, then the clothes would have soaked up most of the blood. You'll have to find his clothes.'

'Hang on a minute, Doctor. You're saying that if he was nude he couldn't have been stabbed, but if he was clothed he might have been?'

'In essence, that's right. There's an outside chance animals might have licked the floor but you'll never get a prosecution on that.'

'Does Chief Inspector Walsh know this?'

Webster peered at him over his glasses. 'Why do you ask that?'

McLoughlin rumpled his hair. 'He hasn't mentioned it.' Or had he? McLoughlin could remember very little of what Walsh had said that first night. 'OK. Supposing he was nude. How did he die?'

Webster pursued his lips. 'Old age. Cold. From the little that's left, it's impossible to say. I couldn't find any traces of barbiturates or asphyxia, but— ' He shrugged, and tapped the photographs. 'Shoe leather. Find the clothes. They'll tell you more than I can.'

McLoughlin put his hands on the desk and hunched his shoulders.

'We've been conducting a murder enquiry on the basis that he was stabbed in the belly. Now you're telling me he could have died of natural causes. Have you any idea how many hours I've worked in the last week?'

The pathologist chuckled. 'About half as many as I have, at a rough guess. I've pulled out the stops on this one. Good grief, man, we don't get cases like this every day. Most bodies have at least ninety per cent of their constituent parts. In any case, until you produce some intact and unstained clothes to prove me wrong, stabbing still looks the most likely. Old men, wandering around nude in search of an ice house to freeze to death in, are quite outside my experience.'

McLoughlin straightened. 'Touché. Any more surprises?'

'Just a little bit of fun which I've tacked on to the end of the report, so I don't want you coming back and accusing me of putting ideas into your head.' He chuckled. 'I had another look in the ice house yesterday. It's been sealed for over a week now and the temperature's dropped considerably. The door's as old as the hills but it still fits perfectly. I was impressed. Obviously an extraordinarily efficient method of storing ice. Very cold and very sterile. Must have kept for months.'

'And?'

The doctor turned his attention to some letters in front of him. 'I've speculated on what sort of condition he would have been in if the door had remained closed until the gardener found him.' He scratched his name in spidery writing on the top letter. 'Surprisingly good, I think. I'd like to have seen it. Purely out of scientific interest, of course.'

He raised his head. McLoughlin and the report had gone.

Sergeant Bob Rogers, who had switched to the afternoon shift after a two-day break and was now on duty at the desk, looked up as McLoughlin came in through the front doors. 'Ah, Andy. The very man.' He held up the description of Wally Ferris that had circulated round the county. 'This tramp you're looking for.'

'Found him. Matter of fact, as soon as I've seen the Inspector, I'm off after him again.'

'Good, then you can bring him in. He's on our missing persons' list.'

McLoughlin walked slowly across the floor. 'You've got Wally Ferris down as a missing person? But he's been on the road for years.'

Rogers frowned and turned the list for McLoughlin to look at.

'See for yourself. The description here fits the one you put out to a T.'

McLoughlin looked at what was written. 'Did Walsh see this?'

'Left it with him the first night.'

McLoughlin reached for the telephone. 'Do me a favour, Bob. The next time you see me too hungover to double-check what that bastard does' – he pointed to his chin – 'hit me here.'

He slouched in a chair in the Chief Inspector's office and watched the thin, bloodless lips dribble smoke. Imperceptibly, the face had changed. Where respect had once fleshed it with a genial wisdom, contempt had uncovered its malice. Phrases registered here and there – 'definitely Maybury' . . . 'young man recognised him' . . . 'in the ice house two weeks' . . . 'tramp must have seen him there' . . . 'you missed it completely' . . . 'writing a report' . . . 'domestic problems can't excuse your negligence' – but the bulk of what was said passed over McLoughlin's head. He stared unblinkingly at Walsh's face and thought about the teeth behind the smile.

Walsh jabbed his pipe stem angrily at his Sergeant. 'DS Robinson is out rounding up Wally Ferris now and by God, there are going to be no mistakes this time.'

The younger man stirred. 'What will you do? Show him a photograph of Maybury and suggest he was the dead man? Wally will agree with you just to get out of here.'

'Staines has already made the identification. If Wally confirms it, we're on safe ground.'

'How old is Staines?'

'Twenty-fiveish.'

'So he was fifteen when he last saw Maybury? And he claims to have recognised him in the dark? You'll never get a prosecution on that.'

'It's a good case,' said Walsh calmly. 'We've motive, means and opportunity, plus a wealth of circumstantial evidence. Mutilation to obscure identity, lamb bones to tempt scavengers to the ice house, the removal of the clothes to hinder investigation, Fred's obliteration of tracks and evidence. With all that and the positive IDs, she'll confess this time, I think.'

McLoughlin rubbed his unshaven jaw and yawned. 'You're forgetting the forensic evidence. That's not so easy to fabricate. Webster won't lie for you.'

Walsh's ferocious brows snapped together. 'What's that supposed to mean?'

'You know damn well – *sir*. The dead man was too old to be Maybury. And what happened to all the blood?'

Walsh eyed him with intense dislike. 'Get out of here!' he growled.

There was humour in the dark face. 'Are you going to tell her defence barrister to bugger off every time he asks a reasonable question?'

'The blood was on the clothes, presumably destroyed with them,' said Walsh tightly. 'As to Webster's interpretation of his skull X-rays, it is just that, an interpretation. The discrepancy between his position and mine is six years. I say fifty-four. He says sixty. He's wrong. Now get out.'

McLoughlin shrugged and stood up, reaching into his pocket and removing a piece of folded paper. 'The missing persons' list,' he said, dropping it on to the desk. 'I took a photocopy. It's yours. Keep it as a memento.'

'I've seen it.'

McLoughlin studied the pink scalp through the thinning hair. He remembered liking this man once. But that was before Anne's revelations. 'So I gather. Bob Rogers showed it to you the night the body was discovered. The case, for all it ever was a case, should have been over by the morning.'

Walsh stared at him for a moment, then took the paper and unfolded it. There were the same five names and descriptions, but with 'Since Traced' scrawled across Daniel Thompson's box. The two young women were of no consequence because of their sex, which left the Asian lad, Mohammed Mirahmadi, who was too young, and the semi-senile Keith Chapel, sixty-eight, who had walked out of his warden-run hostel five months before, wearing a green jacket, blue jumper and bright pink slacks. A tight, cold fist gripped at Walsh's insides. He laid the paper on the desk. 'The tramp didn't come into it until the next day,' he muttered. 'And how could this old man know about Streech Grange or the ice house?'

McLoughlin stabbed at the box with his finger. 'Look at his initials,' he said. 'Keith Chapel. K.C. I rang the warden of his hostel. The old boy used to ramble on endlessly about a garage he'd owned and what a success it was until a woman spread lies about him and he was forced to sell up. You knew all about it. Dammit, it was you who prompted Mrs Goode to tell the story.'

'Only by hearsay,' Walsh muttered. 'I never met the man. He was gone by the time Maybury disappeared. I thought Casey was a name. Everyone called him Casey. It's in the file as Casey.'

'You're damn right it's in the file. For a bit of hearsay, you gave it a hell of an airing. Great story, shame about the facts. Was that about the size of it?'

'It's not my fault if people thought she killed her parents. We just recorded what they told us.'

'Like hell you did! You fed it to them first. Jesus, you even hoicked it out for my benefit the other evening. And I believed it.' He shook his head. 'What did she do, for pity's sake? Laugh? Call you a dirty old man? Threaten to tell your wife?' He waited for a moment. 'Or couldn't she hide her revulsion?'

'You're suspended,' Walsh whispered. His hands quivered with a life of their own.

'What for? Uncovering the truth?' He slammed his palm on to the missing persons' list. 'You bastard! You had the bloody nerve to accuse me of negligence. Those trousers should have registered with you. You heard them described twice in twelve hours. How many men wear pink slacks, for Christ's sake? You knew a man had been reported missing wearing pink trousers. And it wasn't difficult to find Wally. If I'd had that information when I spoke to him— ' He shook his head angrily and reached for his briefcase. 'There's Dr Webster's final report.' He flung it on to the desk. 'Judging by the fact that Wally felt K.C.'s clothes were fit to wear, I think we can safely assume they were neither ripped with a knife nor blood-soaked. The poor old chap probably died of cold.'

'He went missing five months ago,' muttered the Inspector. 'Where was he for the first two months?'

'In a cardboard box in a subway, I should think, just like all the other poor sods this bloody awful society rejects.'

Walsh moved restlessly. 'And Maybury? You know all the answers. So where's Maybury?'

'I don't know. Living it up in France, I expect. He seems to have had enough contacts out there through his wine business.'

'She killed him.'

McLoughlin's eyes narrowed. 'The bastard ran away when the money dried up and left her and his two small children to carry the can. It was planned, for God's sake.' He was silent for a moment. 'I can't think of one good reason why he would have wanted to punish them but, if he did, he must have been praying for a shit like you to turn up.' He walked to the door.

'What are you going to do?' The words were barely above a whisper.

McLoughlin didn't answer.

On his way down the corridor, he bumped into Nick Robinson and

Wally Ferris. He gave the old man a friendly punch on the shoulder. 'You might have left him his underpants, you old rogue.'

Wally shuffled his feet and cast sideways glances at both policemen. 'You lot gonna charge me then?'

'What with?'

'Didn't do no 'arm, not really. Wet frough I was wiv all that flamin' rain and 'im sittin' there quiet as a mouse. To tell you the trufe I didn't click to 'im bein' dead, not for a while. Put 'im down as one of my sort, but wiv a screw loose. There's a lot like that who've 'ad too much mefs and too little whisky. 'Ad quite a chat wiv 'im one way and anuvver.' He pulled a lugubrious face. ''E didn't 'ave no underpants, son, didn't 'ave nuffink 'cept the 'fings 'e'd folded up and put on the floor beside 'im.' He gave McLoughlin a sly peep. 'Didn't see no 'arm in taking 'em, not when 'e didn't need 'em and I did. Bloody parky, it was. I put 'em on over me own cloves.'

Nick Robinson, who had had no success in getting Wally to talk, snorted. 'You're saying he was sitting there stark naked, dead as a dodo, and you had a chat with him?'

'It was company,' muttered Wally defensively, 'an' it was a while before I got used to the gloom in the cave. You see some funny fings in my line of business.'

'Pink elephants mostly, I should think.' Robinson looked enquiringly at McLoughlin. 'What's all this about the clothes?'

'You'll find out. What do you reckon he died of, Wally?'

'Gawd knows. Cold, I should fink. That place is freezin' wiv ve door closed, an' 'e'd wedged a brick against it. I 'ad to push pretty 'ard to get it open. It weren't nuffink nasty. 'E 'ad a smile on 'is face.'

There was a sharp indrawn breath from Robinson. 'But there was blood, wasn't there?'

Wally's old eyes looked shocked. 'Course there weren't no blood. I wouldn't 'ave stayed if there was blood. 'E was in lovely shape. On the white side per'aps but that was natural. It was dark wiv all the rain outside.' He wrinkled his nose. 'Whiffed a bit, but I didn't 'old it against 'im. Dare say I didn't smell too good meself.'

It was like something out of a Samuel Beckett play, thought McLoughlin. Two old men sitting in semi-darkness, chatting – one nude and dead, the other sodden, and in more ways than one. He didn't doubt for a minute that Wally had spent the night with K.C., rambling happily about this and that. Wally loved to talk. Was it a horrible shock, he wondered, to find in the sober morning light that he'd been chatting with a corpse? Probably not. Wally, he was sure, had seen many worse things. 'So did you shut the door again when you left?'

The old man pulled thoughtfully at his lower lip. 'Sort of.' He seemed to be weighing the problem in his mind. 'That's to say, I did the first time. The first time I shut it. Seemed to me 'e wanted to be left in peace or 'e wouldn't 'ave wedged a brick against it. Then that geezer in the shed gave me the whisky, an' I 'ad a few mouffuls, an' I got to finking about proper burials an' such. Seemed wrong some'ow to leave 'im wivout a chance of a few good words bein' said for 'im, wouldn't want it personally, so I nips back and opens the door. Reckoned 'e'd 'ave more chance of bein' found wiv ve door open.'

It would be cruel, McLoughlin thought, to tell him that by opening the door he had let in the heat, the dogs, the rats and putrefaction. He hoped Walsh wouldn't do it.

'And that,' Wally finished firmly, 'is all I knows. Can I go now?'

'Not likely,' said Nick Robinson, 'the Inspector wants a word with you.' He took a firm grip on Wally's arm and looked enquiringly at McLoughlin. 'How about filling me in?'

McLoughlin grinned evilly. 'Let's just say, you got your wires crossed, old son.'

TWENTY-THREE

He folded himself wearily into his car and sat for some time staring blankly through the windscreen. Some words of Francis Bacon kept repeating themselves in his mind like a memory-jerk mnemonic. 'Revenge is a kind of wild justice. The more man's nature runs to it, the more ought law to weed it out.' He rubbed his gaunt face. He had told Anne he sympathised with personal vengeance but he knew now that wasn't true. The end result of an 'eye for an eye' was a world gone blind. With a sigh, he fired the motor and drew out into the traffic.

He lived in a modern box on a large estate to the north-west of Silverborne where every house was depressingly similar and where individuality expressed itself only in what colour you chose to paint your front door. It had satisfied him once. Before he had seen Streech Grange.

'Hello, Andy,' said Kelly. She was standing irresolutely by the kitchen sink, mop in hand, washing the dirty dishes he had left untouched for ten days. He had forgotten how stunning she was and how easily that fabulous body had once been able to turn him on.

'Hello.'

'Pleased to see me?'

He shrugged. 'Sure. Look, you don't need to do those. I was planning to tackle them over the weekend. I haven't been around much this week.'

'I know. I've been trying to phone you.'

He went to the fridge and took out a piece of cheese from among the opened tins of furred tomatoes and sliced cling peaches. He held it out to her. 'Want some?' She shook her head, so he ate the whole lump before looking at his watch. 'I've a phone call to make, then I'll grab a quick shower before I go out.' He waved his arm to encompass the whole house. 'Take your time and take what you like.' He smiled without hostility. 'Except my books and my two boat paintings. You won't quibble over those, will you? You always said they were only good for gathering dust.' So much so that they had been relegated, along with him, to the spare room.

He was on his way to the stairs when his conscience smote and he turned round. 'Look, really, don't do the washing-up. It's not necessary. I'd have done it myself if I'd had the time.' He smiled again. 'You'll ruin your nail varnish.'

Her mouth trembled. 'Jack and me, it didn't work.' She flung herself after him and burrowed her sweet-smelling head into his chest. 'Oh, Andy, I've missed you. I want to come home. I want to come home so much.'

An awful lethargy stole over him then, like the lethargy a drowning man must feel in the moment before he gives up. His eyes looked into the middle distance above her head, seeking straws. There were none. He held her for a second or two, then gently disentangled himself. 'Come home,' he said. 'It's yours as much as mine.'

'You're not angry?'

'Not at all. I'm glad.'

Her wonderful eyes shone like stars. 'Your mother said you would be.'

Straws, he thought, were useless to drowning men. It was the unquenchable longing for life that kept heads above water. 'I'll have that shower, then I'll be off,' he said. 'I'll fetch the books and the paintings tomorrow, and maybe the records I bought before we were married.' He glanced through the sitting-room door at the chromium coffee table, the oatmeal carpet, the net curtains, the white formica wall units and the dainty pastel three-piece suite, and he thought, no one has ever lived here. He shook his head. 'There's nothing else I want.'

She caught him by the arm. 'You *are* angry.'

His dark face cracked into a grin. 'No. I'm glad. I needed a push. I hate this place. I always have done. It's so' – he sought for a word – 'sterile.' He looked at her with compassion. 'Like our marriage.'

She dug her fingers into his arm. 'I knew you'd bring that up, you bastard. But it's not my fault. You never wanted kids any more than I did.'

He removed her hands. 'That wasn't quite the sterility I was referring to.'

She was bitter. 'You've found someone else.'

He moved to the telephone, took a piece of paper from his pocket and dialled the number written on it. 'McLoughlin,' he said into the mouthpiece. 'We've identified the body. That's it, all over the newspapers tomorrow, so if he's any sense he'll lie low. Yes, it'll have to be tonight. Damn right, I want him. Let's just say I take what he did personally. So can you swing it?' He listened for a moment. 'Just make the point that they've got away with murder again. I'll be with you by ten.' He looked up and caught Kelly's eye. Water had gathered in great droplets round the mascaraed lashes. 'Where will you go?'

'I don't know yet. Maybe Glasgow.'

Tears turned to anger, and her anger lashed out at him as it always had done. 'You've left that bloody job, haven't you? After all the begging I did for you to leave, you've left it because someone else asked you.'

'No one's asked me, Kelly, and I haven't left it, not yet.'

'But you will.'

'Maybe.'

'Who is she?'

He found he wanted to hurt her, so there must be some feeling left. Perhaps there always would be. Seven years, however sterile, had left their mark. 'She's my rose,' he said, 'my red, red rose.' And Kelly, who had heard enough of hated Rabbie Burns to last a lifetime, felt a knot of panic tighten round her heart.

Phoebe rocked Diana's shoulder and prodded her into wakefulness. 'We've got visitors,' she whispered. 'I need help.' Somewhere in the darkness behind her came the low growls of the dogs.

Diana squinted at her out of one eye. 'Turn the light on,' she said sleepily.

'No, I don't want them to know we're awake.' She bundled Diana's dressing-gown on to her chest. 'Come on, old girl, get a move on.'

'Have you called the police?' Diana sat up and shrugged her arms into the dressing-gown.

'No point. It'll be over one way or another long before the police get here.' Phoebe switched on a small torch and pointed it at the floor. 'Come on,' she urged, 'we haven't much time.'

Diana pulled on her slippers and padded after her. 'Why are the dogs here? Why aren't they outside? And where's McLoughlin?'

'He didn't come tonight.' She sighed. 'The one night we needed him, he didn't turn up.'

'So what are you planning to do?'

Phoebe lifted her shotgun from where she had propped it outside Diana's bedroom door. 'I'm going to use this,' she said, leading the way downstairs, 'and I don't want to shoot the dogs by mistake. It'll be their turn to have a go if the bastards manage to break in.'

'Lord, woman,' muttered Diana, 'you're not intending to kill anyone, are you?'

'Don't be a fool.' She crept across the hall and into her drawing-room. 'I'm going to scare the shit out of the creeps. They didn't get rid of me last time. They won't get rid of me now.' She gestured Diana to one side of the curtains and, switching off the torch, took up a position on the other side. 'Keep your eyes peeled. If you see anyone on the far side of the terrace, let me know.'

'I'm going to regret this,' Diana groaned, twitching the curtain aside and peering into the darkness. 'I can't see a bloody thing. How do you know they're out there?'

'Benson came in through the cellar window and woke me. I trained him to do it after the first time these yobs had a go at me.' She patted the old dog's head. 'You're such a good boy, aren't you. It's years since I've had you patrolling the grounds and you haven't forgotten.' The sound of the dog's tail swishing backwards and forwards across the carpet was loud in the quiet room. Hedges, unborn at the time of David Maybury's disappearance, crouched by his mistress's feet, muscles tensed for when his turn came. Phoebe scanned the wide terrace for signs of movement. 'Your eyes will soon adjust.'

'There *is* someone,' said Diana suddenly. 'By the right-hand wall. Do you see him?'

'Yes. There's another coming round Anne's wing.' She gripped her shotgun firmly. 'Can you unlock the windows without making a noise?'

For a brief moment Diana hesitated, then she shrugged and applied herself carefully to the key. Phoebe, she argued, knew all there was to know about hell. She had been there. She wouldn't willingly go back a second time. In any case, the adrenaline was racing in her as strongly as it was racing in Phoebe. It was backs-against-the-wall time, she thought, when everyone, even rabbits, showed their teeth. 'OK,' she whispered, as the lock clicked quietly open. She peeped past the edge of the curtain again. 'Oh, lord,' she breathed, 'there are dozens of them.'

Black figures crouched along the edge of the terrace like a troop of apes, but to think of them as such was to demean the animals. It is only man, with his single evolutionary advancement of reason, who takes pleasure in other people's pain. Diana's mouth went dry. There was something unbelievably chilling in mob hysteria where individual accountability was subordinate to the group.

'Hardly dozens; five, six at the most. When I say, "Now," open the door wide.' Phoebe gave a wild laugh. 'We'll put the old adage to the test and wait till we see the whites of their eyes. I've always wanted to try it.'

There was confusion in the huddled mass as they seemed to crowd together about the terrace wall, then separate again. 'What are they doing?' asked Diana.

'Pulling bricks off the top by the look of it. Keep your head down if they start throwing them.'

One of the crouching group seemed to be the leader. He used his arms to direct his troop, half to go down one side of the terrace, half to take the other side. 'Now,' muttered Phoebe urgently. 'I don't want them splitting up.'

Diana twisted the handle and thrust the door open. Phoebe was through it in a second, her tall figure melting into the shadows. She had raised the heavy stock to her shoulder and was about to sight down the barrel when one large hand clamped itself over her mouth and another plucked the gun from her grasp.

'I wouldn't if I were you, madam,' whispered Fred's soft voice in her ear. He kept his hand firmly over her mouth and used his forearm on her shoulder to force her to her knees. Bent double, he laid the shotgun noiselessly on the flagstones then, urging her upright again, he caught her round the waist as if she were no more than a piece of thistledown, and lifted her through the drawing-room windows. He felt Diana's presence, rather than saw it. 'Not a sound,' he cautioned her in a tight whisper, 'and close the window, if you please.'

'But, Fred— ' she began.

'Do as I say, Mrs Goode. Do you want madam hurt?'

Thoroughly shaken, Diana did as he said.

Ignoring Phoebe's biting teeth, Fred hauled her unceremoniously across the room and bundled her into the hall. Diana pursued him. 'What are you doing?' she demanded fiercely, buffeting him around his shoulders with bunched fists. 'Put Phoebe down this minute.' Benson and Hedges, alarmed by Diana's tone, threw themselves against Fred's legs.

'This door, too, Mrs Goode, if you please.'

She caught a handful of his sparse hair and tugged hard. 'Let her go,' she grunted.

With a sigh of pain, he swung round, carrying both women with him, and kicked the door to with his foot. Seconds later the French windows shattered inwards into a thousand pieces. 'There,' he said amiably, setting Phoebe carefully on the floor and removing his hand from her mouth. 'We're all right now, I think. If you wouldn't mind, Mrs Goode, that *is* a little painful. Thank you.' He fished a handkerchief from his pocket and wrapped it round his bleeding fingers. 'Good boys,' he murmured, fondling the dogs' muzzles,

219

'that's the ticket. I don't say I'm not annoyed about another window needing new glass, but this time we'll make sure it's paid for.' He opened the door. 'Would you excuse me, madam? I'd hate to miss the fun.'

Speechlessly, the two women watched his great bulk pad lightly across the broken glass and step out on to the terrace. Beyond, lit by brilliant moonlight, was a scene from Hieronymus Bosch. A grotesque tangle of misshapen figures writhed in hideous and noisy confusion upon the lawn. As Fred, with a curdling roar, charged across the terrace and launched himself atop the mêlée, Phoebe took in the situation at a glance, whistled up Hedges and pointed to one flying fugitive who had managed to pull himself free. 'Off you go, boy.' Hedges, barking his excitement, bounded across the grass, bowled his man over and pranced about him, howling his achievement to the moon. Benson, not to be outdone, waddled on to the terrace, sat comfortably on his haunches and raised his old muzzle in joyous unison.

The row from dogs and flailing bodies was deafening.

'Men!' exclaimed Diana in Phoebe's ear and Phoebe, with adrenaline still running rampant in her bloodstream, burst into tears of laughter.

TWENTY-FOUR

The confusion was short-lived. By the time Diana thought of switching on the drawing-room lights, the half dozen vandals had thrown in the towel and were being herded across the terrace by a panting semi-circle of McLoughlin, young PC Gavin Williams, out of uniform, Jonathan, Fred and Paddy Clarke.

'Inside,' ordered McLoughlin curtly. 'You're all nicked.'

Stripped of their menace by the glare of the overhead lamps, they were an unprepossessing bunch of shuffling, sweaty youths with surly faces and evasive eyes. Diana knew them all by sight as lads from the village, but she could put a name to only two of them, Eddie Staines and nineteen-year-old Peter Barnes, son of Dilys and brother to Emma. She looked them over in amazement. 'What have we ever done to you? I don't even know who most of you are.'

Barnes was a good-looking young man, tall, athletic, an ex-public school boy, now working in his father's print business in Silverborne. He sneered at her but didn't answer. Eddie Staines and the remaining four stared fixedly at the floor.

'It's a reasonable enough question,' said McLoughlin evenly. 'What have these ladies ever done to you?'

Barnes shifted his gaze. 'Which ladies?' he asked insolently. 'Do you mean the dykes?'

Barnes's voice, unaccented, interested McLoughlin. The shouts on the lawn had all carried the strangled vowels of the working class. A slight shake of his head kept Diana quiet. 'I was referring to Mrs Maybury and her friends,' he said in the same even tone. 'What have they ever done to you?' He searched the line of unresponsive faces. 'All right, for the moment you will be charged with aggravated assault on the owner of Streech Grange.'

'We never touched her,' complained Eddie Staines.

'Shut up,' said Barnes.

'Never touched who?'

'Her. Mrs Maybury.'

'I didn't say you did.'

221

'What was all that aggravated assault crap?'

'She's not the owner of Streech Grange,' McLoughlin pointed out. 'Mr Jonathan Maybury and his sister own this property.'

'Oh.' Eddie frowned. 'We thought it was the dyke's.'

McLoughlin arched an eyebrow. 'Do you mean Mrs Maybury?'

'You soft in the head, or what?'

'That,' murmured McLoughlin mildly, 'would appear to be your privilege. Eddie Staines, is it?'

'Yeah.'

'Keep your big mouth shut, you ignorant turd,' Barnes grated through clenched teeth.

A cold gleam lit McLouglin's eyes. 'Well, well, Paddy, you were right. It's the jumped-up little oik who calls the shots. So what's his problem?'

'His mother,' was Paddy's laconic reply.

The boy threw him a murderous glance.

Paddy gave an indifferent shrug. 'I'm sorry for you, lad. If you'd had half your sister's sense, you'd have got by. You'd have raised two fingers to that stupid bitch with her twisted ambitions, and you'd have kept your sanity. Try asking yourself who Emma's really screwing when she comes up here and spreads her legs.' He glanced at McLoughlin. 'Ever heard the expression, a beggar on horseback? A beggar comes into a bit of money, buys a horse to raise himself up, only to find he can't ride the damn thing. That's Dilys Barnes. She came a cropper when she set her sights too high and moved the family into Streech. No harm in that, of course. It's a free country. But you don't, if you've any sense, treat one end of the village like muck because you think they're beneath you, while you lick the backsides of the other end and brandish your painfully transparent family tree under their noses. That way, you alienate everybody.'

Peter's face worked unpleasantly. 'Bastard!' he hissed.

Paddy let it pass. 'People laughed at her, of course. They would. Social climbing's a spectator sport in a place like this, and Dilys was never any good at it.' He stroked his chin. 'She's a very unintelligent woman. She couldn't grasp the first rule, that class is in inverse proportion to its relevance.' His eyes flickered over Peter. 'You'll need a translation, lad. The classier you are the less you have to talk about it.'

Barnes bunched his fists. 'Fuck you, Paddy. Cheap Irish trash, that's all you are.' Fleetingly, McLoughlin had the odd impression that the boy was enjoying himself.

A deep laugh rumbled in Paddy's throat. 'I'll take it as a compliment, lad. It's a long time since anyone's recognised the Irish in me.'

He dodged a flying fist. 'Jesus Christ!' he said crossly. 'You're even more stupid than your mother, despite your fancy education and the puffed-up ideas she's given you.' He wagged a finger at Phoebe. 'It's your fault, woman. You made a laughing-stock of her and, believe me, you don't do that to the Dilys Barneses of this world. She has a poisoned callus on her soul for every slight, true or imagined, that she's suffered, and the biggest and the most venomous is the one you gave her. She's fed her venom to this little creep by the bucket-load.'

Phoebe looked at him in astonishment. 'I hardly know her. She made a scene by the village pond once but I was far too angry to laugh.'

'Before David went missing,' he prompted. 'He did the real damage. He repeated the story in the pub and it was all round the village before you could say Jack Robinson.'

Phoebe stared at him blankly and shook her head.

He reached down to scratch the ears of the old Labrador lying at his feet. 'When Benson was little more than a puppy? Dilys caught him humping her Pekinese.' His eyes twinkled encouragingly. 'Harangued you over the telephone for not keeping him under better control.'

'Oh, good God!' Phoebe clapped her hands to her face. 'Not my Barnes pun. But it was a joke,' she protested. 'You're not going to tell me she took it personally. I was referring to her Peke. The damn thing was on heat and she let it out, reeking of pheromones.'

Paddy's great chuckle boomed about the room, stirring the heightened adrenalin into a responsive froth.

Phoebe's voice shook. 'It was all her fault anyway. She would keep calling Benson a dirty dog.' Quite unconsciously, she took on the refined tones of Dilys Barnes. ' "Your dirty dog should be ashamed of himself, Mrs Maybury." God, it was funny. She couldn't bring herself to say that Benson had rogered her ghastly bitch.' She wiped her eyes on her sleeve. 'So I said, I was very sorry but, as she knew better than I, you couldn't stop dirty dogs poking into smelly barns.' She looked up, caught Diana's eye and laughed out loud. The room quivered.

Eddie Staines, not too bright but with a well-developed sense of humour, grinned broadly. 'That's good. Never heard it before. That why they call old man Barnes "the dirty dog" then? God, struth!' He doubled up as Peter Barnes, without any warning, swung a booted foot and kicked him in the groin. 'Ah, Jesus!' He backed away, clutching his balls.

McLoughlin watched this little sally with amused detachment. 'And presumably Dilys got lumbered with Smelly?' he said to Paddy. The big man grinned. 'For a month or two, maybe. Far as I recall, Dirty Dog stuck to Tony longer than Smelly Barnes stuck to Dilys, but the damage was done. Takes herself too seriously, you see. When you're eaten up with frustrated ambition, there's no room for humour.' His eyes rested on the bitter young face of the boy. 'Respectability,' he said with heavy irony, 'it's a sickness with her. With this one, too. They won't be laughed at.'

And that, McLoughlin knew, was as far as Paddy could take him. He had been suspicious enough of Peter Barnes to set him up, but he had no proof that the lad had struck Anne any more than he had proof that Dilys initiated all the slander against Phoebe. 'She's far too cunning,' he had said that morning. 'She's a type. Pathologically jealous. You come across them now and then. They're usually women, invariably inadequate and their spite is always directed against their own sex because that's the sex they're jealous of. They are completely vicious. As often as not, the target is their own daughter.'

'So why single out Mrs Maybury?' McLoughlin had asked.

'Because she was the first lady of Streech and you buggers dropped her in the shit. For ten years, Dilys has been wetting herself because she can look down on Mrs Maybury of Streech Grange. God knows, she was never going to do it any other way.'

'What did she do?'

'Piled shit on shit, of course. People were ready to believe anything after you lot left, and murder was the least of the garbage Dilys fed them.'

'What a sewer you live in, Paddy.' McLaughlin spoke quietly, his voice level.

The big man surprised him. 'If it is, it's Phoebe's fault,' he had observed. 'She's the focus for it all. Whatever the rights and wrongs, any normal woman would have sold up and moved on. The Grange isn't worth the price she's had to pay for it.'

No, McLoughlin thought, Paddy was wrong about that. The Grange was worth whatever Phoebe had to pay, and she would go on paying because it was cheap at the price. The real cost was being borne by the people who loved her. He glanced across at her with a sudden irritation. God damn the woman! People loved her or hated her. The one thing no one seemed to feel was indifference.

'OK,' he said abruptly into the silence, 'you' – he jerked a finger at Eddie Staines – 'are going to listen to a few home truths. You're not the brightest thing on two legs but you have to be brighter than this dickhead here.' He scowled at Barnes, then held up a finger. 'Number one, Eddie. Mrs Maybury did not murder her parents. Colonel and Mrs Gallagher died because their brakes didn't work, and their brakes didn't work because K.C. hadn't serviced the car properly. Had he done so, he would have found the corroded brake hose. Got that?'

'Yeah, but who corroded it?' asked Eddie triumphantly. 'That's the question.'

'Read the coroner's report,' said McLoughlin wearily. 'Colonel Gallagher took the car to K.C. *because* the brakes felt soft. He wrote a note to that effect and the note, in his handwriting, is in the file. K.C. ignored it.' He held up a second finger. 'Number two. Mr David Maybury walked out of this house alive ten years ago. No one murdered him. He legged it because he had finally run through all of Mrs Maybury's money and he didn't fancy working for his living.'

'So who's arguing? Saw the bugger myself three months ago. Mind you, he's dead now.' Eddie glared at Phoebe. 'Hell of a way to get your own back, lady.'

McLoughlin held up a third finger. 'Number three, Eddie. That man wasn't David Maybury.'

He looked sceptical. 'Oh, yeah?'

'Oh, yeah. It was K.C. And it's not a matter for debate. It is a matter of proven fact.'

There was a long silence. Very slowly, recognition dawned. 'Hell, happen it was, too. Knew I knew him. But that Inspector of yours was damn sure it was Maybury.'

Paddy snorted. 'The only people who are ever damn sure of anything are idiots and politicians. Same difference, some would say.'

They could almost follow Eddie's thought processes in the contortions of his face. 'Still, I don't see it makes much difference. We're back to square one. If it was K.C. she did in this time, then stands to reason she did her old man in ten years ago. The only proof you thought she didn't was that I thought the old guy was him. You follow me?'

'I follow you,' McLoughlin told him. 'But the whole thing stinks. Didn't it occur to you that if it was Maybury this time, then you've been beating up on an innocent woman for ten years?'

'There was her parents— ' He broke off as his brain caught up with his mouth. 'Yeah, well, as I say, we're back to square one now.'

'Anything but. Mrs Maybury didn't kill K.C., Eddie. You did.'

'Cobblers!'

'He wasn't murdered. He died of cold, starvation and self-neglect. You were the last person to see him alive. If you'd offered him a hand he wouldn't be dead now. He needed help, and you didn't give it to him.'

'Now listen here, mister. You trying to set me up or something? The Inspector said he was stabbed in the gut.'

Between the Scylla of Barnes and the Charybdis of Walsh, was it any wonder, thought McLoughlin, that Phoebe had retreated into her fortress? Without a twinge of regret, he rode rough-shod over Walsh's thirty years on the Force. 'The Inspector greased a few palms and was over-promoted,' he said bluntly. 'It happens in the police just as it happens everywhere else. They'll give him early retirement as a result of this cock-up and get shot of him.'

'Jesus!' said Eddie, impressed by so much honesty from a policeman.

'You cretin,' muttered Peter Barnes. 'He's running bloody rings round you.'

McLoughlin ignored him. 'Number four, Eddie,' he went on. 'When you and the scum you associate with come up here for a spot of queer-bashing, you miss the mark. There are no queers living in Streech Grange. Who told you there were?'

'It's common knowledge.' Eddie looked uncomfortable. 'The three dykes. The three witches. They're always called one or the other.' He darted a quick glance at Peter Barnes. 'Me, I'm not into queer-bashing.'

'I see.' McLoughlin transferred his attention to Barnes. 'So it's you who's not keen on queers.' He yawned suddenly and rubbed his eyes. 'What happened? Someone try it on at that school you went to?' He saw the sudden pinching round the boy's nostrils and his brooding face cracked into a grin. 'Don't tell me you enjoyed it, and now you're busting a gut to prove you didn't.'

'Fucking perverts,' the boy blurted out. 'They make me sick.' He spat at Phoebe. 'Fucking perverts. They should be locked up.' A well of loathing seemed to overflow. 'I hate them.'

Something malignant stirred in the depths of McLoughlin's dark eyes. He took a lightning step forward and clamped his hand across Barnes's mouth, digging his fingers and thumb into the soft flesh of the cheeks and forcing the boy up on to the balls of his feet. 'I find you extremely offensive,' he said softly. 'You're a moronic little psychopath and in my book it's the likes of you who should be locked up, not the likes of Oscar Wilde. The only contribution you will ever make to society will be a negative one when you pass your prejudices and your miserably inadequate IQ to a succeeding generation.' He

226

levered Barnes up another inch. 'In addition it makes me very angry to hear these women referred to as perverts. Do you understand me?'

Barnes tried to speak but the words stuck in his throat. McLoughlin dug his fingers deeper and Barnes nodded vigorously. 'Good.' McLoughlin unlocked his fingers and pushed him away with the heel of his hand. He favoured Staines with a friendly smile. 'I hope you can see where all this is leading, Eddie. You do realise I am giving you the benefit of the doubt. I am assuming you genuinely believed these people were guilty of something.'

Eddie's good-humoured face puckered in worried concentration. 'Listen, mister, I just came along to see justice done. I swear to God that's all I came for.' He waved a hand at the other youths. 'That's all any of us came for. We got the call you were letting her off again. This queer-bashing stuff, that's Peter's kick.' He flicked a shy look at Phoebe and Diana. 'Jesus, it doesn't make sense anyway. If you're not queer, why do you go along with it?'

Diana rolled her eyes to Heaven. 'Do you know, I've often wondered that myself.' She turned to Phoebe. 'I've forgotten, old thing, why do we go along with it?'

Phoebe's rich laugh tumbled from her mouth. 'Don't be such a fool.' She looked at Eddie and raised her hands helplessly. 'We've never had a choice. Hardly anyone ever speaks to us. Those who do, know all about us. Those who don't, assume whatever they want to assume. You have assumed we're gay.' Her eyes laughed softly. 'Bar copulating naked by the village pond with a series of men, I don't see how we could ever prove we weren't. In any case, would you have thought any better of us if you'd known we preferred men?'

'Yeah,' said Eddie with an appreciative wink. 'I bloody well would. Mind you,' he continued thoughtfully, 'none of this explains what happened to your old man. If the only reason he legged it was because the money'd dried up why didn't he get you off the hook when he read what was happening to you? It only needed a phone call to the police.'

There was an awkward silence.

'You talk as if the man had a clear conscience,' said McLoughlin at last. Out of the corner of his eye he saw the colour drain from Jonathan's set face. Dammit, he thought. Whichever way you turned, you were always caught between the rock and the hard place. 'It's sub judice, Eddie, which is why we've never released details. But I can tell you this, the minute the man re-surfaces he will be prosecuted.' He shrugged. 'For the moment you'll just have to take my word that it suits his book if everyone thinks he's dead. He was a villain. We'll find him one day.'

Even Paddy looked impressed.

'Jesus!' said Eddie again. 'Je – sus!' He scrunched his foot on some broken glass. 'Listen, lady,' he offered, 'about these windows.' He gestured to the youths behind him. 'We'll clear up and put some new ones in. It's only fair.'

'You can do better than that, Eddie,' said McLoughlin pleasantly. 'It's names we want. Let's start with who attacked Miss Cattrell?'

Eddie shook his head with genuine regret. 'I can guess, same as you can, but if it's proof you need, then I can't help you. Like I said, queer-bashing doesn't turn me on.' He indicated one of his mates. 'Me and Bob took a couple of birds to the flicks that night. I don't know about the rest of them.'

A chorus of denials greeted this statement.

'Not me. I was watching telly with my folks.'

'Jesus, Eddie, I was round your sister's place. You bloody know that.'

'Fuck that. I only heard about it the next morning, same as you.'

Above their heads, McLoughlin caught Paddy's eye and saw his own disappointment mirrored there. The truth had an unmistakable ring about it. 'And what about you?' he asked Peter Barnes, knowing the little bastard would get away with it. 'Where were you?'

Barnes grinned. 'I was with my mother all evening until half-past midnight. Then I went to bed. She'll sign a statement if you ask her nicely.' He raised his middle finger and jabbed it in the air at Paddy. 'That's to you and your beggar crap, shithead.' He giggled and crooked his arm over his other fist, thrusting the finger skyward. 'And that's to your pathetic little set-up. What a joke. It was so fucking transparent, a blind man could have seen through it. You think I haven't creepy-crawled this place, seen the tame fuzz they've got watching over them?' He giggled again.

Alarm bells rang in McLoughlin's head. What the hell sort of psychopath was this boy? A Charles Manson freak? Je – sus! 'Creepy-crawled', he knew, was an expression the Charles Manson Family had used to describe the way they had entered Sharon Tate's house before they murdered her. 'So what brought you up here?' he asked, loosing some handcuffs from his jacket pocket. 'Gives you a buzz, does it, being arrested?'

'It sure as hell gives me a buzz to see you cretins screw up. That's got to be worth a slapped wrist and a fine any day. Hell, it was a bit of high spirits. Dad'll ante-up for the damage.'

There was a moment of silence before Jonathan's cool voice spoke from the shattered window. 'That seems reasonable,' he said. 'In return, I'll ante-up for the damage I'm going to do to you.'

It was the element of surprise that held everyone frozen. Like a slow motion sequence they watched him cross the room, release the safety catch on his mother's shotgun, shove the barrel between Barnes's legs and pull the trigger. The explosion left them deaf. Through a dense cloud of dust they saw, rather than heard, the screams that issued from the boy's writhing mouth. They watched the pool of liquid collect on the floor at his feet.

McLoughlin, stunned, tried to intervene, only to find a pair of thick arms clamped around his chest, holding him back. 'Jon!' he yelled, his voice muffled by the ringing echoes in his ears. 'For God's sake! He's not worth it!'

'Leave him be, sir.' It was Fred's voice. 'He's waited a long time for this.'

Shocked beyond belief, McLoughlin watched Jonathan Maybury drive Peter Barnes against the wall and ram the shotgun into the boy's screaming mouth.

TWENTY-FIVE

Gap-toothed where the windows yawned, its finery ruffled by bird-shot, the old house slumbered on, a silent witness to many worse things in its four-hundred-year history. Within half an hour, three patrol cars had arrived to ferry the culprits to the Station with PC Gavin Williams in firm but reluctant charge. 'It's down to you, Sarge,' he protested. 'You should be taking them in.'

'Nn-nn. They're all yours. I've some unfinished business here.'

'What do I do about Maybury, Sarge?'

McLoughlin folded his arms and didn't say anything.

'Barnes is bound to mention it.'

'Let him.'

'Shouldn't we charge Maybury?'

'What with? Accidental discharge of a licensed firearm?'

'You'll never get away with that. Eddie, for one, knows it wasn't an accident.'

McLoughlin was amused. 'I think you'll find Eddie's somewhat disenchanted with Peter Barnes. Apart from anything else, he doesn't take kindly to being set up as a fall-guy for Barnes's warped sense of humour. He tells me he and his mates were looking the other way when the accident happened.'

Williams looked worried. 'What do I say?'

'That's up to you, Gavin. I can't help you I'm afraid. When the gun went off, I had my back turned, taking down the names and addresses of the intruders. After that I couldn't see anything for dust.'

'Hell, Sarge!'

'I thought you were taking down the names and addresses of all the witnesses to the vandalism. It's standard police procedure in incidents of this sort.'

The constable pulled a wry face. 'And how do you explain Barnes's confession? I mean if it was just an accident why would he want to stitch himself up? Jesus, Sarge, he was so bloody terrified, he was pissing all over the floor.'

McLoughlin clapped him amiably on the shoulder. 'Is that right, Gavin? I couldn't see a damn thing because of the dust in my eyes. So don't ask me what loosened his tongue, because I couldn't tell you, unless it was the shock of the gun going off. Explosions react on people in different ways. Left me temporarily blinded but with my ears working overtime. Some sort of compensation effect, I imagine. Couldn't see worth a damn, but I heard every word the little weasel said.'

Williams shook his head. 'I was in a blue funk. I thought the doctor shot his balls off.'

So did I, thought McLoughlin. So did I. And so it seemed had Peter Barnes. Swept back by the violence of Jonathan's assault and numbed by the blast of the shotgun between his legs which had discharged itself harmlessly into Phoebe's drawing-room wall, he had burst into tears of self-pity as Jonathan rammed the barrel against his teeth and threatened to pull the second trigger. 'I didn't mean to do it,' he babbled. 'I was creepy-crawling the house. I didn't mean to do it. I didn't mean to do it,' he screamed. 'She came back. The silly bitch came back. I had to hit her.'

Jonathan's finger whitened on the trigger. 'Now tell me about nine years ago.'

'Oh, God, help me! Somebody help me!' The front of his trousers was saturated with urine.

'TELL ME!' roared Jonathan, his face white and drawn with rage. 'Someone ransacked this house. WHO WAS IT?'

'It was my dad,' the boy screamed, sobbing convulsively. 'He got drunk with some friends.' His eyes widened alarmingly as Jonathan started to squeeze the trigger. 'It's not my fault. Mum's always giggling about it. It's not my fault. It was my dad.' His eyes rolled into the back of his head and he collapsed on the floor.

Jonathan lowered the gun and looked across at McLoughlin. 'We never knew who it was. Mum, Jane and I locked ourselves in the cellar and waited till they'd gone. I have never been so frightened in my life. We could hear them shouting and breaking all the furniture. I thought they were going to kill us.' He shook his head and looked down at the twitching boy. 'I swore I'd make them pay if I ever found out who they were. They used the house as a toilet and wrote "Murdering Bitch" all over the walls in tomato ketchup. I was only eleven. I thought it was blood.' His jaw tightened.

McLoughlin shook off Fred's bear hug and started to slap the dust out of his clothes. 'That was a hell of a close shave, Jon. What happened, for God's sake? Did you trip on some broken glass or something?'

'That's it, Sergeant,' said Fred impassively. 'I was watching. Could have been quite nasty if young Jon hadn't kept his wits about him.'

'Yes, well, do something with the flaming thing before it goes off again.' He watched Fred take the gun, break it open and remove the second cartridge. 'Oh, for Christ's sake, Barnes, get up and stop belly-aching. You're damn lucky, Dr Maybury had the good sense to keep the barrel down.' He hauled him to his feet and snapped on the handcuffs. 'You're under arrest. Constable Williams will read you your rights.'

The boy was still sobbing. 'He tried to kill me.'

'There's gratitude for you,' said Paddy, shaking plaster from his hair. 'Jon nearly blows his own foot off to protect the little scum and all he can do is accuse him.' He looked at Jonathan's stricken face, saw the obvious danger signals, and glanced across at Fred with a Gary Lineker finger to eye gesture.

Calmly Fred took the boy's arm and steered him towards the door into the hall. 'I suggest we check on the rest of the house, sir. I don't like the idea of Miss Cattrell alone upstairs.' He closed the door firmly behind them.

Half an hour, thought McLoughlin, and it seemed more like a year. He smoothed the stubble on his jaw and stared thoughtfully at the young constable. 'I can't help you, Gavin. You're a good copper and it's not my place to tell you what to do. You must make your own decision.'

The young man glanced through the drawing-room door where Fred was helping Phoebe restore order. 'I agreed to do the patrols with you because of him and the old lady really. They're decent folks. Seemed wrong to abandon them to yobbos.'

'I agree,' said McLoughlin dryly.

He frowned. 'If you want my opinion, the Chief Inspector's got some explaining to do on this one. You should hear what Molly has to say about when she and Fred first came here. The house had been totally vandalised. Mrs Maybury and the two kids were living in one bedroom which Miss Cattrell and the lad, Jonathan, had managed to clean up. According to Molly, Mrs Maybury and Jane were so shell-shocked by the whole thing they didn't know if they were coming or going. Molly says you could still smell the piss even after three months, and the mould on the tomato ketchup had started to grow inwards, into the walls. It took them weeks to scrub the place clean. What's the Chief got against them, Sarge? Why wouldn't he believe them?'

Because, thought McLoughlin, he couldn't afford to. It was Walsh himself who, all those years ago, had created the climate of hate in which this woman and her two young children could be terrorised. For him, and for whatever reason, Phoebe had always been guilty, and his prolonged and hostile hounding of her had led inevitably to others meting out justice when he failed to prove it himself. 'He's a small man, Gavin,' was all he said.

'Well, I don't like it and I'm going to say something. It's not what I joined the Force for. I asked Molly why they didn't call the police in when it happened, and do you know what she said? "Because madam knew better than to ask help from the enemy." ' He scuffed his foot shyly against the floor. 'I'm planning to take Molly and Fred around and about a bit, no fuss, nothing like that, but I'd like them to know we're not all enemies.'

McLoughlin smiled down on the bent head. If Williams wanted to wrap up his affection in the guise of community policing, that was fine with him. 'I'm told she makes a damn good lardy cake.'

'Bloody brilliant!' The young eyes sparkled. 'You should try some.'

'I will.' He pushed the lad towards the front door and the waiting cars. 'It won't do Eddie and his mates any harm to spend the night in a police cell, so book 'em and lock 'em up. If Mrs Maybury wants to press charges in the morning, then we'll fill out all the sheets then. But I don't think she will. She laid the first stone of a bridge this evening.'

'And Barnes?'

'Keep him on ice for me. I'll be in first thing tomorrow morning. I'll take his statement myself. And Gavin?'

'Yes?'

'He would have talked anyway. He couldn't have resisted it. He's too arrogant to keep quiet for long. You'll see. Tomorrow, without any pressure from me, he'll give us the whole works.'

A weight seemed to drop from the lad's shoulders. 'Yeah. Anything else I should do?'

'Bell his parents in a couple of hours, three o'clock, say, tell them we're holding their son, and get them down to the Station. But, whatever you do, don't let them talk to him. Keep them waiting through the dark hours till I get there. Just tell them he's confessed to ten years of persecution. I want them softened up.'

Williams looked doubtful. 'You'll never get a prosecution after ten years, will you?'

'No.' McLoughlin grinned. 'But for a few hours, I can sure as hell make them think I will.'

Paddy was another who took his leave reluctantly. 'You'll have to come out of retreat now,' he told Phoebe and Diana. 'One way and another the door's been forced. It's a damn good thing too. It's time you made a bit of an effort. Come down to the pub tomorrow. It's as good a place as any to start.' He shook hands with McLoughlin. 'Jack in the job, Andy, and join me in starting a brewery. It'll need a strong hand at the helm.'

'I don't know the first thing about brewing.'

'I wouldn't want you for your brewing skills. That's my province. Organise the business, find me customers, get the whole thing rolling. You'd be good at that. I need someone I can trust.'

McLoughlin grinned. 'You mean someone Customs and Excise trusts? You're too anarchic for me, Paddy. I'd be a nervous wreck in three months, trying to remember what I was supposed to be hiding.'

Paddy gave a roar of laughter and punched him on the shoulder. 'Think about it, old son. I enjoy your company.' He left.

Jonathan had retreated to an armchair where he sat in embarrassed silence, studiously avoiding everyone's gaze. His anger had long since abated and he was desperately trying to come to terms with what he had done to Peter Barnes. He could find no excuses for his violence. Fred coughed politely. 'If there's nothing more I can do, madam,' he said to Phoebe, 'I'll be heading back to the Lodge. The wife and young Jane will be wondering how we got on.' Jane had been sleeping at the Lodge with Molly for the past few nights while Fred patrolled the grounds with McLoughlin and PC Williams.

'Oh, Fred,' said Phoebe with genuine contrition, 'I'm so sorry. I am so sorry. I never really thought you were one of them. It was the shock. You do believe that, don't you? I'll take you down for your tetanus tomorrow.'

Fred looked at his bandaged hand, washed, disinfected, cried over and dressed by Phoebe and Diana amidst a welter of apology. 'I think, madam,' he said severely, 'that if one more word is said on this matter I shall be forced to give in my notice. I can stand a lot of things, but I can't stand fuss. Is that understood? Good. Now, if you will excuse me?'

'I'll drive you,' said Phoebe immediately.

'I'd rather the young doctor drove me, if that's all right. There's something I'd like his opinion on.'

The door closed behind them.

Phoebe turned away to hide the dampness in her eyes. 'God broke the mould after He made Fred and Molly,' she said gruffly. 'They never deserved any of this and yet they've stuck with us through thick and thin. I've made up my mind, Di,' she went on fiercely, 'I will brave that wretched pub tomorrow. Someone's got to make the first move and it might as well be me. Fred's been going there for years and no one, apart from Paddy, ever talks to him. I'm damn well going to do something about it.'

Diana looked at her friend's furious face. 'What, for instance? Hold your shotgun on them till they agree to talk?'

Phoebe laughed. 'No. I am going to let bygones be bygones.'

'Well, in that case, I'll come with you.' She looked at McLoughlin. 'Can we do that? It's all over now, isn't it? The Inspector was very curt over the phone but he seems to have absolved us.'

He nodded. 'Yes, you're absolved.'

'Was it suicide?' asked Phoebe.

'I doubt it. He was a confused old man whose memories of Streech survived all his other memories. I think he made his way back here, looking for somewhere to die.'

'But how could he possibly have known where the ice house was?'

'From the pamphlets your husband had printed. If you're touting for tourists, a garage is the obvious place to leave them. On paper, K. C. probably knew this garden better than you did.'

'Still. To remember it after all this time.'

'But the memory is like that,' said Diana. 'Old people remember every detail of their childhood but can't remember what they had for breakfast.' She shook her head. 'I never knew the man but I've always felt very bitter about what happened to Phoebe's parents and the lies he told afterwards. Still' – she shrugged – 'to die like that, alone and with nothing. It's very sad. It may sound silly, but I wish he hadn't taken his clothes off. It makes it worse, somehow, as if he were pointing out the futility of living. Naked we're born and naked we die. I have this awful feeling that, for him, everything that happened in between was worthless.'

McLoughlin stretched. 'I wouldn't get too sentimental about that, if I were you, Mrs Goode. We've only Wally's word for it that the corpse was nude. I think he's probably a little ashamed of himself. There's a world of difference between taking some unwanted, folded clothes and undressing a corpse to rob it.' He looked at his watch. 'Anything else?'

'We'd like to thank you,' said Phoebe.

'What for?'

'Everything. Jane. Jonathan. Anne. Us.'

He nodded and made for the door into the hall. The two women looked at each other.

'You will be coming back, won't you?' said Diana in a rush.

He laughed quietly. 'If I have to, I will.'

'What's that supposed to mean?'

235

Phoebe chuckled. 'I think it means that he wasn't planning on leaving. He can't come back if he's never gone, can he?'

The gun-shot and shouting had dragged Anne from a deep barbiturate-induced sleep to a lighter sleep where dreams enacted themselves in glorious Technicolor. There were no nightmares, just an endless parade of places and faces, some only half-remembered, which fluttered across the screen of her sleeping mind in surrealistic juxtaposition. And, somewhere, irritatingly, McLoughlin was tapping the double-glazing in the windows of a huge citadel and telling her it needed two people to lift it if they weren't to be buried alive.

She sat up with a start and looked at him. Her bedside light was on. 'I dreamt that Jon and Lizzie were getting married,' she said, isolating the one memory from the cloud of others which vanished for ever.

He pulled up the wicker chair and sat on it. 'Given time and room to breathe, perhaps they will.'

She thought about that. 'You don't miss much, do you?'

'That depends. We've caught your assailant.' He stretched out his long legs and gave her all the details. 'Paddy wants me to join him in starting a brewery.'

She smiled. 'Do you like him?'

'He's a bastard.'

'But do you like him?'

He nodded. 'He's his own man. I like him very much.'

'Will you join him?'

'I shouldn't think so. It would be too easy to get addicted to that Special of his.' He looked at her through half-closed lids. 'Jon's going back to London tomorrow. He asked me to find out if you wanted your love letters returned. He says he can try and fish them out before he goes.'

She looked at her hands. 'Do you know where he's put them?'

'I gather they're in a fissure in the old oak tree behind the ice house. He's a little worried about whether or not he can retrieve them. He asked me to give him a hand.' He studied her face. 'Should I, Cattrell?'

'No. Let them stay there.' She raised her head to look at him. 'When I'm firing on all cylinders again I'll take some cement and stick it into every crack in the oak tree so the damn things never see the light of day again. I had to ask Jon to hide them – he was the only one there when Walsh took me away – but he's the last person in the world I want looking at them. Oh God, I wish they *were* love letters.' She fell silent.

'What are they?'

'Photographs.'

'Of David Maybury?' She nodded. 'After Phoebe had killed him?' She nodded again. 'One of your famous insurance policies, I suppose.'

She sighed. 'I never thought we'd get away with it. I kept a record in case the body was found and Phoebe needed a defence.' Her face clouded. 'I developed them myself. Awful, awful pictures, showing David two weeks after Phoebe killed him, showing Phoebe herself, looking so damn mad you wouldn't believe it was the same woman, showing what the vandals did to the house, showing the tomb I built in the cellar. I never want to see them again.'

'Tell me, Anne.'

She took a deep breath. 'David came back the night after the house had been ransacked. It was inevitable he would turn up some time, but to choose that night—' She shook her head. 'Not that he knew, of course. He wouldn't have come back if he'd known. The doors were barred with stacked-up furniture, so he came in through the cellar window. Phoebe was in the kitchen and she heard him stumbling around in the dark downstairs.' Her eyes searched his. 'You must understand how frightened she was. She thought the drunks had come back to kill her and the children.'

'I do understand.'

'She picked up the heaviest thing she could find, the woodchopping axe by the Aga, and when he came through the cellar door she split his head in two.'

'Did she recognise him?'

'You mean, did she know it was David when she killed him? I shouldn't think so. It all happened too fast. She certainly recognised him afterwards.'

There was a long silence. 'You could have brought the police in then,' he said at last. 'With the evidence of what had happened the night before, she could have pleaded self-defence. She would have got off with no trouble at all.'

She stared at her hands. 'I would have done if I'd known about it. But Jon didn't phone me for a fortnight.' She raised her hands to her eyes to block out the nightmare pictures. 'Phoebe has absolutely no recollection of that two-week period. The only thing she had the sense to do before she went into shock was to shove David's body back down the cellar steps and bolt the door. The children have never known about it. Jon only phoned me because for two weeks she had kept them all locked in her bedroom, living on a diet of tinned food that she'd rescued from the larder. He took the key while she was asleep, let himself out of the bedroom and kept ringing my number till I answered.' Tears welled in her eyes, spilling over her tired lids, as she remembered. 'He was only eleven, hardly more than a baby really, and he said he was doing his best but he thought Jane and Mummy needed a proper person to look after them.' She dashed the tears from her eyes. 'Oh God, I'm sorry. It just makes me cry every time I think of it. He must have been so frightened. I came straight down.'

She looked suddenly very tired. 'I couldn't possibly go to the police, McLoughlin. She was completely off her head and Jon and Jane would hardly speak. I thought Phoebe had vandalised the house herself *after* killing David. There was no way of proving which came first. And if I thought that, what the hell conclusion would Walsh have come to? It was a nightmare. All I could think of doing was to put the children before everything else, because that is what Phoebe's father had asked me to do when he set up the trust. And putting them first, I decided, meant keeping their mother out of a prison hospital.' She sighed. 'So, over a period of days, I bought small quantities of grey stone from DIY shops all over South Hampshire. I had to be able to fit it in Phoebe's car. I didn't dare get anyone to deliver. Then I locked myself in the cellar and bricked that revolting, stinking mess that had once been David behind a fake wall.' She gagged on bile. 'He's still there. The wall has never been disturbed. Diana went down and checked after Fred found that thing in the ice house. We were so afraid he had somehow got out.'

'Does Fred know?'

'No. Only Diana, Phoebe and I.'

'And Phoebe knows what she did?'

'Oh, yes. It took a while, but she remembered it all in the end. She wanted to confess about four years ago, but we persuaded her out of it. Jane at fourteen was down to four and a half stone. Diana and I said her peace of mind was more important than Phoebe's.' She took another deep breath. 'It meant we've never been able to sell the Grange, of course. Sod's Law predicts that whoever buys it will want to rip the guts out of the cellar to put in a jacuzzi.' She smiled faintly. 'At times it has been quite unbearable. But when I look at the three of them now, I know it was all worth it.' Her damp eyes pleaded for a reassurance she would never put into words.

He took one of her hands. 'What can I say, woman? Except that next time I tell you how to run your life, remind me that you know best.' He played with her fingers, pulling at them. 'I could use your photographs of the house to smash Walsh and Barnes for what they've done to Phoebe.'

'No,' she said immediately. 'No one knows they exist, except you and me. Phoebe and Diana don't know. Let's leave them where they are. I see death too often in my nightmares as it is. Phoebe wouldn't want it, anyway. Walsh was right. She did kill David.'

He nodded and looked away. It was a while before he spoke. 'My wife came back to me tonight.'

She forced herself to smile. 'Are you glad?'

'As a matter of fact I am.' She tried to extract her hand tactfully from his, but he wouldn't let her.

'Then I'm pleased for you. Will it work this time, do you think?'

'Oh, yes. I'm toying with the idea of leaving the police force. What do you think?'

'It'll make things easier at home. The divorce rate amongst policemen is phenomenal.'

'Forget the practicalities. Advise me, for myself.'

'I can't,' she said. 'It's something you will have to decide for yourself. All I can say is that, whatever decision you come to, make sure it's one you can live with.' She looked at him shyly. 'I was mistaken before, you know. I think you were probably right to go into the police, and I think the police would be the poorer without you.'

He nodded. 'And you? What will you do now?'

She smiled brightly. 'Oh, the usual. Storm a few citadels, seduce a sculptor or two.'

He grinned. 'Well, before you do that, will you give me a hand in the cellar one night? I think it's time that wall came down, and David Maybury left this house for good. Don't worry. It won't be unpleasant. After nine years there will be very little left and this time we'll get rid of him properly.'

'Wouldn't it be better to leave well alone?'

'No.'

'Why not?'

'Because, Cattrell, if Phoebe isn't freed of him, you and Diana will be tied to this house for ever.'

She looked into a private darkness beyond him. How little he understood. They would always be tied now. It had been too long. They had lost the confidence to start again.

He gave her fingers a last squeeze and stood up. 'I'd better make tracks for bed then.'

She nodded, her eyes over-bright. 'Goodbye, McLoughlin. I wish you luck, I really do.'

He scratched the side of his face. 'I suppose you couldn't lend me a pillow? And maybe a toothbrush from the bathroom?'

'What for?'

'I've got nowhere to sleep, woman. I told you, my wife came back. I'm damned if I'm spending another seven years with someone whose favourite colour is beige. I walked out.' He watched her smile. 'I thought I'd shack up with a friend this time.'

'What sort of friend?'

'Oh, I don't know. How about a cynical, selfish intellectual snob, who can't sustain relationships, doesn't conform and embarrasses people?'

She laughed quietly. 'It's all true.'

'Of course it is. We've a lot in common. It's not a bad description of me either.'

'You'd hate living here.'

'About as much as you do, probably. How does Glasgow sound?'

'What would we do there?'

'Explore, Cattrell, explore.'

Her eyes danced. 'Are you going to take no for an answer, McLoughlin?'

'No.'

'Well what the hell are you waiting for then?'

HB 5 X